Once making her home i
Luana DaRosa has sinc
different continents—though her favourite
romantic locations remain the tropical places
of Latin America. When she's not typing away
at her latest romance novel, or reading about
love, Luana is either crocheting, buying yarn she
doesn't need, or chasing her bunnies around the
house. She lives with her partner in a cosy town
in the south of England. Find her on Twitter under
the handle @LuDaRosaBooks.

Susan Carlisle's love affair with books began
when she made a bad grade in mathematics.
Not allowed to watch TV until the grade had
improved, she filled her time with books. Having
turned her love of reading into a love for writing
romance, she now pens hot Medicals. She
loves castles, travelling, afternoon tea, reading
voraciously and hearing from her readers. Join
her newsletter at SusanCarlisle.com.

A THERAPY PUP TO REUNITE THEM

LUANA DaROSA

SECOND CHANCE FOR THE HEART DOCTOR

SUSAN CARLISLE

MILLS & BOON

First published in Great Britain 2023
by Mills & Boon, an imprint of HarperCollins*Publishers* Ltd,
1 London Bridge Street, London, SE1 9GF

www.harpercollins.co.uk

HarperCollins*Publishers* Macken House, 39/40 Mayor Street Upper, Dublin 1, D01 C9W8, Ireland

ISBN: 978-0-263-30628-6

12/23

A THERAPY PUP
TO REUNITE THEM

LUANA DaROSA

MILLS & BOON

For Sir Raptor, the best boy. <3

CHAPTER ONE

THE RECEPTION AREA outside the office of Whitehall Memorial's Head of Neurology was surprisingly quiet. As a neurologist herself, Raquel had heard tales about Whitehall Memorial and, though she had never dreamt of joining this elite group of neurologists and neurosurgeons, she knew plenty who wanted to and none who had. That was how competitive this programme was for medical professionals around the globe. Even sitting in front of the office filled her with the nervous bubbles of impostor syndrome, as if she had somehow swindled herself into the *locum tenens* position they had offered her a few weeks ago.

Though that wasn't the main reason her stomach was tied in a solid knot. Raquel had been accepting short-term placements at different hospitals all over the United States for two years now to fund her research into training seizure-alert dogs.

The Head of Neurology here, Dr Mia Brett, had contacted her about placing a dog with a teenage patient of hers and had offered her a part-time position. Settling a dog with a new handler took several weeks and a lot of spot training, so when that offer had come in, Raquel hadn't hesitated before accepting. A chance to convince the Head of Neurology at Whitehall Memorial of her research didn't come along every day—and she really needed to find some hospitals willing to work with her if she wanted to continue her non-profit work.

She looked down at the Golden Retriever lying in front of her feet with a small smile tugging at the corners of her lips. Raquel had been working with Nesta and several of her siblings, training them to respond to seizures in epileptic patients. Their mother, Lily, had been part of service-dog training facilitated in a women's prison. There, they had worked with diabetic inmates to train dogs to alert to low blood-sugar.

Lily had been responding well to the training but then suddenly had stopped and hyper-focused on a specific inmate to the great confusion of her trainers—until the person had started seizing, thereby revealing what the dog had responded to. Raquel's friend, who had worked at the prison overseeing the project, had given her a call, as she knew that she was studying seizure-response dogs and how to train them.

That had been two years ago and it had been the moment Raquel had started her own business focusing on seizure-response dogs. A dream that was hanging in the balance right now because seizure response was such a new field in neurology and dog training alike, and there weren't many people keen on investing in something so experimental. But after a lot of hustling, cajoling, and pleading, she had found some investors to back her financially with an interest in epilepsy.

These investors now wanted to see that she knew what she was doing—which, on most levels, she did. She knew how to train these dogs, knew what to look out for and how epileptic seizures worked. As a neurologist, she had worked with plenty of patients on several neurological conditions that led to seizures.

What she struggled with was business acumen. No one had told her how hard it would be to run her own business. People spoke about difficulties when chasing their dreams, and on an intellectual level Raquel had understood that. It was the emotional level that was now catching up with her and robbing her of her sound sleep: investors getting nervous that she hadn't signed any new contracts for half a year. Though they assured her they were still interested, they needed to see results to justify the investment.

Two years of spotty contracts had stressed the patience of her investors to breaking point. She was due to meet with them in four weeks to discuss progress—and they had laid out that, if Raquel couldn't get a major hospital or institute interested in her work, they'd pull their investment.

So, this placement was about more than *just* work. If she couldn't impress the decision-makers at Whitehall Memorial, her days of doing research and training dogs would be over. This was her chance. She would be working with the Head of Neurology for the next month on both a specific case to place her dog and as a generalist in the department. There would be opportunities to talk about the benefits of service dogs for neurological disorders and she would have to seize every single opportunity.

The first one being a meeting with Dr Brett to get situated in her new role as locum neurologist and to kick off the meeting with the patient with whom she would place Nesta.

The assistant looked up from her screen and caught

Raquel's eye. 'Dr Brett is ready to see you now,' she said with a smile, then nodded her chin towards the door.

Raquel stood, her grip around Nesta's lead so tight with nerves, she had to will her hand to relax. There weren't many moments in her life when she'd known something extraordinary was about to happen, but she knew in her gut that this moment would be one to remember.

'You got this, girl,' Raquel whispered to the dog, as much as to herself, then approached the door and let herself into the office of the woman who would have the power to decide the fate of her charity at the end of four weeks.

The interior of Dr Brett's office was as modern as the rest of the hospital. She sat behind a glass desk with large windows at her back from which Raquel could see New York City's skyline. Raquel tried not to stare, keeping her eyes on the older woman looking up at her with a smile.

Though Dr Brett seemed to have noticed for, when she stood, she said, 'Dr Pascal, what a pleasure to meet you. Have you been to New York before?'

Raquel took her outstretched hand and gave it a firm shake, whilst shaking her head. 'No, this is my first time visiting the big city.'

'Then, as a native, let me welcome you to New York City. I hope you will have some time to enjoy the sights while you're here,' Dr Brett said as she pointed at the empty chair in front of her. When Raquel sat down, she continued, 'I'm glad you could accept such a short-term placement. Dr Prem won't be out for long, but the way we are staffed even one person less is a noticeable strain.'

At her feet, Nesta settled down at Raquel's silent command, and Raquel caught Dr Brett's gaze travel down to the dog, a bright spark in her eyes. She had already caught her interest—good. That would go a long way to convince the woman they should work together.

'Thank you for the welcome, Dr Brett. I've done many of these placements in the past. The short-term ones are the trickiest to do—even locum doctors like a bit of stability,' she said with a laugh. 'But, since you have a patient for one of my dogs and some additional work, this was an opportunity I couldn't pass up.'

Dr Brett waved a hand in front of her dismissively. 'Please call me Mia. I'm very hands-on in the department and I want to be on the same level with the neurologists on my team.' She paused, her eyes drifting towards Nesta again. 'I don't know how much information you have, but Alexandria is the relative of one of our doctors here, and she herself suggested getting a seizure dog after doing the research. We don't usually see such participation. The research on it is still new, from what I can tell.'

Nervous energy bubbled up within Raquel as she nodded. The lack of research was one reason she was working so hard to gain the recognition of larger institutions such as Whitehall Memorial. An endorsement from Dr Brett—Mia, she reminded herself—would go a long way to convince other hospitals. If she couldn't convince them, then the last two years would have been for nothing. One more thing to add to the list of her failures in life—her marriage sitting on top of that list.

Raquel swallowed the sigh building in her throat, forcing her attention back into the moment. 'I'm here to change that, and Nesta will show you exactly how much your patient's quality of life will improve with this,' she replied, her skin flushing at the approving smile she received from Mia.

'Good, I'm keen to see it. Now…' She opened a drawer under her desk and retrieved a tablet, which she handed over to Raquel. 'There is only one long-term patient of Dr Prem's that needs your immediate attention. She's a prime candidate for deep-brain stimulation and is waiting to finalise the treatment plan before surgery. Other than that, you'll be spending most of your time doing consults for the emergency room, since you requested to work evening shifts. I had all the information loaded onto the tablet. Have a read through it tonight so we can discuss questions tomorrow.'

Raquel took the tablet with a grateful smile, slipping it into her bag. Since Nesta's new handler was a teenager, she needed to have the day time free to do their training at school and after-school activities, leaving only the evening shifts to do the other half of the work she had agreed to. She'd known going in that most of her time would go into the one-off patients, since longer treatment plans needed a consistent neurologist on it—which was why the deep-brain stimulation, or DBS, case had taken her by surprise. Organising surgery for deep-brain stimulation would require coordination with the neuro-surgical team.

Raquel was about to ask for an introduction when Mia got off her chair and waved a hand. 'Shall we go see her? Since you have this afternoon scheduled for your introduction with Alexandria, we'll start your rotation in the neurology department tomorrow.'

They walked out of her office, Nesta, dutiful as ever, padding along behind her.

'Can you call ahead and let Dr Wolf know we are on our way?' Mia said to her assistant as they passed her, who nodded and picked up the phone. 'He is the head of the neurosurgical department, and Alexandria's uncle.'

Raquel's eyes widened in surprise as she absorbed that information. Just the person she needed to see about her new patient. If he was involved in setting his niece up with a service dog, maybe he too might consider giving her an endorsement for her charity. Those two people together carried a lot of sway in the medical world and could open a lot of doors for her if she proved herself good enough in her time here.

So, the head of one of the most prestigious neurosurgical departments in the US was a Dr Wolf… She searched her memory for a neurologist or neuro-surgeon named Wolf, trying to remember if she had ever heard of him or read some of his research. But the only picture that came up when she thought of the name 'Wolf' was a blurry one of her brother's best friend—Christian Wolf. He *was* a medical doctor, but not in the neurology field. Wasn't he a plastic surgeon…?

A tendril of warmth unfurled in her chest, sparking alive a feeling that Raquel immediately stomped on to kill it before it could derail her thoughts. Now was not the time or place to think about her high-school crush who also happened to be her brother's best friend, and to whom she hadn't spoken or seen in fifteen years.

Her brother, Ramón, still lived in Puerto Rico and had never left their home country—unlike Raquel, who'd been excited to leave and see the world when she'd landed a spot at an American college. And a part of it had been because of Christian and the stories he'd told about living all over the globe. Coming from a small island nation, her horizons had expanded by several magnitudes when she'd arrived in the United States.

Though the kernel of gratitude towards her brother's best friend remained, most of her feelings for him were wrapped up in a tight ball of chaos that she'd shoved into a dark corner of her mind, never to be examined again. Because, when Ramón had brought Christian home after school and invited her to hang out with them, Raquel had fallen under his spell almost immediately. And, the longer she had spent time with him, the more convinced she'd become that he had feelings for her too. So much so that she had acted on what she'd sensed between them and kissed him during a slow dance at his prom—only for Christian to back away.

As an adult, thinking back to their time together, she had asked Ramón if he'd sensed something between them back then, but her brother had always refused to talk about it. He said that, since they were still very much best friends, he wouldn't gossip about his *hermano*. All Raquel knew was that Christian had gone on to train as a plastic surgeon somewhere on the west coast. She shoved the thoughts of Christian away into the dusty corners of her mind where they belonged. This Dr Wolf was her priority, not the boy she used to like.

They approached a reception desk, and the assistant sitting behind it waved at them as they approached. 'Dr Wolf asked me to send you right through,' he said in a chipper voice.

A lump appeared in her throat as they approached the door, and she swallowed hard to banish it. She knew what to do, knew what to say, and had the utmost confidence in Nesta and the value she provided. There was no way she should be nervous now, when she had never in her life believed in anything more than what she was doing with these dogs.

Raquel knew where these feelings were coming from—her ex-husband. She had met Tom in her last year of medical school and married him not even a year later. He'd been the owner of a medical device start-up company that was now worth quite a bit more money. The company's meteoric rise had coincided with their divorce and, even though she knew it had been necessary for them to separate, part of her ached at seeing the success he'd achieved once they had made that decision. It was as if she'd been holding him back.

But they had been holding *each other* back. Tom might have spent less time building his company than he had wanted to so he could be with his wife, but Raquel had also put her own career aspirations on hold, giving them the flexibility to uproot their lives and move whenever they'd needed to. They had both believed it to be a good idea when they'd spoken about it. The ramifications of what it meant to devote her life to the success of someone else had only become apparent to her when they had split up.

Because of that decision, she was further behind in her career than her peers and fighting to keep her head above water. Maybe she should never have taken the leap into her own business, knowing how hard it had been on Tom. But seeing him succeed without her, while Raquel had been left with a broken heart and a career in tatters, had triggered something in her: a fighting spirit. She *needed* to leave her mark on something meaningful, and she knew that her non-profit work would be it—if she could also convince other people of the same.

The thoughts kept bubbling up inside her, and Raquel once more pushed them away, focusing on the moment at hand. If she could impress Mia and this Dr Wolf, they could be her staunchest allies in bringing in a contract with Whitehall Memorial for her investors.

Much like Mia's office, this one was in the same clinical, modern style with large windows making up an entire wall. Though, unlike earlier, this time Raquel noticed nothing inside the office—nothing except that blurry picture in her mind's eye that now came into focus with a sudden ferocity that pushed the air out of her lungs.

Because standing up from behind the desk to greet her was Christian Wolf.

'Are they coming?' Alexandria stood close to the door, peeking through the window now and then to look at the foot traffic outside her uncle's office.

Christian looked up from the patient file he'd been working on all morning. The scans weren't very encouraging. A brain tumour was causing his patient to have seizures in a rare form—the seizures only took place in certain parts of the body. A colleague from the neurology department had sent him the case, along with the scans, to see if Christian could remove the tumour after the team at a smaller hospital in Arizona had declined to do the surgery—the risks of it going wrong were too great.

This wasn't the first time a smaller team had elected to send him a patient. Christian had worked hard to craft a reputation for his unparalleled skill as a neurosurgeon. Most of his patient roster now comprised people who were sent to him from all over the United States—a fact that made him proud, he had to admit.

When he had first started his career as a surgeon, his goals had been a lot different. He'd wanted to help people, of course. But he had thought that he would do that by giving people the looks they desired by fulfilling their visual fantasies of themselves—help them attain their ideal self.

Then his brother had got sick, changing Christian's life for ever. He'd quit his job in Los Angeles and moved to New York to be with his niece and him throughout the progression of his Huntington's disease diagnosis. Anthony's wife had taken off shortly after the birth of their child, leaving him all alone to care for his now-teenaged daughter, when they had received news of his diagnosis.

Christian had not hesitated, and had even changed his specialty, as he'd wanted to learn more about neurological diseases and how to support his brother and niece. Without a cure, all they'd been able to do was live life to the fullest until the day had come for them to say goodbye to Anthony. That had been three months ago, and the loss burned as hot today as it had back then. Though he knew he would eventually become Lexi's guardian and would step into the role of father figure for the rest of both of their lives, he still felt under-prepared—ill-suited, even.

Especially as Lexi had special needs herself. The seizures had begun when she'd been four years old, and it hadn't taken long for her to be diagnosed with epilepsy. One of his most pressing concerns with her diagnosis was how to give his niece the freedom a thirteen-year-old craved without endangering her. The discussion of summer camp had come up. With all her friends going, she wanted to sign up as well. Only, the location was upstate and, with her seizures being unpredictable, how could he make sure she was safe?

Hours of research in medical journals and countless conversations with his colleagues in the neurology department had yielded precious few leads, and the frustration within Christian had grown. He was used to being the person with a plan, so not knowing how to help his niece get the life he wanted her to have was something he struggled to reconcile within him.

His confidence at being her new father figure was already shaky. Not being able to help her with her needs had only compounded the sense of failure that rose within him in the quiet hours of the night.

It had been Lexi who'd made him aware of the existence of seizure-response dogs—a shortcoming of knowledge he'd rectified the moment he'd heard of the concept. When he had spoken to Mia—who oversaw his niece's ongoing treatment as her neurologist—about the potential of Lexi getting a service dog, she had done a similar deep dive into the world of seizure-alert animals. It hadn't taken her long to find an organisation specialising in training these dogs, and Hannah, the liaison he'd been speaking to via phone and email, had confirmed that a trainer would bring a dog.

Ever since they had confirmed the date, Lexi had been a bundle of nervous excitement. Today, the day when she would finally meet her service dog, had by far been the most exhausting. After finishing school, she'd come straight to hospital, where Christian had found his niece in his office after his surgery. Now she was loitering at his door and staring outside, to the great amusement of his assistant, Dino.

'Sit down, Lexi. Hannah sent over the schedule when we confirmed the appointment and gave us a timeframe, not an exact time of day.' He scrolled through his emails and clicked on the one from Hannah. His eyes flew to the first line after her greeting paragraph:

Meet and Greet with Nesta and Alexandria. Four p.m.

There were different appointments on the spreadsheet Hannah had sent over, spanning the next four weeks, but Christian had been happy to leave the rest of the plan to his niece and the dog trainer. He'd asked how much of his involvement would be necessary, so that he could talk to the chief and potentially clear his schedule, and had to admit he'd been happy to hear that his involvement would be minimal. Though guilt had mingled with the relief, only deepening the doubt in his parenting skills. Because of how busy he was, and how his job had him working such irregular hours, he'd never felt suited for the father role. Surely a father was supposed to be right there with his child, experiencing every moment with them?

Lexi jumped when his phone rang and ran to his desk, hopping from one foot to the other as he picked up the phone and said, 'Dr Wolf speaking.'

He listened to his assistant on the other end, then nodded. 'Thanks for letting me know. Send them right through when they arrive.'

Lexi's eyes grew wide at his words and she raced back to the door to press her forehead against the glass, surveying everyone who walked by his office. Christian chuckled at her excitement, then closed the email. Hidden behind it were the patient scans he'd been looking at all day. He wasn't any step closer to working out how to perform this surgery, or if surgery was even the best option at this point.

'I can see Nesta! She is *so* pretty,' his niece said, earning a confused look from him that she couldn't see with her forehead pressed against the door.

Christian lifted his head, trying to see past his niece. Though the dog would no doubt be interesting, he was more keen on seeing the trainer. With the dog needed to perform such specific tasks, he wasn't sure what kind of person to expect.

Lexi backed away from the door as footsteps echoed on the other side of it, coming closer to his desk in two big leaps, and then the door swung open. Dr Mia Brett walked in first and behind her a short woman in a curve-hugging jeans and a loose shirt that hid most of her upper body's curves. Not that this was a problem. The jeans were showing enough for an errant mind to fill in the blanks—like his at this very moment.

He forced his eyes up to her face, which was framed by straight, black hair, and he started when he looked into brown-green eyes that completed the woman's familiar appearance. Eyes that were staring back at him with an expression as surprised as he felt.

'Raquel?' he asked, his brain not able to comprehend that the person standing in front of him might be who he thought she was.

But when she nodded he couldn't stop the smile from spreading over his lips. He got off his chair, his trance at her sudden appearance broken, and gave her a quick hug. 'I haven't seen you in…what?…fifteen years? What are you doing here?'

She returned the hug, her hands coming to rest on each side of his shoulder blades, and her fingers left tiny tendrils of warmth behind as he stepped away to look at her. Then his eyes snagged on the lead in her hand and followed it all the way down until he saw the Golden Retriever sitting at her heel.

Before Raquel could say anything else, Lexi came up to both of them, eyes sparkling with joy as she looked at the dog. 'Is this Nesta?' she said with quiet reverence.

Raquel gave a short laugh and then nodded. 'Yes, this is her. You'll get plenty of time to get to know each other, but for now we have some things to discuss.'

Had he been in contact with Raquel all this time and not known? No, the person in the email was Hannah, and he didn't remember her ever having mentioned the trainer's name. There was no way he would have read the name without feeling something, was there?

Though it had been well over a decade since they had last seen each other, there had been a time when he'd seen Raquel every day while visiting Ramón. With both his parents being important ambassadors for the United States, they had moved a lot in his youth, and one of those moves had brought them to Puerto Rico for three years, just as Christian had started high school.

Ramón had taken the new kid under his wing almost immediately, introducing him to his friend circle and his family within the first week. Christian had never received such a warm welcome in any other place, and it was a memory he cherished to this day—along with the deep friendship he and Ramón still shared. Though they didn't see each other often, they texted almost daily to keep up with each other's lives.

Raquel had been close to her brother as well, and all three of them had often ended up hanging out. Though their initial meeting had been only through Ramón, it hadn't taken them long to establish a friendship of their own, to the point where Christian had been just as excited to see her.

Maybe too excited, when he thought back to that time. Because his family had moved around so much, he'd never been good at making permanent connections, so when he'd become aware of the magnitude of his feelings for Raquel he hadn't known what to do with them—knowing that it would only be a matter of time before he would be gone again.

When it had become clear that their feelings for each other were mutual on the night of his prom, he'd lost courage—too scared of what would happen if he wanted her too much but couldn't have her.

A lack of courage Christian had lamented over the years, especially when facing the failed relationships in his adult life. Would they have made it through the stressful medical school years or would she have been another casualty, another sacrifice he'd have had to make to get to where he was now?

The thoughts rushed through him as they stepped away from each other, the smile on her face bright but tentative. She had not been expecting him, either.

'Erm…wow, okay. This is very surprising.' She stared at Christian for a few breaths, then she lowered her gaze to Lexi. 'You're Alexandria, yes? I'm Raquel, both a neurologist and a dog trainer. It's lovely to meet you and I can't wait for you and Nesta to get to know each other. Did you read all the materials Hannah sent through to you?'

Lexi nodded, her mind too focused on the dog in front of her to notice anything untoward going on between her uncle and her dog's trainer.

Christian took a deep breath, willing the flutter in his chest to calm as he processed the sudden appearance of Raquel and all the long-lost emotions stirring from somewhere deep inside his memory—a task that tested his will power when her deep-set eyes locked onto his once more.

'Está bien si nos sentamos allí?' she asked him, pointing at the sofa, and he nodded.

'Por favor, ponte cómoda.' He started towards the seat when he caught Lexi's gaze and she looked at him, bewildered.

'I didn't know you spoke Spanish,' she said, arms crossed in front of her chest and indignation lacing her voice.

'Oh yeah, I learned it in Puerto Rico, where I met Raquel. Your father might not have mentioned it because he didn't come with us, since he was in college when your grandparents moved us to Puerto Rico. We were suggesting we sit down and talk.'

Though he'd become fluent in Spanish during his time in Puerto Rico, he didn't get many chances to practise any more in his day-to-day, and the right words didn't come to his mind as easily as they used to. That was something Ramón loved to make fun of whenever they spoke on the phone, their conversations living in that beautiful intersection where English and Spanish met and became 'Spanglish'.

A tiny flutter rushed over his niece's face at the mention of her father, breaking through the excitement of the day. He knew this day was especially important to her, and it pained her not to have her father by her side to see this through with her.

Christian's heart ached, and he took a seat by her side as they spread out around the sofa and loungers on the far side of his office. Anthony might not be here, but *he* was, and he would be for every other milestone, filling in as a father for whatever Lexi needed. If only he had the same confidence in his fathering abilities that he had in the operating room.

CHAPTER TWO

RAQUEL'S HEART WAS racing in her chest, her pulse so loud she could hear it roar in her ears as she walked over to the sofa and sat down. And across from her sat Christian Wolf: Ramón's best friend and the man for whom she'd pined for the entire three years that he'd spent in Puerto Rico.

He was the relative of her new patient! How had his name never come up in the process? She cast her memory back, thinking about all the times she had communicated about Alexandria's case, which hadn't been that often... Though she loved working with dogs and patients alike, she didn't enjoy any of the paperwork or having to be on the phone.

No, Raquel wanted to spend her time actively working on the dog training and on placing her dogs with a patient. That was when she had hired Hannah, a college student looking for some extra cash. She was the one who handled all the administrative work and only sent Raquel whatever she needed to know about the patients she was working with. Which meant that Christian's name might never have come up.

Oh God, why did it have to be *him*? This was so not the moment to accidentally bump into her high-school crush. No, that should have happened at the height of her career, as she was expanding and was able to carefully choose her hospitals, rather than come here cap in hand, convincing them why they should work with her. Not now, when she was still feeling so tender and vulnerable from her divorce just over two years ago that a strong wind could pick up and blow her away. Not when the work she'd dedicated her life to ever since was on the brink of falling apart underneath her hands. That was not a mind frame in which she wanted to talk to Christian Wolf, who had apparently abandoned his plans of becoming a plastic surgeon and had instead risen in the highest echelons of neuro-surgical experts.

Raquel forced in a deep breath and then set her eyes on Alexandria. She needed to stay anchored in the moment and remember what she'd come here to do. It didn't matter that it was Christian sitting opposite her. She still needed to convince Mia, through her work here and in her department, that she knew what she was doing—that she was worthy of a further contract. No more contracts meant no funding, and without funding she'd be shutting down her charity in four weeks, leaving her with…nothing. Nothing but the shreds of her career mingling with the cold ashes of her marriage.

Except now there was Christian. When she had flown in, she wouldn't have guessed that he might hold the keys to her continued success. If she showed him the work that went into her dog training, if he could see first-hand how much a service dog would improve his niece's life, surely he'd use his influence to put in a good word with Mia and the hospital? Raquel would never want to use her brother's friendship with Christian to sway him, but if hard work on her part impressed him she'd not turn away his help.

'Okay, let me talk you through what we're going to do in the next four weeks,' she started, her focus on Alexandria. 'I trained Nesta from very early on to help you in case of a seizure. We picked her because her mother, Lily, who was trained to be a low blood-sugar alert dog, began reacting to a specific person in her surroundings having epileptic seizures.'

Mia sat up at that. 'How could a dog not trained in detecting seizures react to them?' she asked.

Raquel opened her mouth to answer, when Alexandria cut in, 'There's no such thing as a seizure-alert dog. Or at least, they haven't figured that out yet. They can train dogs to respond to seizures in a specific manner. Like, if I'm seizing, she can push a button to alert Chris or lie next to me so I don't get hurt.'

Raquel looked at the well-informed teen and decided right away that she liked her. Not only had she done extensive research about the service animal she was about to receive, she was also not shy about calling out misconceptions—something that would come in handy on the journey to come. Though people understood the concept of a service animal, not so many understood what that really entailed, and how to behave around one of them. Alexandria would spend a lot of time explaining to people why Nesta was with her, even though that was nobody's business.

'That's correct. I have worked with many dogs that can accurately alert to a seizure but, since the research behind it is not solid, I cannot promise you that. Dogs can alert to changes in scents that are undetectable to humans, and it's not out of the question that there is a change of smell when people have seizures,' Raquel continued, borrowing the words from the sales pitch that she had memorised. 'The primary focus on my dogs' training lies on how they respond to seizures and what we want them to do in specific situations.'

She looked at Alexandria, who beamed at her with anticipation. This was one of her favourite parts of the job—matching a patient with their dog and watching them become an inseparable team.

'Can you tell me more about your seizures, Alexandria?' she asked, coming to the point she needed to get across to both Christian and Mia. If they saw Nesta in action, there was no way they could refuse her more work.

This was the first time she saw the teen look unsure of herself. Alexandria glanced over at Christian, who gave her a reassuring nod, before she turned her gaze back to Raquel. 'I mostly have absence seizures where I black out completely and come back after a few minutes. They weren't so inconvenient in the past, but now...' She paused, looking down at her hands. 'When I'm walking, I sometimes don't stop. Last time it happened, I almost ran into traffic. If my friend hadn't been there...'

Alexandria's voice trailed off, and Raquel could fill in the rest. As a neurologist, she had worked with plenty of people with different seizures. Absence seizures were far more frequent in children and adolescents than in adults, who tended to suffer from focal seizures impacting specific parts of the brain. Most people retained awareness of a seizure happening, and some could even tell it was about to happen. What made absence seizures so difficult to deal with was the loss of agency and not knowing what was happening.

She had read Alexandria's file before coming here, knew exactly what her day-to-day looked like and had studied her seizure diary. But it was still important to hear this information from the patients themselves. Through conversations, she could often discern clues and habits that her patients hadn't even thought worth mentioning.

'Thank you for sharing that,' she said with a smile. Though this was Alexandria's daily life, Raquel could imagine sharing these things with a stranger wasn't the easiest. If they were to be successful in bonding her with Nesta, they needed to be comfortable sharing each other's confidence.

'With absence seizures, Nesta can help in different ways. If you are sitting or lying down in a public space, she is already trained in supporting you by keeping your head off the ground or lying beside you so you don't get injured. She can also alert help in case of a seizure and no one is around. This can be a button at home or something you carry with you. As long as she can access it, she can press it.'

Raquel looked at Nesta, who lay next to her with her head on her paws. 'If you are walking, we could put a harness on Nesta and get you used to following her lead wherever you are going, and when she senses your seizure she will stop, and stop you from walking any further. One thing to consider with that is how conspicuous this is. Service dogs, by design, draw attention to themselves, but that also means people will become aware when both of you suddenly stop.'

Raquel opened her bag and pulled out some props she used whenever she was pitching her service dogs. One of them was a lanyard with a laminated card on it. 'Something like this has worked for other patients I work with. It has instructions clearly written on it to leave you be, though some good Samaritans aren't really able to walk away without doing something, as you've probably experienced yourself already.'

She chuckled when Alexandria sighed, overly dramatic, while rolling her eyes. 'The amount of times people call ambulances for one of my harmless seizures is *so* bad. They always have to call my uncle, who can usually convince them I'm fine to go.'

'There's still a lot of awareness work to be done around seizures and what non-medically trained onlookers should actually do,' Raquel said with a nod. 'That's something I'm working on, alongside raising the profile of seizure-response dogs.'

Another line from her pitch deck…and she looked at Christian and Mia to gauge their expressions. Christian nodded, his expression one of deep understanding, that made her wonder about the relationship between he and his niece. Was he her primary-care physician or potentially more? She would have expected Alexandria's parents to be present at this meeting.

She swallowed hard when his blue-grey eyes caught her gaze for the first time since she had launched into her explanation. She remembered that hue so well; she had spent countless hours looking at him during their time in high school, fantasising what it would be like to see those eyes every morning when she woke up.

A reality that had never come to pass—had never had the chance to, really. They had never spoken about the spark between them—had never even addressed how he'd rejected her kiss the night of his prom—and, when he had left Puerto Rico, it had faded back into non-existence.

Now, as he looked into her eyes, warmth bloomed in the centre of her chest, glowing in an all too familiar way, and Raquel almost shook her head. This was not the time or place to think about her relationship with Christian. She needed to talk to him, yes, but not about the spark. *Never* about the spark. That had turned out to be nothing more than a figment of her imagination—Christian's reaction to her advance during their teenage years was proof enough of that.

'Who is her primary care-giver?' she asked, striking a conversational tone so it wouldn't seem as if she was prying, and purposefully avoiding the mention of any parent, as she guessed there was some history she didn't know about.

In any other circumstances, she wouldn't have been concerned about that but, since she knew Christian, she wanted to be more delicate. Alexandria had to be Anthony's child. Was he not here because he'd asked his doctor brother to handle her medical decisions, or were there other reasons for his absence?

The answer became apparent when the room went quiet. Christian frowned, and Alexandria looked down at her lap, where her hands lay curled up.

'She lives with me,' he said, and Raquel fought the urge to ask what had happened. Though she had never met Anthony, she'd heard enough about him to be sympathetic to the pain she sensed radiating from them both.

'When we place a dog with a minor, the adult becomes just as much the handler. You will have to support Alexandria as she gets used to Nesta and go on this journey with her. A dog is difficult to maintain, even one as well trained as Nesta. She still needs to go to the vet and can get sick, like a family dog would.'

Some people she spoke to didn't know how much maintenance went into a dog. They believed, because of the training, they would miraculously take care of themselves, but these animals needed just as much attention.

But Christian didn't seem surprised by that information. He nodded towards his niece with a smile. 'Lexi has already put me through the service-dog handler boot camp with all the information you sent over,' he said, the fondness for his niece giving his voice a softer timbre.

Then he looked back at Raquel, who held her breath so it wouldn't stutter when his eyes swept over her. 'You'll stay with her for a month to train the dog specifically to Lexi and her needs, right?'

Raquel nodded. 'That's right. I'll accompany Alexandria for the rest of the afternoon to see if Nesta is catching her seizures, should they happen, and we'll take it from there. I spoke to her school already, to arrange access to her classroom, and submitted all the documentation they needed for their security checks. They said they would get in touch with you.'

Christian nodded. 'They did.'

'Okay, then.' Raquel got up from her seat and moved on to the bitter-sweet moment that always came when handing over a dog. She loved all of them, but was equally excited for them to fulfil their purpose and become a team with their new handler.

Alexandria squealed when she realised what was about to happen, and from the corner of her eye Raquel saw Christian get to his feet as well, an admonishing hand raised at his niece. 'Be careful, Lexi. We've had you seize from too much excitement before,' he cautioned her, and Raquel's heart squeezed when the excitement in his niece's eyes banked.

What an awfully heavy burden to live with, to have to restrict her own feelings in case they might cause a seizure. She gave Alexandria a few moments, then held out Nesta's lead towards her. The teen hesitated, the excitement bubbling back up in her as she closed her fingers around the lead. Dutiful Nesta walked over to her new handler, sniffing at her hand and nuzzling it with her nose in a greeting.

Raquel smiled broadly. As part of her training, Nesta knew to get accustomed to her new handler's scent right away.

'We will learn in the coming weeks if Nesta can alert you to seizures. She's trained to grab your attention if she detects anything unusual, and we'll have to show her what the right action is once she alerts, because otherwise she will keep alerting you. She will either poke you with her nose in your leg or paw at you with her front paw.'

Because they had so little research on how dogs alerted for seizures, they relied on the dogs to fall back to other response training to alert properly. Though she believed in Nesta's abilities, she didn't want to make any promises she couldn't back up with actions. Getting her to respond in certain ways was far more beneficial and predictable than trying to train her to alert.

'What's your plan for the afternoon?' she asked Alexandria, who was staring at her dog with wide eyes and trying to contain her joy with visible effort.

'Just some homework and waiting for Chris to be done with work.' Raquel almost laughed at Alexandria using her uncle's name without putting the title of 'uncle' anywhere in that sentence. Just another of the many culture shocks she'd got used to since moving to the United States. If she called one of her *tías* or *tíos* by anything other than that, her mother would have thrown a *chancla* at her head.

'You can stay in my office. I have consultations for two more hours and then we can go home,' he said and then looked at Raquel. 'You should…'

Nesta sat up straight, drawing their attention to her as she raised her front leg and scratched at Alexandria's leg. They looked at each other, wide-eyed, as she alerted to something. Christian was immediately by his niece's side.

'Are you having a seizure?' he asked her and frowned when Alexandria looked at him.

'No…but I…' Her hand went up to her chest, pressing down on her sternum. Then she walked over to the seat she had just occupied and sat down. She took a shaky inhale, then her face went blank, her grip around the dog's lead loosening. That didn't deter Nesta. She had kept up with her handler and was now putting her head in her lap. Alexandria grasped at her in what looked like an automated gesture and kept staring ahead.

'Oh, wow…she alerted.' Raquel breathed and caught both Christian's and Mia's attention. 'That will go a long way to give Alexandria some control over her life.'

She looked over at Christian. His expression was tight with concern—an understandable reaction. No matter how well trained he'd become as a doctor, things were so much tougher when they involved family. Mia, however, was watching Nesta closely and nodded to herself as the minutes went on.

Nesta lifted her head and Alexandria unfroze, releasing a deep breath. When she looked around, she noticed all three adults in the room staring at her, as well as the dog slowly backing away from her and sitting down by her feet. 'Oh, no…' she mumbled, and the skin on her cheeks turned rosy.

Christian walked over to his niece, crouching down in

front of her. Raquel looked away to give the girl privacy. They would experience a lot of these moments together in the coming weeks, but that didn't make it any easier.

'Do you remember the dog alerting you?' she heard him ask, and Alexandria's nod sent a wave of pride rushing through Raquel.

A beep echoed through the office and drew her attention to Mia, who had pulled her phone out of her pocket. 'I'm needed elsewhere,' she mumbled, mostly to herself, but then raised her eyes at Raquel. 'Fascinating application of your medical degree, I have so say, Raquel. Please keep me informed about the progress and check in with me tomorrow about your assignments for the neurology wing.'

Raquel's heart skipped a beat at that, and she nodded with more enthusiasm than necessary. Having her work acknowledged by one of the leading figures in neurology was a thrilling feeling. She stepped forward to shake Mia's hand as they said goodbye. From behind her, she heard Alexandria whisper something to her uncle. Rustling followed her words, as well as the soft patting of Nesta's feet on the wood floor. She whirled around just to see the teen vanish behind a door nestled between two book cases.

'Bathroom,' Christian said next to her, almost making her jump.

'Oh…okay.' A tentative smile spread over her lips as she looked at him undisturbed for the first time since their surprise reunion not even an hour ago. She had to crane her neck to do so, their difference in height similar to what it had been fifteen years ago.

Grey streaks wound themselves through his blond hair, mostly clustering around his temples. Grey had also invaded the stubble on his cheeks, giving him exactly the look she had always envisaged on a successful neurosurgeon who could also be the star of his own show.

His gleaming white shirt and spotless trousers shone a big spotlight on her own comfy jeans and the over-sized shirt she'd chosen to wear on the flight. Because of a delay to her flight, she hadn't yet checked into her hotel or got more presentable—something that hadn't bothered her until this moment, as his eyes slowly raked over her, taking her measure.

A shiver clawed through her, the muscles in her stomach tightening with the sensation of a sudden drop. Before she could say anything to excuse her looks, he said, 'Have dinner with me tonight.'

Her eyes rounded at the sudden invitation and how it sent excited sparks skittering across her skin. Dinner with Christian? This was the first moment they'd had together alone, and this was what he chose to say?

'Christian, I—'

'You are coming over to the apartment, right? To settle them in?' He paused, as if he wasn't sure about his invitation. 'Lexi told me you and Nesta would need to spend time in all of her usual surroundings.'

'Oh…yes.' She hadn't even thought that far ahead. But, if Alexandria lived with her uncle, that naturally meant she would spend some time at Christian's place. The excited sparks intensified their zigzag trajectory across her skin, settling in a pinch behind her navel.

'How come she lives with you full-time? What happened to Anthony?'

Pain flickered over Christian's expression, a brief loss of his composure that he quickly regained, but it was enough for her to notice.

'He…' Christian started, then stopped when the lock on the bathroom door clicked.

He shot her a quick look as he said in Spanish, 'Something to discuss after dinner when we're alone. You'll stay?'

Raquel stared at him, her insides in a disarray of conflicting emotions. There were several excellent reasons she shouldn't stay for dinner or let any of their past closeness slip into this arrangement here. Not only were the feelings she'd once had for Christian long gone, she couldn't let an echo of them interfere with her assignment. Not only was his niece her client, they were also colleagues now.

But she also genuinely wanted to know how his life had been until now. She might have had unrequited feelings for Christian all those years ago, but he was still her brother's best friend. There was no harm in hanging out, was there? Ramón had probably already told him all about her life.

'Okay, sure,' she said with a nod as Alexandria emerged from the bathroom with Nesta by her side, colour returning to her face.

Christian nodded and the smile he shot her hit her very low in her body, where it sent electric ripples through her. 'Great. Then I'll see you two in a few hours and we can head home for dinner together.'

CHAPTER THREE

THE GENTLE CLINKING of ice-cubes against glass filled the air as Christian reached for his drink to take a sip. Having Raquel sat across from him at the same table was a strange sight, and he didn't quite know how to interpret the low buzz filling his veins that had grown louder throughout the evening.

When they had arrived at his apartment, he had excused himself and retreated into the office to do some more work before dinner. Though he had soon figured out that the familiar voice drifting through the closed door was enough to distract him from the charts he'd meant to update and had given up on his task.

Raquel Pascal had re-entered his life without making a single noise, as if she had wanted to drift in and out without ever being noticed, though he knew that this characterisation was unfair. When she had entered his office, her shock had been genuine. She hadn't expected to see him. Somehow, they had both been in touch with each other through several proxies and hadn't even known.

The low hum of awareness in him roared alive as he followed those thoughts. Christian had been cautious with his feelings for her fifteen years ago, as he hadn't wanted to risk his friendship with Ramón by getting too close to his sister. He'd thought Raquel wouldn't be interested anyway, until the night of the prom, when she had tried to kiss him. By the time that had happened, he'd already accepted a place at a college in the US and known he'd be leaving Puerto Rico behind. With the added complication that his feelings were focused on his best friend's younger sister, his young adult self had chosen to take the easy way out and leave before anyone could get hurt.

Not that he was now reconsidering his feelings. Though his life was different, it was far more complex. He had dedicated his career to helping his brother and niece, one of which he had already failed. He would not disappoint the other. Hell, the only reason he was even following those thoughts was because he was so dedicated to Alexandria's wellbeing that he was willing to try anything to give her the life she wanted—to be the father figure she needed. The thought sometimes paralysed him. How could he take care of her when he didn't know the first thing about being a parent?

The last thing he wanted to add to that were ancient romantic notions he knew would lead him nowhere. That he sensed the connection clicking back into place—that he felt as if it had survived all this time—mattered little.

He glanced at the empty seat at the table where Lexi had sat as they ate dinner, keeping the conversation on the topic of Nesta and their training together. They had finished, and Lexi had quickly excused herself when her best friend, Annie's, name had flashed across the screen of her phone—leaving Christian alone with Raquel and the storm of emotions and memories she'd brought up in him.

'Thanks for dinner. That was quite impressive. I didn't realise they did room service for apartments,' Raquel said into the silence, taking a sip of her own glass.

'They do in this apartment building, and the services they offer had a lot to do with why I moved here with Lexi. My schedule is unpredictable, and I didn't want her to live off Chinese takeout and pizza whenever I'm not around,' he said, chuckling into the amber liquid in his glass.

Raquel joined in with his laugh and the sound dropping from her lips rolled over him in an electrified wave, uncovering memories of her buried in the sands of time. That laugh had once filled her brother's room when she'd come over to butt in on their 'bro time', as Ramón had weirdly insisted on calling it. Her brother had tried to get rid of her but, even though he had never said it, Christian hadn't minded her intrusion. He'd welcomed it, really.

'I hope you don't take this the wrong way, but you sound like a dad,' she said in between laughs, her eyes alight with the kindness her words meant to convey.

He could see that, could hear it and in his mind, and he could even rationalise it for the compliment that it was, yet it stung and he couldn't quite keep his expression neutral. 'Father' was a role he'd come into unwillingly. He'd much rather his brother were still alive to do the honour, for he'd been a far better father than Christian could hope to be. Fatherhood had never been something his career-driven self had considered, not when he spent more time working than at home. That had never sounded like a fair life for a child or a spouse, so Christian had found his peace knowing that he would have neither.

Now he was confronted with his shortcomings every time he got home too late to say goodnight, or had to ask the teachers to call him with any updates because he couldn't attend school at the usual hours.

'Sometimes it still feels strange to think about Anthony... He died of Huntington's three months ago, after struggling with it for several years. As it got worse, I stepped in and helped care for Lexi,' he said, sharing a safe version of the inner battle raging within him ever since they had said goodbye to his brother. Though he and Raquel had been friends at one point, his struggles to identify as a parent weren't something he would ever be comfortable discussing with her—or with anyone.

Especially not with her. Not with the warm tendrils of their past moments floating towards him the moment he'd seen her stand in the door of his office. He didn't have enough time for Lexi; there was certainly nothing left with which to indulge feelings like that.

'I'm so sorry to hear that, Christian,' she said, clutching her hand over her heart as a frown pulled at the corners of her eyebrows. 'Is that why you work as a neuro-surgeon now?'

Christian raised his eyebrows in surprise. 'How do you know I changed specialties?'

A shade of peach crept onto her cheeks, the colour only enhancing an already beautiful face. He remembered her features well, and had sometimes fantasised about tracing them with his fingers as he looked at her across the room. Had wanted to slide his hands through her silky-looking hair and tug on those black strands as he held on to her.

There'd been subtle changes to her. Lines had appeared around her eyes, ones he hoped dearly were from smiling. Her brown-green eyes were more distant, something he could understand very well. Life rarely let someone pick their path and they were littered with obstacles to be overcome—each one chipping something away.

Her eyes were not hardened, though. He still recog-

nised the bright spark coming through her shy exterior
as she said, 'I remember someone telling me you went to
LA to become a plastic surgeon after med school. It must
have been Ramón, though I don't recall the conversation.'

An electric current sprung into existence between
them, sending small jolts of energy through his body
as they looked at each other. From the small intake of
breath, he could tell she sensed it too. That a part of their
connection should remain alive to this day was strange
when it had only been an infatuation—and a distraction
now, when he barely had his life together enough to become an impromptu father.

Yet somehow speaking to her about Anthony wasn't
as daunting as it was with other people. Maybe that infatuation was still good for some things.

'That's right. I'd already been playing with the idea
of changing specialties when we learned Lexi had epilepsy, and my decision firmed up with Anthony's diagnosis. I moved to New York and into the apartment next
door from theirs. Stayed there until the day he became
too sick to live on his own.'

'Quite the beautiful tribute to make to your family.
And it worked out well for your career.' The look she
gave him heated his skin as she continued, 'I mean, look
at you. Head of Neurosurgery at Whitehall Memorial.
My neurology friends in med school only ever dared to
whisper the name.'

He chuckled at that. 'I can't believe we ended up working in the same field by sheer happenstance. I don't remember you ever saying you wanted to become a doctor.'

Raquel looked down into her glass as she shrugged,
and the collar of her oversized T-shirt shifted at that slight
movement, gliding down her shoulder and exposing the

skin underneath, that deepened into a dark gold in the dim light of the dining room. Would it be as soft to the touch as it looked?

'I don't think I decided until the end of secondary school, and even then it was almost more a "why not?". I know that sounds kind of dumb, because people usually see being a physician as their calling. But that feeling didn't awaken in me until I was in my third year. One of my professors asked me to join her for a volunteer position she did at the weekend when her usual med student had to drop out.'

She smiled as she looked up, her white teeth gleaming in the low light and showing the joy buried underneath that memory. 'That's when I first saw dogs used as therapy animals. Other volunteers were there with us, including an animal refuge that would place part-time dogs with inmates to train them. It did wonders for the rehabilitation of the human and the animal couldn't have lived a better life.'

Christian couldn't help but smile at her recollection, her words making clear how much that moment had meant to her. 'But you went ahead with your neurology residency anyway? Or did you know at this point already that you wanted to do what you are doing now?'

'I finished my traineeship as a neurologist and then I…got married.'

'You're married?'

His blood immediately chilled at her words, his eyes darting to her hand, but there was no wedding ring on her finger. Not unusual for a medical professional, though; jewellery wasn't safe when working in a hospital and wedding rings often stayed at home.

But Raquel shook her head. 'Not any more. It was

fantastic for a bit, and then mostly bad for the rest of the time, before we could finally admit to each other that we should never have married.'

Her voice didn't sound like her own as she said that, but like some far away version of herself. As if she was merely an onlooker, commenting on someone else's marriage. He'd expected hurt, not this strange…detachment.

'I'm sorry to hear that, Raquel. That must have been difficult for you,' he said, lacking better words to say. He'd never got serious enough with anyone to contemplate marriage, and now his life was all about work or his niece, with little room left for romance.

'Ah, don't be. I'm catching up with everything now that I'm free to do so. Sure, the hustle would have been easier in my mid-twenties rather than in my mid-thirties, but no use crying over lost time.' She put on a smile, though he still detected her shift in mood behind it. She might try her best to not dwell on it, but he sensed the topic was harder for her than she let on.

'Yeah…seizure-response dogs. That's an interesting way to use your MD.'

That was a story he was interested in knowing more about. People often changed their specialties, he was the proof of that, but it was rare to find someone who had gone through so many years of medical training just to leave it behind. What an enormous sacrifice.

'Yes, that's a reaction I get a lot from colleagues,' she said with a chuckle that rolled over him like a familiar and warm breeze. 'Ever since that day with my professor, I volunteered with different charities that used animals to help people heal from illness, and it sparked an interest in me. Neurology is and will always be my passion, and the longer I thought about it the more solid the idea of combining animal therapy with neurological conditions became. Which is why I'm here.'

There was genuine excitement in her voice, and he wasn't sure if it was because of the subject or because she was here—with him. He didn't have the heart to question it, so instead he said, 'But you are also still working as a neurologist part-time, from what Mia told me. How come?'

The joy in her eyes banked, her expression falling, and regret twisted in his gut at the sight. He didn't need to see the small shake of her head to know the answer to his question. 'If you don't want to talk—'

'No, it's fine. My problems won't become any better or worse if I refuse to speak about them,' she said with a rueful smile.

'Well, I agree they won't get worse, but maybe they can get better if you have someone to listen to you,' he replied, meaning every word.

With his own problems looming, he understood too well how much mental pressure that could build up.

'Ah, what is there to say?' Raquel took a sip of her wine, expelling a deep sigh into the glass. 'My business is a charity, so at the end of the day my only goal is to cover my costs and pay what little staff I can afford to have at the moment. The research into how service dogs can help with seizures is not as extensive as other areas, so naturally people who might need them don't always know that's an option. And, because it's such a new area, medical insurance companies rarely help with the cost, which makes having a seizure-alert dog a privilege, when it should really be a basic need if it helps people function independently. I mean, you saw it for yourself today. Nesta put your niece in a safe position and guarded her until it was over.'

Christian had seen it and the possibilities that had unravelled in front of his eyes had been magnificent. The independence the service dog would bring Lexi would do so much to improve her quality of life. She could go out on her own for a walk, or meet her friends without him having to arrange transport for her, or track down other parents to see if they could help.

'You work on research *and* training?' he asked her, curious to learn more about her work.

Raquel nodded and the light catching in her glossy, dark hair slipping over her shoulder drew his eyes towards it. He slowly raked his gaze back upwards to her face, noting every dip and plane of her chest and collar bone. Why, he didn't know. He didn't *need* a mental map of the points of Raquel's flesh that interested him, yet now he had one anyway.

'That's part of my work, yes, and also where my MD comes in quite handy. While working part-time in different hospitals, I also published my first paper on this subject last year. Getting it peer-reviewed was an adventure in and of itself.' Her eyes dropped to her glass, vanishing behind her thick lashes. 'But that's only the start. Once I have more to show for it, I can get other neurological institutions and hospitals involved.'

'You have me convinced, Raquel. What I saw today was impressive and I can think of a few of my patients that may benefit from a seizure-response dog.' His words were genuine, not ones to flatter her. Though he knew some of his patients wouldn't be able to afford it as easily as he had, he would still make the recommendation. That it might help an old friend boost her business would be a fortunate side effect.

Christian was not prepared for the spark lighting up in her eyes when she heard him say that. Had the stray thought he had verbalised meant so much to her?

'I can't even tell you how much an endorsement from you would mean to my business. I mean…you are the Head of Neurosurgery at Whitehall Memorial. You're *someone*. Your interest and business might be enough to satisfy my investors and give me more time to work on other connections.'

An endorsement? Christian stopped to consider the words that had bubbled forth from her with a nervous energy he was familiar with. What did she need his endorsement for?

But something else she had said that caught his attention—how she was funding her business. 'You have people backing you financially on top of still working yourself as a neurologist?' he asked, and her eyes grew grim.

'Yeah, but not for much longer. My investors are nervous about me not signing on with major hospitals. They say they are still very interested in the research that I plan to do, but if they don't see larger institutions like hospitals and neurological centres giving me contracts, they will withdraw their funding at our next meeting—which is in four weeks.'

She sighed again, rolling her head up and staring up at his ceiling. 'That's why I accepted the locum placement here. One, to earn money I can put towards my charity, but also to show Mia the quality of my work. If I can get her to commit to giving me a contract, my investors would be happy. They know that Whitehall Memorial investing in this research would get others across the country interested.'

He was glad that she was looking up at the ceiling, for his neutral expression slipped for the duration of a heartbeat before he slipped it back on. She was hoping to enlist the help of Mia. As respective department chairs, they worked together often enough that he had established an easy-going relationship with her. From observing her reaction earlier today, he knew she was interested in Raquel's work.

But giving Raquel a contract for more work wasn't up to her alone to decide. Sarah Frazier, the Chief of Medicine at Whitehall Memorial, would have to sign off on the budget required, and he doubted she would sign off on something this experimental. Though Whitehall Memorial was at the forefront of medical innovation, Frazier had always put more emphasis on things that showed quick results—cutting-edge surgery and headline-grabbing procedures.

From his research into seizure-alert dogs, he knew that, even though the foundation was solid, the research was years away from seeing any breakthroughs—especially considering how few people were putting their effort intro research in the first place. Though Whitehall was known for their commitment to science, their own investors would want to see a more solid approach to their pro bono projects.

He frowned when he realised Raquel was potentially wasting her time. Her hard work deserved recognition and a reward, but how could he help with that? Raquel had asked for an endorsement, which he was more than happy to give, but would that be enough to guarantee her success?

And why was he suddenly deeply worried about her success in the first place?

Had she over-shared? Her mind raced when Christian remained quiet, not saying anything about the information she had just shared. Raquel straightened her neck and the look Christian shot her over the dinner table sent her heart rate through the roof. It was a calculating look, one of intent—though what he intended to do, she could only imagine.

'Anyway, this is the story of the last few years of my life and what brought this unexpected reunion upon us.' She swallowed when he remained silent, his blue-grey eyes narrowed on her and gleaming with…something… that she couldn't describe. It sent flashes of heat and chills through her body, her thigh muscles tensing with the sudden rush of awareness washing over her.

'Are there any other avenues you are pursuing outside of getting a contract with Whitehall Memorial?' The question was too specific to be a random one and his tone of voice had her stomach plummeting through her body. Did he already know something she didn't?

Her dream had been hanging by a thread for a while now, and Raquel had forced herself not to look at it too closely or she knew she would have a daily breakdown. Because of how little funding she'd had to begin with, she'd had to pick up as many locum positions as she could afford while spending the time outside work on her charity, training dogs and researching as she placed them with patients.

The guarded look on Christian's face almost had her

bursting into tears, but she took a few focusing breaths before asking, 'Do you know something I should know?'

His fingers traced the rim of his glass in an uncharacteristic sign of nerves, which only deepened Raquel's concern. She had been clear with Mia that she wanted to explore the opportunity of an official collaboration between her charity and the hospital. How was that already at risk when she hadn't even started her first shift?

'Mia seems interested enough, and I will say that she'll be an important person to win over if you want a formal partnership with Whitehall Memorial. Our pro bono budget is a very sought-after commodity, so your argument has to be air-tight.' He raised his eyes to hers, sympathy shining in his blue-grey gaze.

Raquel's heart pushed against her chest, making each breath harder than the last one. She'd known that it wouldn't be easy to get a contract, but she had worked too hard on putting everything together after her divorce that she couldn't give up, even if the odds were slimmer than she thought.

'I have all the documentation here. It's a long shot, I get that, but the data are there, the benefits are undeniable and...' This was her last chance to secure funding for her charity. Without a contract the remaining investors would pull out and her dream would evaporate into thin air. She *had* to succeed here—there was no other option. She could not fail again, the way she had failed her younger self when she'd put her career second—the way she had failed in her marriage. Adding another thing to that list would be too much for her to bear.

Raquel surged to her feet as a sense of panic gripped her. 'Let me show you the papers I published. In them you can...' The rest of her words died in her throat when

Christian wrapped his hand around her wrist, pulling her to a stop.

She stared at him, wide-eyed, her heart stuttering inside her chest as his fingers tightened around her arm. 'Take a deep breath, Raquel,' he said, his voice low and steady.

She did as she was told, pain shooting through her chest as she forced air into her lungs. 'Good,' he said, the tone of his voice skittering down her spine in a warm spark. 'Now take another one.'

This breath was easier than the previous one and her heart found its rhythm again, its only disruption Christian's sudden proximity.

'You've been running yourself thin trying to keep this passion of yours alive, haven't you?' he asked, and Raquel bit down on her lower lip when mist sprang into her eyes out of nowhere. It was a simple fact he'd voiced—one people would easily see if they merely glanced in her direction.

She couldn't remember the last time she'd had a moment to herself—whatever she had to give went straight back into her charity. Raquel knew it was worth it, and she'd work even harder if it meant that she could keep doing this research and training the dogs. She was tired, yes, but not exhausted enough to throw in the towel.

Still, just the simple acknowledgement of her efforts created a tiny crack in the thick walls she kept around herself. A shudder raked through her body when he let go of her hand but remained standing close enough to her that the scent of his cologne drifted up her nose.

'Tell me what's at stake. I want to help.' The calm and assurance in the words cracked the exhaustion she'd been holding at bay over the last few months. There was so much to do, so many people to convince and partners to meet, that she hadn't had time to come up for air in the last two years.

And even though she was more than willing to make these sacrifices, to give even more despite running on empty, something about being seen by Christian in this moment—of all people—broke through her defences.

Raquel hung her head as tears spilled out of her eyes and she couldn't stop her shoulders from shuddering with each shaky breath that turned into a sob. 'I've devoted the last two years of my life to this cause, and I would have given it even more if I hadn't made the mistake of getting married. This is the first thing I've done all on my own since my divorce, since putting my career on hold for someone else. This is *all* I have to show I'm not a complete failure as a person.'

The words spilled out of her between sobs, and under any other circumstances she would never have allowed herself to show such weakness in front of anyone. But something about Christian's presence was soothing, lulling her into a sense of safety. He had been her confidant before, and had listened to her as she'd spoken about the trivialities of school drama.

The connection between them had remained intact, she realised, as she leaned on it and let her exhaustion take over.

'Sorry, I'm a bit of a mess,' she huffed out as she tried to get the tears to stop, and froze when Christian stepped closer.

She looked up just in time to see him wrap his arms around her as he pulled her into a hug that had her heart slamming against her chest. Warmth flooded through her, invading every corner of her body and instantly setting her at ease. His hand traced lazy circles over her back, his fingers leaving trails of hot sparks bouncing under her skin, and she inhaled his scent with a shuddering breath.

'I can't promise you that there will be a contract at the end of your placement here, but I will do whatever I can to convince the chief; you have my word,' he said, his words soothing her exhaustion as much as his touch.

His face was so close to hers, his breath grazing over her heated cheeks, and for one moment she fantasised about what it would be like to lean in and finally claim that kiss he had denied her fifteen years ago. But then Christian stepped back, breaking the spell he had her under, and emptiness rushed into the space they had shared a few seconds ago.

'Thank you, Christian,' she said quietly when she found her voice again, swiping the hem of her over-sized shirt over her eyes to dry the tears streaking her cheeks. 'Look at me, prattling on about my problems when we should have been talking about work.'

Christian blinked, seemingly unaware of what she meant, so she added, 'She assigned me to Dr Prem's cases and said one was a perfect candidate for deep-brain stimulation. I meant to bring it up when…'

She shrugged, not sure how she should characterise her sudden outburst of emotions. It would be hard to look him in the eye tomorrow after how she had spilled her guts unprompted, yet she couldn't help but feel lighter than she had in weeks.

'Oh…' Christian straightened, then his eyes darted to the clock hanging on the wall. Raquel followed his gaze and gasped at the time. They had been talking for hours.

'Actually, never mind that. I didn't realise it was already so late. We can talk at the hospital,' she quickly said when she realised where his hesitation came from. He must have been exhausted himself, yet had been kind enough to let her ramble on.

'Let me call you a cab,' he said, and the protest died in her throat when he looked at her, her eyes showing no compromise in this regard, so she simply nodded, thankful that she didn't have to work out her own way back to the hotel.

She gathered her things as he spoke on the phone, slowly drifting towards the door while sending him the occasional glance as he spoke in a quiet voice. He gave her a one-sided smile as he turned round.

'You're going to accompany Lexi to school tomorrow, right?' Christian asked, and Raquel noted the distance he left between them this time as he came to a halt several feet away from her.

She nodded, pushing that thought away. There'd been no deeper meaning to his hug other than that of an old friend comforting her. 'That's right. The teachers will need a briefing on Alexandria's needs and how Nesta plays into them. It's also good to observe her in her normal environment.'

Talking about work helped her calm her frayed nerves, focusing on the things she could control rather than the torrent of different emotion that was creating a tight ball of chaos in the pit of her stomach.

'I'm usually up early to get some work done before school drop-off. Why don't you come by earlier and we can discuss the case before you leave for school?' He glanced at his phone when it vibrated. 'They're ready for you downstairs.'

'I...' Raquel wasn't sure if she should spend more alone time with Christian. If this evening had taught her anything it was that he'd scaled her usual defences with ease. The stress of her two jobs had been something she'd struggled with for the last two years, yet she'd managed to keep it all inside until he had asked her a simple question—until he had looked at her and actually seen her.

That could be dangerous. Her emotions were already volatile, and throwing her old flame into the mix with all that was going on could only be a terrible idea.

Despite all of that, she felt herself smile and nod. 'All right. I'll see you in the morning,' she said and, when she glanced over her shoulder as she walked out of the door, she saw his eyes linger on her until she entered the lift.

CHAPTER FOUR

CHRISTIAN SAT IN his home office, staring blankly at the screen. He'd got up before Lexi, the way he usually did, but instead of focusing on the medical paper in front of him his mind kept straying towards Raquel. To the softness of her hand when he had held it between his. And the bow-shaped mouth just slightly parting as he'd pulled her into his arms. The scent that had enveloped him as he'd held her close, reminding him of the sun and the beaches in Puerto Rico.

He closed the document on his screen, giving up on writing the pages. It would have to wait a few more days until he could settle back into his routine. Just now, Raquel's sudden appearance still felt too raw, too real, for him to stick his past feelings for her back into the box inside his mind, where they belonged.

Their reunion needed to stay professional and platonic. Anything else was out of the question for him. His focus needed to remain on Lexi, who didn't get enough of his attention as it was. There was no way someone else could fit into his life—not without significant sacrifices. And Christian could never ask anyone for those—especially not Raquel.

When he'd warned her about the slim chance of getting a contract with Whitehall Memorial, he hadn't expected such a visceral reaction. Though she had shared little with him, he could read between the lines how much she had sacrificed to get to this point—and that it all stood on the brink of nothingness again.

Christian was determined to help his old friend in what limited capacity he could. Throughout their conversation, something hot had stabbed him in the side whenever she'd brought up her past experience. There had been a man lucky enough to marry her, only to make her put her life on hold for him. As someone who was in a similar situation—having to do what was right for Lexi took priority over anything else—he couldn't imagine robbing her of her spark like that. What selfish person would do such a thing?

With a deep sigh, he pushed himself off the office chair and strode into the kitchen, pressing the button of the coffee machine. The coffee grinder came alive with a whirr and soon the black liquid poured into the cup he'd shoved under the nozzle. Grabbing milk from the fridge, he sat it down on the kitchen island while waiting for the coffee to finish.

Christian was surprised to hear that Raquel had been married—and the relief washing over him when he'd heard about her divorce mere seconds later was a reaction he wasn't prepared to examine any more closely. They hadn't seen each other in so long, and had never even been a couple, so he had no business feeling this strange attachment he sensed between them. When he'd seen the distress on her face, he hadn't been able to fight the urge to wrap her in his arms. And then he'd had to fight the impulse to kiss her—not just for how she was helping Lexi attain a better life, but because of *who* she was to him.

Had been, Christian corrected himself as he poured milk into the coffee mug and gave it a distracted stir. Raquel wasn't someone he had pined over in a long time, so what was reviving itself inside his chest was no more than an unresolved strand of their relationship. Nothing to worry about, because what was there to give? Neither of them were leading lives that made them available to each other.

The entrance buzzer going off ripped him from his contemplation, and he tapped the screen. 'Yes?'

'Good morning, Dr Wolf. I have a visitor down here for you. Ms Raquel Pascal?' The voice of the concierge filtered through the speakers.

'Please send her up.' He paused and then added, 'And it's Dr Pascal.'

'Oh…' The line went quiet for a moment, then he heard the concierge clear his throat. 'Very well; I will send up Dr Pascal, sir.'

The speaker went silent, and he went back to his coffee. He took a sip, savouring the familiar taste and the jolt of caffeine that would shortly follow, needing it to shake him awake when his night had been haunted by Raquel, the softness of her hands and that hint of lavender and coconut he couldn't forget about. He was about to wait at the door when he looked at his mug, putting it down again. Then he grabbed a new one off the shelf and pressed the button on the coffee machine, which began grinding up beans again.

A faint knock came at the front door, and he walked up to it, opening it. Raquel stood on the other side, eyes still bleary from the early morning.

'Sorry to make you get up so early,' Christian said by

way of greeting, then stepped aside to let her in, gently closing the door behind her.

'It's okay. I'm flexible with clients' needs,' she replied, her eyes darting over him with a quick glance, and the blush appearing on her cheeks was such an exquisite sight, he had to ball his hand into a fist to stop himself from reaching out to touch her.

'Do you drink coffee?' he asked, clearing his throat to shoo away the intruding thoughts.

'I'm a millennial—which means at this point I'm probably thirty-five per cent coffee,' she replied, a smile tugging at the corners of her lips when he chuckled. Talking to Raquel was just so simple. It wasn't like talking to his patients or his colleagues, or even other parents in Lexi's class—as little as he did to begin with.

No, things with Raquel were just…easy. And easy was something he hadn't felt ever since Anthony had been diagnosed so many years ago.

'Good,' he said, then walked over to the coffee machine. 'Do you take anything with it?'

'Just some milk,' she replied, and watched as he grabbed the milk jug again and poured some of it into the mug intended for her.

'A woman after my own heart,' he said as he handed her the mug, then raised it. 'Enjoy.'

Raquel mimicked his gesture, then put the mug to her full, dark-pink lips and took her first sip. The moan coming from her lips set off something within Christian, something low and primal in the pit of his stomach, and he quickly distracted himself with his own mug. He glanced at the oven clock, then nodded towards his office. 'Let's go talk. Lexi is going to be up in half an hour to get ready for school.'

She nodded as they walked to his office, and when Christian waited at the door for her to pass him he caught another nose full of her scent, feeding the primal thing awakening in his stomach without meaning to.

Shoving those thoughts away, he pointed at the sofa in the corner of his office and took a seat on a lounger next to it to bring a safe distance between them. Though them working together had come as a surprise, he couldn't let that throw him off his game. Raquel was here to help Alexandria get a better life and work on the cases assigned to her. Their collaboration was purely professional.

His eyes lingered on her, despite his own warning in his head, dipping down from her face and over her body. A cream blouse was tucked into her high-waisted jeans, accentuating the flair of her hips even as she sat down. When his gaze wandered back up to her face, she looked at him with widened eyes and a sparkle illuminating them. Heat expanded in his chest with every breath and Christian momentarily forgot why they were sitting here in the first place—and why he shouldn't throw her over his shoulder and make good on the promise that had sparked alive between them so many years ago.

He snapped out of the distracting fantasy when Raquel cleared her throat and said, 'So, deep-brain stimulation…?'

'What…? Oh, right. The case. Let me get the chart.' That had been why he'd asked her here, to discuss their first case together, something that was now looking far more complicated than he'd expected. He couldn't keep his thoughts straight when she was near him. He was veering into dangerous territory. His main responsibility was to Lexi, to give her the life his brother hadn't got a chance to give her. The interest in Raquel should be based on what she could do for his niece, not how she hadn't left his mind since she'd appeared in his office yesterday.

A singular focus had brought him this far ahead in his career. The ability to ignore everything around him and to hone in on the task ahead of him helped him get through multi-hour surgeries of extreme difficulty. Yet he couldn't have put Raquel out of his mind to save his own life.

He got up and retrieved a tablet from his office, tapping on it as he strode back, and handing it to Raquel, who received it with a smile that instantly brought back all the heat he had just banished from his body.

'Dr Prem and I had already agreed on surgical intervention for his case before he left unexpectedly. He diagnosed Evelyn Crane with Parkinson's disease two years ago and she has been coming for her regular check-ups every month,' Christian said as he sat back down, once again wringing back control over the sensations in his body.

'I see... I assume, now that someone is there to accompany her through all of pre- and post-surgery, you want to get started in the next few days?' Her hazel eyes narrowed as she scrolled through the patient's chart and bit down on her lower lip with a hum as she read on. 'I read through bits of her chart last night, but I was lacking some context. It says we have moved her to stage-two Parkinson at the beginning of the year. What's your standard for stage two?'

Christian shook his head as he stared at the point where her teeth had dug into her lip, a small red mark tinting the brown skin. 'I believe stage-two patients still keep most of their mobility, but the stiffness now manifests in both sides of the body and difficulty walking increases or develops. But it's been a while since I've been this deep in diagnostic work, so best ask Mia for any specifics. In Evelyn's case, though, her mobility is severely restricted and, with the unexpected delay, we don't want to waste any more time.'

'Mia wasn't kidding when she said she needed me to hit the ground running,' she said, breathing out a laugh. 'Though stage two sounds similar to how I would have defined it. What's left to do for Evelyn to get her into surgery?'

'Dr Prem noted a pre-op check with her but by now that's outdated. That'll be your first step to get her in. Chances are Mia already asked someone to schedule an appointment, since she had to postpone the surgery very last minute,' Christian answered.

He had received a message from Mia, along with the other neurosurgeons in his department, that the new locum neurologist would take all of Dr Prem's patients for the duration of his compassionate leave and that all non-critical surgeries would be postponed until then.

'I'm meeting with Mia later today after my appointment with Alexandria. I'll get her booked in first chance I get and start constructing the post-surgical care plan today,' Raquel said, handing him back the tablet. 'Thank you for providing the context. I know we could have spoken later but I… It's always a bit nerve-wracking to step into a brand-new hospital, and I want to leave an excellent impression on Mia.'

Christian took back the tablet, a smile tugging at his lips at the vulnerability in Raquel's words. They hadn't seen each other in so long, yet she hadn't forsaken the habit of opening up to him. That alone pulled at the wall of responsibilities he'd created to hide behind. Maybe he could trust her with his thoughts, too—let her see just a bit of the struggle he was going through with Lexi and his self-doubts.

Christian pushed that thought aside before it could take root. He could not be as selfish, as her ex-husband had turned out to be. She deserved a lot more than he was able to give and opening up to her would only serve his own needs—not hers.

'What is your morning with Lexi looking like?' he asked, not ready to let go of their conversation just yet. Though he couldn't let her see the thoughts bubbling beneath the surface, her presence alone was soothing.

'I hope that her day won't feel much different. I'm going to stay mostly in the background and observe her with Nesta, mainly to note any alerts or potential responses that we should enhance with training. She's done a great job of adapting to Alexandria on instinct alone. With the right enforcements here and there, she will make a steadfast companion to your niece for many years.' The spark entering her eyes as she spoke about the dog was enchanting, and with it came the low hum of awareness as he leaned forward to rest his arms on his thighs.

'I've not seen her so excited or smile this much. Her moods have been dark ever since Tony passed away,' he said, and regretted it immediately as the sparkle in her eyes vanished. As the heat in his veins diminished at the thought of his brother.

'How are you holding up with everything? It can't have been easy.' The sympathy in her expression was almost too much for Christian to bear.

It was a familiar sentiment, one he'd seen in way too many faces over the last three months, and it always brought up the sense of inadequacy that had haunted him ever since he'd taken Lexi into his care. It was something no one saw in him because he kept that part carefully hidden. But now he sensed it bubbling up as those hazel eyes bore into him, wringing the truth from his lips.

'I…never thought I would be a father. Never wanted it enough. Now I'm responsible for the life of my niece and I just don't know if I'm doing enough,' he heard himself say, surprised at how easy it was to open up to this woman sitting next to him.

Her features softened, and she leaned forward to reach out for his hand, wrapping her fingers around his. The warmth of her skin banished the chill gathering inside him and sent a trickle of heat down his arm.

'That must be frightening,' she said in a low voice that made his head shoot up to meet her gaze.

It was frightening, and before Raquel had made such an unexpected return in his life it had been all Christian could think about. He might be doing his best, but was he doing the right things? Would Lexi understand that he'd worked so hard to give her a life in which she would never want for anything? Or would she only ever recall all the times he hadn't made it in time to pick her up from school and had had to ask Sam—a retired nurse who sometimes acted as Lexi's care-giver when he couldn't—to look after her?

He barely remembered his own parents, who had lived such intense career lives as diplomats that he'd been mostly raised by whichever nanny they could find in the country they had currently been in. Even in retirement, they had taken up some volunteer work for the government, working until their final days together.

His work ethic mirrored the behaviour his parents had modelled for him growing up, but that had come with the drawback that they had been rarely around. Anthony had been different, and had been present in his daughter's life. He hadn't been a workaholic, like Christian. Would Lexi grow to resent him for his absence, the way he'd sometimes resented his parents for theirs?

But Raquel... Something about the simple acknowledgement that his situation justified his fear set the pressure on his chest at ease whenever he spoke about the topic. He looked down at where her fingers were wrapped around his and twisted his hand around so their palms were lying against each other. Her fingers flexed open, as if she was ready to let go of him, but then they curled back in, gently grazing his skin.

'It is,' he said, and let his thumb drift over the back of her hand. 'I rarely get people who understand that.'

She exhaled with a soft sigh, her lips parting as if to say something, when the shuffling of feet and paws on the wooden floors drifted through the quiet air. Raquel snatched her hand back as his own spine stiffened at the sudden sound, and he swallowed a curse as he examined the situation he had let himself get into.

This was exactly why he doubted his skills as a father. What was he doing, holding hands with the woman who was training the service dog of his niece? No matter what relationship they'd had before this moment, he knew as a medical professional that anything between them was beyond acceptable. She was here to do a job, not explore what could have been between them had he shown a bit more courage fifteen years ago, and told her how he felt, instead of leaving her hanging because he'd been too scared to be open with her.

Christian got to his feet just as Lexi walked past the

open office door, looking first at him and then Raquel, with eyes still heavy with sleep.

'Good morning,' he said before she could say anything. 'Raquel is ready to take you to school and spend the morning with you, so you better get ready.'

His touch lingered on her hand whenever Raquel let her mind wander, which had been way too often ever since she'd left Alexandria's school building to head to Whitehall Memorial for her first shift.

The morning had gone without any incidents, for which she was grateful. As expected, Nesta had drawn many eyes and whispers towards Alexandria and her, but the girl was already showing her expertise as a service-dog handler in avoiding unwanted attention and educating people who tried to disturb Nesta while she was working. Though Raquel would have loved to claim that the rule about not petting a working dog was common knowledge, there were always enough people who tried to do just that, and needed to be taught about the boundaries surrounding service dogs.

Nesta had curled up under Alexandria's seat for all the lessons in the morning, only standing up once when a seizure happened. As with the first day in Christian's office, the Golden Retriever had shoved her head between the girl's hands on her lap and had lain there until she came back into consciousness.

The teacher had momentarily stopped when Nesta had moved, drawing more attention to Alexandria than necessary, but Raquel had waited until after the class to talk with the teacher and tell her she should resume lessons if Nesta was simply guarding Alexandria.

'Nesta knows what's considered a medical emergency

and will alert someone to the fact if her handler needs medical attention,' she had said, which had drawn an impressed whistle from the teacher's lips, and filled Raquel's step with a spring for the rest of the morning.

That was until she crossed the threshold of Whitehall Memorial and all the complicated feelings she had shoved into a box in the depth of her being popped out once more. What had she been thinking, grabbing Christian's hand like that? The touch had sent jolts of electricity up her arm that had left trails of flames underneath her skin.

Not only were they temporary colleagues, Christian was also technically her client, since Alexandria was a minor. Those two things combined were enough to make any semblance of their past feelings of each other off-limits—if there even were any feelings from his side. There hadn't been fifteen years ago... But there was no way she imagined the tension between them now. His hand had lingered on hers, his fingers drawing soft circles on the back of her hand that she could still feel now.

Then again, those had been her exact thoughts all those years ago, only for him to pull back at the last second and tell her he didn't see her in a romantic light.

Raquel shook those thoughts off when she walked through the doors leading to the neurology department. 'I'm here to see Dr Brett. She asked me to come here about my shift assignments,' Raquel said when she reached the desk in front of Mia's office.

The woman behind the desk looked up at her, then scanned the screen in front of her. 'Mia is seeing a patient in Room 301. She asked me to send you there when you arrive and to wait outside until she comes out.'

They weren't meeting in her office. Raquel raised her eyebrows in surprise, but nodded and walked down the corridor, noting the numbers on every door until she understood in what sequence they were. She didn't have to wait long for Mia to emerge from the room and stood up straight when the tall woman approached her with a sincere but tired smile. 'First day for you, Raquel. Are you excited?' she asked as she came to a halt in front of her.

She nodded, holding her hand out and shaking Mia's in greeting. 'Yes! Alexandria and I had a great start this morning, and I'm keen to fill in wherever you need me.' Though she knew she would have her roster of patients to take care of, she wanted Mia to know she was available for her in whatever form she needed. The more impressed the Head of Neurology was with her, the easier it would be to get her endorsement. This wasn't the first time Raquel had needed to hustle on one job to make another come along.

'Ah, you will regret saying that by the end of the week, I promise you,' Mia said with a wry smile, then waved her along as she strode down the hall. 'Since you're working the late shift for the month we've contracted you for, your primary responsibility outside of your patient roster will be consultations in the ER.'

'I might only be here temporarily, but I'm here to help,' she reiterated as she glanced up at the woman.

'Sorry for not meeting you at my office. We had a last-minute appointment come in for the patient of Dr Prem's I told you about, so I wanted to take you straight to her. Evelyn Crane?' She looked at Raquel, who quickly nodded, and was thankful Christian had taken the time to talk her through his thoughts.

'What good timing. I was actually going to schedule her for an appointment after our meeting, since she was ready for surgery when it had to be postponed because

of staffing. I spoke to Chr… Dr Wolf…this morning to
see if he'd already assigned anyone on his team to join
the case.'

'How do you know Christian again?' Mia had been in
the room when she'd had her unexpected reunion with
him, and the way she looked at her left the impression
that she had been curious about their connection since
yesterday.

'He and my brother are best friends, funnily enough.
Though I didn't know he worked here and he wasn't the
reason I came here.' She didn't know why she felt the
need to add that last part, but something about Mia's presence told her she was all about her patients and wanted
to see that reflected in her staff.

'Huh, interesting. You train the dogs from early on,
but you also still practise medicine. You've got a lot on
your plate,' Mia commented as she resumed her walk.

Raquel worried her lip. Revealing to Mia that she
needed to work to fund her dog-training efforts wasn't
something she had planned to do, so she wouldn't seem
desperate. But thinking on the fly and coming up with
a better sounding version of the truth wasn't something
she'd ever been good at.

'I partially fund my charity work, so I have to keep
working as a neurologist as well,' she finally said as the
silence stretched on. If the truth was something that
would cause Mia to shy away, then she was never going
to give Raquel her support in the first place.

But, to her relief, the woman only nodded, understanding where she was coming from. 'There's not a lot of research around seizure-response dogs,' she said, her tone
more curious than sceptical.

'That's what makes securing funding much more difficult. Investors fear the uncertainty, regardless of how much it can improve the quality of life of the patients. It doesn't help that I'm some unknown doctor doing this research on the side. Investors are all about the Mark Hendersons and Christian Wolfs of this world.' Raquel bit her lip again to stop herself from showing too much self-pity. That would not help her win Mia over.

'So, you were saying about Evelyn...' she said, steering the conversation back to where it had started.

'Ah, yes. Since we knew you were starting, we called Evelyn and scheduled her this appointment.'

Mia stopped in front of a closed door. 'I asked Christian to swing by as well, so he should arrive at any moment. Get yourself acquainted with the patient before he arrives, and page if you need anything.'

The Head of Neurology took her phone out of her lab coat and glanced at the clock with a sigh. Then, with only a tight smile as a goodbye, she turned around and left the way they had come from. Raquel hesitated for a few heartbeats, staring down the corridor where the woman had just disappeared, then looked back at the closed door and raised her hand to knock.

Christian's morning was occupied by extracting a tricky tumour that was compressing his patient's eye nerves and causing visual impairment. Losing himself fully in a unique surgery with a complicated plan of action was exactly the kind of distraction he needed to forget about the conversation he'd had with Raquel early that morning. To forget how much he had shared about himself; how thoughts he hadn't voiced to anyone came out unbidden simply because she was there. And how he felt seen for the first time in so long simply because she had acknowledged the struggle within him.

That tactic had worked until this moment, as he stood in front of an examination room in the neurology wing with his hand hovering on the door handle. Mia had left a message with the OR nurse that she'd scheduled a consultation with Evelyn Crane, now that her new neurologist was up and running—not knowing that it was this neurologist who had him piling more work onto his plate so he didn't have to deal with the bubbling heat inside him.

Her faint laughter filtered through the door, raising the fine hair along his arms as he remembered how much he'd relished that laughter when they had been teenagers. Though it sounded different now, deeper and richer, the tone was the same, the brightness of it intoxicating enough for him to crave more. He wanted to hear the breath of that laugh graze his skin; wanted to swallow the sound with his own lips...

Christian exhaled sharply, driving those thoughts away. Their past relationship didn't matter in this situation, not when they would work so closely together, both at the hospital and at home. He needed to remind himself of that whenever the heat surged through his veins. This wasn't about him. It was about Lexi and how he could live up to his responsibilities as her guardian and father figure.

He flexed his fingers several times before balling them into a fist and knocking on the door. The murmuring went quiet and then he heard her soft and accented voice say, 'Come in.'

Though he had steeled himself, his blood still heated when he stepped into the room and saw her standing next to their patient, who lay on the examination table with several electrodes stuck to her chest. She hadn't changed clothes since he'd last seen her, and his eyes lingered on the roundness of her hips before he looked back up to greet the patient.

'Evelyn, I'm Christian Wolf. You might still remember me from your pre-surgical check with Dr Prem, where we were walking you through the steps of the surgery.'

He didn't reach out to her so as not to disturb the readings of the vital monitor, but stepped closer to where Raquel was noting down things on the tablet. Evelyn gave a weak smile and he could tell she was trying her best to control the tremors that had started the moment he'd introduced herself.

Raquel noticed the woman's increase in stress as well, for she laid a soft hand on the patient's arm and smiled at her. 'I just finished talking Evelyn through the latest update. Thankfully, her medication works well after cycling through different combinations. I've already drawn some blood and sent it off to the lab. Barring any flags from the lab, we are good to schedule the surgery.'

Christian nodded, then pointed at a door leading to an adjacent consultation room. 'Evelyn, you don't mind if Dr Pascal and I quickly go over our notes to make sure we have all of our plans in order?'

The woman shook her head, and then he looked at Raquel as he pushed down the door handle and stepped through into the other room. She stood up and walked over to him, her hand holding out the tablet for him to have a look. His eyes drifted down, lingering on the delicate fingers as they wrapped around the piece of equipment, and more unbidden fantasies sprang to life in his brain. When she had stepped past him, he closed the door and turned around to face her.

This close to her, he could see each individual long lash as she blinked up at him, her scent surrounding him as it had back at his place and transporting him to places he couldn't go. They were *colleagues*.

'I hope you don't mind. I find it best to discuss things away from the patient's ears and come back with a united solution,' he explained, about the sidebar he had just pulled her into.

'Of course, I thought as much. What do you want to talk about?' A soft pink dusted her cheeks as she looked up to him and he fought the urge to reach out to her.

'What's the desired outcome of the surgery that can't be achieved through non-surgical means? You said her medication is working well, so maybe surgery is no longer the best option?' he asked as he took the patient chart and looked at the blood test results she had indicated. Christian hadn't changed his mind about the surgery, but it never hurt to stress-test ideas and force a deeper analysis of the proposed medical procedure.

Raquel seemed to understand the purpose of his question as she paused to consider. 'The mix of medication the patient is on shows increased stress on her liver function, and in time it could also affect her kidneys. If we want to avoid future renal failure, or even the need for dialysis down the road, deep-brain stimulation is the best option to preserve the quality of life she currently has.'

He nodded, letting her words roll around in his head as he considered the risks of surgery. The only problem with that was the subtle scent of earthy lavender that kept pulling him out of his contemplation and back to the woman in front of him—and how he wanted to bury his face in her neck to revel in that scent.

This was *not* good. They were in a professional environment and seeing a patient together. All he was supposed to note was her recommendation as a neurologist in referring a case to his department. Something that she was doing with such excellence and care that it was even harder to keep his mind focused on the things in front of him. Even though she had only learned about Evelyn's case this morning, she didn't shy away from advocating what was right for her patient.

'Is the patient aware of the risks involving the surgery?' he asked to put his mind back into medicine mode.

'Of course. She's struggling with the decline of her mobility and is at the point where anything seems worth the risk.'

Christian took a deep breath to calm his nerves, then handed the tablet back to her. 'Good. Let's schedule the surgery. If you get in touch with my assistant, he will shuffle some things around so we can go ahead the second your aftercare plan is locked into people's schedule.'

Raquel looked up at him through those dark lashes he had been counting mere moments ago, and the smile lighting up her face almost tore through the leash of control he'd put on himself. 'I'll start putting the plan together to hand over to your team. But it'll have to be next week, because I'm flying to Puerto Rico for Ramón's...'

She paused, their looks of surprise matching each other's as they both realised what she'd been about to say: Ramón's wedding. A deeply intimate and romantic setting that he suddenly realised they would attend together, just when he'd thought he could keep his distance from her.

'You're going too, aren't you?' she said, cutting the tension with a low chuckle.

'I have to admit, I had forgotten about it until you

brought it up.' Which was strange, because he had spoken to Ramón two weeks ago about the timing of everything on the day. Back then Raquel had played on his mind as well, though he had decided not to worry about their reunion until he was there. Strange how that had turned out...

'I guess, then, we'll plan the surgery for the day after we get back. That should give me enough time to put together the post-surgery plans and get all the other teams involved.'

She turned around and pushed the door back open, and then threw him another smile over her shoulder as she said, 'And thanks for stress-testing my diagnostic plan. I appreciate you looking out for me.'

CHAPTER FIVE

'I CAN'T BELIEVE this mass of greenery just exists in the middle of Manhattan.'

Raquel looked around her, turning on her heels several times over as she took in the grandeur of Central Park—and how different it was from her home in Puerto Rico. Her family lived on a rural estate where the entire Pascal clan owned several adjacent houses and land parcels that formed a considerable portion of the land there. She loved walking around the bushes and forests at home, finding the nicer spots and marking them so she could find her way back whenever she had to escape her family—which happened often enough whenever she went back to visit.

'It's pretty impressive,' Christian agreed, taking in the same view as her.

He walked next to her with a considerable enough distance between them for her to notice this as a deliberate act, and she was grateful for it. Grateful and also unbelievably annoyed at the distance.

As part of the training for Nesta and Alexandria, they had agreed to spend the day together in an open spot with enough strangers in their space so they could observe how dog and handler reacted in various situations. This wasn't nearly as crowded as a train or a small venue, but still something different from school, which was a controlled environment. Watching Alexandria with her dog filled Raquel with pride and confidence that this placement would go off without a hitch. The girl's preparation around the subject of seizure-response dogs and her own condition shone through every interaction they had with each other.

But spending the day with her meant also spending the day with Christian, with whom she had been exchanging charged looks from the moment they'd met. Or maybe that was her over-active fantasy deceiving her again. She thought she'd sensed his gaze lingering on her in the quiet moments between them. But, then again, she'd believed the same thing fifteen years ago, only to have her heart broken. Was the electricity between them real or was she seeing things again?

'Do you come here often?' she asked, to distract herself from the turmoil kicking off within her.

'Not as much as I should. You know the life of a medical professional: we rarely get to keep ordinary hours, and when we do it's spent poking our noses into the latest research or doing something else to keep on top of our game.' He paused and chuckled. 'It's such a stereotype, but I guess it's true that you never really appreciate what your city has to offer until someone comes to visit.'

Raquel joined in with his laughter, willing away the tension between them. 'Try running your own business on top of your regular job and you'll take any chance you get to go outside and touch some grass.'

The sideways glance he shot her set something off in the pit of her stomach. Why had she thought that an outing with him was a good idea? But, regardless of their connection, it was something necessary for her work with Alexandria.

They both looked ahead to where Alexandria was holding onto Nesta's harness as they walked along the winding path. The people walking past them didn't seem to notice the dog or the girl, except for children here and there who pointed and asked questions. But, unlike many other training sessions, Raquel hadn't had to intervene once so far. When it came to enforcing service-dog boundaries, Alexandria was already doing that all on her own.

His hazel eyes focused on her as he turned his head. Her heart tumbled inside her chest when she detected his attention on her, his expression unreadable. The only thing she noticed was a distinct softness around the usually hard lines of his mouth, as if he understood her struggle to find her path. Even though she knew he couldn't. Not really. Though she and Tom had been in love at one point, they had never learned how to express themselves to one another, which had led them to make wrong assumptions about the other person until they had both sacrificed so much of the life they'd wanted to lead in an attempt to make the other one happy.

Raquel had claimed a lot of the blame for herself, only later seeing how much her willingness to put herself second had cost her. Before getting married, she had thought about the idea of working with dogs, the way her mentor at medical school had. Something about that vision of the future had sent thrills of excitement through her. But Tom's start-up had taken all of their attention as a couple. So she had told herself to be patient—another year didn't matter—only to find out that she should have been more ambitious. If she had held onto her own convictions, she could only imagine how far along her charity would be by now.

How could Christian understand this when he didn't even know about it? Yet somehow his eyes conveyed just that he did.

'Is it that way because of your ex?' he asked.

Raquel swallowed, the fluttering in her stomach dying down and turning into a heavy stone weighing her down. Her mouth went dry and her brain went into immediate crisis control. Admitting how much of herself she had lost in her marriage was too painful for her. She'd freely admit that she'd had a late career start with her charity work, but always left out the reason why.

'Yes… I put a lot on hold for my marriage and I made Tom a priority over growing the career I wanted. But most of the responsibility lies with me. I decided to support him above anything else, so I have to be the one to own this. He never asked me to do anything, but I thought that a good spouse would put their partner ahead of themselves, no matter the cost. It's what I'd seen growing up with my parents and my *tíos* and *tías*. They all had such successful marriages…'

She pressed her lips into a thin line to stop the words from pouring out of her mouth. But his presence was so reassuring, even after so many years, that she fell into the habit of sharing her every thought with him. 'I'm better off by myself. That's a lesson I learned the hard way, and I don't plan on repeating it. Ever.'

Christian's step faltered as he looked at her, picking up on the visceral edge of her words as she almost spat them out. In front of them, Nesta stopped, her body blocking the path ahead and preventing Alexandria from moving on. Not that the girl would have. She remained rooted to the spot, wide-eyed and staring to her side, where a cyclist had just collided head-on with a woman pushing a pram.

* * *

Christian's legs moved before he had any time to think. In two strides, he was next to Lexi and looking her over. 'Did you get hit?' he asked, and relief flooded his body when she shook her head, her knuckles turning white where she gripped Nesta's lead.

'Stay here with Nesta,' he told her, then turned round to the people lying prone in the grass to assess the situation.

Several people were coming over to the scene, but a quick scan of their faces told him no one was here to help. No one except Raquel, who shot past him and knelt down next to the turned-over pram. He hurried over to her and, by the time he was on his knees, the cries of a baby pierced the air. His blood ran cold. He'd only seen the collision side-on, but that was enough to understand the speed at which it had all happened—and what that speed could do to an infant.

Raquel scooped the infant up, its head coming to rest in the crook of an arm. With the skilled hands of a physician that still remembered the first aid steps for young children, she checked for any injuries, moving both arms and legs to test out the range of motion or any reactions outside of the shock that had rattled it to tears.

Christian left her to it as he inspected the mother with similar precision. Her face was scrunched into an expression of pain, her left hand clutching her right elbow, and when he held his ear close to her face he heard a soft groan of pain coming from her.

'Ma'am, can you hear me?' he asked, and the pain-filled moan became louder, but her eyes remained squeezed shut. 'She is semi-conscious, most likely struggling with the shock and pain of the impact. Potential injury on her right arm.'

Before he could decide on the next points of action, he needed to triage the last patient. One course of action was already clear. As he moved over to the cyclist, he pointed at one of the onlookers. 'Call an ambulance and tell them there has been a crash involving a bicycle and a pedestrian.'

The man nodded, fumbling for his phone as Christian focused his attention on the situation at hand. The cyclist's face began moving just as he knelt down next to him, hinting at a loss of consciousness for the few minutes he'd spent looking at the woman behind him.

He ran his eyes over the man's body, scanning for obvious injuries, and frowned when he noticed a large piece of the helmet missing. A quick look around didn't reveal the missing piece anywhere nearby. Though the helmet had surely prevented a more catastrophic injury, chances were that the patient's unconsciousness was because of a traumatic head injury.

Christian withdrew his phone from his pocket and turned on the torch before leaning over the patient. 'Sir, please open your eyes if you can hear me. I'm a doctor. You've been in an accident.'

He paused and watched the eyes of the man flutter open briefly before they closed again, his head falling to the side. Christian reached out, righted his head and then used the torch to check pupillary responses on each eye.

'Normal response, which makes damage to the brain unlikely. A concussion seems more likely,' he mumbled, mostly to himself, then turned round to find Raquel.

She had got to her feet and righted the pram. The baby lay inside it now and Lexi stood next to Raquel, looking at the woman with a face of concentration as Raquel spoke to her too softly for him to hear. But his eyes widened when Lexi grabbed the handle of the pram and pushed it to the side, before beginning to rock it back and forth, with Nesta at her heel.

Raquel gave a tight smile when she faced him and stepped towards him. 'The baby is fine, thank goodness. No signs of any head or spinal injuries,' she updated him. 'The child is in shock, so I asked Alexandria to rock her while we treat the mother.'

Christian nodded, then looked towards the woman on the floor. 'The cyclist lost consciousness on impact. I want to do a concussion assessment before the ambulance arrives. When I checked the woman over, she was conscious but not alert. With the force of the impact, I'd be worried about any spinal trauma.'

'I'll check on her now. Did you already call emergency services?'

Christian gave her another nod and ignored the heat her small smile caused to erupt in the pit of his stomach.

A drawn-out groan pulled his attention back to the moment, and he kneeled back down to inspect the patient, who seemed more alert now. 'Hey, my name is Christian. Can you tell me your name?'

The man's eyes moved behind his closed eyelids. When his eyes finally opened, his gaze was unfocused for a few moments before they found him.

'Dylan,' he pushed out between clenched teeth, his breath becoming more laboured as he tried to focus.

'Okay, Dylan… You were in an accident. Do you remember what happened to you?' Though this was a general question, it was also part of his concussion-assessment questionnaire. Loss of memory was a common side-effect of both losing consciousness and a concussion. So, while the question wouldn't rule out either, he'd at least have a good idea where the man's mental state was at.

Dylan took a laboured breath, his eyes falling shut for a second before he opened them again. 'I… I was on my bike when someone jumped on my path. I had to swerve and…' His voice trailed off, his brow furrowing as he tried to recall the next part. Panic entered his eyes when the memories wouldn't come and Christian laid a calming hand on his shoulder.

'It's okay. It's not unusual to forget the seconds before a crash. Your brain is trying to protect you by going into shock. Do you feel any pain in your head?' Christian knew the question to be vague and that it wouldn't be easy for the patient to pinpoint specific locations of his pain after such a crash. But getting to focus on isolating specific body parts would help them understand if there were any serious injuries that needed treatment right away. There were no outward signs of massive trauma, but that meant little if they couldn't see what lay beneath the surface.

'I…crashed?' he asked, his eyes wide as he absorbed information. He tried to move his head to the side to inspect his surroundings, but winced when he moved too quickly, another symptom Christian noted and filed away for later examination. This could either be neck pain, indicating a spinal contusion, or it might be part of a concussion that was throwing off his sense of direction.

Christian reached out to stabilise his neck and prevent him from turning his head. 'Try to avoid sudden movements until we've checked you out. Are you experiencing any nausea? Blurry vision?'

Dylan looked up at him, and he could see that his eyes were coming in and out of focus as he stared at him.

'Yes,' he said with a slight dip of his chin. 'What did I crash into?'

Christian paused for a second. Telling his patient that he had crashed into a mother with her child would only cause unnecessary distress and potentially worsen his condition. More information about what happened could wait until after a thorough neurological assessment at the hospital. So he said, 'Dylan, chances are you are suffering from a concussion. I cannot rule out whether you also have spinal trauma. Try not to move, as it might exacerbate your injuries. An ambulance is already on its way.'

As if to confirm his words, the sound of a siren approaching pierced the air, and Christian looked up just as Raquel approached him. Behind her, he spotted the woman, her eyes open, sitting upright, while still clutching her left arm.

'She dislocated her elbow when she tried to break her fall with her hand outstretched. Otherwise, no neurological signs of a concussion, head or spinal trauma. Considering the speed at which it all happened, she got lucky,' she said, and then her head turned toward the approaching sirens. 'Will they be able to get here, or do we need to move them?'

'We're close to one of the larger entrances. Moving Dylan without securing his neck and spine is not an option. He most likely has a concussion and some spinal contusions,' Christian replied in a quiet voice so as to not further stress out his patient. The shock would wear off soon enough, and it would be best if he was on his way to the emergency room by then.

Raquel gave him a nod and another encouraging smile that cascaded through him in the warm breeze of familiar want he'd been trying to fight off ever since she'd stepped back into his life. Despite working hard to achieve professional greatness, his life was a mess, and the last thing he needed was to drag someone else into it. Not when he was still coming to terms with becoming his niece's guardian and how unprepared he felt for that. Raquel invading his every thought and making it hard to focus wasn't something he could afford just now. Maybe if things settled down in a few years, when Lexi was older...

He pushed those thoughts away, as he always did when they threatened to take over, and focused on the situation at hand. But, despite the mental reprimand he'd just given himself, his eyes drifted towards where Raquel sat on the grass, talking to the other woman in a low and soothing voice. A tingling spark appeared in his chest as he observed the gentleness with which she had handled the situation from the very beginning.

It was something he'd noticed in her treatment with Lexi as well—she always spoke to her on equal terms and ensured that everyone was comfortable and bought in, every step of the way. That kindness and intuition was what had drawn him towards her all these years ago, and something within him brightened at the realisation that, whatever had happened to her in life, it hadn't extinguished this force of good within her.

Though he knew that *something* had happened to her. Hearing about the struggle in her marriage had torn at his heart, and the bitterness in her voice had almost been too much for him. He'd wanted to ask more, despite knowing that he shouldn't. Her lack of interest in relationships after what she had been through matched his own stance. So why had disappointment stabbed at him when she had said that?

The appearance of the ambulance at the gate nearest to them ripped him out of his contemplations and he walked towards the vehicle with an arm raised, waving them towards their location. Two paramedics jumped out of the ambulance once it came to a stop, one walking to the side to open the back door, while the other one approached him.

'We have three victims of a bicycle collision, two adults and an infant,' Christian explained as they walked over to the two adults on the grass.

Raquel joined him when she saw him approach with the paramedic and raised her eyebrows at him in a silent question. When Christian nodded, she listed her findings.

'First examination of the female patient shows a dislocated elbow, but no signs of head trauma or spinal injuries. She could sit up on her own but complains about severe pain. She pushed her child out of the way, so there was no direct impact on the baby. I couldn't make out any external injuries and, when examining each limb, they all had full range of motion and caused no visible discomfort to the child.'

Done with her part, she looked over at Christian, who continued, 'Male patient is showing signs of head trauma, most likely a concussion, though we weren't able to rule out other causes in the field. The tenderness in his neck and low mobility is concerning, so he needs secured transport.'

The paramedic nodded. 'We'll have to get another ambulance out for the woman and her child, since they seem to be less critical,' he said, then he turned round and walked back to the ambulance, where he gave his colleague some instructions before jumping back into the driver's seat to radio for support.

Raquel sighed with relief and the sound of it vibrated

through his bones. 'When we planned a training session in a crowded place, I hadn't expected that,' she said with a chuckle.

'I'm impressed with how calm Nesta remained, with all the noise and shouting,' he said, and delighted at the blush rising to her cheeks at the compliment.

'She's a great service dog, and I'm very proud of her,' she replied, and it took all the strength he had within him not to reach out and brush his fingers over her face to see if her cheeks felt as warm and soft as they looked.

His fingers twitched at his sides and he balled them into a fist when Lexi approached them as if she'd heard them talking about them. Her hand was still tightly gripping Nesta's lead and, though her expression was rattled, he realised she was okay. Once the woman had recovered some more, Lexi had left the pram with her and wandered over.

'Did you have a seizure?' Raquel asked when she too noticed her expression.

'I think so, but I can't be sure. I don't have any recollection of it. Normally I have people around me to confirm what happened, but with both of you busy...' Her voice trailed off and Christian's chest squeezed tight as he realised it was guilt straining her words—guilt that she needed his attention.

'That's even more of a testament to your new companion, Lexi,' he said, swallowing the thickness that threatened to coat his voice. She had gone through so much with her diagnosis, and then losing her father, he didn't want her shouldering yet another thing such as guilt at requiring his help.

'Chris is right. Even though things were happening around you, Nesta kept you safe until you were back in control. It shows you two will make a great team for many years,' Raquel chimed in, crouching down to be at eye level with the Golden Retriever. 'Scenarios like this one are the reason we are doing these things together. Not to make you feel bad, but to make sure that you and Nesta know how to react, so that you can lead a more independent life.'

Lexi's expression softened at that, relief shining in her eyes that he felt reflected in himself, where it mingled with the other source of warmth that had cropped up in the last few days. Watching Raquel work with his niece affected him more than he was willing to admit, painting a picture of a future he wasn't ready to consider. How could he think about any of that when he didn't even have enough time to wish her goodnight every day?

'Shall we continue our walk or are you too exhausted to go on? We can take a break and plan something else for another day,' Raquel said to Lexi, who looked at Christian with an enquiring look.

'Up to you, sweetie. What would you prefer?'

Lexi looked down at Nesta, who sat by her side and stared up at her with enormous eyes. 'There's an ice-cream place I hoped we would reach because they serve ice-cream for both humans and dogs. Maybe we can go there before we go home?'

A sheepish smile appeared on his niece's face, and he laughed. 'Sure. Let's go get some ice-cream.'

CHAPTER SIX

'LATE NIGHT?'

Raquel jumped at the sudden sound of a voice, and breathed out a sigh when Mia sat down next to her. She gave the piles of paper stacked on the table a once-over before looking back at Raquel with a questioning look.

'I'm putting together Evelyn's team for her surgery in two weeks. She will need physical therapy, speech therapists…potentially even psychotherapy, depending on how well the surgery goes. Since I'm new to Whitehall, I have to read through a lot of documentation to find the right people for her.'

A week had passed since she'd begun working in Whitehall Memorial's neurology department, and the learning curve had been as steep as she had expected. Though everyone was kind and willing to answer her questions whenever she had any, Raquel didn't want to rely on her colleagues for ever. The point of a locum doctor was that they could pick up the loose threads easily enough and run with them until the hospital had resolved their staffing issues.

But this wasn't any hospital, and the pinnacle of what neurology had to offer came with overflowing schedules that made it almost impossible to assemble a team in such a short time as two weeks. She would need to finalise her plans and sync up with Christian about them before the end of the week. After that, she would spend the weekend in Puerto Rico for her brother's wedding, and then there'd be only a few days between her return to New York and the surgery.

The thought of Christian sent a cascade of explosive heat through her body, and Raquel suppressed a visible shiver. Something had changed between them that weekend in Central Park, and she wasn't sure how to put it in words. 'Change' might not even have been the right word. It was more like the strand of a potential future had unravelled in her mind's eye. A future where they could work side by side—and potentially more.

The admiration he'd expressed for her hard work had sent her heart soaring, the appreciation for it evident in his words and actions alike, as he'd involved himself with Alexandria and her training. It was so different from where she had been in life after her divorce, when she had begun her healing journey.

That glimpse of what life could be like caused great trepidation within her because, even though she tried to ignore it as much as possible, she knew those feelings, knew what they meant and how she was not at all prepared to heed any of it. That had been why she had shared so much about her ex-husband when she usually didn't. Not to deter Christian from acting on the tension between them, but to remind herself that she had been there before, and that she had lost too much time and too much of herself in her failed relationship to go back there.

Could she trust herself to keep the fragments of herself she had clawed together intact if she let herself sink into those feelings? Her healing journey was far from over…

'In case you need any help.'

Raquel looked up with wide eyes, blinking several times as her mind shifted back into the present, those words hanging in the air. Had Mia been talking this entire time? A dreadful flutter dispersed the butterflies circling the pit of her stomach, and her brain went into overdrive as she scrambled for something to say.

'You were off in your own world, weren't you?' the other woman said, and Raquel blew out a deep sigh.

'Sorry about that. I promise I'm not usually so easily distracted. This is an important case, with the Head of Neurosurgery involved, so I really want to nail it. Which makes it even worse that I wasn't listening to you.' Raquel buried her face in her hands as the tension from the last few days washed over her. The weekend in Puerto Rico would be exactly what she needed to get some distance between Christian and her, and to refocus her on her original goal—impressing the people at Whitehall Memorial enough that they would want to work with her dogs and her going forward.

Though Christian would be there as well, she would be busy with her future sister-in-law and the rest of the bridal party. The maid of honour had already emailed her the itinerary and there was only one afternoon of free time before the wedding. She could hide for an afternoon.

'I said, if you need any help to put the team together, let me know. We can check the schedules and see if we can move anything,' Mia said, an understanding smile on her face, as if she had heard every single word of Raquel's inner monologue. 'Don't put so much pressure on yourself. Is this *just* about the surgery?'

The flutter in her stomach intensified and she bit down on the insides of her cheeks to will the heat shooting to her face to disappear—to no avail. There was no way Mia knew about her thoughts around Christian. How could she know? They hardly interacted with each other at the hospital, so where would Mia get such an idea?

'I...' The aggressive vibration of her pager saved her from going any further. She picked up the device and squinted at the small screen as a message appeared. 'They need a consultation at the ER,' she said, leaving the papers on the table to retrieve later.

She paused at the door, then said the words bubbling up in her chest. 'Thanks for offering to help. I think I will take you up on that.'

'Any time,' Mia said, raising her hand in a short wave as she left.

Christian frowned as he stepped into the emergency room, no longer used to the planned chaos surrounding him. He had been about to leave for the day when he'd received a page from the ER to go down there for an emergency consultation. His blood had gone cold, as his brain filled in the blanks of such a page, believing the worst had happened. But Lexi had picked up her phone on the third ring and he'd quickly told her he had received a page and would be late, so as not to worry her.

Now he glanced around, not seeing the charge nurse behind her desk to tell him who had paged him and why. As the Head of Neurosurgery, he handled the shift assignments on his team and who was on pager duty for the ER for each eight-hour shift in a twenty-four-hour period. He rarely put himself on the list unless there was a staffing shortage forcing him to do so. So the fact the nurse had paged him rather than whoever was on pager duty was either an oversight or something serious enough had come in to require his attention.

The nurse rounded the corner with a stack of clipboards under her arm just as he approached the desk. He swiftly stepped up to help her when it looked as if she was about to drop some clipboards, took some and set them down on the counter before looking at her.

'Someone paged me for a consult, Steph. Where do you need me?'

The nurse furrowed her brow, glancing at the monitor behind her desk and scanning its content. 'Oh, the new person in Neurology *insisted* we page you for this. We told her we have someone from your department on call, but she said you would want to be involved.'

'Raquel paged me?' That would have stabbed fear into his heart had he not already checked in with Lexi. Who could she possibly be seeing? Whoever it might be, he knew Raquel wouldn't page him for no reason.

After the tension he'd sensed in the park, he'd made the conscious effort to spend as little time around her as possible, or he might lose all sense of self simply by looking at her. The rest of the day had been thankfully uneventful, and it had afforded him a glance of what his life could look like if he dared to expand his family—to let someone into the place where he didn't let anyone tread.

This was in relation to their relationship as medical professionals and nothing else, even though that too had affected him on a deep level as he'd watched her handle the entire crash site with precision and empathy, assuring both mother and child when they had just been through a traumatic event. Not only that, she had calmed Lexi as well. Raquel was taking more and more of the fear away and replacing it with confidence that his niece could lead a life like anyone else.

'Dr Pascal? Yes, she just took the patient to get a CT,'

Steph said, and he nodded in thanks before disappearing down the corridor towards the CT.

His heart skipped a beat when he knocked on the door and heard her voice calling him in, and he took several steadying breaths before he pushed the door open. Raquel stood behind the radiologist, who sat in front of the monitor as the CT whirred alive.

'Ah, good, you're here. Sorry for paging you without context, but I had to get the patient in here to confirm my diagnosis. I think we are looking at a brain bleed,' Raquel said when he walked up to her.

She sent him a sideways glance, and he wondered if it was because of the intentional distance he kept between them. Her scent was already drifting up his nose, making it harder to focus with each breath. How had things escalated so quickly from when she had unexpectedly re-entered his life? Christian thought they had left their youthful feelings for each other behind because, even back then, nothing had ever happened—because he hadn't let it go anywhere.

But her presence alone was intoxicating and so enticing that he wished he was in a position where he could give in. Only he knew he couldn't. Not with Lexi just settling in and learning what a more independent life could look like. He had barely enough time to spend with her; he could not be so selfish as to take what little he had and divide it by another person. No, this was no more than an idle fantasy he needed to shake off.

'Is this about an emergency surgery? I can give you the name of the resident on call,' he said, reaching for his phone, when Raquel stretched out her hand.

'I think you want to take this one. It's Dylan.'

Christian furrowed his brow, thinking through his patient roster and looking for the name, when the realisation hit him. 'The cyclist that crashed in Central Park?'

Raquel nodded. 'He came in complaining about worsening headaches, sensitivity to light and dizziness that is getting progressively worse. I gave the paramedics our names in case the ER where they took them needed to get in touch, and I guess they told him where to find us.'

'A brain haemorrhage?' Christian thought back to the initial examination, remembering the large piece of helmet missing just above the forehead. Dylan had complained about a headache and nausea, which could have been the signs of a traumatic brain injury—something he had noted with the paramedics. 'Do you know if the hospital did a CT scan on him when he was first admitted?'

Raquel shook her head. 'It wasn't here, so we don't have any notes. When I asked him, he said they asked him a few questions and then put him on strict rest for a week to recover.'

'They *didn't* scan his head after they saw a chunk of helmet missing?' Christian felt his temper flare and took a few breaths to calm himself.

The image popping up on the screen in front of them saved him from showing his anger at the blatant mistreatment of his patient. The radiologist leaned forward, as did he and Raquel as several more pictures appeared, showing them a 3D perspective of Dylan's brain…

'There it is,' the radiologist said, pointing at the screen with his pen.

Raquel placed a hand on the shoulder of the radiologist and leaned forward. Temper flared inside Christian's chest again, but this time for reasons wholly unrelated to his patient and any of his treatments. He balled his hand into a fist as he tamped down on the surge of emotions and forced himself to look at the scan in front of him instead.

'He's bleeding into his frontal lobe,' he said, and noted with way too much satisfaction that Raquel withdrew her hand before taking a step back.

'Dylan must have been bleeding since Saturday,' she said, eyes wide with shock.

'We have to get him into surgery right now. I'll let them know we're coming in with a patient. Can you make sure the scans get delivered to the right OR?'

Raquel nodded, and he dared to smile at her, if only to ease the worry in her eyes. 'Thanks for paging me. You did the right thing,' he said, and wished he could reach out to underline the meaning of his words with a gentle stroke of her cheek.

But that wasn't the reality he lived in, so instead he let his hand drop and spared her one last glance before heading out to rally a team for emergency surgery.

Raquel could feel her pulse in her throat as she stared through the window in the scrub room into the OR. The charge nurse at the ER had ushered her into one of the examination rooms, where a familiar-looking face had lain on a bed, squeezing his eyes shut to block out the fluorescent lights.

Fearing the worst, she had immediately begun her examination and dug deeper into the treatment he had received in hospital. If they had diagnosed him properly and he had actually followed the advice, there should have been no reason to be back in the emergency room now. But he had said, despite following the advice for bed rest, and even calling in sick when he really couldn't afford to take more days off work, his pain had only worsened to the point where he'd wanted to seek out *them* specifically.

Her heart squeezed tight at the thought of the pain he'd gone through since Saturday, and she was glad that Christian could be the one to perform the surgery when he'd been the one to help him after his collision. A small part of her had been hesitant to page him in favour of following the protocol the charge nurse had introduced her to, which was to page the person on pager duty. That would have been the easy way out for her as well, as it would have meant not having to deal with Christian.

Their connection was becoming increasingly problematic to the point where she almost believed coming to New York had been a mistake. But how could she have known? He hadn't been involved in her hiring, and the college kid working with her part-time had been the one to set things up with Lexi. Though she'd had several opportunities to work out that Christian worked at Whitehall, she had taken exactly none of them. Just as he had never looked her up either, or he would have known she was one of the few people in the country capable of training seizure-response dogs.

But, despite more than a decade passing without them seeing each other, the feelings that had never manifested between them surged back up—burning hotter and wilder with every moment they spent together.

Raquel knew she should step away—both from Christian and the window she was staring through—but couldn't will herself to do either. She knew she shouldn't be lurking around the scrub room. She'd come over here to deliver the CT scans they had taken not even half an hour ago, and had meant to leave, when the activity in the OR had grabbed her attention.

The anaesthesiologist had just finished putting Dylan under, and she watched as Christian picked up the scalpel. He looked at the monitor in front of him, which would show the scan of the brain with the location of the bleed. Then he looked down and placed the scalpel on the patient's scalp with no hesitation.

Raquel couldn't see where he was cutting or how long the incision was, only that he put down the scalpel moments after and stretched out his hand to request another instrument.

Her eyes rounded when he brought the bone drill down on the exposed skull, and even through the glass she could hear the muffled grind as he cut through the bone. Was it near where the piece of helmet had been missing? Raquel stood on her toes, craning her neck further and pushing herself up with the help of the sink, just to catch a glimpse of the surgical field. After everything they had been through on Saturday, she *really* wanted to see Dylan over the finish line and into recovery—despite not being able to contribute in the OR.

Whether it was because she was trying too hard to see what was going on, or because Christian turned when he was handing the drill back to the OR nurse, Raquel didn't know, but their eyes locked onto each other's. She stood there frozen and watched as his brow furrowed. Then he turned his head and said something to one of the neurosurgical interns observing the operation. Her heart skipped a beat when the intern nodded and then walked towards her, stopping at the small intercom that connected the OR with the scrub room.

'Dr Wolf says you are welcome to observe the surgery,' the junior doctor said. 'You just have to scrub in.'

The intercom went silent, mirroring the lack of any

coherent thought going on in her brain. Then a shower of hot sparks burst alive in the pit of her stomach and she suppressed the urge to shudder. He was inviting her to observe the surgery... In all the things that had flashed through her mind the moment he'd caught her spying on his surgery a few moments ago, this hadn't been a remotely likely outcome.

When the intern remained standing in front of the intercom, she hurried over and pressed the button to say, 'Thank you! I will be in now.'

By the time Raquel was done scrubbing her hands down to her nails, Christian had already opened the skull and was now looking at the exposed brain. When she entered the OR, he waved her over to his side.

'I hear you wanted to observe fixing a brain bleed close up,' he said to her in a low voice that rumbled through her and set her entire being askew with unbidden want.

How was it she couldn't think straight when she was near this man? For the first time in her career she'd been invited to observe brain surgery and yet a few words out of his mouth had her thinking completely unrelated thoughts. Such as what his voice would sound like as he growled her name just as they...

'Where did you hear that? You must have some very unreliable sources,' she said, and prayed that he hadn't heard the wobble in her voice that betrayed all the inappropriate thoughts rattling around in her head.

'It's been quite some time since I had a neurologist follow me into an OR.'

She looked at him as his eyes remained trained on the open surgical field in front of him. 'Has this happened before?'

The crinkles appearing around his eyes were the only

indicator of his smile, with his mouth hidden behind the surgical mask, yet she could still feel the heat it caused to stir in her body. Was she kidding herself, or had he sounded flirtatious?

'It's not easy when you're one of five people in the country that can operate on a glioblastoma multiforme with only a microscope and some scans.' A chuckle trickled through her which accompanied Christian's words and mingled with the storm of butterflies already raging in her stomach, bringing her into further disarray.

He was *definitely* flirting with her, yet her brain latched onto what he had just said.

'With a microscope? You don't use computer guidance on a GBM?' In her career, she had diagnosed a few of these tricky malignant tumours. They were an aggressive form of cancer and, because of their rapid growth, they invaded healthy tissue in abnormal forms, making it almost impossible to separate the tumours from their surroundings.

Even *with* computer guidance, they were almost impossible to get. Without them, it would seem impossible.

'Why would you do it without a computer, though?' she asked. 'Wouldn't it be better to have it as a back-up?'

Christian remained quiet. Then he put down the forceps he'd been using to inspect the brain lesion caused by the haemorrhage, to map out the extent and what their best course of action would be. He shot her a sideways glance that slid through her entire body and only incited the brewing storm within her further.

'When the glioblastoma is complex enough, even lasers and computer models can get confused, as there are too many signals to interpret. That is why it remains necessary for surgeons to understand how to navigate these tumours with and without the help of different tools.'

He looked around the room as he spoke, imprinting his knowledge on the interns and residents assisting in the surgery today. All eyes in the room were bright, their attention all on Christian as they absorbed his words.

The command he exerted on the room was palpable, the respect each staff member afforded him tangible in the air, giving Raquel a sense of awe. She'd known this man as he'd entered adulthood, had known all his childish flaws and goofy ideas that he and her brother had cooked up. And, though she had sensed a connection that went deeper than the superficial back then, the man standing next to her was on a whole different level.

Could she even keep up with him if she wanted to? Not that she *wanted* to. There was no way someone as valued as Christian would look her way for more than a second, when she couldn't even get her own research off the ground without holding down a second job. Someone of his calibre wouldn't have needed help to convince a prestigious hospital to give him a contract in the first place. What made her think she could be with such a successful man when her own husband had had to divorce her to find success in life? There was clearly something wrong with her.

The torrent of self-doubt the storm within her was turning into was stopped dead in its tracks when Christian's gaze finally landed on her, those light-blue eyes sparking with excitement and something else. A familiarity that spoke of the time they had spent together—that he, too, remembered her, maybe even fondly.

Raquel willed herself to breathe as her body tensed

with the electric shock of their connection—a jolt to her system that he had conveyed with only a flick of his eyes towards her. How was this even possible?

'Neurology noted intense headaches, light sensitivity and a recent fall from a bicycle on the patient's notes, along with these scans showing a dark shadow on the patient's frontal lobe. All this led us to confirm that a brain haemorrhage was the most likely diagnosis and, with the deterioration of the patient, surgical intervention was the most promising course of action. Can we visually confirm the diagnosis?'

He raised his voice as he spoke, addressing the junior doctors in the room, who all stepped forward to look at the exposed brain. Raquel took a step to the side to give everyone the opportunity to inspect it after having a look at it herself. Though she had seen many brains in her training years, they had mostly been those of cadavers for them to work on in med school.

'With the haemorrhagic lesion confirmed, what are our next steps?' he asked when everyone had shuffled back into their place.

'Removing any blood clots that might cause a tamponade and cauterising the wound,' one intern in the back said, after their resident had prodded them with an elbow to get them to speak up.

'Correct. Blood clots can cause serious issues down the line, like strokes, if certain parts of the brain are under-supplied with blood.' Christian nodded, then looked at the resident to his left. 'Apply suction to the lesion and use forceps to dislodge any clots in the area.'

Raquel watched as the resident received the aspirator and a fresh pair of forceps before following Christian's instructions. If there was any hesitation on the resident's part, she couldn't detect it. But, then again, how could anyone feel insecure with someone like Christian as their teacher? She had no business standing inside an OR, yet he'd sensed and seen her curiosity and had brought her in rather than let her stand on the side lines. Just as he was bringing the junior neurosurgeons in as participants in the surgery, rather than showing them how to do it.

'You should feel the blood clot dislodging. But, if you don't, a tell-tale sign of the clot vanishing is…' He stopped when the aspirator in the resident's hand emitted a sputtering sound and blood flowed up the nozzle. 'This. Let's patch up the wound. This young man needs to get back on his bike so, the faster we get him into recovery, the better.'

Raquel glanced in his direction, but Christian's attention was on the procedure, giving her an unobstructed view of him and some time to observe her old flame. Even with the mask, she could see the expression of intense focus on his face and knew that he took his work seriously. But, more than that, in the last few days he'd shown that he never forgot the human behind every case—something that happened way too easily with higher-ranking doctors in large hospitals. At some point it became as much a numbers game as a profession of healing others.

But he was right there, worrying about a patient who had said he couldn't lose any more work, and ensuring he got the care he needed both medically and on a deeper level.

It would be so easy to fall for this man. If only there was space in her life for that possibility. But with his work here and hers taking her all over the country—not to mention the double shifts she was pulling as a neurologist and dog-trainer—romance was the last thing on her mind.

Even if he made it so incredibly easy to see a future with him.

CHAPTER SEVEN

IT WAS ALMOST eight by the time the surgery was over, and Christian still needed to write the post-operative notes and hand them over to his staff member on night shift. Though the brain haemorrhage wasn't as severe as others he had worked on, he knew Dylan had suffered that injury several days ago—and had only now received the medical attention he'd needed.

He needed to thank Raquel for her quick thinking on that day. If she hadn't given the paramedics their names and told them which hospital they worked at, he might have been turned away again. He knew most of his colleagues were trying to make the best out of a difficult situation, since not all hospitals had the same funding and staffing as Whitehall Memorial, but it bothered him to know how easily they had dismissed Dylan after he'd suffered a traumatic brain injury.

Seeing Raquel through the window of the scrub room had been unexpected, and he'd reacted before he could even think about whether he wanted her so close to him in surgery. With the way she'd been on his mind, and fantasies of her distracting him whenever he sat behind his computer to work on his papers, he'd half-expected the burning heat of his attraction to her to take over.

But nothing of the sort had happened—quite the op-

posite. The shock that the unexpected page had caused
in him still hadn't worn off and, though he'd been in
enough situations where he'd had to shake things off, her
presence had been...calming. Unexpected, yes, but she'd
also soothed away any worries that had been clinging to
him. An effect that wasn't wholly unknown to him, but
one he'd forgotten over the years until the person who
had inspired that sense of security within him had come
back into his life.

Christian glanced around the empty operating room.
He'd left the post-operative care to the most senior resident so he could get home. Though Lexi was old enough
to look after herself for an evening, he still didn't enjoy
being away for so long. Her having the company of the
service dog now made him rest easier, he noticed. He was
glad he could already see the desired effect on his niece
and her companion, with all the training and effort she
and Raquel had put into Nesta.

He shook his head with a sigh, his gaze travelling up
the wall to check on the time, his eyes stopping as they
met an intense brown-green set staring right at him from
inside the scrub room—again.

An unbidden heat flared up within his chest as his
eyes bored into hers, seeing a spark of *something* inside
them that had him tense and loose all at the same time.
Whatever that something was, it was dangerous—and
he *had* to have it. There was no other alternative, despite that small voice in the back of his mind telling him
that there absolutely was. The other path lay beyond the
door at his back rather than through the one leading to
the scrub room.

But Christian didn't want to heed that voice. Not when
it had done precious little to prepare him for the life he

now led. When it had stopped him from going all the way with this woman over fifteen years ago. What would life have looked like if he'd had her to raise his niece with? He'd seen them together already, their thoughts and feelings more aligned than he could ever have achieved on his own. There was so much she could teach him but, with time as limited as it was, could he afford his attention to sway?

His feet moved before he could think otherwise, opening the door to the scrub room and walking to where Raquel waited for him. She crossed her hands behind her back, pushing out her chest as she looked up at him.

'Thank you for letting me watch,' she said, her voice lower than usual and hitting him right in the pit of his stomach, where it whipped up a storm.

'You were trying very hard to participate, so I thought I could lend you a hand. After everything you've done for me,' he replied, taken by surprise at the gravel in his own voice.

What was happening right now? They had hardly interacted in the surgery. All his attention had belonged to his patient and the junior doctors he was in charge of training. Yet he'd noticed her presence, her scent dancing at the edge of his attention and calming his senses after a long day and an unexpected surgery. He'd known she was there and that had been enough to...

Christian didn't know how to complete that thought because he didn't know what he wanted from her. Didn't know what *she* wanted, for that matter. Not a relationship; she had said as much. Then what was it he was picking up between them? Where did this tension come from? He wasn't interested in something permanent. Not while Lexi didn't get enough of his time.

'I don't remember the last time I observed a surgery. Even though our two disciplines work hand in hand, I only ever get to see the result.' A small smile appeared on her lips, and he almost staggered at how much he wanted to lift his fingers to her lips to trace them.

'You're always welcome in my OR, Raquel. Just say the word and I'll make sure there's space for you.' And he meant it. Today was no doubt an outlier. Emergency surgery always put him on edge, as he preferred his day planned out, from surgery to post-op care. But, even without the element of surprise, he sensed something within him that responded well to Raquel's presence.

'Thank you. Since we helped Dylan immediately after his accident, it was nice to see him through this part as well.' She paused, and he watched, almost mesmerised, as she chewed on her lower lip in a sign of shyness that he hadn't seen her exhibit in a long time. He knew the gesture so well from when they'd been teens, but she portrayed more confidence now than back in the day.

'What's the matter?' he heard himself asking, wanting to understand the shift in the air he was sensing. He also didn't want her to go, now that the conversation seemed concluded. Anything would do to keep her in his presence so he could at least attempt to get his fill of her—though he knew that to be virtually impossible.

'I was thinking about Ramón's prom night...or I guess *your* prom night,' she said after some hesitation, throwing him back to a time he hadn't thought about until very recently.

His mouth went dry, his skin tightening as the memories of their almost-kiss came back into his mind. Clearing his throat in an attempt to get rid of the huskiness coating it, he said, 'That's a strangely specific time to think about right after brain surgery.'

Raquel chuckled at that, the sound so bright and warm that he had to bite down the instinct to wrap her into his arms so he could absorb that sound with his mouth. 'I've been thinking a lot about our time together back then. How awkwardly I danced around my feelings for you, wondering if you felt the same way…and never quite finding the courage to say something to you. The moment I finally chose was at the end there, when I tried to kiss you…'

Her voice trailed off just as a ringing began in his ears. What was she saying? Was she really about to discuss this? When he'd left Puerto Rico, he had found his own closure, knowing that they would probably only ever see each other around events in Ramón's life, such as the wedding, and would most likely easily move on from their infatuation.

'Raquel… I'm not sure…' he began, but stopped when she shook her head.

'I'm not trying to…start anything. Just…' She paused, letting out a sigh that revealed the same tension he sensed building within him. 'There's an air around us, and I've been ignoring it, wishing it away, but that didn't make it easier to deal with and to…be around you. It might just be me, and that's fine. I just don't want to repeat the same mistake by thinking what I feel matches what you feel and acting on it—because getting rejected by you again will break me.'

The ringing in his ears grew louder with each word Raquel said, his heart skipping several beats and then ratcheting up the pace to catch up with the missed ones. His brain went into overdrive as he examined the situation from every angle, trying to understand where this sudden confession was coming from—and fighting how much of a chord that struck within him.

He'd spent too much time lamenting the moment when their feelings for each other had been so tangible that he had almost said something—only for his insecurity to get the better of him. What would have happened if he'd misinterpreted her signals? The fear of losing her had been just as real as losing his best friend. How could he have told Ramón back then that he had fallen for his sister?

But their time had come and gone, had it not? There was no rewind button, no do-overs for them to take advantage of. They weren't the people they used to be in high school. If a relationship was out of the question for both of them, what was the point of standing here and discussing something that wouldn't matter in either of their lives?

Yet, despite all of that chaos swirling within his head, his blood heated at her words and desire reared its head, drowning out any rational thought or resistance inside him. All his senses honed onto her, picking up her scent in between the soap and sterilisation liquid in the scrub room. He noted the ragged breaths coming in and out of her slightly parted lips—lips he needed to feel under his fingers, on his mouth, grazing along his skin...

Christian couldn't turn away this time, he needed to give in to the sensation bubbling up inside him. Give in, even though he knew what was in front of him was not long term. They had both said that and had meant it, too.

'Where is this coming from?' he forced himself to ask, to buy his brain some time to catch up and avoid potential missteps that might jeopardise their working relationship. Though every cell in his body was screaming to give in, it wasn't just up to him. His life was not entirely his own to decide…

Raquel took a deep breath, her arms slackening at her side and her eyes coming back to his face—and widening at whatever she saw in there.

'I… Forget I said anything. This was dumb. What on earth was I even thinking, saying anything just after an intense surgery…?' she mumbled, then turned on her heels and stepped towards the door.

The heat of desire cascaded through Raquel and collided with the burning sensation of embarrassment at the absolute word-vomit she had just unleashed on Christian. The man had looked as though she had just surprised him with the worst news he could receive in such a situation. Never had she regretted something this fast after doing it.

She had got caught up in a moment she shouldn't have, sharing way too much of her inner monologue, and why? Because she sensed a connection? A connection she'd been wrong about when they'd been younger and she had tried to kiss him, only for him to back away. What had possessed her to go for a re-enactment of that night right in this moment?

Raquel didn't even know what her end goal had been in spilling her guts. She still meant everything she had said about not wanting a relationship with anyone. Her career was in a precarious situation, her charity always one day away from losing all its funding, and every day was a fight for survival. A relationship simply wouldn't have the space it needed in her life.

So what had that been about—some no-strings closeness? Or was the desire to close the circle they had opened all these years ago driving her? It didn't matter, because

Christian's reaction showed her that, not only wasn't he interested, he was also absolutely horrified that she might believe otherwise.

She was about to pull the door open when his hand wrapped around her elbow, stopping her in her tracks. Then the world tilted under her feet as he spun her round and pressed her against the door. His body covered hers, and Raquel had but one moment to look up before his mouth came down on hers in a kiss that had been fifteen years in the making.

Her body went loose underneath his, his hands coming down on her hips as he pushed her further against the wall. The fine hair on her body stood on end as his fingers drifted under the seam of her scrub top and brushed over the bare skin of her midriff. That small touch was enough to draw a throaty moan from her, her back arching as she leaned into the touch.

The taste of Christian exploded through her mouth as their tongues met, both of them urged on by the fever pitch of the moment—earth, rain and comfort all wrapped into one tangible sensation taking hold of her body. How long had she wanted this to happen?

The trickling sparks through her body met the heat his kiss ignited in her core and created a burning fire that turned her insides to lava. Lava that Christian directed into different places as his hands explored more of her skin under her shirt. Her own hands dug into the fabric of his top, holding on to him so as to not drift away in the sea of sensations and desire engulfing her.

Raquel didn't know why she had waited for him here. After the surgery, the interns had transported Dylan back to the recovery unit of the neurosurgical department, and Christian had held back two of the residents to give them instructions. She knew at that point that she should leave and get some rest. Tomorrow would be her last shift before taking a four-day break to attend her brother's wedding in Puerto Rico, and she had already vowed to herself to do her best to avoid Christian, whose lips were now trailing down her neck as he buried his face in her hair.

'This has been all I've been able to think about since you walked back into my life,' he said in a low growl, his lips brushing over her skin with each word uttered. 'Can I ask something of you?'

Raquel tried to speak, but her words turned into a moan when his hand caressed her back and pushed her against him. A question…when they were in the middle of this? His touch wrapped her brain into the luscious fog of their passion for each other and even contemplating what the question could be was an almost insurmountable effort.

So she simply nodded and gasped at the intensity in his eyes when he leaned back to interlock their stares. There was no hesitation, only a vision of unbridled desire—desire for *her*. That thought shook her deeper than she wanted to admit, when she had spent years believing that he had rejected her.

'I can't stop thinking about you—about how much I want you. So much of my time went into checking myself around you.' He took a deep, shuddering breath that matched her own. Then he brushed his lips over hers again to underline his point, setting off another avalanche of sparks within her.

'There was no question in there.' She breathed against his skin when he retreated only far enough to look at her.

His eyes flared open when he realised it too, and the grin appearing on his lips melted her insides further down. Dear God, how had she ever resisted this man in the first place? That smile had her doomed even before she knew it.

'My question is,' he said, and pulled her into another long and passionate kiss that had her gasping for air when he let go of her again, 'Do you want me too? One night to lay it all out.'

He was thinking of this as a temporary thing. Maybe that was what she needed to move on with her life. One night in which they could reclaim what they had missed in the past and what they had clearly been thinking about all these years.

Would she be able to walk away from him afterwards? Tension rippled through her at that thought, and it was enough for Christian to notice. His hands dropped from her back, where they had been stroking in long, tempting circles, and he took a step backwards. The air rushing into the space now created between them was cold, causing a different kind of shiver to claw down her spine.

'Did I…go too far?' The flames in his eyes banked, and Raquel's heart twisted inside her chest. She raised her hands to placate both him and herself.

'No, you didn't. *I* was the one who started to talk about the past and that I've regretted not saying anything before I tried to kiss you.' She took a deep breath, trying to quell the raging fires of passion and fear inside her into something she could understand—and communicate. 'I…want you too. All of this has been unexpected and fast. I'm not in a position in my life where I can give a lot, so…'

Her voice trailed off and the expression rippling over Christian's face was one of relief. Had he been worried that she would demand more of him? That her confession about her past regrets had been to get him to commit to her? Even though that had never been her intention, the relief in his eyes struck at a place inside her she kept safely hidden away from view. Why did it feel like part of her had wanted him to *want her* in a deeper way? That stood in direct contradiction to what her head was telling her.

'I'm not here to talk you into a relationship. This is not about that. We have some unresolved tension between us, and maybe this will help both of us move on.' He didn't step closer but lifted his hand to her face to run his knuckles over her cheek and down her neck. Heat traced the arch of his caress, mixing with the cold that had risen from her stomach.

A part of her wanted to run away, knowing that if she gave in to him now she would only sink in deeper. That was something she couldn't risk. There was too much at stake for her to let herself be that vulnerable. Last time she had done that, it had set her back several years with the things she wanted to achieve—all because she believed she and her husband had been a team, working towards the same thing. One night was all she had to give. But was one night enough to get from this man all she wanted, that had slipped away so many years ago?

The fire in his eyes was still sparking and she glanced around. 'Where do you want to do this? I think what we're doing here right now is against so many different hospital regulations,' she said, and chuckled when his eyes widened.

He stood up straight, creating some space between them again as he followed her gaze. 'I hadn't thought that far ahead,' he said with a wry smile. 'In fact, I had planned none of this when I stepped in here.'

Raquel huffed a laugh at that and stepped away from

between Christian and the wall—because she knew if he kissed her again she would do whatever he wanted right then and there. She sensed him following her with his eyes as she took a few steps around the scrub room to calm her racing heart. Were they really going to do this?

'No need to rush. We'll be in Puerto Rico this weekend. I don't know about Ramón, but Clara has a tight schedule for her side of the bridal party,' she said, and part of her hoped this was enough to give them the opportunity to back out if they changed their mind.

But his eyes lit up with an almost lethal intention, and she gasped when he stepped closer to her again, forcing her head upwards to keep eye contact. 'Your brother doesn't have any plans for his groomsmen except to help him get ready. He sent me both of their schedules, so I know we both have the afternoon of the first day off. Will you be staying at your cousin's house with the rest of the bridesmaids?' he asked, so close to her face that she felt his breath grazing her skin.

The molten lava inside her surged through her body again at his words. The romantic setting of Puerto Rico was something she'd wanted to avoid, yet her body responded at the thought of being with him there—or anywhere. Except…

'My family will be crawling all over the house. There's no way we…'

Raquel stopped talking when he swiped his thumb over her lips before bending down for a soft brush of his mouth against hers. 'Ramón and the groomsmen are staying at a hotel at the request of the bride-to-be. Seems like she didn't trust your brother not to sneak into her room for their night apart, so they banished him from the property.'

A hotel room? That was a possibility she hadn't considered. Her heart flipped inside her chest as their plans suddenly became real, and she took a deep breath, steeling herself for her answer. 'Okay, let's see what happens in Puerto Rico,' she said, and swallowed a yelp when Christian hauled her back into his arms, before his mouth came crashing down on hers again. The kiss contained all the wants and desire she couldn't put into words, making her both excited and fearful about their weekend together.

CHAPTER EIGHT

THE HEAT IN Puerto Rico was an entirely different beast from that in New York, and Christian realised by the pinch in his chest how much he missed his former home. Though he'd only spent three years of his life here, this was the place where he had the fondest memories.

The thought of Raquel summoned back up the flames he'd been nurturing inside him, and each breath fuelled it, stoking it higher and higher. The memory of their kiss didn't help to quell what stirred within him, even though part of him knew that what they were doing was risky.

Christian had not once factored his relationship with Ramón into any of the decisions he had made in the last few weeks ever since Raquel had appeared back in his life—unlike fifteen years ago, when his affection for his sister had been a cause of his hesitation. He'd believed his affection for Raquel no more than youthful exuberance, but he now wondered if he had found something truly unique then but hadn't been mature enough to understand the rarity of their connection.

Not that it mattered now. The link between them might still be alive, but their lives were too different now. There was no reclaiming what they had lost. The attraction was the only thing remaining in the way to some closure, because they had both shared enough to see that they weren't compatible on a personal level. Christian had too much going on with Lexi and needed to devote all his time to her. Raquel, on the other hand, wasn't in a position to be with him in New York. Her work with seizure-response dogs required her to go wherever she was needed, picking up other work as a neurologist when she needed it.

She'd said that she regretted the way her marriage had set back her career. Her struggle was something that kept him up at night. She had said because of her experience that relationships weren't an option for her just now, but he was dying to know what had happened between them to change her mind about companionship so drastically. Deep down inside, he knew he shouldn't be curious about that. It wouldn't help their situation—quite the opposite. What if he learned too much about her? Learned how to heal her? It would make it so much harder to let go...

But that wasn't the only barrier. Why was he even thinking about her when he himself had so much work still to do? When he couldn't even be the father figure Lexi deserved? His mind drifted to Anthony—not for the first time in the last two weeks. Would he have been proud of what his younger brother had achieved or distraught about how much he had sacrificed to get to where he was in his career? Would the doubt in his own parenting abilities have been less if he had spent less time climbing up the career ladder?

'Did you solve it?' The familiar voice ripped him out of his contemplation and he blinked as his eyes raked over Raquel from head to toe.

All the self-doubt wrapping itself around his chest dissolved the second he beheld her. The floral dress she wore clung tightly to her upper body and flared out at the hips, accentuating her hourglass curves.

'You're stunning,' he said, as no other thought had space in his brain but this one, and she rewarded him for his directness with an exquisite blush dusting her cheek bones. A flush he planned to bring out many times over while they were in Puerto Rico.

'I… Thank you,' she said with a tentative smile.

They stared at each other for a few moments as the world faded away and only that tangible hunger that had sprung alive between them existed, ready to be acted on. Christian's nerves were so taut, he was ready to throw her over his shoulder and abscond with her to his room— only to emerge for the ceremony when they were both needed in the bridal party.

'Sorry, what did you ask me?' he said, to distract himself from the thoughts dominating his mind ever since their kiss.

'Oh… I made a joke. You looked lost in thought and so I imagined you were working on a tricky tumour extraction in your head. I asked if you were any closer to solving it.'

Christian huffed a laugh at how wrong she was about where his thoughts lay but decided to play along, and he said, 'I was about halfway done cutting around the tiny blood vessels in the brain when you approached me.'

Raquel laughed as she glanced around the room. The wedding guests had all been put up in one of the houses owned by her extended family near the farm that her uncle and cousins operated.

'I was about to go for a stroll down the beach. Would you care to join me?' she asked, and his heart pounded against his chest at the question.

They'd discussed keeping a low profile when her family was around them, including their plans for this afternoon. Just to be safe, Raquel had wanted it to look as if they had bumped into each other, so as not to set any unnecessary rumours loose. They wouldn't come back here, but rather would walk to his hotel, where they would be away from prying eyes.

Christian got off his chair and held his arm out towards her. 'It would be my pleasure to escort you.'

The beach was a five-minute walk down the road from her uncle's house and, the moment she arrived there, Raquel felt some of the tension within her uncoiling. Though she loved her family with all her heart, being around the extended Pascal clan stretched her nerves thin—especially when her *tíos* and *tías* poked their noses into her life and asked questions she preferred not to answer. Though she'd got divorced more than two years ago, some of her family still looked at her with pity.

A few heads turned as she held on to Christian's arm and walked out of the front door, but Raquel couldn't bring herself to care. All she could focus on was the butterflies rioting in the pit of her stomach that sent her nervous system into overdrive as her fingers grazed over his arm. Such an innocent gesture caused an unreasonable tumult within her, yet she remained powerless to stop it. Maybe she even enjoyed it a bit. *Okay, a lot.*

The memory of their kiss had been with her ever since she'd stepped out of that scrub room. It had stayed in her dreams and in the morning after as she'd woken up tense and with an ache only something—*someone*—could soothe away. That they had agreed to do just that didn't help. What had sounded like a good idea in New

York seemed different in the light of the Puerto Rican sun. Was the weekend of her brother's wedding the right time finally to give in to Christian?

A lump appeared in her throat as the thought bubbled up, the butterflies intensifying their bouncy dance inside her.

'Were you keen on getting out for a bit?' he asked, sensing her discomfort.

Raquel bit her lip. 'Was it that obvious?'

'Not sure if calling it "obvious" is fair. Maybe I'm good at sensing your mood,' he replied with a shrug, way too casually for how his words affected her.

Sensing her mood? What a dangerous thing to say when she was already at the edge of a cliff, just waiting for the signal to jump—right down towards him. The last two weeks had been nothing short of a fantasy taking shape in the real world. She'd been surrounded by professionals who understood her, patients who'd needed her help both as a doctor and as a dog trainer and now the most gorgeous man she had ever known—past and present—was slipping his hand into hers as they strolled down to the beach. The picture in her head was too perfect to last. There was an air of fragility around everything, and she feared that one tiny breeze would send it all toppling down. Something such as them finally sleeping together…

'It's been a while since I've been back, so everyone is keen to catch up with me. It gets a bit repetitive to recap the last few years of my life, especially when it involves…'

Her voice trailed off when she realised what she'd been about to say. The last thing she wanted to talk about was her ex-husband. *Especially* not with Christian holding her hand. Though their separation had been mutual and mostly amicable, the relationship had left wounds on her she was still working out—even two years later.

Christian looked at her, his expression unreadable, and she held her breath in anticipation of a question about her ex. Would she ruin the mood if she refused to answer anything? She had shared some of her thoughts, but she sensed that saying more would put her in dangerous territory. They were already far too close for something they had both said could only be one night—one night to get some closure.

To her relief, he said nothing as they strolled along the beach.

'Did you see Ramón yet?' she asked, to change the topic to something slightly safer. Her brother was still a concern in her mind. If he got wind of anything going on between them, he would be relentless. He'd been the one to orchestrate she and Christian going to the prom together and she feared he would try his best to play match-maker, even at his own wedding.

'The groomsmen had breakfast together though, going by how enthusiastic Ramón was acting, I assume Clara was the one to set it up,' he said with a playful smile. 'It was hard to focus on what was going on in front of me. My thoughts have been…very distracting.'

Heat flared in her cheeks as he shot her a sideways glance loaded with his intent, and her hand tingled where he grasped it. 'If he finds out about us, he's going to lose his mind. So will Clara, though differently. She'll not take any disruption of the wedding kindly,' Raquel said, hoping that reminder would douse her own want for Christian.

'It'll be our secret,' he said, then his gaze trailed towards the water. 'It's been far too long since I've been back here.'

Raquel followed his gaze and watched as the water rose onto the beach and retreated again in a familiar rhythm. Her parents' house was close enough to the beach for her to have gone there a lot growing up—though that beach was a lot more popular with both locals and tourists, so she'd never been as undisturbed as they were here.

'You and Ramón don't meet up often?' she asked, though she probably knew the answer already. Her brother would have mentioned his best friend coming to visit him here.

He shook his head. 'You know how it is. We always talk about hanging out on the phone, but then the timing never lines up. First, I was too busy with med school and my internship, then Anthony got sick, and now with Lexi it's hard to get away.'

She nodded, recognising a lot of the things he listed as reasons she hadn't come to visit for quite some time, either. 'The doctor life is not an easy one, especially if you're sharing that time with someone else,' she said and dared to lean into him a bit, their arms brushing against each other as they both looked out onto the water.

'Or something else. I spend way too much time at work. I can't imagine what it must be like to have two jobs.'

She laughed at the awe in his voice. 'I wish I had enough funding for my charity work that I didn't need to work as a doctor on the side. Don't get me wrong, I love working with patients, and I'm glad I have that income, but if I could live off my charity work I wouldn't hesitate to do that.'

'It's not an easy life you chose,' he said, and Raquel

shivered when his arm came around her shoulder, drawing her closer to him.

'Life has a tendency to choose for us, don't you think?' She knew her life wasn't an easy one, but she could see how his wasn't either. 'Who is looking after Lexi while you're away?'

'Sam is staying at my apartment until I get back. She's a retired nurse that got into child care for kids with special needs. She used to look after Lexi when Anthony was still alive, so she's familiar with Lexi and her needs. Whenever I need help during the day, or when I'm stuck doing an extensive surgery, she is always available to check in with Lexi.'

He paused and shot her a glance. 'With Nesta, I'm hoping she'll become more independent. Though it sometimes feels like I'm treating the symptoms and not the disease.'

Raquel furrowed her brow as she looked up at him. 'What do you mean by that?' He couldn't mean treating her epilepsy, because he knew that was impossible with current medical advances.

He turned towards her, one hand still intertwined with hers while he raked the other one through his hair. 'I know I'm the problem in her life, yet all I can give her are solutions that are bought with money. What she really needs is a father, but I can't even do that for her...'

His voice trailed off and Raquel's heart squeezed tight at the agony written on his face. During the entire two weeks they had spent together, she had sensed something brewing beneath the surface, a restlessness and self-doubt that didn't fit with the picture of the confident surgeon she knew him to be. This was about his guardianship?

'You...don't think you deserve to be her father?'

* * *

The simplicity of her words struck Christian in a raw spot buried deep inside his chest. The self-doubt had been eating him up ever since his brother had passed away and he'd become Lexi's guardian, and he wished he'd had more guidance from Anthony—or anyone, really. His career had always been far more important to him, and he hadn't wanted to subject someone to the life of a high-calibre surgeon, in which they would rarely see him at dinner time and he would already be out of the door before anyone else woke up.

'Ever since she came into my care, I've hated when people talk as if I'm her father. I have not nearly done enough to deserve such a title, and I can see it in her eyes too.' That was the hardest thing to live with every day. He saw it every time he didn't make it in time to say goodnight or when he had to send Sam to help her with a school project. Christian tried hard to be the father figure she deserved, but he wasn't even close to reaching his brother's status. Anthony had made parenting seem easy.

'Christian…that's just not true,' Raquel said after a few beats of silence, and these words, too, lashed him like the strike of a whip, even though she had said them with a calm gentleness.

'I know what I see when…' He stopped when Raquel shook her head.

'You should know you can't possibly know that unless you two have had that conversation. Not making any assumptions based on what we believe we see in people's expression or body language is something we're taught as medical professionals to ensure our diagnosis is as accurate as possible. Why don't you give Lexi the same courtesy?' Her hand was still wrapped around his, sending tendrils of warmth into the storm raging inside him.

How had they even arrived at this topic? These doubts were a secret he kept deep down inside himself, dealing with any outbursts that arose. He had never thought about sharing his insecurities in the light of day like this; hadn't trusted anyone deeply enough to do so. Until Raquel had walked back into his life and something he'd long lost had slotted back into place.

A lightness spread through him, calming the storm with her help. Instead of saying anything, he faced her, wrapped his arms around her shoulders and pulled her to his chest. With his face resting on the top of her head, he dug his nose into her hair and took a deep breath, further calming himself and anchoring him in this moment. 'You're right.' He breathed out and smiled against her hair when he noticed the shiver shaking her body.

'You should talk to her about this. Children are a lot more perceptive than you think, and she might have picked up on things even though you've tried to shield her,' Raquel said, her voice slightly muffled by their embrace. 'But I can promise you, she looks at you with nothing but adoration and love. I've spoken to her enough to know that she understands well what you do when you're not home—and that you are trying your best. What else can you do?'

What else could he do than try his best? The impact of those words pushed the air out of his lungs as they shattered a deep-seated fear inside his heart before taking the fallen pieces and rebuilding it into something new—confidence—knowing that, if he was trying to be the best father figure he could be, he was doing right by

Lexi. If he worked hard and listened to her needs, they would find the way—together.

Raquel was right. He should talk to her about it.

He pulled away so he could look at this woman who had appeared back in his life out of nowhere, and was now bringing order into the chaos he'd been battling ever since his brother's passing. The woman from whom he had walked away because back then he had been too afraid to talk to her—wanting to avoid pain by not taking a chance. Just as he'd tried to do now. Instead of speaking to Lexi, he'd fed on his own insecurity and let it rule him.

Those brown-green eyes had him in a trance, soothing away all his doubts and making him forget what had held him back in seeking his happiness with her. Why had he ever thought he had to choose one thing over the other?

The spark in his eyes sent a bolt of lightning chasing down Raquel's spine. The delicious intent she'd seen in them since their kiss was still there, yet it mingled with something else, something deep and soft that took all the remaining breath out of her lungs.

'You're all I can think of since you showed up in my office, Raquel.' His voice was deep, coated in the desire she sensed mirrored in her own body. The words hit a soft spot inside her, a place she hadn't looked at or cared for since her divorce—believing it too warped and broken to let anyone see or touch it. Though hearing these words sent a jolt of fear through her, she didn't back away from it, but rather accepted the words and how light they made her feel.

'Me too,' she said and closed her eyes when his face drifted closer to hers. Their foreheads touched as he wrapped his arms around her shoulders to pull her even closer to his chest.

'Do you think we are far enough away not to cause a scandal if I kiss you right now?'

Raquel didn't even look before she said, 'We're far enough.'

She *needed* to know that the kiss at the hospital had not just been a product of her ancient feelings for this man, but that their connection was something real. Especially if she was about to let him further in than she had let anyone else since her ex-husband. She knew the parameters around their encounter, knew she couldn't fall for him or she might go too deep, too fast and lose herself all over again.

Her thoughts stopped chasing each other when his grey-blue gaze narrowed as his face came closer, and then fire erupted underneath her skin as his lips closed over hers. Her hands fisted into the fabric of his shirt to steady herself as much as to pull him closer.

His scent mixed with the saltiness of the sea and the earthy tones of the sand underneath them, combining into a smell that spelled safety—home. After being adrift for so many years, trying to reclaim the life she wanted for herself, Raquel had found something that just...fitted. Someone she'd had in her life all these years, hidden away under layers of missed chances and insecurities. Her reaction to Christian was so strong, the kiss they shared so *right*, that she couldn't remember what had kept them apart in the first place. Had they simply not been the people they'd needed to be to fit together the way they did now?

Raquel shuddered when she opened her mouth for his pleading tongue, giving in to him with both her body and her mind. Her hands began to wander, slipping under his shirt and relishing the feel of muscle and skin underneath it. The subdued growl she got at her caress drove a hot spear of need right into her core.

His hands wandered up her back and he threaded his fingers into her hair, pulling her head back and deepening the kiss until she clung to him for dear life. Only when both their breaths left them in panting bursts did he let go of her mouth. His lips brushed over the shell of her ear as he asked, 'Do you want to continue this at the hotel?'

CHAPTER NINE

CHRISTIAN COULDN'T REMEMBER the last time he'd had to be discreet when taking a woman to his room. He was thankful that the only people he knew in this hotel were the other groomsmen. It would have been so much more difficult to find some time alone with Raquel if they'd been surrounded by her family. How could anyone find some closeness under these circumstances?

Though what he felt for Raquel was more than just closeness, and this would be more than just sex. She was...in a completely different league...and his youthful feelings for her had not only come back with a vengeance, they had matured with him and presented him with a dilemma he didn't want to think about too closely. Not when Raquel was looking at him with undiluted hunger as they stood in front of the closed door of his room.

A grin spread over Christian's lips, one that turned positively feral when he opened the door to his room and pulled Raquel through it. He pushed the door closed the second she had stepped through it, grabbing her by the waist and hauling her against the door in an imitation of their first kiss in the scrub room.

He put all the want and desire he'd been holding back into this kiss, its pace more frantic than the one they'd shared before.

Raquel yelped when her feet lifted off the ground, and she wrapped her legs around his midsection to keep her balance—exactly the way he had wanted her to react. As he deepened the kiss, he pushed his hips against hers and relished the shudder racking through her body as his hard length pressed against her.

'*Dios...*' she breathed out, her hands gripping his shoulders as his mouth left hers to trail down her neck, leaving gentle kisses everywhere he went.

Dios indeed. Her skin was so soft against his lips; her scent was one he wanted to lose himself in for the rest of his life, along with the gentle gasps and mewls dropping from her lips at every one of his touches. He wasn't worthy of that reaction, but for her he would try to be. For Raquel, who had seen through the barriers of his own insecurities to see the real him, and who had led him there with kindness and patience.

He would try his best—just as he would in every other aspect of his life—even if it could just be for this one night.

Christian's head dipped lower, his lips brushing over her collar bone and down the front of her dress, where he paused to look at the swell of her breasts pushing against the dress's neckline, that distracting, concealing piece of fabric.

'Are you planning on wearing this dress later?' he asked, earning himself a confused look from Raquel.

'I...no, I just put this one on for our walk,' she said, her voice no more than breathless sighs. He could hear how much effort it took for her to focus on this seemingly unrelated question and a part of him relished that he'd already mentally exhausted her—when they were only just getting started.

'So I don't have to be careful and hang it in the closet to avoid any wrinkles?' He knew the answer already, but asked anyway. The more he could distract her, the sweeter it would be when he got back on topic.

To underline his question, he placed her legs back on the floor and stroked his hands down her sides, as if admiring the cut of the dress. He caught the bob of her throat with a glint of primal satisfaction.

'No, rip it off my body if that's what you want to do.' Raquel's voice grew louder, her eyes coming back into focus. A grin spread over his lips when he saw the fire in her eyes instantly reignite and, instead of saying anything else, she gripped the hem of his shirt and pulled it over his head. Then she tossed the shirt onto the floor without giving it another glance.

Christian chuckled. 'I see... I think I can do that.' But, even though everything inside him was taut and ready for that moment, he wanted to draw it out just a bit longer—in case this truly was one night and nothing else. He needed time to commit every dip and curve of her body to memory. To preserve this moment as the special occasion it was.

Raquel had meant it when she had said that he should rip the dress off her body. So, when instead he took her by the hand and tugged her after him, her insides burst into flames that she knew would never die down. She had been burning for this man for far too long. One time would not be enough—maybe even a lifetime would be too short to conquer the depth of desire she found within her.

It was a strange sensation that she was wholly unfamiliar with. Not a single one of her past relationships compared to the energy thrumming through her whenever Christian touched her. Was this simply because of the many years of anticipation? Or was there something different about them? Was their attraction to each other somehow built differently?

She wasn't sure how to answer that question—wasn't sure it mattered. This was their one opportunity. After that, Raquel would leave Whitehall Memorial and find a new assignment while Christian would stay in New York. Even if Mia or the chief agreed to give her a contract, that would only bring her back for a few weeks at a time.

Their timing had always been bad and the present was no exception. All she could do was enjoy the moment they'd been granted right now. If he wasn't so adamant on teasing her until she exploded from anticipation alone.

Raquel kicked off her shoes as he pulled her towards the bed, where he sat down at the edge and looked up at her. 'Turn around,' he said and the gravel in his voice had her obeying without a second thought.

She inhaled sharply when his hands touched her legs just underneath her knees and then began sliding higher, slipping under the hem of her dress and over her thighs until his fingers reached her butt. He let out a sharp hiss when his fingers dug into her flesh and that sound was enough to drive her already heated core to new temperatures.

Not only was Christian touching her so intimately, but he had the same reactions to touching her as she had to him. He *desired* her. All thoughts emptied out of her head when his right hand slipped along her hip to her front, his fingers brushing over her lacy underwear. His other hand slid down her thigh again in a gentle caress, then he wrapped his arm around her waist and pulled her down towards him.

'Christian, wha—?' Her yelp swallowed the rest of her sentence as he guided her down to sit on his lap.

His right hand was still brushing over the triangle of fabric covering her, increasing the pressure on the ache building there. He spread out his fingers as she squirmed, her body no longer hers to command and desperate to increase what little friction he was offering her.

He huffed a laugh, his face close enough to her that his breath grazed her heated cheeks. 'Spread your legs for me,' he said, his voice lower than she'd ever heard it.

There was no resisting that command. Her muscles moved of their own accord and her knees fell open with her legs draped over each of his. The flame inside her rose higher as his erection pressed against her backside, telling her he was enjoying this just as much as her. Raquel shuddered at that thought and shook more when his low laugh rumbled through her. He kissed her neck and nipped at her earlobe as he said, 'Getting to do this to you is so much hotter than you can imagine, Raquel.'

Her breath stuttered as she released it, each one ratcheting her heart rate higher and higher. She opened her mouth to reply, but the only thing her throat could produce was a long, drawn-out moan as his fingers pressed down on her. Raquel couldn't stop her hips from bucking, that spot sensitive enough that she could feel his fingers even through the fabric of her underwear.

'You are so cruel, Christian,' she huffed out, her head falling down on his shoulder. His eyes met hers when she cracked one open to look at him. The smile spreading over his lips was primal. This was driving him just as mad.

His free hand came up to her face, drawing her mouth towards his in a passionate kiss. Just as his tongue slipped into her mouth, he slid his fingers under the seam of her underwear and over her.

Her body tensed then loosened up, only to tense again as he stroked her, his fingers coaxing out moan after throaty moan which his hungry lips swallowed whole as he kept kissing her. Raquel forgot where she was, and what the reasons had been for her to deny herself this moment, because right here and now she couldn't understand why she had hesitated—or any of the reasons she had repeated over the last few weeks of why she shouldn't let the attraction to Christian overwhelm her.

'Open your eyes, sweetheart,' he said, the tempo of his fingers steady, even though the urgency inside her was rising exponentially. 'I want to look at you.'

Look at her? Her mind was too scrambled from teetering between pleasure and pain to understand what lay behind his request as Christian kept up his rhythm. Her eyes fluttered open and, as she stared into the blue eyes glazed over with undiluted want for her, she understood what he meant.

A loud moan burst from her throat and her muscles clenched tightly as he brought her over the edge with one last stroke of his fingers. His arm tightened around her waist and pressed her closer to him, holding her through her climax. All the while he kept pressing kisses onto her neck, her cheek and behind her ear. His breaths were as heavy as hers, each one grazing her cheek in a hot sear.

She turned her head to look at him again, eyes wide and struggling to come up with the words to say. She didn't need to, for Christian leaned in and kissed her, gently this time, before smiling at her.

'Thank you for letting me do this,' he said as his right hand slid up her body. 'This has been a fantasy of mine for a long time.'

Raquel blinked as she absorbed his words, her brain still finding its way back to earth after getting scattered among the stars. 'Thank me? Christian, I…' Her voice trailed off when she heard the zip of her dress being pulled down. The light pressure the fabric kept on her torso eased as the zip slipped further down until Christian reached the bottom.

The fabric rustled as his hand pushed it off each shoulder, leaving a kiss in each spot where he touched her. Any post-climax drowsiness vanished as he exposed more of her skin to the cool air of his room, and her passion-addled brain told her to let him take the lead. It had worked so well just a few moments ago.

But, if they had only this moment with each other, should she be content with just taking orders? Something inside her had awakened with his touch, a desire to be more, to have more with him.

Before Raquel could overthink it, she stood and peeled the dress off her body. It fell to the floor with barely a rustle, and as she stared at Christian, she reached behind to unclasp her bra, throwing it on top of her dress. Then, as she stepped out of the dress pooling around her ankles, she pushed her underwear down her hips and felt it slide down her thighs as she took another step.

Goose bumps prickled all over her skin when Christian's hot gaze raked over her, his bare chest heaving with each breath. He didn't move as she straddled him, but hissed when she palmed his erection through his trousers.

'You are so beautiful, Raquel,' he whispered into her

ear as she worked her palm over him, his throaty moan almost enough to send her over the edge again.

She wound her fingers around the waistband and pulled forward enough for her fingers to grasp the button. Raquel flicked it open with a quick motion and her mouth went dry when she looked down at his considerable size.

Her lips parted, her tongue darting out and licking her lips as the sense of anticipation within her heightened. This was everything she'd ever wanted from him. One night to let loose, to explore what they had missed so many years ago. They couldn't reclaim the past, but at least they could have this.

When she stood up naked in front of him, Christian lost all sense of self and time. He could only focus on the gorgeous apparition in front of him, standing there in all her glory and wanting him. *Him.* That thought almost undid him right there and then. What had he done to deserve any of her attention? Hadn't he been the one to run away from her all those years ago?

He'd left because he hadn't had the courage to tell her how he felt and hadn't wanted to risk rejection, but had rather chosen to do it himself then. That was a mistake he would undo today, right here. He would choose her and would continue to choose her as long as she would have him. Christian couldn't get back the years they'd missed, but he could start marking the right choice today.

He raised his hands to her face, pulling her closer to him until his lips were on hers, to put all the feelings bubbling up in his chest into that touch. There would be time to talk about things, but right now he wanted to be present in the moment…with Raquel.

'Let me get out of these clothes,' he whispered against her cheek when he trailed kisses down her jaw. Then he wrapped his hands around her hips and stood up.

Raquel yelped as she quickly wrapped her legs around him to keep balance and, just as she adjusted herself, he turned around to put her back down on the bed. One pull on his waistband and his trousers and boxers were on the floor, on top of her already discarded dress.

She held her hand out when he looked at her, like a siren beckoning him, and he was ready to surrender everything he was to her for one moment of bliss. Seeing her lying on the bed with her hair spread out, it surprised him he wasn't on his knees, worshipping her until she could no longer move. There was still time for that later...

But now he needed to feel her all around him. Christian turned with a wink, shoving his hand into his toiletries bag and coming back up with a condom. The urgency with which he ripped the package open and rolled it over him betrayed the need rising hotter and hotter within him, and was only stoked to a higher level by Raquel's darkened eyes watching his every move.

When he turned back to her, the glint in her eyes removed the last shreds of self-restraint he had put on himself. He got into bed with her, his body covering hers as he settled down between her legs. Raquel moaned as his full length pressed against her slick heat, and he had to take several deep breaths to calm himself. He hadn't felt such excitement and need with anyone in his past. Drawing out his own satisfaction in favour of hers was the most exquisite torture, and he wanted to do it over and over again.

Raquel wrapped her legs around his waist once more,

her hips grinding against him and conveying her own urgency. Her arms came around his neck, pulling him down towards her and onto her lips in a passionate kiss that matched the movements of her hips.

'Christian, enough playing around. *Te necesito*,' she moaned into his ear, and his arousal only heightened at her use of Spanish.

I need you.

How long had he yearned to hear those words from her? He hadn't even known how much he was missing out on her until she had returned to his life. It had been like seeing the stars again for the first time in over a decade.

'Such impatience,' he replied with a teasing grin. She answered by grinding her hip against him again, seeking the thing he was denying her.

Christian hissed, swallowing the curse building in his chest. This woman really would be his demise. There was absolutely no way this was going to end well, not with everything they had discussed and all the boundaries they had trampled over in their mad dash to this moment. But Christian couldn't care about it. Not just now, as he shifted his hips and slid into her with a groan of pure satisfaction.

Raquel contracted around him, a matching moan dropping from her lips as he rocked in and out at a gentle pace to start with as they looked into each other's eyes. The spark of unbridled desire he saw within the hazel eyes urged him on to pick up the pace as he kissed her deeply. Her tongue greeted him in her mouth, dancing around him and taking what little breath he had left in his lungs.

Christian didn't care. Whatever was his to give, she could have it, and if he didn't have it, he would find it somehow. As the tension in the pit of his stomach built, he realised that there was nothing he wouldn't do with this woman. She'd only have to ask and he would give it to her.

'Raquel, I...' He didn't know how to end the sentence. Didn't know how to say what was happening inside him. How could he tell her what he sensed bursting out of his chest whenever he looked at her? They had agreed there would be no more than this one time. Wouldn't it be selfish to say anything when they had both established this as their boundary?

Instead of saying anything, he buried his face in her exposed neck as her head fell backwards, and let his mouth wander. He brushed his lips against her pert, dark nipple before encircling it with his mouth and lavishing it with attention.

Raquel bowed off the bed at this touch, her huffed breaths turning into loud moans as he brought her closer to her second release as she brought him just as close to his. Her nails dug into his shoulders, trailing further down with each thrust, and he didn't doubt there would be some marks left on his skin afterwards. Not that he cared. If those were the only thing he would carry away from all of this, then he would cherish them for the rest of his life.

'Christian... I'm going to...' His mouth swallowed the rest of the words as he came back up to press his lips on hers in a passionate kiss that sent them both over the edge of the cliff.

A tremble shook his body as his vision filled with bright flecks and stars. He remained on top of her for several heartbeats before wrapping his arms around her and rolling with her so they lay side by side. His heart threatened to explode as he took in the flush of her cheeks and the still passion-glazed eyes that looked back at him with such warmth.

How was he supposed to be satisfied with only one moment?

CHAPTER TEN

ONE TIME WASN'T ENOUGH. Raquel knew it the second Christian had rolled off her. The quiet satisfaction had only lasted for a few minutes before the need had reawakened. The scheduled rehearsal dinner had forced them to leave the room—an almost three-hour affair that had had Raquel writhing at the thought of being back in his bed.

That had been yesterday, and she had woken up with a pep in her step she'd struggled to keep under control as she had joined the rest of the bridesmaids to get ready for the ceremony earlier that morning. Thankfully she had been able to focus all her attention on Clara. Getting the bride ready for her big day had put any thoughts of Christian aside, until the moment that she watched her now sister-in-law walk down the aisle and towards her brother with a smile so bright it had melted her heart.

Then her eyes collided with Christian's and all the memories of their night together had come rushing back, heating the blood in her veins. She'd sensed his stolen glances raking over her during the ceremony, and had replied to some of them with a sneaky wink of her own when she'd been certain no one was paying attention to her—which was throughout the ceremony. All eyes had been glued on the bride and groom, the bridal party little more than background actors in her brother's fairy-tale wedding.

That served her well enough, given that she didn't know what exactly was going on between them—or what had been brewing for the last two weeks. Their attraction wasn't surprising. She had pined for him all throughout his time in Puerto Rico, and now she'd come to understand that this time the feelings were mutual.

Their compatibility on a physical level was unlike any she had ever experienced. Watching Ramón get married to the woman he'd been in love with since his university days sparked an ache inside her chest that was hard to put into words. Raquel had had that moment herself when she'd married her ex, though that romance had been a lot more whirlwind and, in hindsight, had not been the right fit. Part of her wondered if she had been so desperate to recreate that feeling she'd had with Christian all those years ago that she had been willing to settle for Tom, the next-best thing.

But that hadn't worked out and the sacrifices she had made had shaped her life now. A life into which she couldn't fit someone like Christian. She had once built her life around her spouse and had lost so much of herself in the process.

It didn't matter how explosive their connection was, or how dread pooled in the pit of her stomach when she thought about the end of this weekend when they would have to go back to their normal lives.

Was she right to let him go when she had only just got to know him again?

Around her, the after party was in full swing. The newlywed couple sat at the same table as the rest of the bridal party and her, receiving many of the guests for personal congratulations and well wishes.

Every now and then she caught Christian's eyes on her and she wasn't sure if the hunger in his eyes was imagined or real. If Ramón picked up on anything going on between them, she would not hear the end of it. Her family already considered her the sad, divorced spinster who preferred the company of dogs over men. If suddenly a handsome neurosurgeon entered the mix, she would never see the end of the meddling.

What she and Christian had was not intended to be permanent. How would that even have worked? Her work would not let her settle down and he needed to be in New York with his niece.

'The DJ is ready for the first dance,' Donna, the maid of honour, announced next to Raquel, ripping her out of her thoughts. 'Ramón and Clara are going to kick us off and then the bridal party will join them halfway through, just as we rehearsed. Is everyone good with this? The videographer is rolling already, so let's make some nice memories for our lovely couple.'

Raquel's eyes widened at the woman's instructions. She had completely forgotten about that part of the evening. During the rehearsal dinner, Clara had announced that she wanted the entire bridal party to join the first dance for the traditional *danza criolla*.

Raquel had only half-paid attention to those plans, since most of her brain had still been scattered among the stars at this point from the mind-bending orgasm Christian had recently given her. One she was keen to repeat tonight after they sent off the couple on their honeymoon, though she knew the smart choice would be to avoid him going forward. What was the point of dragging it out when they were going to end up separated again? They'd got the closure they longed for. Now it was time to move on, right?

Except, in a couple of minutes, she would find herself pressed against him on the dance floor. She didn't know whether Clara knew about their connection, but she suspected as much, since she had paired them up for their dance.

'We'll keep it up for two or three songs, give people enough time to join us on the dance floor and then Clara and the bridesmaids are taking some pictures inside. So don't linger around too long.' Donna made a point of looking at every single bridesmaid at the table and getting an acknowledgement of her words.

At least she wouldn't have to dance for long but she knew that being pressed against Christian for several songs would have her begging for more at the end.

Their eyes met over the table, and Raquel gasped at the pure masculinity of his smile. The spark in his eyes was enough to convey his intentions for later and sent a cascade of hot sparks tearing through her body. She dared a quick glance around and noted that no one was paying them any attention. If they had, they would have seen the message written in his eyes: Christian was going to devour her tonight.

Applause erupted around her when Ramón and Clara got up from their chairs and walked onto the dance floor just as a medium-paced song began to play. While the guests gathered round to watch the pair, Donna motioned them all to get up and into position, sending a pointed glance towards a man standing behind a camera on a raised platform.

Raquel had to suppress an eye-roll as she got off her

chair, the fabric of her peach-coloured dress rustling in unison with the other bridesmaids'. Someone held onto her chair as she got up, pulling it away and giving her enough space to navigate round the other women all getting ready.

She turned to find Christian standing behind her chair, blue-grey eyes narrowed with the same promise she'd seen just a few moments ago. Raquel took the arm he offered her and levelled a stern look at him that threatened to melt away under the fire of passion in his own eyes.

'You have to stop looking at me like that, Chris,' she hissed quietly as they made their way to where the maid of honour stood.

Christian had the gall to look at her with feigned innocence as he asked, 'Like what?'

'Seriously?' She tried her best to look disapproving, but felt the chuckle bubbling up at the corners of her mouth. 'You look like you are about to claim me in front of my entire extended family.'

His eyebrows rose at that, and Raquel shivered when he folded his free hand over hers. A mischievous twinkle entered his eyes. 'I didn't know I was allowed to do that.'

'You are *definitely* not,' she replied, but couldn't stop the quiet laughter from spilling over her lips. He needed to stop saying things like that or she might believe that they had a chance at a future together.

'I guess I'll have to make up for it later,' he said, and the wink he gave her with those words shot a spear of hot desire through her chest as the memories of last night poured back into her consciousness.

'Christian…'

'Go, go, go.' The half-whispered instructions of the maid of honour interrupted her and, the next moment, she was moving towards the middle where her brother and sister-in-law were already twirling on their feet, eyes only for one another, and unaware that their bridal party was joining them.

Christian seemed to have paid more attention to the instructions given out last night, judging by the confidence with which he placed himself in the ring of people, pulling her into his arms. One hand landed on her hip while the other one grasped her hand, and then he began a sequence of familiar steps that were mirrored all around them.

Raquel went along as he led them through the dance, still stunned from the awareness and need thrumming through her at the lightest touch from the man who was now spinning her round on the dance floor. 'How do you know the *danza criolla*?'

With as many relatives as she had, she'd learned all the traditions of a Puerto Rican wedding early on—including the *danza criolla*.

He laughed as they spun further, each step steadfast and with the beat of the music—as if he, too, had grown up with the rhythm of this dance. 'I don't know if you remember, but my parents were diplomats. They made a point of learning the most common traditions in the countries they were serving in. Not all of them survived in my brain, but I knew I had to eventually dance at Ramón's wedding.'

They swayed around the couples, skirts billowing as the groomsmen whirled their partners around. The next move brought Christian's face closer to hers, igniting the sleeping embers in her core. There was something about his expression, something soft and warm, wrapping around her as he looked at her.

'Was your wedding anything like this?' he asked, and her breath hitched in her throat.

'We… No, it wasn't,' she replied, struggling to find the right words at the unexpected question.

The thought of answering any questions about her marriage brought instant unease to her stomach, but something was different today. Thoughts about Tom were never comfortable, and she had also actively avoided talking to *anyone* about this for so long—because her family's prying felt invasive, as if they were entitled to a piece of her story.

Christian showed none of that in his face. He wanted to know her and had asked so many questions about her life without hyper-fixating on the one thing she thought she had failed at. They'd agreed to be with each other this weekend—so why not treat this like a safe space? Something deep inside her told her he would never betray her confidence.

Was she a fool to believe that feeling?

'We couldn't afford a wedding straight out of med school, and I didn't want to ask my parents for the money. I know they would have paid for everything, but…something inside of me stopped me from asking for it.' She swallowed the lump appearing in her throat. 'I think deep inside some part of me knew that this—that he—wasn't who I was supposed to be with.'

An expression fluttered over Christian's face, too brief for Raquel to understand it, yet it shot an icy trickle down her spine.

'But you went through with it anyway?' he asked, his eyes fixed on a point above her head as they shifted on the dance floor without missing a single beat.

'I wish I could tell you why. Tom was just…there. We

met in med school, got more serious about it and then that seemed like the next logical step. I grew up thinking that perfect was unattainable—that you make sacrifices for the people you love, that you…compromise. My mother or my *tías* spoke about how they'd had to make the choices that were right for their marriage—that I shouldn't expect everything to just fit without having to give some.'

She huffed out an unamused laugh as she looked back at her memories. 'Tom had met his business partner in my last year of med school, and that's when he mapped out the next decade of our lives. Because of what I'd heard my relatives say my entire life, I thought, as the spouse, my job was to fit into whatever vision he had come up with.'

Raquel couldn't hear his soothing sounds of encouragement over the loud music, but the vibration travelled from his arm down to hers, soothing the torrent the memories of Tom caused in her. She had never answered the question as to why she worked so hard, why she'd only begun her charity work so late in life, because she was scared of how people would see her. If they knew how willingly she had gone along with a proposed plan without even questioning it or speaking up, how could they trust her?

'I know that sounds really dumb and that's the reason I normally don't talk about…' She stopped talking when his hand tightened on her hip, his steely stare boring into her.

'A good spouse would have checked in with you and not just considered your wishes but worked on how to achieve them—together,' he said, his low voice curling around her as if they weren't dancing in the middle of many other couples. 'Don't explain the disrespect you suffered away. You deserved to be consulted about your life's direction, and you shouldn't take all the blame onto yourself.'

Raquel blinked several times as his words sank within her like a stone in water. Even after two years she still carried the weight of her failed marriage with her. 'You think I should have stood up for myself?' she asked, but he shook his head with a gentle smile on his lips.

'I think you deserve someone who will stand up for you unprompted.'

The world faded away under her feet, the noise around them dimming until it was just the two of them dancing to the sound of a muted band, their instruments not loud enough to get through to her as she got lost in Christian's eyes. She'd always blamed herself for what had happened—she knew only how to find the flaw within herself—and had built the last two years of her life in a way to avoid that vulnerability.

Would you stand up for me?

The question clung to her lips, begging to be released, but what if the answer was yes? She didn't know what she would do with that information—how she would react. They weren't supposed to mean more to each other than they already did.

'What about now?' he said, saving her from her own turmoil.

She blinked again in confusion. 'What do you mean?'

'Would you want a wedding like this now?'

'There's no chance I will ever get married again.' The answer flew out of her mouth before she could even contemplate it, and the snort following her words was the result of a defence mechanism she had developed in the years of her unhappy marriage and throughout the divorce process. Raquel had lost so much of herself to Tom and his ambitions that, the moment she had been freed of the pressure, she'd barely recognised herself.

She wasn't sure she recognised herself now, either, as she looked up at this gorgeous man to whom she had just opened up and watched the curious spark in his eyes bank.

Tension rippled around them, and she flinched as the crowd around them cheered, some of them joining them on the dance floor. Something about her words hadn't sat well with him—didn't sit well with her just now. Was that truly how she felt or was this the reaction borne out of years full of regret?

'Raquel, I was calling you for a solid minute.' The rapid-fire Spanish pierced through her thundering thoughts, and she turned her head to see Donna waving at her with the impatience of a woman who had been ordered to carry most of the stress of the day so the bride didn't have to.

'Sorry, I didn't hear you. The music was so loud,' she replied and got an incredulous look from her.

'Yeah, right,' she said, her eyes flicking over to Christian, who had released his grip on her and stood some paces away.

'I have to go take some photos,' Raquel called over her shoulder when Donna wrapped her hand around her wrist and pulled her in the direction of the main house. 'I'll be right back.'

Christian wasn't fast enough extracting himself from the dance floor and ended up fielding one dance with an elderly woman who complimented him on his very capable hands and proceeded to ask him about his life's history when he mentioned being a doctor.

He knew that his occupation, along with no visible ring on his finger, made him prime real-estate in situations such as these, where older relatives had their younger charges to care for and needed to make good matches— one reason he avoided weddings, though there was no way he would have missed Ramón's, even with all the inconveniences.

As the music changed, Christian took the opportunity to take his leave before Abuelita Rosana could find her niece, who he 'just had to meet'.

He scanned the outside area where the reception was in full swing and found a group of comfy chairs tucked away in a corner, with no one in sight. *Perfect*. He could lie low until Raquel returned from the bridal photo-shoot and then…

His chest tightened as he thought about the night they had spent together. Even though there had been little sleep, he was buzzing from the energy Raquel summoned in him. He knew a lifetime would not be enough to sate his desire for this woman, and that thought frightened him. Part of him had wanted to tell her about the growing feelings, had wanted to know if she felt it too. His heart had fluttered when she'd opened up to him about her marriage, sharing with him what had happened— only for it to crack at her words.

There's no chance I will ever get married again.

His mood had dropped considerably by the time he plopped down on the chair, his thoughts circling around his feelings for Raquel and their inevitability. This was exactly what they had agreed to, and what she had told him only confirmed what she wanted from him—a physical relationship and nothing more.

A glass of amber liquid appeared in front of his vision, the ice cubes clinking against the glass as Ramón sat down on the chair next to him.

'*Salud!*' his best friend said when Christian grabbed it from him and put the glass to his lips.

Christian gave it a sniff, picking up hints of fruit and sweetness. The liquid burned in his throat when he took a swig. 'Pitorro…' he said with an appreciative nod. 'We've already arrived at that part of the reception?'

'Abuelo brought his finest Pitorro today. Proofed in a cask that had some sweet wine in it,' Ramón said as he took another sip.

'Explains the hints of fruit.' Christian took another sip, savouring the flavour on his tongue before swallowing.

His first experience with Pitorro had been at sixteen, when Ramón had sneaked some of his father's supplies into his room. Because of its home-brewed nature, the spirit was usually a much higher proof than commercial rum—which had made it hard for a sixteen-year-old to appreciate it.

They sat in companionable quiet for a while before Christian said, 'You did it. Congratulations, brother.'

Ramón looked at him with a half-smile. 'Easiest decision I ever made, Chris. It was like everything in my life led me right to this moment.'

Christian's chest constricted at those words as his own situation came back to the forefront of his mind. That kind of stalwart conviction was something lacking in his life. Not a single thing that had ever happened had felt as though it was on purpose, to lead him to a grander thing. Life just happened around him while he tried his best to adapt to it.

A stab of jealousy buried itself in his side. He'd seen the looks Ramón shot at his wife many times over, each one full of the love and loyalty that bound them together. A tether so strong even he could see it.

Was he tethered to someone like that?

A face surfaced in front of his mind's eye at that question, one he immediately pushed away.

'You should tell her how you feel,' Ramón said out of nowhere.

Christian's eyes whipped up from where he had been staring into his drink while contemplating his best friend's words. 'I don't know—'

'Yeah, you do, *mentiroso*. You've been in love with Raquel since the day you met her one and a half decades ago, and judging by what I've seen today those feelings haven't gone anywhere.' Ramón leaned back in his chair as Christian narrowed his eyes at him.

'You should be too busy at your own wedding to notice anything going on in my life, Ramón,' he replied, to evade the question.

What was he going to tell his best friend—that he and his younger sister had decided on a weekend affair? That he was desperately falling in love with her? Apparently, he already knew that.

'It wasn't me who clocked you. You know the *tías* on both sides keep track of any eligible bachelor and bachelorette, so they marked you the moment you set foot on this property. They seemed to have...noticed some glances and touches here and there, and came to me for some answers.'

Of course they hadn't gone unnoticed. With so many

people around them, Christian would have hoped that their familiarity looked like nothing more but an old friendship rekindled for this wedding.

'What did you tell them?' He hardly dared ask that question and breathed out a sigh of relief when Ramón snorted.

'Nothing. I care for you, *hermano*. Sending my *tías* as match-makers would not have the desired outcome for any of us,' he said, taking another gulp of his rum.

'I… There's nothing going on between me and Raquel.' The words didn't sit right with Christian, but he forced them out of his mouth anyway, because at the core they were true. They had slept together, and he would never be the same person who he had been before meeting her—before being with her. But she didn't want more from him and, if it hadn't been clear from the start, he definitely knew now.

He wouldn't be the one to force a change where she didn't want one, even though everything within him had changed the moment she had walked into his office. He was still in love with Raquel, that feeling from so long ago having survived all the hardships in his life, maturing into something precious and rare.

'Not everyone can have what you found…' he said when movement from the door caught both men's attention and Clara appeared, still in her white dress, her eyes darting around in search of her husband.

That look laid bare a deep yearning within Christian for someone to look for him with such an expression of anticipation and love in her eyes as Clara showed now. If only…

His heart stopped in his chest when Raquel stepped out behind Clara, her eyes searching as well, and when their gazes collided her face lit up with unveiled affection, her lips widening into a smile that had him struggling to draw in his next breath.

Could it be?

He got up from his chair without much thought when he felt a hand encircle his wrist, holding him back. Ramón stood as well, his expression serious.

'You can say there's nothing going on as much as you want, Chris. But you better be careful with my sister's heart. She's been through a lot and she has the scars to show for it. She won't trust you unless you mean it. So be serious about her,' he said, before letting go of his hand just as Clara joined them, throwing her arms around her husband and ending their conversation.

CHAPTER ELEVEN

THE BUTTERFLIES IN Raquel's stomach had become a constant companion ever since arriving in New York almost four weeks ago. They bounced against her insides with an unrelenting viciousness as she approached the scrub room outside the theatre where she would be part of Evelyn's surgery. The day to insert the probes had finally come, getting her patient one step closer to the quality of life she deserved.

She swallowed her nervousness as she pushed the door open and found two of the OR nurses already busy scrubbing in, while part of the surgical team was already setting up inside the operating theatre—Christian included.

The weekend in Puerto Rico seemed like an elaborate dream conjured up by her lonely brain. But she knew her imagination couldn't have been this vivid and colourful. What had happened between them last weekend had altered her world for ever.

And now it was over. They had spent their nights together, sharing their affection with one another, until they'd arrived back in New York. Neither of them had said anything as they had kissed one last time at the airport, a silent understanding passing between them. As agreed—it was over.

Since then, their interactions had been purely professional and, though part of her hurt at the coolness between them, she knew they were doing the right thing, leaving what had happened in Puerto Rico.

This morning had been her final meeting with Alexandria and Nesta. Christian had been there too, and Raquel had wondered for a moment if he'd already had a conversation with his niece about the struggles in his heart.

Raquel had no hesitation closing out this assignment as successful. Both dog and handler had made such amazing progress during her time here and Raquel felt confident that they would remain an inseparable team for many years to come—as well as brilliant advocates for her work with epilepsy patients and their service dogs.

Evelyn would be her last patient at Whitehall Memorial. She still had a few patients to see after that, but Dr Prem was already back from his compassionate leave and taking over most of the workload. There was nothing left to do but to hand over anything remaining and then talk to Mia and the Chief of Medicine about potentially giving her a contract. If she left New York with a commitment from the hospital to sponsor several dogs for patients who needed them, she would call her time here a success. She could not show up to the meeting with her investors empty-handed.

Though that wasn't the only thing weighing on her mind as she prepared to leave New York behind. Raquel had no regrets about what had happened between them. How could she? Christian had shown her she was still a woman with needs and wants, despite her best efforts to pretend otherwise. What she couldn't accept was the depth of her feelings for him.

These last few days had shown her that her best efforts to remain detached and uninvolved had failed. Instead of the usual elation of new opportunities appearing on the horizon, dread filled her with each passing day as she realised she'd have to leave New York by the end of the week—leave Christian and that glimmer of warmth she'd sensed growing inside her chest ever since she'd first seen him again. It was a feeling she'd been denying vehemently for the last weeks, but could no longer. Not when she woke up every day with a head full of dreams about the future—and they all involved him. They involved Alexandria, too.

She was in love with Christian. Christian, who hadn't looked at her with anything but professionalism since they'd come back from Puerto Rico because, unlike her, he knew how to play by the rules they'd set.

She stepped to the sink with a silent sigh leaving her chest, getting her head into the task ahead of her. The probes for the deep-brain stimulation had to be placed with the patient awake, making it a tricky and risky surgery.

Raquel was here to ensure they put the probes in the right parts of the brain. Christian and his team of surgeons would handle the entire surgery but, because Evelyn would be awake, they could get her input on the placement and test the effectiveness of the deep-brain stimulation as they did the procedure.

By the time she was done scrubbing in, the OR was buzzing with activity.

'Patient is on her way, Dr Wolf,' the leading nurse said after hanging up the phone on the wall.

'Good, thank you for the update. Can we put the cortical mapping we did yesterday on the screen? We should go over the surgical plan one more time.'

Christian's voice stood out amongst the thrum of other

voices and noise around her, like a beacon flashing its light just at her. Her ears immediately perked up and her eyes found their way to him of their own accord, no matter how adamant her brain was about *not* looking at him.

He stood in front of a screen at the side of the OR, where another physician stood with a tablet. Several pictures appeared on the larger screen, all showing a cross-section of Evelyn's brain with different areas lit up in various colours.

'We're aiming for this area for the probes to lessen her tremors. My primary concern is how close it is to some of the speech mapping we did. Did Dr Pascal see those? We should…' His voice trailed off as he looked around.

An electric current shot through her body when their eyes met, his eye round in surprise before narrowing slightly and unearthing some memories from this weekend she had worked hard to suppress for today.

'Would you mind looking at this, Dr Pascal?' he said, his tone not betraying if his reaction to seeing her was anything like hers to him.

She pushed down the nerves bubbling up inside her and stepped closer to look at the pictures presented. Her arm brushed his and for a few moments his hand hovered over her back as if he was going to place it on the small of her back. But then he simply cleared his throat, taking an extra step.

'For the probes to be most effective, we'll try to place them as close to these areas as possible,' Christian said, pointing to an area at the back of the brain. 'We should look out for any speech issues when we place them, since those regions touch.'

Raquel nodded, forcing her mind back into focus and willing herself to ignore Christian and anything that had happened between them. It was done. They had both agreed to it from the very start.

'I'm going to go through both mobility and speech exercises with Evelyn while you place the probes. Any irregularities will be clear during the procedure, giving us plenty of opportunity to correct it,' she said, then turned when the large double doors of the OR opened to admit Evelyn for her surgery.

'This is going along great, Evelyn. How are you feeling?'

Christian's voice was muffled behind his mask and, with the noise of the suction and the bone saw, Raquel hardly heard his words. She looked at the intern standing closest to her with an eyebrow raised in a silent question. The man stepped closer and repeated Christian's words to Evelyn.

Her eyes darted to Raquel's, and she gave an encouraging nod. 'You can tell me and he'll be able to hear you,' she said to the woman.

'I'm…very nervous. The sounds are…jarring,' Evelyn said, her eyes wide enough to see the whites.

They had administered a sedative to calm some of her nerves, but they had to be careful during awake surgery not to go too heavy on them or they wouldn't be able to check the probe placement with her.

Raquel looked at the surgical team standing behind Evelyn. They had drilled small holes into her skull to place each of the three probes and Christian was attaching the stereotactic frame onto the skull to hold the micro-drive in place.

This was a lot more detail than she usually had about a surgery but, with Evelyn being the one big case she'd worked on here in New York besides Alexandria and

Nesta, she wanted to be fully informed and involved. The surgical team had been very accommodating of her thirst for knowledge, and part of her wondered how much of the influence was because of Christian. Had he told his team they needed to teach her more than usual with a neurologist collaborating on a case?

She snapped back to attention when Christian made eye contact with her.

'We're about to place the first probe. There should be a reduction of tremors as a result of it,' he said, and she nodded before shifting her attention to Evelyn.

'Evelyn, can you stretch out your arms in front of you like this?' Raquel mimicked the movement, fully extending her arms in front of her with the palms facing up.

The older woman mirrored her, though as soon as she moved her arms tremors shook them. A nurse rushed to her side when the IV attached to her arm clattered against the metal of the pole holding it and untangled the cannula. Raquel gave her a grateful smile.

'Take it slow and easy. We should see an improvement in a few seconds,' Christian said from behind, then whispered something Raquel couldn't hear.

Evelyn let out a small moan as she struggled to extend her arm when the tremor suddenly died down. Raquel's eyes went wide for a second before focusing back on her patient. 'They turned the probe on. Can you try extending your arms again with the palms facing up?'

Raquel still stood there with her arms in front of her as she watched her patient do the same with noticeably fewer muscle spasms than before.

'Can you try turning your palms downwards for me?' she asked when Evelyn had fully extended her arm and watched as she did just that.

'Amazing job, Evelyn. Looks like we have the first probe in the right location.' Christian turned his head to look at the monitor to the side, his eyes narrowing. 'Can we test if we are too close to the speech area?'

Raquel nodded. 'I'm going to show you some pictures. Can you tell me what you see?'

She dropped her arms to her side and grabbed a stack of large flashcards from the table set up next to her. She turned the first card round and showed it to Evelyn.

'A house with yellow walls,' the woman said, and Raquel nodded, her smile growing bigger under the mask with each correct answer until Christian spoke up again.

'We're on to the next probe. You are doing great.' They followed the same steps as with the first probe, each time testing a different motor function the probe was supposed to improve, and checking the adjacent brain regions to make sure they were not interfering with any other neurological functions.

By the time they were ready to close up, Raquel had been standing in front of Evelyn for several hours. Pain lanced through her legs and lower back when she could finally move again once they had wheeled the patient out of the room.

'I don't know how you all do it,' she mumbled to no one in particular and started at the familiar voice next to her.

'You get used to it. I think you were also holding a lot of tension in your muscles while standing there. You have to be as relaxed as possible. If you tense up, you'll feel it tenfold the moment you let go,' Christian said as he peeled off his mask and tossed it.

'I'll remember that for next time. Whenever that will

be,' she said, and schooled her face to neutrality as a small but sharp pain lanced through her side at her own words.

This was it—their last moment together. The only thing left to do was to discuss with Mia the potential of a contract. Her bags were already packed and waiting in the hotel room she had called her home for the last month. But, as far as she and Christian were concerned, there was nothing left between them. They'd had their closure in Puerto Rico, had dared to take even more than that.

Why was it so hard to walk away in this moment?

Raquel willed her feet to walk away, summoning the words of their last goodbye so she could leave this chaos of her ancient feelings far behind. It didn't matter how deep she had let Christian sink inside her. It wasn't relevant that her heart beat faster just looking at him, that his touch still lingered on her skin even days later.

'I…' Why was it so hard to speak? Her throat tightened around the words, her heart begging her to hang on to this moment—to this man—when she knew she couldn't. 'I think…we're done here. We signed off Nesta this morning, and I just have one more meeting with Mia.'

Raquel didn't know how to say goodbye—not with everything swirling around between them. She didn't know whether to address it or to move away. What she did know was that she couldn't admit her feelings to him. The risk of rejection was too great, the scar of him rebuffing her advances fifteen years ago still hurting. He might have admitted to the attraction brewing between them, but he hadn't mentioned his feelings turning romantic. Raquel had been wrong about his feelings for her before.

'Do you have a few minutes to meet me in my office?' he asked, his voice flat and not betraying anything beyond his words.

Was this about his endorsement for her service-dog work? Or a more *personal* goodbye? When she had first arrived, he'd promised to support her with Mia and the chief in her mission to gain a contract here. But she had assumed he would do whatever he could in the background to sway his colleagues.

'Sure, let me clean up and I'll meet you there,' she said, her brow furrowed when Christian simply nodded and walked off, leaving her puzzled over his request to meet and the abrupt departure.

He couldn't let her go. Not without a fight, not without throwing everything he had at it. He'd rather go down trying than walk away from the woman he'd loved for most of his adult life. Christian hadn't even been aware of that; he had denied the feelings for so long, and believed that every relationship he had attempted ever since had failed because he wasn't a relationship person. Turned out the reasons they had failed were because none of those women had been *her*.

Raquel.

The realisation had bubbled inside his head all week and really struck him when they had met this morning to sign off the outstanding paperwork for Nesta to officially become Lexi's service dog. With her training concluded, there wasn't any reason to be around him any more, other than the one case they had together—which was now done. It was in that that he realised he needed her to be in his life—for good.

He'd lacked courage around his feelings in the past and he didn't plan to make that mistake again. She might reject him for going back on their agreement, and that was a risk he had to take. But it was better to know where he stood with her rather than play out this fantasy in his head of what their lives could look like together if they only showed enough conviction for each other.

There was one topic that gave him pause. Before surgery, he had attended a budget meeting with all the department chairs and the chief to discuss new plans—including new contracts. Mia had floated the idea about some pro bono work with Raquel's charity to give access to service dogs to people who normally could not afford them, at which point he had voiced his agreement with the plan and shared his own experience with it.

But Chief Frazier had shot that idea down, citing other uses for their pro bono budget that would have a greater impact. Though impressed with Raquel's research, Frazier wanted the budget to go to something more tangible than research around seizure-response dogs. Christian's heart had cracked in half at the news. He knew how much a contract meant to Raquel and that the future of her charity hinged on her being able to show interest from a major hospital with a neurology focus. Without a contract from Whitehall Memorial to show her investors, Raquel would lose what little investment she had left.

Mia had been just as disappointed to hear the decision, and had wanted to keep Raquel around for her excellent work. So, when Christian had proposed an alternative solution that didn't need any budget approval, the Head of Neurology had needed little convincing.

They were going to hire Raquel and let her run her research part-time. That should satisfy any investors and would give her the official backing of the hospital. All he needed to do now was convince her that this was the right move for her. Not just because he selfishly wanted her to stay near him—no; *because* he loved her, he wanted her to be successful regardless of how she felt about him.

He sat down behind his desk only to jump up again almost immediately, pacing in front of the floor-to-ceiling windows of his office as he waited for her to arrive. When she finally knocked on the door, his heart rate was elevated—from the nerves or the pacing, he couldn't tell.

'Come in,' he called, then crossed the office in five big strides and came to a halt in front of her.

She dipped her head back to look up at him, eyes wide and filled with a determination that set off the yearning he'd struggled to contain ever since arriving back in New York, after the weekend in Puerto Rico that made him realise he didn't want to spend a single moment apart from her any more.

His lips parted, looking for the words he wanted to say, but they mixed with the message that he *needed* to tell her. A lump formed in his throat—one he couldn't swallow. There was so much to say, but all he wanted to do was...

'Christian, are you...?' He swallowed the rest of her words when he slid his mouth over hers, pulling her into a kiss that had been bubbling up inside him all week as he had tried his hardest to stay away from her.

Raquel relaxed against his arms as they came around her, her eyes drifting closed to get lost in his kiss. Her nerves had been taut as she'd arrived here, with her brain running through every possible scenario that might have led to this meeting. She didn't even know if this was about hospital business or their personal relationship.

Had he changed his mind about their arrangement? That thought had sent her into a tailspin of emotions, with both excitement and dread warring within her for dominance. What if he wanted more? She didn't let herself contemplate that question too long because thinking about it meant coming up with an answer—and that was an impossible task. Raquel didn't know what she would do if that was what he wanted to talk about.

His arms tightened around her, his hands diving into her hair and pulling her head back further to deepen the kiss. Their breaths mingled as they left their lungs in short bursts, and Raquel didn't know how much time had passed when he finally pulled away from her. The absence of his mouth on hers left a noticeable emptiness as yearning rushed through her.

He rested his forehead on her shoulder and the circle of his arms around her tightened to squeeze her closer to him. She wrapped her own arms around his midsection, returning the embrace and letting his closeness calm her. She still had no idea what they were doing, but just being near him was a balm on her nerves and filled her with a sense of security. Whatever happened to them, she could be grateful that he'd given her as much as he had.

'Christian...' she began but stopped when his chest expanded to release a deep sigh.

'There's no contract for you. I got the news about it earlier this morning,' he finally said, and the warmth he'd conjured in her body left with each beat of her heart until an icy shiver shook her.

'What?' The closeness of his embrace had suddenly become confining, each breath harder than the next. She put her hands on his chest, pushing him away and side-stepping when he gave her space. 'They told you?'

'I was part of the budget meeting this morning when

they made the decision,' he said, his expression one of regret as he looked at her.

Raquel's mind went into overdrive as she processed the news and the moment leading up to him sharing it with her. 'Why did you kiss me?' That wasn't what she would have expected before hearing bad news. Had he meant to use her affection for him to soften the blow?

Christian let out another sigh, messing up his hair as he raked his fingers through it. He stared up at the ceiling, as if he had to contemplate his answer, and the mixture of affection and desperation she glimpsed in his eyes when he looked back at her had her heart stopping inside her chest.

'Because I'm in love with you, Raquel. I knew the moment you walked through those doors the first time that my feelings for you haven't changed. I...wanted you to have this contract—want to give you *anything* you desire on this planet.'

The earth underneath Raquel's feet shook and she forced breath into her lungs despite the pressure on her chest making it almost impossible. The words she had feared—had dreamed of in the quiet hours of the night— floated in the room between them and mingled with the news of her charity's demise. The two opposing feelings knotted themselves into a tight ball of chaos, making it impossible for her to understand where one started and the other one ended.

She took another step back, hoping that some space would help her clear the mess inside her mind.

'I have something else to offer. Not what you had hoped for coming here, but a close second—a job here at Whitehall Memorial. Mia was as disappointed as I was when the chief decided against our proposal, so we came up with something that we, as heads of our departments, could approve. She would be willing to hire you as a full-time neurologist and give you half of your time for research.'

He paused, the hopeful glint in his eyes tying an invisible string around her chest and constricting her breath even further. 'You could stay here and we...'

He didn't finish his sentence, and Raquel was thankful for it, for she didn't know how to sort through the onslaught of information. He wanted her to stay—had even arranged a job for her so that she could remain by his side. He hadn't been able to give her her first choice, but had found another way for her to get what she wanted—and for him to get everything he wanted. His career, his own department and now...her.

Desperate fear wound its icy grip around her heart, squeezing tighter and tighter until it shattered under the pressure. Physical pain radiated through her body and she took another step backwards as she stared at Christian with wide eyes.

'You're saying that the only way I can keep the funding for my work is if I stay here...with you? You thought that's what I wanted, after everything I told you about my marriage?' The situations felt so similar to one another, Raquel had a hard time telling them apart. She had put too much of her life on pause just to serve the needs of her ex-husband, and because of that she'd had to work twice has hard to catch up with her peers, who had years of experience—all for a promise that *soon* it would have been her turn. Only, soon had never come.

Would it be the same here? She'd agree to stay here, stay with him and be happy with whatever time was left for her research after her commitments to the neurology department. Could she risk giving Christian that kind of power over her?

Her heart had fluttered when he had professed his love to her and screamed at her to say the words back, to acknowledge the truth she felt within her. But now this other thing was right next to the truth in her heart, casting shadows and doubt on the sincerity of his confession.

'What? That's not… No, Raquel. I didn't offer this to you to *trap* you here in New York. How could you even think that?' Genuine hurt rippled over Christian's face, hurt she felt mirrored in her own chest.

'Why else would you package the information the way you have? First, you tell me I'm not getting a contract, when you knew this would mean the end of my charity work because my sponsors will pull out. Then you tell me you love me and that you have a solution to my problem that benefits you disproportionately more than me.' The words bubbled out of her mouth, all her insecurities and wounds from her past relationship laid bare between them.

'This is… What are you accusing me of right now?' His expression turned hard and impossible to read.

'I'm not accusing you of anything. I just…' Her pulse hammered against her throat, the rush of her blood deafening in her ears and making it so much harder to think. She didn't know where this conversation was going, only that she needed to get out of there or she would risk getting stuck again. She couldn't—not when she had sacrificed so much of herself the first time, only to be left with nothing at the end.

'Thank you for the offer, but I will find my own way,' she forced out as the panic crept further up and into her throat, constricting her vocal cords so much that every word became agony. She needed to leave—now.

'Raquel, wait. I think you're…'

Raquel didn't—couldn't—stay to let him finish. The fear of repeating her past mistakes gripped her tightly, making all the decisions for her with no other consideration. Before she could change her mind, she pushed the door open and fled down the now familiar corridor of Whitehall Memorial. Where she would go, she didn't know but, without the chance of a contract, she had no more reasons to stay in New York.

CHAPTER TWELVE

A RHYTHMIC SOFT clicking against the marble floor startled Christian out of his shallow sleep. He bolted upright, only to find Lexi and Nesta staring at him. His niece raised her hands in a placating gesture.

'It's just me,' she said into the quiet of the apartment.

His gaze shot to the window. The sky was only just turning light as dawn approached.

'You're up early,' he mumbled as he shook off the last vestiges of sleep.

'It's the first day of summer camp, and the bus leaves early.'

Guilt flooded through him at the reminder. Summer camp had been the whole reason for them to look into Nesta, yet it had slipped his mind that today was the day Lexi was leaving. His entire week had been a whirlwind of working and sleeping, his mind constantly seeking out distractions so he wouldn't think about the one person he knew he wasn't allowed to think about.

'Do you…?' He didn't even know how to ask the question without seeming like an absent parent-figure in her life. How could he have let his heartbreak consume him so wholly?

'Annie's mum is picking me up. Don't worry about it.' He looked at his niece, surprised at the mature tone in her voice as she stepped closer and took a seat on the sofa he had just been sleeping on. 'What's wrong with your bed that you're not sleeping in it?'

Christian let out a breath and shook his head. She was way too observant for her age. What *was* wrong with his bed? He didn't have a straightforward answer for that, only that in the last week it had been easier to work himself so hard that he could only get past his door before collapsing from exhaustion. A tactic he thought worked well to get his mind off Raquel and the last moment they'd had together.

She'd left straight afterwards, not giving him another chance to explain himself. He wasn't sure if he'd even been able to find the right words to do so. All he had wanted to do was to give her a choice—to show her *he* was a choice, if she wanted him. Though, after replaying the conversation in his head over and over again, he understood where he had misstepped.

He had packed too much information into one conversation and hadn't given her enough time to consider anything before spilling his feelings for her. In fact, he shouldn't have said anything about loving her and should have left that conversation for a more appropriate time. It had just…surged out of him thoughtlessly.

Now he was paying the price for it.

'Nothing is wrong with it. I've just had some late nights and end up passing out,' he said, digging up a small smile that he hoped would put Lexi at ease. The last thing he wanted was for her to pick up on the trouble he'd caused himself—and Raquel.

Lexi pursed her lips and gave him a scrutinising glance that reminded him so much of Anthony, it pushed all the air out of his lungs. 'Uncle…'

Christian's heart sank at the word. She'd not used that word many times to address him—usually when either of them was in trouble. Was she upset that he'd forgotten about camp? 'I'm sorry I forgot about your summer camp. I'll make sure to pick you up.' He grabbed his phone and opened the calendar app to set himself a reminder. His eyes roamed over the day's schedule and paused: there were no surgeries planned for today.

'That's not what I wanted to talk about. I'm…worried about you.' Her voice turned soft and a delicate frown appeared on her face.

Christian put his phone down to look at her. 'Me? Why are you worried about me? I'm fine.'

The lie came as easily as if it were the truth. It was the phrase he repeated to so many people over and over again whenever they asked him how he was. Yet he could see in her eyes that she wasn't buying it.

'I don't get upset if you forget certain dates at school or what my friends' names are. You're a busy doctor and you don't have a lot of time for a niece you had to take in against your will…'

Ice spread through his veins as her words sunk in. For the second time in a week, his world was ripped out from under his feet. Did she think that he'd been forced to take her on, when he thought of it as nothing but a privilege to have her as a niece?

He'd let his insecurity around being the best possible substitute parent he could be get in the way of *actually* being a good parent to her. Raquel had helped him realise that in Puerto Rico, and he'd promised himself that he would talk to Lexi about it. He'd planned to have that conversation soon but then things had happened with Raquel…

His priorities needed to change, starting today. Christian wouldn't accept that his behaviour had led Lexi to believe she was unwelcome in his life.

'Lexi, my sweet. You are not here against my will. I'm so glad that the two of us get to be a family, and that you would think even for a second that your presence is a nuisance tells me I haven't been showing up for you enough.' He reached out to take her hand in his, forcing her to look at him. 'I'm sorry I've been working so much. It's not about you, it's about some other things going on...'

Lexi's frown eased. 'You've not been working so much because you've been avoiding me?'

'No, nothing of the sort. What made you think that?'

'You've just been so...withdrawn ever since Raquel left, and when she was here you were much more...present. I thought it had to do with her being around and helping out. Once she signed Nesta off, you were at the hospital all the time, and I...'

Christian clenched his jaw to swallow the curse building in his throat. He had been so wrapped up in his own misery that he hadn't even seen how it was affecting Lexi. 'I'm sorry, Lexi. I promise I'm going to do better.'

Nesta stepped up to his niece, laying her head on her lap and pushing her head under her hands. He watched as Lexi buried her fingers in her golden fur and gave the dog a gentle rub.

He tensed, watching for signs of a seizure, but then his niece shook her head. 'Nothing is happening. Nesta sometimes just senses when I'm upset or emotional,' she said, with a loving gaze towards the dog.

'Are you happy with your dog? Is she everything you had hoped she would be?' he asked, ignoring the stab of pain in his side at the thought of the dog and how much effort Raquel had put into research and training.

Lexi's face immediately lit up, and she nodded. 'She's amazing. Sometimes it's difficult to get people to understand what she does, but she's been alerting and shielding me from day one. It's like we were meant to be together.'

The pain in his side flared across his body at her last sentence, the words hitting him so much deeper than she could possibly understand, yet there seemed to be knowledge in her eyes as she looked at him.

'Nesta and I are a team. Like you and Raquel were when we were out in the park and you had to help those people. She improves my life and I try to do the same for her. We wouldn't be able to do these things by ourselves, right?' she continued as she stroked the dog's head, oblivious to the torrent of truth she had just unleashed on Christian.

Christian struggled to find the words to reply, to cover up the shock her words had put him in. Raquel had made his life so much better in the last four weeks and, instead of doing the same for her, he had tried to sell *his* proposed solution to her rather than giving her what she wanted. How could he not have seen it until this moment? Was it too late to fix it?

'Are you okay?' Lexi asked, her brow furrowed as she looked at him.

The buzz of the doorbell saved him from having to answer that, and his niece surged to her feet. 'That's Annie.'

Christian got up as well and wrapped Lexi in a hug. 'Thank you for telling me how you feel. Have an amazing time at camp and I'll be there to pick you up. Maybe then we can talk some more about this.'

He walked her to the door, where her friend was waiting. The second the door closed behind them, Christian sprinted back to the sofa and grabbed his phone. He swiped to the side, bringing up his contact list, and pressed on the first contact. A quick glance at the clock told him that no one would be happy about this, but there was no time to spare.

The line rang several times before Ramón answered the phone. *'Hermano, sabes qué hora es?* Your house better be on fire right now.'

'I know it's early... I messed up, Ramón, and I need your help to fix it.'

'Hermanita.'

The voice of her brother filtered through the closed door and Raquel turned around in bed, slamming the pillow over her head to drown out both the afternoon sun and Ramón's knocking. He'd been at her door every hour, wanting to talk.

That was the last thing she wanted. Talking had led her into this situation to begin with, and she knew it wouldn't make her feel better. Nothing would ever make her feel better. There was a hole inside her chest that was eating everything it touched, everything that had once brought joy and laughter into her life.

She had lost everything. Her charity work had lost its funding and the man she loved was living his best life without her—because she had left. Her fear had kicked in at the sudden path that had opened up in front of her, forcing a decision she hadn't even considered making. Christian felt the same way, and had wanted her to stay in New York with him, but the information had come at her so fast—too fast—and her flight instinct had won.

Not knowing what to do with her broken heart and

spirit, she had bought the first ticket back to Puerto Rico and had taken up residence in her old bedroom, while living on frozen *pasteles* that were still left over from her brother's wedding.

What she hadn't expected was for her brother to be here. That threw a wrench into her moping and eating plans for the foreseeable future. Because he also had a relationship with Christian, he probably already knew some version of what had happened in New York.

Another knock thundered through the room. 'I swear, *por Dios*, if you don't open *esta porta ahora mismo* I will take it off its hinges.'

Raquel ignored his threat—until she heard the sound of a power drill rattling the door. With an irritated sigh, she shoved the blanket off her and stalked to the door, unlocking it and pulling it open. 'Ramón, *estás loco*? Why can't I have a moment of peace *en esta casa*?'

Their sentences were coming out in a mixture of English and Spanish, as they tended to when they were fighting with each other. They had used English growing up to speak in secrecy in front of their parents, but their vocabulary hadn't been wide enough to have fluent conversations.

'Why are you even here? Aren't you supposed to be on your honeymoon?'

Ramón leaned against her door frame, power drill dangling from his hand. 'Oh, hi there, Sis, it's nice to see you too. When did you get back to Puerto Rico?' he said, ignoring her question.

Raquel scoffed, then turned around to stalk back into her room. 'I don't need you to clown about.'

'I'm just saying… You got back here a week ago and I haven't seen you for…about a week.' Ramón followed her into the room and remained standing as she flopped back onto the bed. 'What's going on? Why aren't you working?'

Raquel sighed and suppressed the urge to run away—again. Between how things had ended with Christian and her work woes, her mountain of problems had become so high she didn't know where to start.

'I'm not working because… I didn't get the contract I needed from Whitehall Memorial, so now my investors are backing out. Without funding, I can't keep research-ing and training dogs.' Admitting to her failure out loud broke her heart all over again. She buried her head in her hands and let out a long sigh. 'I've worked so hard to get this off the ground, and now it's all over.'

'Sucks that your investors backed out, but that doesn't mean it's all over, does it? Can't you find new investors?' he asked, and she looked up with her eyebrows raised in surprise. He understood where she was coming from…

'I'm just not sure it was meant to be any more, Ramón. Like…shouldn't it be easier, in that case? It's been so hard to fight for this at every turn and I'm exhausted. If it was truly meant to be, wouldn't it be easier?' Those were the words she had been agonising over since coming back to Puerto Rico—coming to terms with the fact that her dream might truly be over.

Losing her investors meant starting from scratch again and finding someone who believed enough in her re-search and passion to fund her. If it was right, wouldn't it be easy?

She looked at her brother, who leaned against the wall with his arms crossed in front of him. 'I don't think any-thing worth having will be easy to get,' he said after some contemplation.

The words sank inside her like a stone, casting a new perspective on her struggle. But before she could say anything Ramón continued, 'Let's say you fell in love with someone many years ago and it didn't work out. Then you meet them again and that connection is back. You still have the same feelings, but now you think the struggles of life made you a different person—which is true, but that doesn't make it *not* worth trying.'

Raquel let out a shuddering sigh and curled up into a ball on her bed. Of course he knew about Christian, and how much of her heartache actually came from that source? 'How much do you know?'

Ramón snorted, as if offended by the question. '*Hermanita*… I knew what was happening between you two when we were in high school, and I also saw you two making eyes at each other all throughout my wedding.'

That weekend felt like a lifetime ago, one in which they had been free simply to enjoy their time together with no consequences.

'I'm sorry, I didn't realise we were this obvious,' she said, covering her face with her hands to stifle the groan dropping from her lips. Each time she thought she had reached the highest limit of her pain, some stray memory of Christian popped into her head, filling that space in her chest with bleak sorrow.

'Why are you back here, Raquel? What happened between you two?' Ramón's voice was soft as he approached the bed, sitting down at the edge of it and wrapping his hand around her wrist to pull her hand away from her face.

'After he told me that there wouldn't be a contract for me at Whitehall, he told me he loved me and offered me a job so I could stay in New York—if I wanted to.' She'd gone over that conversation so many times, it was seared into her brain and she doubted it would ever leave her.

The primal fear that had gripped her still chilled her blood, the similarities between the situation with Christian and her failed marriage so stark.

'Okay…and that's a bad thing?' her brother asked, genuine curiosity the only thing she could detect in his voice. Everything was so messy and convoluted inside her, she wasn't sure anyone could understand what had happened to her in that room.

'It's not that it's a bad thing. No… It's just the way he presented it. He told me how he felt and my heart almost burst at hearing him say that, words I've been longing to hear from him. But then he offered me a job, when he knew how hard it had been for me to get where I was after my marriage fell apart…'

She paused, looking at her brother, who nodded in understanding. 'I get it. He messed up his pitch. So you left New York and came here to process. What do you want to do now? Because eating *pasteles* and scrolling on your phone for hours on end will not get you funding for your work or back with the man you love.'

'What do I…?' Her voice trailed off as she considered the question she'd been avoiding for the last week. All she had wanted until now was to wallow in her own sadness at both the opportunity lost and the man she loved gone from her life once more—all because he'd messed up his pitch…?

Raquel paused, pushing away the hurt wrapping itself around her whenever she thought back to that moment so she could look at it from a new angle. Her past experience with her ex-husband had influenced a lot of her decisions after their divorce and, judging by her own reaction, she was still making choices because of him. The realisation thundered through her, making her sit upright.

'*Dios*, I'm an idiot. I thought…he would be just like Tom because that's all I've ever known. But he said the job was there regardless of what I said, so I could still work with my charity part-time while working out my next steps.' She stared at her brother wide-eyed. 'I could still take the job and say no to being with him.'

Ramón raised his eyebrows in surprise. 'Is…that what you want?'

'What? No!' Raquel scrambled off the bed, the sudden urge to move surging through her body. She had wasted so much time with self-pity when all she'd needed to do was to take a step back and consider the intention behind his actions rather than how Christian had presented things. But the fear of her past trauma still had such a tight grip on her, she would always have to a remind herself that people were different—that Christian was different.

'What are you going to do?' Ramón asked when she began rifling through her bag for clothes.

'I don't know… I need to tell him how I feel. I didn't say it when he said it. Who knows what he's been thinking this last week? Oh, my God, I can't believe I ran away like that.' Her thoughts were a jumble of words and emotions, all of them bouncing around in her head uncontrolled.

She stopped when Ramón let out a sigh of relief and said, 'I'm so glad to hear that. This could have turned out terribly.'

'What could have?'

'Well…' He paused, a sheepish grin spreading over his lips. 'I maybe kind of went and picked him up from the airport earlier today… And he may be waiting outside right now…'

Heat exploded through her body as his words sank in, followed by a wave of cold that set loose a storm inside of her. '*Dios ayúdame*, has he been listening to our conversation all this time?'

Soft footsteps sounded outside the room and there stood Christian, clearing his throat. Dark shadows circled his eyes, as if he'd been struggling to sleep in the last few days—something Raquel found mirrored in herself. The nights had been the hardest when everything was quiet and thoughts kept chasing each other.

'Ramón!' Raquel turned towards her brother, who was already halfway across the room.

'I'm sure you two have lots to talk about,' he said, then shrugged and scurried out of the room, closing the door behind him.

Awareness of Christian's proximity to her flooded her body, and she froze in place as he looked her over. There was a slight hesitation, a moment where unspoken words passed between them to form an understanding of their feelings for each other.

One moment Christian was still looking at her from across the room, then he was hauling her into his arms and squeezing her tight. She lifted her head to find his mouth already waiting for hers in a kiss that stole all the breath from her lungs.

'I'm sorry I ran. I feared what it meant to stay with you—of repeating my past mistakes. I…'

Christian interrupted her with another gentle kiss, his lips barely brushing over hers, yet that contact was enough to send shivers down her spine.

'I was too focused on telling you how I feel, I didn't

stop long enough to consider how *you* would feel. I'm never going to let that happen again, Raquel.' He whispered the words against her neck, his warm breath making her shudder. 'I'm all in. I'll do whatever it takes to make your dreams in life come true.'

Raquel leaned back, untangling her hands from his hair so she could take his face between them. Her thumbs brushed over his cheekbones and she smiled as she looked at the man she loved. 'I love you, Christian. Let's build a life we've both been dreaming of. Together.'

EPILOGUE

THE SOUND OF yelping puppies filled the air. The new litter of Golden Retriever puppies was settling into its new home with the mother. Over the next few weeks, as the puppies grew larger, they would go through some gentle testing Raquel had designed to determine if they would make suitable seizure-alert dogs.

'What happens to the ones who don't do so well?' Lexi asked, and Raquel looked up from the large pen to look at her stepdaughter.

'We're partnering with a programme that lets inmates raise dogs to teach them accountability for someone beside themselves.' Raquel chuckled when Lexi's eyes widened. 'It's a great way to boost rehabilitation, and the dogs lead a joyful life with their owners.'

Though she always wanted to keep the whole litter for herself, she knew that not all of them would have the necessary attritbutes to become a service dog. It became that more important that they had a plan for the puppies who wouldn't stay with them.

Next to Lexi, Nesta raised her head off the floor, sniffing at the dog pen in front of her before lying back down. It had been almost a year since she'd flown Nesta to New York to place her with Lexi. When she had accepted that job, she couldn't have imagined that she would be in this position a year later, with an entire training and research facility all to herself.

Or that she would end up marrying the love of her life not even two months after meeting him again.

As if her thoughts had summoned him, Christian appeared through the door and she couldn't help but smile at him. He wore a form-fitting shirt with the logo of her charity printed on it and she had to suppress the urge to immediately rip it off his body—an urge that hadn't lessened over time, as she'd thought it would.

'How are we doing in here?' he asked as he stepped closer, laying one hand on each of their shoulders.

'Good. Leblanc is settling in well with her puppies and they're resting after their travels,' Raquel said, with a glance at the pen in front of them.

'I set up a live stream of the puppies. There's already a few hundred people watching,' Lexi added, pointing at a camera set up at the far side of the room, and Raquel's heart swelled inside her chest.

They had gone back to New York together and waited for Lexi to get back from camp before discussing what they wanted their life as a family to look like. It was Lexi who'd suggested what they had ended up doing—moving to Puerto Rico and putting all their effort into researching and training seizure-alert dogs.

Raquel had feared asking such a sacrifice from Christian and Lexi, but they hadn't viewed it that way. They had been as enthusiastic about her work as she had been. And, with Christian's connections in the medical world, they had found new investors and many smaller hospitals interested in working with them all across the United States. He'd accepted a position at a hospital in Puerto

Rico and split his time between her charity work and his neurosurgery.

The effort these two had put into making her dream come alive in front of her had been a humbling experience—and one she would endeavour to pay back for the rest of her life.

'So… I have something I wanted to share with you two while I have you here,' she said, her heart racing as she said the words. She had been sitting on the news a few days now, just waiting for the right moment to happen.

Christian looked at her with a puzzled expression, but Lexi's face immediately lit up, as if some intuition had already told her what the news would be.

Raquel took a calming breath, her hands resting on her stomach as she said, 'I'm pregnant.'

* * * * *

SECOND CHANCE FOR THE HEART DOCTOR

SUSAN CARLISLE

MILLS & BOON

To Sophia.

The last but not the least. I love you

CHAPTER ONE

PEDIATRIC NURSE BAYLEY DODD stood in front of the cardiology floor nurses' station listening to the other nurses at her back talk in animated whispers. Despite trying to concentrate on the child's chart in front of her, Bayley couldn't help but overhear the chatter.

"I heard he's tall, dark and handsome." A nurse released a heavy sigh as if she'd seen her favorite movie star.

Another said, "I've been told he's recently divorced."

"I saw him. He's dreamy," one more breathy feminine voice offered.

Bayley endured it as long as she could. She turned and held the electronic pad in a grip across her chest. Pulling her face into an exaggerated silly schoolgirl face and batting her eyelids, she used a falsetto voice to say, "Oh, I hope he asks me to the prom."

Gaining no laughter and registering the widening of the eyes of the other women, who all looked beyond her shoulder, Bayley's face sobered. Her gaze met one of the nurse's. Bayley winced and mouthed: *He's right behind me?*

The nurses each gave slight nods before they mumbled something about needing to check on their patients and flushed like a new IV line, disappearing in three directions. Bayley couldn't help but make fun of people who acted so caught up in the mystique of the gorgeous new doctor. She'd heard he had left his private practice. That the hospital was lucky to get him. She didn't care how he looked or where he came from as long as he loved children and did his job.

Atlanta Children's Hospital had a well-known and busy cardiology department. A new staff member was always welcome. She was working as a nurse for now, but she hoped she'd be back here next year as a doctor. She just had to finish her final year of medical school first.

Bayley had waited to turn around as long as she could. She had to do it sometime. Slowly she made her move. The doctor stood an arm's length from her. His lips were a tight line. Yep, he'd heard every word she'd said. Why couldn't she be swallowed by the floor?

"Hello."

His voice made her think of flowing warm caramel candy. Smooth and tasty. Bayley glanced up. And farther up. The new doctor stood tall. With blond hair cut tight on the sides and longer on the top, he appeared to be an alpha male who kept up with the latest fashion. Something that Bayley couldn't afford to do. She let her hair grow in order not to spend the money for upkeep on a style. Paying for medical school took priority. Along with her father's needs.

What held her attention was his eyes. They reminded her of being at the beach when a storm rolled in, all dark gray. Exciting and intimidating at the same time.

"I'm Dr. Hunt."

His tone held no note of humor. This was a somber man who had serious things on his mind. He didn't have time for silly nurses or her comic routine. She didn't believe in aggravating staff members. That only made them more difficult to work with. She pulled the wrinkles out of her scrub shirt. "Hello. I'm Bayley. I'm one of the nurses on the floor this evening. How can I help you?"

"I'm looking for a patient. Johnny Smith. Apparently they have changed his room since I was given the list."

"Johnny is in Room 325. I can show you." She started in that direction.

His voice stopped her. "I'd like to see his chart first."

She handed him the tech pad she held. "You can find it all right on here. You do have a log-in number?"

He took the pad from her and quickly touched it. Glancing down, he scrolled through a few pages using his long finger with trimmed nails before handing the pad back to her. "Thank you." He looked at her name tag. "Bayley." He started off down the hall.

"Hey, sir." He looked back. "Johnny's room is this way." She pointed in the opposite direction. "I'll show you. I was headed there before you came up. I've been attending him for the last week."

Dr. Hunt offered her a half smile and nodded. His long legs carried him past her and down the hall, his sparkling-white lab coat flapping as he went. Bayley had to hustle to keep up. "Johnny is Dr. Mario's patient."

For a large man he stopped quickly. She almost bumped into him. He looked at her. "I realize that. I've been asked to consult. Tell me what you know about the patient."

She resisted the temptation to go up on her toes so she would be taller. "As you must have read, Johnny has cardiomyopathy. He collapsed at school. He is being evaluated for a heart transplant. And is one very unhappy teenager."

His look turned indulgent. It rocked her back on her heels. If he really applied his charm, he would be a force that no one could resist. Including her. Maybe the reputation that preceded him had merit.

"You are coming in with me." His attention remained on her. It was more a demand than a question.

"Yes. I've gotten to know this family. I'd like to introduce you, if you don't mind. They're stressed to the max."

He waved a hand toward the door. "After you."

She appreciated his understanding. Yet she wasn't going to get wrapped up in the lore of the new handsome doctor. She had her father to worry about, school and a job. There was no time or energy for a romantic encounter with a doctor or any other man. Between nursing school then medical school and seeing about her father, there had been little time left to consider a relationship.

She'd accepted that years ago. Her father had been injured in an industrial accident while at work, leaving him using a wheelchair. Just weeks after he came home her mother had left them, never to return. Bayley had had to grow up quickly. She became caregiver and household manager far too young. Because of her responsibilities, the only lasting bond she'd ever known had been with her father.

Bayley entered the patient's room. She made sure she wore a smile. This patient and his family needed all the encouragement they could get. A blunt doctor at this point could tip their emotions and hope over the edge. Dr. Hunt might be the type to do that.

The lights were off in the room. Johnny lay in the hospital bed playing a video game on the TV. He had deteriorated over the last few weeks. Staying in the hospital on bed rest hadn't helped. The teenager needed a new heart. He needed it soon.

"Johnny, I'd like for you to meet Dr. Hunt. He's here to check you out at the request of Dr. Mario."

The boy barely looked her direction as he continued to fight off some imaginary cartoon characters on the TV, his fingers moving quickly on the controller.

His mother, who sat in the corner, stood and came to the bedside. "Johnny, don't be rude."

Bayley's heart went out to the boy. He didn't care if he was rude or not. All he wanted was to feel better so he could be out with his friends having a good time. At the beginning of his hospital stay the room had been filled with them. Now they wandered in occasionally. The days had become longer for Johnny, and more unhappy.

Dr. Hunt moved to face the TV. "*Revenge of the Aliens.* Have you found the door to the O'Shazia, on the frosty level?"

Johnny's eyes brightened, looking at Dr. Hunt with budding respect. "How did you know about that?"

"I play the game all the time with my nephew. I also have a gaming room. I'm on level seven right now."

"Wow, you must be good."

Bayley smiled. The new doctor had managed to impress the unhappy teen.

Dr. Hunt shrugged. "It's like anything, a little practice and a little forethought can make you better. Do you want me to give you a hint on this level?"

Johnny nodded. "Sure."

"Pick up the key that's inside the jewel box."

Johnny made a few clicks.

Bayley's head swam. This man in his starched-collar white button-down shirt, expensive-looking shoes and belt, and navy slacks with a crease looked nothing like the unkempt, dirty-tee-and-shorts gamers from the pictures she'd seen. There must be more to Dr. Hunt than his good looks and dressing style. Who was the real Dr. Hunt?

"That's right. Go over there. Open the box. The key's inside."

The boy made some fast movements with his fingers. "Got it."

Johnny's mother stepped closer to Bayley.

The two males continued to talk about a world Bayley'd had no idea existed.

The mother leaned toward her and whispered, "What do you know about this doctor?"

"He's new on staff. All I've heard is he's really good. He's supposed to be a big deal. And very smart."

The mother looked from Dr. Hunt to her son and back again. "I'm supposed to trust him?"

Bayley glanced at Dr. Hunt. "I believe you should."

"I'm going to take your word for it." Johnny's mother didn't sound convinced.

Bayley did believe the hospital hired quality personnel. Would the hospital feel that way about her when she finished her medical degree? Only one more year of training and she could be on the medical staff. Not as a cardiologist but a general MD. They just had to survive financially until then. Her father's workplace compensation had covered them through her attending nursing school and she'd worked as many shifts as she could around her classes. But paying for medical school proved more difficult with her father's increasing medical problems. They'd barely made it through the month. Her only chance of finishing school depended on winning the Wilcott-Ross scholarship. It would change her and her father's life. She'd be able to afford to finish school and find a place to live where her father could have a better quality of life.

Dr. Hunt finished his conversation with Johnny then turned to them. He extended his hand to the mom. "I'm Dr. Hunt. It's nice to meet you. You have a fine son here. We'll get him all fixed up and out of here soon."

That bit of hope put a smile on the mother's face. "I'll hold you to that."

He returned the smile. Bayley's stomach fluttered and the smile wasn't even for her. No wonder Dr. Hunt was the talk of the cardiology department. When he took the dark snarl off his face and smiled, he became movie star glamorous. No wonder people were falling at his feet. She might, as well.

"Johnny, would you mind if I give you a quick listen?" Dr. Hunt asked.

"Okay." The teen paused the game.

Dr. Hunt removed his stethoscope from his neck. Seconds later he listened to Johnny's chest. With a practiced movement he wrapped his stethoscope around his neck again. "Has your appetite lessened?"

The teen nodded.

"And how about your energy?" the doctor asked.

"Yeah."

Dr. Hunt nodded. "How about your weight? Any changes?"

"I've gained a little."

Dr. Hunt pursed his lips. "Okay. It was nice to meet you, Johnny." He stepped toward the door, glancing back at her. "Thanks."

"No problem." Bayley moved to the IV pole. She admired Dr. Hunt's broad shoulders as he stepped into the hall and quietly closed the door behind him. He had a nice bedside manner. He would do.

Jenson continued down the hall. The nurse had been protective of Johnny. He could almost see her claws come out when she'd admonished him to go easy with the boy and his family.

He didn't acknowledge the looks from the nurses he passed while he looked at the numbers on the doors until he found his next patient. The longer he remained on staff the more patients he would have on the floor. He needed to see this one before he had to attend the weekly heart catheterization conference starting in fifteen minutes. After the meeting he would be headed home.

He intended to have a nice quiet night, maybe find a good pickup game of basketball in the park down the road. In his old life his family would have been horror-struck if he had been out playing with just anyone in the park. Because of his family name, how it might look would have made it impossible. His father always thought Jenson should be at the club playing tennis or golf with the right people.

The best outcome of the destruction of Jenson's marriage was his new living environment. He had bought a little condo an older part of Atlanta. It was a quarter of the size of the uptown, ultramodern apartment he and his ex-wife, Darlene, had shared. His new place was set up like a man cave, all to his liking, including a video game room. He smiled at the memory of the look on the nurse's face. What was her name? Bayley. When he had started discussing video games with Johnny, it had almost been comical.

She had listened at the side of the bed while he had talked to Johnny with a quirky smile on her lips. What she didn't know was he'd spent far too much time playing games in the last year because of the shame he felt over not being able to hold his marriage together. His father had accused him of being a hermit. The darkness had lessened somewhat when he had resigned from the clinic. Being alone suited him just fine.

Finished with his last patient, he exited the child's room and headed toward the nurses' station to order a change in the girl's IV dip. Bayley swerved around him in a blur of pink scrubs and flying brunette hair in her hurry up the hall.

"Whoa" He stopped himself before they crashed.

Over her shoulder she called in a firm voice, "Come with me. Room 318."

Another nurse hurried right behind her.

He didn't hesitate before doing as she said, following her into a patient's room. Bayley already had her stethoscope out and was listening to the small baby's chest.

"He needs adenosine," she said. He raised an eyebrow at her, surprised. "I'm a medical student as well as a nurse," she informed him as she stood back.

The other nurse worked at removing the child's one-piece outfit.

"What going on?" Jenson unwrapped his stethoscope from his neck.

"The telemetry is showing arrhythmia. It's two hundred. BP one-thirty over ninety."

"How old?" Jenson put the earpieces in place.

"Sixteen days. Just out of ICU," Bayley replied.

Despite the number of people talking in the room and him looking down at the patient Jenson recognized Bayley's voice. He nodded then listened to the child's heart rate. The stream of the baby's heartbeat alarmed him. He looked at Bayley. "What was he doing when this started?"

Bayley looked at the woman standing at the bedside. She said, "He's just been lying here asleep."

"He's going to be fine," Bayley assured the mother. "We're just going to give him a good checkup. While we do I need you to move out of the way."

The mother looked stricken, but she stepped back and took a chair against the wall without further questions. Jenson hated he had little time to comfort the woman. He had her child to care for. Taking a second, he said, "Everything's gonna be fine, ma'am. I'm Dr. Hunt. I just need to examine your baby, then we'll talk." Despite the seriousness of the situation, he tried to put a soothing note in his voice.

"I want a full blood panel with electrolytes," Jenson ordered softly to the nurses beside him.

Bayley flushed the IV, preparing to pull the blood. Five vials were placed on the bed beside her by another nurse. He was impressed. Bayley took care of the blood draw swiftly and efficiently. Obviously, this emergency routine had been practiced. Everyone knew their responsibilities.

Jenson wrapped his stethoscope around his neck. "BP?"

"One-ten over eighty-three," a nurse watching the monitor said.

"Push adenosine. Then put him on digoxin along with his routine meds."

Jenson continued listening to the child's heart. "The

heart rate is coming down." He removed his stethoscope. "Bayley, what tests should be ordered?"

"I'd start with an EKG and ECHO."

He liked the sound of confidence in her voice. "Then see they are ordered, and I'll sign off on them." He looked at her and then at the others. "Good work, everyone."

Then he turned to the woman waiting. "You're her mother?"

The mother nodded.

"Do you mind stepping out into the hall with me?" He held the door for the terrified parent and followed her out.

He nodded to Bayley. "Keep me posted on how the child is doing."

Bayley watched Dr. Hunt walk toward her from one end of the hall a couple weeks later. In just a few interactions she had become just as enamored with him as the other nurses. They still chased him, but he remained professional. With each patient he was good-natured and thorough.

She couldn't help but be impressed with his demeanor. He had calmly and confidently taken care of the baby in distress weeks earlier, giving orders with authority and certainty. More than that, he'd been tender in his care of the scared mother. Every doctor should handle an emergency with as much skill. She also appreciated him giving her a chance to learn by asking her what she would do. The child had been discharged without further episodes a week later. So far, he hadn't returned to the hospital.

She'd learned from Johnny that Dr. Hunt stopped in to see how Johnny's gaming was going a couple of times a week. The other women might be enamored with his looks but what she found most attractive were Dr. Hunt's medical skills and compassion.

She watched until he entered one of his patient's rooms.

One of the nurses nudged her with her shoulder as they sat behind the nurses' station.

"Uh, what?"

"Dr. Scrumptious."

"Surely that's not what y'all are calling him now?" Bayley rolled her eyes.

"I was just thinking by the way you were looking at him you might think he was scrumptious."

Bayley shook her head. "You're crazy."

The nurse wore a teasing smile as she stood. "I'm just telling you what I saw."

Bayley still sat behind the nurses's station catching up on her charting when a shadow loomed over her. She glanced up to see Dr. Hunt look down at her.

"Hey, Bayley. I'm the floor doctor this week. I understand you'll be doing rounds with me."

Bayley looked around. The two other nurses sitting beside her listened with interest. They weren't missing anything he said or did.

"Uh, yes. Are you ready now?"

"Yes." He picked up a charting pad.

"May I finish this last note?"

"Sure. I'll read over a chart. I'll be right over here." He moved to stand just to the side of the desk but out of the way of any traffic.

A few minutes later she joined him. He started up the hall. "You seem to know the patients well. That makes you a valuable resource."

One of the nurses giggled when she passed them.

"I guess so." She had no choice but to agree. She wasn't

used to being singled out. She'd always been the little mouse in the corner going unnoticed. She glanced over her shoulder to the nurses watching them. They quickly looked away. She needed to get this back to business. "Let's begin at 301, then."

"Thank you for agreeing to do this."

Like she had a choice.

"I'm happy to. The more experience I have, the better my chances of finishing medical school."

Jenson stopped at the first patient's room. His gaze held hers. "I think you're a very interesting woman, Bayley."

Her mouth worked like a fish's.

"We have a patient to see. Tell me about him."

She almost got whiplash from the sudden change in topic.

"His name is Ronnie Prichard. He'd been admitted for arrhythmia." She looked at the chart on her pad. "He is thirteen and unhappy about being here. He has had an EKG, X-Rays, ECHO and blood panel. All look normal."

"Okay, let's go see him." He knocked on the door and entered. "Hey, Ronnie. I'm Dr. Hunt. I'm here to check on you."

Bayley followed Dr. Hunt into the room. She stood at the end of the bed as he stepped close to the boy.

"What're you working on?" Dr. Hunt moved nearer. "It looks like a model of a car."

Ronnie had pieces strewn across the rolling tray that had been pulled over the bed.

"It's going to be a model of a Formula One car." The boy showed Dr. Hunt the box top with the picture of the assembled car.

Dr. Hunt took it. "Nice." He handed the box back. "You like racing I'm guessing."

The boy nodded and smiled.

"Who is your favorite driver?" Dr. Hunt asked, but his focus had turned to the monitors.

Ronnie went into an explanation about a man Bayley had no idea existed. But that didn't matter because it was the first time she'd seen Ronnie so animated since he'd come to the hospital.

She studied Dr. Hunt. He really had a way with kids. She could only respect that. He was the type of doctor she wanted to become. His gaze met hers. He smiled and she returned it. What would happen if he really turned that charm on her? She'd probably be a puddle at his feet.

Dr. Hunt brought the conversation back to his examination. "Do you mind if I listen to your heart for a moment?"

Ronnie shook his head.

"Would you sit forward for me? I promise this won't hurt. It won't take long."

The boy did as Dr. Hunt asked.

Finished, Dr. Hunt said, "I look forward to seeing how that car is coming along tomorrow."

The boy smiled.

Bayley exited the room first. Dr. Hunt wasn't far behind. "You were great with him. I don't think I've heard him say ten words in the last three days."

Dr. Hunt shrugged. "It's all about finding common ground."

She could learn much from him. They moved to the next patient. Outside the door Bayley once again told Dr. Hunt about the patient they were going to see. They continued to visit patients until all twenty-six were seen.

With each patient Dr. Hunt sound as interested in them as he had been Ronnie and Johnny. They had spent extra time in Johnny's room, but Bayley hadn't minded.

He stopped walking and faced her. "You always smile when you're with a patient or a parent. And when you're making fun of me."

Her cheeks hearted. "I'm sorry about that."

"Hey, I'm just teasing. You should smile and laugh more often. If I've learned anything about life, it's that it's too short not to laugh and do what you enjoy."

"And that is?"

"For me, gaming, basketball, and action movies. How about you?"

"School and taking care of my father is all I have time for."

He started for the stairs. "When you take fun out of your life it leaves it pretty hollow. Thanks for your help today. You were great."

CHAPTER TWO

THREE WEEKS LATER Jenson walked down the third-floor hallway in the direction of the nurses' station. He hadn't been sure what his reception would be when he joined the staff of Atlanta Children's Hospital. So far it had been very warm. But he had no interest whatsoever in dating a woman despite all the attention the nurses gave him. He did his best to ignore it.

Oddly Bayley didn't appear susceptible to his looks. Some other members of staff acted silly when he came around, but Bayley didn't seem impressed. He was happy about it but it still pricked his pride. Why wasn't she interested in him? Somehow it made him want to get her attention.

Until recent developments he'd never thought he might be working as a staff doctor at a hospital. His life had been mapped out for him. That was until his ex, Darlene, pulled her last stunt. She'd left him no choice but to make a change.

The day he walked in to find his wife and Brett, his best friend, in bed had been the day he'd decided to leave the clinic.Regardless of the fact that the clinic had been started by Jenson's grandfather. Jenson had to move on. He had been too stupid to see it coming, or maybe too busy to care.

He shook his head violently, as if trying to get water out of his ears to remove thoughts that were unhealthy and unconducive to him starting a new life. His total attention now rested on keeping his nose to the grindstone and emphasis on his career—on building his life around what he wanted and what he enjoyed instead of obligation to his father.

That's what had brought him to a hospital that didn't have his name on it. That wasn't under his family's control. He wouldn't have to work with Brett and be reminded of his betrayal every day.

He went in search of Bayley. He didn't have to look far. He found her sitting behind the staff desk, fresh-faced, with her hair pulled back in a tail behind her head, a few freckles dotting her nose.

"Excuse me, Bayley. My patient in 329 needs to have a bandage changed."

Bayley quickly pushed the chair back and stood. "I'll take care of that right away."

"Thank you." He headed to his office. After a little paperwork he would be on his way home.

An hour later, he backed his car out of his parking place. From the corner of his eye, he saw a flash of blue color. Was that Bayley running across the lot? He looked again. It was Bayley. Her hands were clutching something to her chest as she headed for the bus stop just outside the exit. Seconds later she disappeared from sight behind a line of parked cars. He turned toward the entrance to find her picking herself up off the pavement and grabbing the bag she'd held in her arms.

The bus pulled away without her. Bayley's shoulders slumped. She looked in the direction of the departing bus.

He drove up beside her and rolled down the passenger-side window. "Are you okay?"

She glanced at him then at the disappearing bus. "Yeah. I just missed my bus."

"You aren't hurt, are you?"

Bayley gave him a sheepish look as she dusted off her bag. She pushed back a lock of hair that had come loose. "Just my pride."

He could well understand wounded pride. For some crazy reason he couldn't fathom, he asked, "Would you like a ride?"

Her look was almost comical as her eyes widened and her brows lifted. If it hadn't been for the desperation in her eyes, he'd have bet she planned to turn him down.

She glanced in the direction where the bus had been then met his look. "You don't have to do that. I'll just catch the next one. It'll be by in thirty minutes."

"You won't be late if you wait that long?"

Bayley quirked her mouth to one side. "Yeah, I'll be really late."

"Then quit arguing and get in. I'll take you to where you need to go." He leaned over the passenger seat and pushed the door open.

"I don't want to cause you any trouble." Her nose wrinkled with uncertainty.

Bayley was cute when she did that. Which he shouldn't be noticing. A car pulled up behind him. "The only trouble you're causing is a traffic jam."

"Man, if I don't, I'll be late for my advisory meeting," she mumbled more to herself than him as she grabbed the door handle. She plopped her bottom in the seat and pulled the door closed.

"Buckle up."

Bayley pushed her well-used black bag to the floor then went to work on her seat belt. She really was attractive in her frustration. More of her hair, normally held back in a tight grip, now fell around her face in thick locks of curls. He'd never seen her so out of sorts. On the floor she acted and looked professional at all times. This Bayley interested him. And she shouldn't. He had sworn off women. "Where to?"

"Emory University." She settled into the seat.

His brows rose.

She looked at him. "I have a meeting with my medical school advisor."

He pulled into the traffic.

"Do you need help with directions?" She gathered her hair, bringing it under control. He rather liked it the other way.

"No. I went to school there too."

"Then you know the Lanier Building." She leaned against the door, gazing out the windshield.

"Sure do. Spent a lot of time there." Back when life seemed simple. Before Brett and Darlene had brought his life to a screeching halt. He and Brett had been friends since middle school. They'd gone to college and medical school together. Since Brett's family couldn't afford it Jenson's parents had even helped pay his way. Darlene had been on the fringe of his life for years since their fathers had been business partners. It was only natural they'd start dating. And marry. After all, as his father had put it, she would be a "suitable wife." But that was in the past. Better forgotten.

He glanced at Bayley. "You'll make a great doctor. Calm in an emergency, good with the patients, thorough. If you ever need a reference, you let me know."

She gave him a quick smile. "Thanks. I might take you up on that. And thanks for the compliment."

They said nothing for a few moments.

He looked at Bayley. She sat with her hands clasped in her lap. They were nice hands with long fingers. What was she so uptight about? "You okay?"

"Yeah. I just hate being rushed."

He returned his eyes to the road. "We'll be there in a few minutes." Then it occurred to him. "Did I make you late because of my order to change the bandage?"

She gave him a sheepish look as if she didn't want to answer. "No, that wasn't your fault."

"You shouldn't feel like you have to do and oversee everything." He stopped for the red light.

"Sure I should. If something happens to a patient I need to know why when I'm the lead nurse for the day. I carry the responsibility." Her voice had taken on a strong note.

"Agreed, but others carry responsibility as well." Like Darlene and Brett for their disloyalty. Or him for his lack of attention to his marriage. "You shouldn't do their jobs when you know they can."

"Let's just say we generally agree to disagree. I was just helping out."

"That I can appreciate but don't let people take advantage of you"

She shifted and looked at him. "Sounds like you've had some experience there."

"Let's just say I was taken advantage of and ended up in a messy divorce that too many people had an opinion on. I've heard enough gossip to last a lifetime." Because of his ex, his family name had been dragged through the social pages, and not in a positive manner.

"I'm sorry you were hurt. People can be harsh even when they don't intend to be."

The last thing he needed was her sympathy. Over the last few months, the pain had started to dull. "I have to admit they had good material to work with. Wife and best friend/coworker have an affair under the nose of the too-busy-to-notice husband."

Bayley hissed. The space between them turned quiet. "I'm sorry. No one should endure that kind of betrayal."

Why was he unloading this kind of baggage on her? Jenson maneuvered the car through a turn. He didn't talk to anyone about his marriage. He wanted it forgotten.

"Agreed."

Soon he pulled in front of a three-story building with a 1960s design.

"You can let me out right here."

He stopped along the curb. She didn't hesitate before she opened the door and gathered her belongs. "Thanks for the ride. I really appreciate it. I was gonna have a hard time explaining why I didn't make it on time." Her mouth formed a line. "They're the ones who should be ashamed. Wedding vows should be honored."

"Thanks."

She climbed out. "I appreciate the ride."

"Glad I could help. Do you have a way home?"

She leaned in to answer him. "I'll take the bus."

"Don't you have a car?"

She huffed with humor. "No such luck."

"I could loan you one of mine for a while, if it would help out." What was he saying?

She looked at him as if he had two heads. "No, thank you. Do you go around loaning your cars to people all the time?"

"Well, actually, no." In fact, he couldn't figure out what had made him suggest it. "It's just that you seem to need one and I have an extra car."

"That must be nice," she said far too sarcastically for his taste.

Her "Thanks again" eased his agitation. "You were a lifesaver."

He watched her hurry into the building. He liked the way she held her head high, as if she knew exactly who she was and liked herself. She was an interesting person whether she knew it or not. His gaze dropped to the swing of her hips in the scrubs. He smiled. That part of her wasn't bad either.

Bayley, along with a couple of her classmates, walked out of the medical school building and into the darkness. The only light came from the lamps along the wide sidewalk and the streetlamps farther away. Beneath one of the lights sat a sleek black luxury car she recognized. Jenson leaned against it with his arms crossed over his chest and one leg over the other at the ankles. Her heart fluttered. What was he doing here?

He wore a pair of gym shorts and a faded T-shirt. His hair looked as if he'd run his fingers through it more than once. Nothing like the usually impeccably groomed Jenson she saw at the hospital. She rather liked this look. He had a little bit of a bad boy appeal to him.

Bayley hadn't been too sure about getting a ride from him earlier. She had been working hard in the last few weeks to remain as professional as possible around Jenson, uh, Dr. Hunt. But the more time she spent with him doing rounds and working with patients, the more she liked him. He had an appealing way about him that had nothing to do with his good looks and everything to do with charisma. He had managed to draw her in.

Then he'd made matters worse by sharing part of his personal life with her. He had a wounded soul. She'd hurt for him listening to him talk of his broken marriage. She'd wanted to take Jenson in her arms and ease his pain. But something about the rigidness of his body had said he wouldn't have appreciated that.

The last thing she needed in her life would be the additional complication of growing to care for Jenson Hunt. Caring for her father and trying to finish medical school had her plate full. Romance could wait. She had work that still needed doing.

She shook her head. Why was Jenson here? Surely he'd gotten over his guilt about being involved in making her late for the bus. The patient who'd needed his bandage replaced had been someone else's responsibility, but that nurse had been busy, so Bayley had done the job herself. Those extra few minutes required to cajole the patient into letting her take the old bandage off had cost her at the bus stop.

After she'd climbed into his car earlier and sank into the leather seat, she'd questioned how many people had seen her do so. She would know soon enough. Word would get around. Being the talk of the floor, or the whole hospital, wasn't her idea of fun. Based on their conversation earlier Jenson would enjoy being the center of gossip even less than her. Yet here he was again. What was going on?

"You know that guy?" a male student asked.

"Yeah." She nodded to her friends. "I know him. I work with him at the hospital. He's a cardiologist. He gave me a ride this afternoon when I missed the bus.

Which I'll do again if I don't get moving, but I need to see what he wants."

She exchanged goodbyes with the other students then started toward Jenson.

As she approached, he stood, his arms at his sides. "Bayley."

She liked the sound of her name onis lips. The letters sort of rolled sweet and smooth, like cream. She shivered. This wasn't the time in her life to think like that about a man, especially this one. Romance had to wait. The bitter notes in his voice earlier had made it clear what he thought of relationships. Plus she had her life planned out. She was so close to the prize and she wouldn't be distracted now. Yet here he was. She couldn't ignore him. Or the extra *pat-pat* of her heart at the sight of him. "Hey there, what're you doing here?"

"That's a warm welcome." His voice had dropped to a low and gravelly tone that had her heart picking up speed again.

"I didn't mean it like that. I'm just surprised to see you."

"You said you wouldn't have time for supper. I just finished playing basketball and was hungry, so I thought I'd stop and get us some burgers. That maybe I could make up for almost making you late. I feel like I had a part in causing your fall since I'm the one who asked for the bandage change which made you late"

Was he really that nice? "You shouldn't feel bad about that. We're all good."

"Good to hear."

She looked down the street. "Well, I've got to go or I'll miss my bus."

Jenson motioned toward the car with his head. "What

about those burgers? You sure you don't want one?
They're hot."

He tempted her. Too much and in too many ways. Not
just with a burger. She pursed her lips while taking a moment to think.

He pulled a paper bag out of the car window and shook
it. "Come on, you know you want one."

Her stomach growled. She hadn't eaten in hours.
"Okay, I'll join you, but then I have to get home."

His eyes narrowed while a worried look came to his
face. "You don't have a husband waiting on you, do you?"

Her neck stiffened. "No. My father."

Jenson exhaled. "Good to hear."

Jenson knew exactly why her answer had caused him to
sigh with relief. He would never do to another man what
had been done to him, or put another human through that
soul-breaking pain. In fact, he should have asked Bayley
sooner if she was involved with someone, but the subject
hadn't come up at work. And tonight he'd been working
off gut feelings and not thinking straight.

After the mess his past life had been, he couldn't afford
to make those types of mistakes. Trust wasn't something
he could give easily again. He needed to get his mind
right around Bayley or any other woman. Ask the hard
questions up front. Let them know he wasn't looking for
happily ever after. He'd already learned that was a pipe
dream. "Nothing permanent" was his plan.

He needed to get a grip. All he wanted was to have
a burger with a coworker. A simple friendly burger. He
had started to make more of this than he should. "There's
a bench over there. Why don't we sit before the burgers
get cold."

Her dark brown eyes flickered in that direction. "Okay. I've got another hour before the next bus."

"I'll drive you home." There he'd said something before thinking again. He did that too often around Bayley. "You don't have to worry about the bus."

"You better be careful here or you're gonna spoil me," she teased.

Something about Bayley made him believe she should be spoiled but never had been. "Why do you ride the bus anyway?"

She squared her shoulders. "Maybe because it's faster than walking."

"So you really don't own a car?" He just couldn't imagine not having a car. Heavens, he'd had one since he was sixteen and at one time owned four automobiles at the same time.

"Not any longer. Most people don't own a fancy car like yours. But if you must know, ours broke down, and since I'm the only one that uses it, I decided we could save money by me riding the bus."

He didn't ask anything else. He had no concept whatsoever of riding public transportation. That was something he'd never had to do. Paying for medical school had never been an issue either. They were from two different worlds. Maybe that's what intrigued him about Bayley. He handed her the sack. "You take this, and I'll get the drinks."

She took the paper bag while he reached inside the car window and pulled out a drink holder. "Lead the way."

They crossed the street, which at this time of the day remained empty. They entered the grassy park area.

Bayley placed the bag in the middle of the bench, which was located under a large tree. Her book bag went to the ground. She sat at one end of bench. He took the other and handed her a drink cup, then placed his drink on the ground next to the leg of the bench. "How was your meeting?"

"Good. She wants a report on a couple of my cases."

"I have no doubt you'll give exciting ones."

Bayley giggled. He liked the sound. "Yeah, something like that. Maybe not exciting but certainly important."

"That I can't dispute." He opened the sack, pulled out an aluminum-wrapped burger and handed it to her. "By the way, I saw Ronnie Prichard in clinic today. The arrhythmia medicine is working well. I don't think he'll need a pacemaker for a long time to come."

"That's great news." She took the burger. "Thanks for telling me."

"No problem." He removed the paper from his burger.

She gave him a head-to-toe look. "Were you really playing basketball just down the street?"

"Yep. I catch a couple of pickup games a week if I can. Good exercise. Gives me a chance to get out."

"Interesting. I hadn't expected that. I didn't see you as the kind of guy who'd play at a local park." She took a bite of her hamburger.

Until recently he hadn't been. He'd spent what little spare time he'd had at the country club seeing and being seen. Mostly because it had been what Darlene had enjoyed. He unwrapped his burger. "I'm not sure if there was a compliment or an insult in there."

She smiled. "Maybe a little bit of both. I'm just trying to put all the pieces together and figure you out."

"Is it important that you figure me out?" He took a bite of his burger.

"Yes. No. I don't know. You came with a lot of talk, but I've found you easy to work with and a good doctor."

"Thanks for that. I try to be both."

She took a draw of her drink. "But I have to admit I'm curious about you leaving the prestigious Hunt Clinic to come to work at the hospital."

Jenson braced himself. He might as well spill it all since he'd said so much while bringing her to campus. "I couldn't work at the Hunt Clinic any longer."

Bayley leaned forward. "Why?"

He took a deep breath. "Because I couldn't face my former best friend every day, knowing I'd caught him in bed with my wife."

"Oh."

"Yeah. Oh."

Bayley touched his arm briefly. "Again, I'm sorry."

He shrugged. "It's over and done with."

"Is that kind of thing ever over? The scars will always be there." She studied her hamburger.

Was she speaking about herself?

She dipped her head to the side. "How long were you married?"

"Eighteen months." Eighteen more than he should have been. He guessed he might as well get it all out since she already knew the punchline. "I thought I was in love but I quickly found being married to Darlene was nothing like dating and having a good time with her. In fact, the good times stopped. I thought it had to do with my work schedule. You know how that is."

Bayley nodded.

"Turns out she was secretly in love with my best friend." The words shouldn't have come out sounding so bitter at this point but he couldn't help it. "I'd tried to make it work. I took time off when I could find a spot. Bought little gifts. The marriage limped along. Until I took half a day off to surprise her and I was the one who got the surprise."

"It made it all worse that you were betrayed by your best friend."

Jenson touched the end of his nose. "Bingo. It wasn't until I moved out that I realized I hadn't truly loved her. If I had I wouldn't have given up so easily. I just wish it hadn't ended the way it did."

"It sounds like losing your best friend hurt worse than the loss of your marriage."

"I hadn't thought about it that way but I guess it did. Leave it to you to point that out."

Bayley took a sip of soda through her straw. "How did your family react?"

"My father gave lip service to understanding but wasn't pleased with me leaving the clinic. I didn't care. I left Darlene and the clinic as soon as I could. My father is still trying to get me to come back. I couldn't stay. Many of the people working there knew what was going on. I think my father might have even suspected.

"It took me about a year to get untangled from my ex-wife and the clinic. I did travel work until the job at the hospital opened."

"And Brett and Darlene now?"

"As far as I know they're still together. He works at the clinic still." He paused. "I try to know as little about them as possible." He wasn't sure he wanted Bayley to know so much about him. Or analyze him this closely. "Why're you going to medical school at your age?"

"I get it. Time to change the subject."

He gave her a wry smile, returning to his cool hamburger.

She grinned. "As opposed to before I became ancient?"

By her sarcastic answer he knew he'd asked that wrong. "That's not exactly what I meant."

"I know. I'm sorry. I really wanted to go to med school right out of college, but it wasn't in the picture at the time. Instead, I worked my way through nursing school. When the university offered night school classes I entered." She looked away for a moment. "Now I've got to win the Wilcott-Ross scholarship, or I won't be able to finish."

Jenson winced. The scholarship was overseen by a foundation that his father sat on the board of. It was one of his family's philanthropic ventures. Jenson only attended the gala as a supporter of the cause, not as a member of the foundation. He had no influence where the scholarship was concerned, and even if he had, it wouldn't be ethical for him to use it to help her.

And Bayley wouldn't appreciate any interference. She struck him as the type who only wanted help based on merit. Still, it would be a shame for her not to become a doctor. She had so much talent. "I'll keep my fingers crossed for you."

"Thanks. I can use all the good thoughts I can get." Her voice had turned wistful.

He watched Bayley bite into her burger. She had a sweet mouth with a plump bottom lip. "It's nice to have someone to share a meal with. A friend."

"Friend." She sounded like she was rolling the word around as if testing it.

He liked being around her. Was there anything wrong with them being friends? It would stop there. He'd promised himself never to trust another woman. He'd learned a soul-crushing and humiliating lesson at the hands of his ex-wife. He and Bayley would just enjoy each other's company. He would keep his emotions locked away.

He glanced over to find Bayley studying him. "Hey, you're staring at me."

"I was just wondering what put that snarl on your lips. Is that how you look at all your friends?"

Jenson plastered a smile on his mouth, pushing ugly memories away. "I'm sorry. I didn't realize I was snarling. What I was really thinking about was how much I like being around you. I like working with you."

Her eyes widened. "Well, thanks. That's nice to hear. Tell me, with your name and your credentials, why you did you come to Children's? I'm sure you could have gone to another private clinic or a hospital in another city. Mayo perhaps?"

"Why, Bayley Dodd, are you a snob?"

She put down the cup she'd been drinking from with a thump. "I am not!"

He cocked his head to the side. "Sure sounded that way to me."

"I'm just stating a fact. We both know your family is well-known around the city, the state."

He pushed the wrapper down on his burger and looked at it for a second. His jaw had pulled tight. Surely she knew him better than that, even after a short amount of time. "To begin with, I didn't go into medicine for money and I'm not practicing for it now. I thought you knew me better than that. And my family lives in Atlanta. My parents and my sister and her family."

Bayley placed her hand on his arm. He looked down at it then at her.

"I'm sorry. I'm the one who misspoke. I wasn't accusing you of anything. I think you're a wonderful doctor.

I'm proud to work with you. You're happy at Children's? You'll be staying?"

"Yeah, I'm very happy at Children's. And I have every intention of staying for a long time," he said with confidence. "It would take something really earth-shattering for me to even consider leaving."

"Not even to make your family happy?"

His look met hers. He said in a firm tone, "Not even for that. I'm done with working at the clinic."

She nodded, looking impressed.

Jenson liked that idea. Something about Bayley pulled at him. Jenson smiled. His ego couldn't help but appreciate her admiration. She laughed. He did as well.

"You have a nice laugh," she said.

It felt good to laugh. He hadn't done it in a long time. And certainly not with a woman. His divorce had chipped away at any humor in his life. Like water dripping on rock, it had slowly taken the fun away and he had failed to notice, until it was too late.

"There you are thinking again. What's going on?"

Bayley read him too well. He had to be careful around her. She saw more than he intended. "I was just thinking maybe I'd like an ice cream for dessert. Want to join me?"

Her lips went into a line. She shook her head. "I better not. My father will be waiting on me."

"Aren't you old enough not to be waited up on?" Bayley seemed devoted to her father.

"I like to think so, but my father likes to know I'm home safe before he goes to sleep."

"I guess a daughter never grows up in a father's eye. I know my father still wants to know what my sister is doing and she's married with a family."

"Would you be protective of a daughter?" She watched him expectantly.

"I guess so if I had one, but that's not going to happen." That chance had gone by.

"Don't you want children someday?" She asked the question nonchalant as if just making conversation. He liked that. Too often women had asked him things as if interviewing him for a husband position. Bayley only sound interested.

"I did at one time." A failed marriage had ended that idea.

Bayley watched him a moment. "You're still young enough to try."

"Thanks. I'm glad to know you still think I have the ability. I'm not too ancient."

She raised a hand, her palm toward him. "Hey, I don't know about that. That's getting into a personal area I'm not qualified to comment on." Bayley shook her head. "Nor should I. In fact, I need to shut up and go catch my bus."

"Forget the bus. I'll take you home."

"That's not necessary. You've paid any debt by bringing me supper and giving me a ride to class."

"Look, it's not a big deal. My car's right there. I'm right here. You need a ride." Why was he set on taking her home? Because he wanted to spend more time with her. Bayley made him think and feel—neither of which he had done in a long time.

CHAPTER THREE

"WHAT'RE YOU DOING?" she asked when Jenson stepped from the car in front of her apartment complex.

"I'm walking you to the door." He came around the vehicle.

She started up the walk. "I can get to the door just fine."

He fell in beside her. Was she ashamed of the place? It looked like a typical apartment complex with paint peeling in a couple of places, and rows of doors three stories high. The stairs were in the center of the building. "I was taught to walk a woman to the door when I brought her home."

"This wasn't a date." Her tone was firmer than she'd intended.

"That doesn't matter," Jenson said casually. "What matters is I see you safely inside."

Bayley had to admit his old-fashioned manners were touching. No other man she'd gone out with had shown such concern. "I don't want to be the one to get you into trouble with your mother."

He grinned. "I appreciate that." He took her bag from her. They headed toward her front door.

There, she reached for her bag. "Thanks for the meal. I guess I'll see you tomorrow."

"I imagine you will."

The door to her lower-level duplex opened. Her father sat in his wheelchair watching them.

"Hey, Dad," Bayley said.

"I had started to worry." He looked from her to Jenson and back again.

"I should've called. Dad, I'd like you to meet Dr. Jenson Hunt. Jenson, this is my father, Russell Dodd."

"Hello, sir. It's nice to meet you." Jenson extended his hand.

The men shook hands. Bayley didn't miss how strong and firm Jenson's hand looked next to her father's frail and thin one.

She needed to say more. "Dr. Hunt and I work together at the hospital."

"It's Jenson." He gave her a pointed look and smiled at her father.

"I believe you mentioned him." Her father rolled back into the house.

She colored. Even in the darkness she feared Jenson could see her face.

"Why don't you come in?" her father encouraged.

Jenson stepped in the direction of his car. "Thank you but I better be going. I just wanted to make sure Bayley got in safely."

Her father nodded. "Thanks. I appreciate that. I hate it when she's out so late after dark."

"I can understand that. Good to meet you, sir. See you later, Bayley."

She watched Jenson walk away for a moment then closed the door. What an unexpected evening it had been.

"He seems like a nice fella." Her father rolled farther into the living room.

"He is." More so than she would have ever dreamed he would have been. "He brought me a burger for dinner. We ate in the green area across from the med building."

"Mmm."

She felt her father's attention on her. "And then brought me home."

"Well, that's nice. I'm glad you're seeing someone."

"Don't start getting any ideas, Dad. I don't have time for that right now. I still have training to complete and the scholarship to win. I don't need my life complicated by a man. Especially some man that'll never work out for me."

Her father's brows rose. "Why would you say that?"

"You did hear his name? It's Jenson Hunt. As in the society Hunts. As in the Hunt Clinic. They're the ones a wing of Central Hospital is named for." Her voice rose as she spoke.

"That doesn't mean he couldn't be interested in you. I fear what happened between your mother and I holds you back from relationships."

"It does not!" She reached into her bag for the papers she needed to review and put them on the table. "Dad, I know you love me, but it'd never work out. We don't even think on the same plane." Bayley started toward the kitchen. She needed to get her father's medications and him into bed before she wrote her paper. As much as she'd enjoyed her dinner with Jenson, she really didn't have time for such things.

Her father came closer. "It has been too long since I saw you with a young man. I'm afraid you're scared to get serious about anyone."

She ignored that statement and continued to gather her father's evening medications, which had become rote over a twenty-year period.

"I was just getting ready for bed, but I didn't have the energy to push myself up out of this chair."

She needed to start looking for help. Her father was getting weaker. Years of inactivity had created its own problems. In a perfect world he could have a new procedure that might relieve the pressure on his spinal cord and give him a chance for a more active life. "I'm sorry I'm late. I'll help you."

She moved behind the wheelchair and pushed him down the narrow hall. Their place hadn't been built for a wheelchair. They were just scraping by until she could save enough money for them to move. If she could just win the scholarship, she might have enough for a deposit on an adapted built home where her father could get around freely. Then she'd save for that surgery. The first step was to win the Wilcott-Ross scholarship.

"When is your doctor's appointment tomorrow?"

"At three."

She parked him beside the bed. "Good, I'll meet you at the clinic after my shift at the hospital. You can get to the bus okay?"

"Gary next door said he'd be home and would help me." Her father, with well-practiced form, pushed himself up on his arms and flung himself onto the bed.

"Perfect." Bayley waited for him to situate himself on the mattress.

He pushed back to the pillows. "Now back to Dr. Hunt. He seemed like a really nice man."

"Dad." She gave him an exasperated sigh. Her father was correct: Jenson was a nice guy. Much nicer than she'd expected.

"Just trying to make conversation."

"Oh, really. You look tired. Let's get this medicine in you and off to sleep you go."

"You do know I'm the elder and the father here. I fear because of me and what your mother did you've had to grow up too soon. Haven't gotten to have your own time, a chance to fall in love."

"I have no interest in love."

Her father picked up his glass of water from his bedside table after accepting the pills from Bayley. "Don't say that. It hurts my heart."

Her father's hand shook as he swallowed and replaced the glass. He was slowly fading. Bayley couldn't stop it without a lot of extra money for surgery. Her father's health had been erratic at best over the last six months. She worried about him while she was gone, which meant she spent no more time away than necessary. Between school and work she was gone a lot already. Dating didn't fit in.

"I haven't seen you with a smile that large on your face in a long time."

Putting her hands on her hips, Bayley glared at him. "Daddy, don't start."

"What?" He gave her his most innocent voice.

"You're making a big deal out of nothing. There's nothing more than one coworker helping out another between Jenson and me."

His eyes twinkled. "I just think that you're protesting too much."

Her father was a Shakespeare fan despite his blue-collar upbringing. He'd always been an intellectual person. She'd gotten her love of learning from him. If her mother had given Bayley any attributes, she had no idea what they were since her mother hadn't stayed around long enough for Bayley to find out. "Funny, Daddy, really, really funny."

"Is there some reason why you can't be interested in a man?"

She adjusted the covers. "Actually, there is. I don't have time for such nonsense."

"Honey, that kind of nonsense you don't prepare for. It just comes along and slaps you in the face."

"You make it sound very attractive." She tucked the cover under his chin.

He met her look. "It can be with the right person."

The one thing she could credit her dad with was he'd always been an eternal optimist. Regardless of the fact his wife had left him with a very young daughter and he'd spent most of his life in a wheelchair, he'd always stayed positive. If it hadn't been for neighbors and friends helping out, she might not have been able to live with him. Even with their struggles through the years their number one goal had been to remain together.

"Honey, you can't let what happened between me and your mom affect your relationships." He shook his head. "Your mom had issues before we got married and during our marriage. When I lost my ability to walk, it was more than she could take. We all have weaknesses. Your mother's were greater than most."

"She should've been able to deal with you being in a wheelchair if she loved you." Bayley adjusted his phone and lamp so he could reach them.

"Some people aren't as strong as you are." Her father patted her hand.

"It's more like some people care about their own lives more than they do about others. They don't care who they hurt." She didn't even try to keep her bitterness out of her voice.

"That's true, but I don't want you to think you can't have a strong and a good relationship because of the example that I've set."

"Dad, you're my example of what love is." She kissed him on the cheek. "I want somebody like dear old Dad."

Her father chuckled.

She walked to the door and put her hand on the light switch. "So far I just haven't found anybody that lives up to you."

Her father's eyes turned concerned, his face sobering. "I'd hate to think I was holding you back."

"I'll let you know if you're ever holding me back. Until then you should consider yourself the best father in the world." He had been. Her father had always been in her corner.

"I love you and I want the best for you. I appreciate your kind words but one day you're gonna have to open your heart and let someone in."

She took a deep breath. "Yeah, but that won't be until after I've finished medical school. I'd say you're stuck with me until then. And I have to have you settled in a place other than this dump."

"It isn't a dump. You've done a great job of making it a home." His voice turned sad. "It may not be what we once had but we're doing okay. None of it matters when you're with people you love."

"Dad, you have always seen the glass half full. That's one of the things I love most about you. I just wish I'd gotten more of that spirit."

"That's because you work, go to school and see about me. You don't spend enough time on yourself. Why don't you invite that doctor to dinner one night? He seemed nice enough."

Would Jenson come if she did? She and her father lived humbly compared to his wealthy lifestyle. "I don't think that would be a good idea. We're just friends."

"Since when do friends not eat together?"

Why was her father pushing this? "Since my focus is work and he's not interested."

Her father pursed his lips in thought. "He must be a little interested or he wouldn't have brought you home."

She did like Jenson. He wasn't anything like she had expected. Except for his good looks. The rumors about those had been spot-on. His personality had been a positive surprise. She enjoyed working with him. Truth told, she had enjoyed their burgers together. Had been flattered he'd brought them and given her a ride home. It had been nice to have a man's attention.

Bayley hated to admit it but for the last week she'd hoped Jenson would be waiting when she left the medical building. Tonight her heart jumped when she saw him walking up the sidewalk. It shouldn't have but it did. High.

Jenson was a nice guy. What was wrong with coworkers seeing each other outside of work? Single coworkers. What could possibly go wrong? A lot, but she had no intention of getting involved with him. They could keep it friendly. It would stay that way.

"I wasn't expecting you. You keep surprising me." Her mouth ran away from her.

"Now, about that ice cream you passed on last week. You have time for it tonight?"

She probably should turn him down, but she wanted

to go. "Sure. I just need to make it quick. Dad will be waiting."

Jenson took her bag from her. He matched her pace to the car. There he opened the door and she slipped inside.

He wore a T-shirt with some writing on it, but it was so faded she couldn't make out the words. His slim hips held up a baggy pair of gym shorts. His calves were thick and strong looking with a dusting of hair. White socks and tennis shoes were on his feet. He should seem like any other guy, yet he stood out among them, both in his smarts and his looks. Jenson was a man who didn't go unnoticed.

Bayley stepped out of the car after Jenson pulled into the parking spot in front of the ice cream parlor.

He held the door open as she entered. "What're you going to have?"

"I'm having mint chocolate chip with a waffle cone. How about you?" She headed toward the line for the counter.

"Wow. You didn't have to think about that, did you?" Jenson grinned.

"Nope." She smiled as they moved forward in the line.

He stepped up beside her. "I'm going to have vanilla."

Bayley whirled. "Vanilla! Surely you can do better than that?"

"I like vanilla. It's a good solid flavor that goes with everything. My mother always served it."

Bayley shook her head. "That's just sad. You should try living a little."

"Okay, smarty-pants. You pick something out for me. But it can't be mint chocolate since you're getting that."

"Now you're talking." She put some space between them and studied him.

He looked around them. "Bayley, people are waiting on us."

"Let them go around." She waved the couple behind them on.

"What're you doing anyway?"

She continued to study him. He had a tiny mole on his chin in just the right place to kiss. Not an idea she should be contemplating. "I'm trying to figure out what type of flavor you are."

"I'm not going to wear it." He chuckled.

"Hush, I'm working here. Tall, good looking."

His brows rose. "You think I'm good looking?"

"Please." She smirked. "It's not like you don't already know that. Nice full lips."

He leaned down so his gaze met hers. "Now you're getting personal."

"Serious."

It was his turn to smirk.

"And charming. But still a little too sad."

"Why would you say that?" He looked away.

What did he not want her to know? "Because I've seen it in your eyes."

"Enough of this. Pick an ice cream or I'm going to have vanilla." He stepped forward when another couple would have gone around them.

Her shoulders straightened and she pushed her chest out. "I think you're a banana-pudding-in-a-cup guy. Yes, that's it. Make it a large because you're really going to like it."

"And said with such confidence. What if I don't like it?"

She waved a family around them. "Then I'll buy you half a gallon of vanilla."

He tilted his head down, surveying her. "You're that confident?"

"I'm that confident." She stepped up behind the family. When it was their turn to order, she didn't hesitate to tell the woman behind the counter what they wanted.

"Where did you get all this knowledge of ice cream?"

"I read a magazine article about telling people's personality from the ice cream they chose. It said it was a good way to find out about your date. Not that we're dating." She waved a hand. "It was just a silly article."

"I wouldn't have taken you for a women's magazine reader." He quirked one side of his mouth in doubt.

"I don't often but I was waiting on Dad while he was at a doctor's appointment and picked it up." She glanced at the girl filling their order.

"So what did it say about a man who picks vanilla?"

She shook her head and wrinkled her nose as if she smelled something bad. "You don't want to know."

"That bad?"

She nodded. "Yeah, pretty bad. But after tonight you won't be a vanilla guy anymore. You'll have found your true ice cream."

He chuckled. "That all sounds ridiculous."

"You just wait and see." She held her head high.

"I'll admit a confident woman does appeal to me."

With their ice cream in hand, they found a two-person table on the sidewalk outside the parlor.

Bayley licked a drip forming on her ice cream cone. "Mmm." She glanced at Jenson. He watched her intently. "Something wrong?"

He shifted in his chair. "No."

She looked at the cup in his hand. "Go ahead. Tell me what you think."

Jenson spooned the ice cream and placed it in his mouth. Slowly he pulled the plastic utensil from between his lips.

Too slow for her comfort. She was far more interested in his amazing lips than she should have been. The breath she hadn't realized she'd been holding came out at the same speed as the spoon. She swallowed, working to regain her equilibrium. "So, what do you think?"

He made a show of rolling his tongue around, tasting and testing.

Bayley couldn't help but lean forward, engrossed in the show.

"It's good. Really good. You were right. It is better than vanilla. In fact, it's almost better than anything I've ever tasted."

She laughed, something she hadn't done enough of lately. Maybe she was the one who was too serious. "I'll resist the desire to say I told you so."

He grinned back. "Thanks. I appreciate that."

They spent the next few minutes enjoying their ice cream.

Bayley finished her cone. Picking up a napkin, she wiped her mouth. "That was good. Thanks for asking me."

Jenson dropped his spoon into the empty paper cup with a thump. "You were right. I needed a large. Thanks for getting me out of my comfort zone."

"No problem. I'm glad I could help. This has been nice, but I need to get home. Dad will be waiting on me." She checked her watch.

"Then we should get going." Jenson picked up their trash and placed it in the receptacle.

Bayley grabbed her bag and joined him. He took her

bag as they headed toward his car, and then followed her to the passenger-side door.

"Bayley."

"Yeah?" She turned to him.

"Are you saving that ice cream on your lip for later?"

"Oh. That always happens." She licked her upper lip. "Gone?"

His gaze had lowered and darkened. "No. Do you mind if I help?"

"Please." She raised her chin.

Her heart quickened as his face came closer. Seconds later his lips touched hers. Her body zinged with awareness. The tip of his tongue traveled along the line of her upper lip, stopping in the corner for a moment to brush back and forth.

Bayley's knees shook. Her hands went to his forearms. She held on. Wow.

Jenson pulled back and licked his lips. "You know, that mint chocolate is good. Or maybe it's just you."

She blinked. "Why did you do that?"

He shook his head as if clearing it then shrugged. "You looked so cute with ice cream on your face that I just wanted a taste."

"You shouldn't have." But she had liked it. Too much. "Why?"

She leaned her head to the side. "Because we work together. We're friends. I don't have time for a relationship."

Jenson stepped back, a panicked look coming to his eyes. "One kiss doesn't a relationship make. I won't be going there again. My ex-wife cured me of that."

"Then we agree? We're just friends?" She opened the door of the car.

"Agreed."

She climbed in while he walked around the car. His kiss had been sweet. Despite it being short, every nerve in her had been firing. The idea of not having that experience again saddened her. Still, it had to be that way. Reliving it in her dreams would have to satisfy her. But if he tried again, could she resist him?

CHAPTER FOUR

Jenson walked down the hall anticipating seeing Bayley. It had been three days since he'd kissed her. A kiss that had heated his blood when it shouldn't have. It had been the sweetest, tenderest and most seductive of his life. One he shouldn't have given.

He couldn't believe the amount of time he'd spent thinking about kissing Bayley again. Memories of that soft sound she made when he pulled away still echoed through his mind. Why had it shaken him so?

He entered the patient's room where he had been told Bayley would be. She stood at the bedside of the patient. He'd planned to speak to her and ask how she had been doing but she was involved in a procedure.

She glanced at him. A tense, worried look covered her face before she returned to urging the patient, "Kristy. You must lie still. You can't move."

"Stop. It hurts." The girl tried to pull to the side, but Bayley held steady.

"I know, sweetheart," she cooed. "Just a few more seconds and it'll all be over. Hang in there."

He checked the PICC line crew's placement of the intravenous line that would lead directly to the girl's heart and drip much-needed antibiotics into her system. Kristy had endocarditis. The medicine would save her life, but it would take time and patience. Along with a few more weeks in the hospital.

Bayley put her hand on the ten-year-old girl's arm when she moved slightly. "Just remain still, sweetie. They're almost done."

Jenson moved to the end of the bed in clear view of the girl. "Kristy, did you know that Bayley knows everything about ice cream? She can even tell you the kind that matches your personality."

Kristy looked at Bayley and back to him. "Personality?"

"The type of person you are. Like how we know you are brave. Look how still you're being. I heard you get good grades, so you're smart. Do you like books, sports, or both?"

"I like books."

He had the child's attention. "Okay. Do you like to play outside?"

"I like to hike."

Jenson nodded as if giving that thought. "That sounds like fun. Why don't you ask Bayley what she thinks is the best ice cream for you?"

Kristy looked to Bayley, who made a show of thinking by raising her face to the ceiling and her index finger to her chin.

"I need to think about what I know about you." Bayley glanced at the group working with Kristy's other arm.

Jenson noted they were almost finished. "Whatever she says I'll order, and we'll test to see if Bayley is right."

"Ooh…" Bayley pursed her lips in a most appealing way. "Now the pressure is on. I say your ice cream flavor is strawberry/blueberry."

"What do you think, Kristy? How does that sound?" Jenson asked, looking away from Bayley to not ponder what her lips had him thinking about.

"Good."

"Then I'll order it." He pulled out his phone and placed an order. "Done."

"We're done here too," one of the PICC line crew announced.

Jenson watched Bayley visibly relax.

"Kristy, you are my hero. You were so brave." He patted her leg.

"That was no fun," the girl said.

Bayley, with a glassy look to her eyes, nodded. "No, it isn't. I'm sorry you had to go through that."

Jenson couldn't believe how personally involved Bayley became with her patients, to the point she felt their pain. Now she had him participating. It felt good. "Kristy, I'm Dr. Hunt. I need to examine you, but you need to rest right now. I'll do it when I bring you your ice cream."

He went out the door and Bayley followed, closing the door behind her.

She sagged against the wall. "Whew, that's always rough. No matter what you do, you can't make the child happy. And the PICC line is necessary." She looked at him. "You were great in there. I don't know if Kristy would've let them finish if it hadn't been for you. Thanks."

A wry smile formed on his lips. "I have to admit it was a first for me."

"You did some quick thinking in there."

He liked the way she looked at him as if he was

her hero. He'd never seen that expression on Darlene's face. Ever.

She stood, seeming to gather herself. "We better start rounds."

"I think we can see a couple of patients before I have to go down and get the ice cream."

"You really ordered some?"

"Of course I did. I'd never lie to a child about ice cream. In fact, I don't lie. I think trust is earned. Is of value. I take that seriously." Something Darlene and Brett hadn't subscribed to.

Bayley shook her head. "Then we better get started on seeing patients. I don't want the ice cream to melt."

Jenson chuckled. Just another thing he liked about Bayley. Her ability to bounce back. To not let life or a difficult time get her down for long. He could take a lesson or two from her.

Bayley had almost made it out of the staff door to the parking lot when she heard, "Hey, Bayley." It was Jenson headed her way.

"What's the hurry? Are you late for the bus again? I can always drive you."

"No, my neighbor called. He found Dad on the floor in the kitchen. Seems he was reaching for something and fell out of the wheelchair. She said he has a pretty good lick to the forehead. They've gone to the emergency room."

"Come on, I'll drive you. You won't want to waste time on the bus."

This time she didn't even hesitate. "I really appreciate it. I'm worried about him."

She hurried to Jenson's car.

Inside he asked, "What hospital?"

"Central Atlanta Hosptial I'm assuming you know where it is."

"Yeah. I've been there a few times." That was the hospital his family had helped build.

Bayley bet he had been there. After all, an entire wing had been named after his family. She clutched her hands in her lap, anxious to see her father. Jenson moved smoothly and confidently through the heavy afternoon traffic.

"Tell me about your dad. What kind of accident put him in a wheelchair?" He glanced at her. "If you don't mind."

"I don't mind. It happened so long ago." She paused a moment. That day she remembered too well. Even as young as she had been, she had known it was the beginning of the end of her parents' marriage. Just months later her mother had left. "He got hurt at work. An iron beam swung around and hit him in the back."

Jenson winced. "He had to have been lucky not to have been killed."

"He was. Very lucky. He followed the safety regulations, but still, accidents happen. His spinal cord was crushed."

"I'm sorry to hear that. I'm assuming you've had countless doctors look at it. There are new innovations in back care."

"Yeah. We've seen all we can afford. I know of a new procedure that sounds promising, but it takes money. After I start practicing, I'm going to save up for him to have it done. I believe he can gain some mobility." She worked to keep the sadness out of her voice.

"He doesn't act bitter."

Pride filled Bayley. "The great thing about my father is he always sees the cup half full. He's not, despite how life has treated him, a bitter old man."

"That's nice to hear. It isn't an attribute everybody can manage."

Bayley watched Jenson for a minute. Had his divorce made him bitter?

Soon they were pulling into a reserved parking spot outside Central Atlanta Hospital.

Bayley looked around them for a security guard running toward them. "You sure about parking here? I don't want you to get towed."

"These two—" he pointed to another empty space "—are my family's spots. You give enough money, and you get parking places."

"Good to know." Not that she would ever get one. Or think she should have one. Entitlement must be nice. But Jenson had never acted that way. Interesting.

They headed toward the doors beneath the sign reading Emergency.

At the department desk she said, "I'm here for my father. Russell Dodd."

The man behind the desk looked at a computer screen. "Mr. Dodd is in Exam Room One. He's in X-Ray, but should be back in a few minutes. Just have a seat. Someone will come get you." He waved a hand toward a couple of plastic-covered chairs.

They took the seats.

"You know, in all the years I've worked here, I've never once sat down. It really isn't very comfortable."

She tapped his leg. "Well, there you go. You're getting a new life experience hanging out with me."

He placed his hand over hers and gave it a gentle squeeze. "Not one I'm sure I wanted."

"You don't have to—"

"But I am. He's going to be fine."

"Thank you for being here. Visits to the hospital have started to happen too often. I need to win that scholarship. That way we can afford to move to a wheelchair-friendly apartment, so he'll quit having accidents trying to get things off the shelf."

Jenson continued to hold her hand. "That's a worthy goal but until then, what're you gonna do?"

"The same as we've been doing. Getting by the best we can." She looked toward the door where a staff member should soon appear to call her back. Jenson's hand felt warm and reassuring. Somehow, just his touch eased her mind.

"It's gonna be fine. Hang in there. You'll get to see him in a minute."

"Thanks for driving me. And coming with me and staying with me. I have no trouble with an emergency at work but make it with my dad and I fall apart." She sucked in her bottom lip.

"I never thought to do anything different."

She didn't doubt his word. "You know, you're a really nice guy."

He bumped her shoulder with his. "Was there ever any question about that?"

She laughed. "No, I guess there wasn't. The female staff didn't give much thought to that, they were so interested in your good looks and money."

"That's not what you see in me, is it?" His gaze met hers, held.

He sounded and acted as if her answer really mattered to him. "Well, that, and more."

"More?" His brows rose and his eyes sparkled with curiosity.

She grinned. "Fishing for compliments?"

Jenson's face sobered. "More like reassurance. I hope you see more in me than my looks and wealth."

"I promise I do. Look at where we are right now. That's points in your favor."

"Nice to hear." He paused a moment. "Would you tell me about your mother?"

Bayley's body stiffened. She didn't want to talk about her. "I'd rather not."

"Will you make an exception for me?" He gave her a pleading look.

A bitter taste entered her mouth. "She doesn't matter. Hasn't in years."

"Do you know where she is?"

"No, and I don't care." Her tone lacked the ring of sincerity she'd worked at.

"You missed her, didn't you?"

Bayley hated that she had. She forced the words out. "I used to."

"She's part of you."

"I'm nothing like her." Bayley bit the words off.

His eyes widened. "I've never heard you speak to or about anyone that way."

Bayley hung her head.

"You don't have to if you don't want to."

"I just don't do it very often." She gave him a tight smile. "But since you're so nice… My mother left six months after my father had finally come home from the hospital after the accident. During the months before she left there was a withdrawn quietness that hadn't been there before the accident. It was almost worse than the shouting and screaming of before. My parents had disagreed a lot.

"Then one morning my mother dressed for the day,

pulled me into her arms for a tight hug and whispered, 'I love you, honey. I can't stay or I'll die.'"

Jenson ran the pad of his thumb over the top of her hand in a reassuring motion.

Bayley stopped herself short of crying. "With that, she walked out the door and never looked back. I know. I watched her from the window. A man in a fancy car, an earlier model of yours, waited at the curb. My mother got into the car. The man drove my mother away."

"I'm so sorry. That had to have been horrible."

Bayley didn't understand any better now than she had then how her mother could have left them. "I don't believe my mother knew what true love was. To walk out and leave her husband just home from the hospital after an accident, and your only child. What type of person does that?" She glanced at him. "Maybe her new boyfriend didn't want a child around to worry about?"

"I'm sure you had nothing to do with it."

She turned to him. "How can you be so sure?"

"Because who wouldn't want you?" He gave her hand a squeeze.

"You're just saying that. But thanks. Mother had always liked the finer things in life. Whatever my father could provide hadn't been enough. When he got hurt, money became tight. I was young but I could understand that. It doesn't matter. My dad and I have made out just fine."

"I know he's proud of you."

"I know it too, but I still worry that I won't know how to be a good wife and mother because I've had the poorest example."

"I don't believe that. But maybe we aren't so different after all." His voice held sadness.

"How's that?"

Jenson's gaze met hers. "We were rejected by women we believed should have loved us."

She pursed her lips. "I wish we had something else in common."

A staff member came out the doors of the emergency examination area and called, "I'm looking for the Dodd family."

Bayley jumped to her feet. "Here." She started toward the door then turned back to Jenson. "You don't have to wait on me any longer."

"I'll wait here and make sure you don't need anything." He sat back in his chair.

"Then you might as well come back with me." Bayley had to admit it was nice to have his support and she hated to leave him out here alone.

Jenson hurried to join her. They were led to an exam room where her father sat in bed with his back supported. There was a large white bandage on this forehead. Bayley raced to him.

"I'm fine, honey. I'm fine."

She hugged him.

"I just have a couple of stitches. I did something stupid, trying to reach for a can of soup. I pushed up too far and next thing you knew I was tipping over. I hit my head on the corner of the lower cabinet. I knew better."

"Well, you had me worried. I'm glad it wasn't more than a few stitches." She looked at the bandage on his head.

Her daddy looked past her. "Dr. Hunt. Nice to see you again. Sorry it had to be under these circumstances."

"Jenson saw me running out of the hospital and offered me a ride." He had without a second thought. Had sat with her in the most depressing of places. Why would a man like that need reassurances about his worth? Because his reckless, uncaring ex-wife had made him feel that way.

"I appreciate you bringing my daughter down here," her father said.

The nurse entered. "Mr. Dodd, we're going to be releasing you now. I need you to follow up with your family doctor in a few days. Your doctor can remove the stitches."

"I've got my own nurse, soon to be doctor living at my house. She'll take care of it. This is my daughter, Bayley." Her father wore a proud look as he touched her arm.

"Hello," the woman said. Looking at Jenson, her face brightened into a large smile. "Dr. Hunt. It's nice to see you. We haven't seen much of you around there."

"Hi, Jean, it's nice to see you." He looked at Mr. Dodd.

The nurse refocused, turning serious again. "I'm sure I don't need to tell either of you—" she looked from Bayley to Jenson "—about concussion protocol, but I must. You're going to need to watch him for any unusual actions, pupils being a different size or vomiting. He can sleep but you'll need to wake him every hour." She gently waved a few papers. "It's all written right here."

Bayley took the papers.

Jenson stepped to the door. "I'll go get the car and bring it around."

Bayley said, "You don't have to do that. You've done enough. We'll get the bus home."

"You're not going to take your father home from the hospital on the bus." Jenson's tone allowed no argument. "So don't argue. I'll meet you out at the entrance." He opened the door.

Her father said, "That's the kind of guy you need.

Somebody who'll stand up to you and talk sense when you need it."

"We're just friends." Except for that kiss.

"Sometimes friendship turns into more."

Her father watched her too closely. She nervously straightened his sheet over him. "Dad, don't start seeing things where they don't exist."

"He's here with you, isn't he?"

She couldn't argue with that.

They were waiting at the exit when Jenson drove up. He helped load her father into the front seat, then the wheelchair into a trunk that wasn't built for large items. Bayley got into the back seat.

Jenson calmly carried on a conversation as he drove with ease through the evening traffic. At their apartment he helped her father inside. Jenson stayed in the living area while she settled her father in bed.

"Do you feel up to having some soup?" Bayley asked her father.

"No, I'd just like to rest."

"You know, I'm gonna have to wake you up every hour or so." She fussed with his covers.

"I heard what the nurse said. Maybe Jenson would like soup and a sandwich. He probably missed his dinner." He pushed her hands away. "My covers are fine."

"Dad, I'm not going to encourage him. We're just friends."

Then why are you so nervous about Jenson being in your home?

She returned to the living area.

Jenson stood looking at family pictures on the wall. "I'll leave you to take care of your dad. Please call me if you need me. I'll be glad to come take a few hours of waking him up if that would help."

Had he overheard what she'd said? "I don't think that'll be necessary. I really appreciate you driving me to the hospital and us home. You're a good friend." She gave him a quick kiss on the cheek.

That put a smile on his face. "I'll check in tomorrow and see how your father's doing."

Despite her words to her father, her feelings were moving toward liking Jenson Hunt too much.

Jenson walked through the group of people standing on the sidewalk to enter the Intercity Clinic early on Saturday morning. When a note came through the hospital email requesting volunteers to help one weekend a month, he'd written back he would be there. It might be interesting to practice other medicine besides cardiology once in a while.

This clinic looked nothing like the shiny modern clinic his family owned. No metal and glass. Instead, the clinic was located in an old storefront in a strip mall. He pushed through the door. The waiting area was a small front room with mismatched chairs lining three walls. Each was filled with someone waiting. An old-fashioned desk was set to guard the hallway that went straight to the back of the building. Behind the desk sat a heavyset woman, probably in her midfifties. She appeared formidable.

As he approached, she continued her discussion with a mother holding a baby on her hip. The woman behind the desk's actions were a novelty for him. Those he worked with usually gave him their attention immediately. He hadn't realized until that moment he had that expectation. He wasn't proud of the fact.

Growing up as he had with wealth and privilege, he'd come to expect certain responses from people. From the time he had been a teenager and girls had started flocking to him, he'd anticipated them. Having Bayley keep him at arm's length, and after being humbled by his ex-wife, he had learned the Hunt name and looks didn't open all doors. Strangely, that didn't disturb him.

The woman behind the desk finally glanced at him. She waved a hand. "Take a seat. I'll be with you as soon as I can."

"I'm Dr. Hunt. I'm here to help out today."

The woman's eyebrows rose. Her gaze traveled down then up again. She gave him a little bit of a smile. She nodded her head to the side toward the hall. He got the idea none of her movements had anything to do with his good looks or what he was wearing, instead his ability to understand the type of patients seen at the clinic. "See Dr. Rothchild. He'll give you your assignment."

"Thanks."

Jenson just made out the woman's muttered "They're going to eat you alive." He continued walking down the hall. Movable walls created cubicles used as exam rooms on each side of the hallway.

Halfway to the back of the building someone slammed into his side.

"Ho." He automatically reached out. Looking down he saw Bayley staring at him. He'd had no idea she would be there.

She gave him a sheepish look. "Hey. What're you doing here?"

"You sure do ask me that a lot."

She grinned and took a step back. "You keep popping up."

Bayley looked glad to see him. He like that idea. Her kiss on the cheek had been nice. He had overheard her comment to her father about them just being friends. It was true, but he wanted a little more. Not too much, but more. More touching. More kissing. More happiness. More peace, which he felt around her.

He looked up and down the hall. "This time I came because there was a request for help."

"I've been working here for years in my spare time." She pulled at her scrub shirt, which he'd noticed she did often around him. Did he make her nervous?

"I don't think you have much of that, but I bet you're here every weekend."

She looked away. "Yeah, something like that."

When did she do something for herself? "Is there anything that you don't do?"

"I don't take too many vacations on the Riviera."

He chuckled.

A dreamy look came over her face. "I've always wanted to see the Riviera."

"I have to admit it is beautiful." The idea he'd like to show it to her popped into his head. No, no, that wasn't what he should do.

"You've been?" Amazement and eagerness brightened her eyes.

"Yes, I did some traveling in Europe when I was in college." At the time every kid he knew traveled, saw the world.

"That's my dream."

A sadness fell over their conversation. "Well, maybe one day soon, you can do it."

Bayley shook her head. "I don't think that'll ever be in the cards for me."

"You never know." Why did he suddenly feel guilty for having traveled?

"Bayley!" a male voice called from a cubicle.

"I need to get back to work." She pointed to the short balding man wearing a lab coat. "That's Mike Rothchild. The doctor in charge today. He'll get you started. Hey, Mike. Help's here." She called then turned to Jenson, "See you around."

"Hey, is there always a line for people to get in?"

"Yep. Saturdays are crazy around here." Bayley headed off with a wave over her shoulder.

Dr. Rothchild stopped and waited on him.

Jenson hurried down the hall. "I'm Jenson Hunt."

The men shook hands. "Nice to meet you. Pick up a folder and go to the exam room indicated on the outside. I wish I had more time to chat. Let me or Bayley know if you need help. She really runs the show around here anyway."

"I'm not surprised."

The older man chuckled. "Let me know if you have any issues."

Jenson worked through the folders, but the patients kept coming. The need was great. With the exception of when he'd done an ER rotation in medical school, the patients he saw could afford care. These apparently couldn't judging by the amount of time they were willing to devote to coming to the free clinic. He had done some serious work with long hours but today there wasn't a minute for him to drink a bottle of water.

Why hadn't he done something like this before? He should be ashamed of himself for not doing so. This wouldn't be his last time. The need was too great to ignore.

It was a little after lunchtime, a meal which he had

yet to have, when Bayley stopped him in the hall with a hand on his forearm.

"I have a patient I want you to see. I know there's something heart-related going on but I can't put my finger on it. I don't hear any irregular beats but something doesn't sound right." Her grave look met his and she implored, "Will you see him?"

When Bayley looked at him like that he'd do anything for her. "Sure, let me see my next patient, then I'll be right in."

Bayley nodded. "Thank you." She left as quickly as she'd appeared.

He noted what room she entered and continued to the one where his patient waited. Fifteen minutes later he knocked on the door Bayley had entered. He found Bayley talking to a woman sitting in a chair against the wall. He assumed she was the mother of the boy who sat on the exam table. The woman clutched her hands in her lap when he entered.

Bayley's hand rested on the towheaded boy with the sunken eyes's thigh as if to make sure he wouldn't fall. She quickly turned to him but spoke to the mother. "Angie, this is Dr. Hunt. He's going to look at Georgie. I want him to see if he can figure out what's going on."

Bayley looked at him. "I've seen Georgie a few times in the last six months. One time for an upset stomach. Another time for a cold. He's been losing weight and now his energy level is low." This time she bent to the boy's level. "Georgie, will you let Dr. Hunt listen to you?"

Jenson stepped closer. "Hi, Georgie. Why don't you just lie down here for me?" Jenson placed a hand at the boy's back and guided him down on the table. "Now, I am just going to listen to you. Just lie still." He placed his stethoscope on his chest. "Then to your lungs, now your belly." He pushed at the boy's stomach and palpated his liver before he returned his stethoscope to listen to his heart again. There it was. He heard it.

He looked at Bayley. "Do we have any lab work on Georgie?"

She shook her head. "No. We don't have a lab here. I wish we did."

"He should be seen at the hospital right away," he said as much to the mother as Bayley.

The mother stood looking distraught as she clutched her bag to her chest.

"Georgie, will you put your hands on top of mine?" Jenson turned his palms up.

The boy placed his hands on Jenson's. The dusky blue of his nail beds had just begun to show. Jenson looked at the mother. "Have you ever been told Georgie has a heart murmur?"

"No." The words came out as a weak sound.

Jenson looked at the mom. "Your son needs to be in the hospital for some tests."

Tears filled her eyes. "I can't do that."

"What do you mean?" Jenson asked in disbelief.

The mother sank into the chair. "I can't afford to take him to the hospital."

Jenson glanced at Bayley, who looked distressed. "Don't worry about that. All will be taken care of. We just need to get Georgie well. Nothing else matters right now."

"You're sure?" It was the mother's turn to have a look of disbelief.

Bayley went to the mother and placed a hand on her shoulder. "You can trust Dr. Hunt."

The mother nodded. "We'll go get some clothes—"

"I'm afraid Georgie needs to go to the hospital right now." He looked at Bayley and nodded toward the door. "Bayley and I are going to step out into the hall and get things ready to go."

Bayley followed him. Out of earshot of the mother and child he said, "Please call for an ambulance. Let them know I'll be right behind it."

"What's wrong?"

"Georgie is in heart failure. He needs medicine and probably surgery. It's not going away."

Bayley looked toward where the boy and mother waited. "Angie is a single mother. When she said she can't pay she meant it."

His gaze met hers. "I'll see about it. Right now we need to get that boy into the hospital."

Relief washed over her face, relaxing the tightness around her lips. "I'll get the ambulance and tell Dr. Rothchild where you've gone."

He nodded. "You did good, Bayley. You're going to be an excellent doctor. You were smart and you went with your gut."

The next hours went by in a whirlwind. Bayley checked in with her dad then headed to the hospital as soon as she could get away from the clinic. She spent the hours after Georgie had been loaded into the ambulance wondering how he was doing. It seemed like forever since Jenson had driven away as well.

He was a hero. Adding to that, he intended to see to it that Georgie's bill would be paid. That was easy to do when someone came from his background. She wasn't that fortunate. Yet she did what she could when she could.

She found Jenson in his office. He had his head down looking at something on the laptop in front of him. Knocking lightly on the door, she waited. He looked up. Jenson looked as tired as she felt. "Hey. How's Georgie? What's going on?"

"He's in surgery."

"Surgery! So soon. Angie must be going nuts. I need to find her." She started out the door.

Jenson stood and came around the desk. Taking her arm, he had her sit in the only chair in the room besides his. "Take a minute for yourself. Angie is fine. One of the social workers is sitting with her. You can go to her in a few minutes."

"What was his final diagnosis?"

"Patent ductus arteriosus." He leaned his hips against the deck edge.

"A hole in his heart. It looks like I should have been able to diagnose it."

"Don't beat yourself up about it. The murmur was very faint. You knew something wasn't right and asked for help. They'll patch the PDA and Georgie should start growing and be just fine. If it hadn't been for you he might have been too sick to have surgery."

"Thanks for that." Bayley leaned back in the chair.

Jenson crossed his legs at the ankles. "How's your father doing? I didn't even have a chance to ask you."

Bayley pushed her hair out of her face, tucking it into the band. "Much better, but I remind him every time I leave that he's not to reach for anything above his head."

"Do you think he does as you say?"

She looked at him with a tired smile. "Not even for a second."

Jenson chuckled. "I figured as much too. I know where you get that strong will from now."

She sat straighter, hands on the end of the chair arms. "I'm not strong-willed."

"Right now is a case in point." Jenson smiled.

Bayley huffed, then grinned. "You've been so great these last few days I feel like I owe you something for a thank-you."

He shook his head. "You don't owe me anything. I'm just glad I was around to help."

"I still appreciate what you've done for Dad. And Georgie. I knew something was wrong with him. I just couldn't put my finger on it, and you figured it out right away. You're handy to have around."

Jenson's eyes sparkled as a smile formed on his perfect lips. "That might be the nicest compliment I've ever had."

"Well, you're welcome, and it's true. Isn't there any way that I can say thank you?" He deserved whatever he requested.

He didn't say anything for a while as if thinking. "I could use a home-cooked meal."

Bayley straightened. "That I can do. How about coming to dinner on Saturday night? I know Dad would like to see you. He asks about you almost daily."

"That sounds good. I look forward to it. Now, let's go check on Georgie and Angie."

CHAPTER FIVE

BY SATURDAY EVENING Bayley had become nothing but a ball of nerves. When she should've been spending the day writing a paper due the next week, instead she had been making and remaking a menu, hoping she'd settle on one that would impress Jenson. Why that mattered so much she couldn't figure out.

But being born with a silver spoon in his mouth, Jenson probably had the finest cook in town. The best she could hope for was to fill him up. She had decided on roast beef and potatoes, corn and homemade rolls. Chocolate cake would be dessert. Since they were all her father's favorites she knew how to cook them well.

Her father rolled into the living room. "Something smells good in here."

"I hope so. I'm sure Jenson is used to fancy cooking and mine is plain Jane. That's all I can offer."

Her father chuckled. "I don't think he's coming over here for just food. I wouldn't worry about it too much."

She put down the hot pad on the counter. "Daddy, I don't want any matchmaking. This is not a date. This is just two friends, coworkers getting together. And you'll be here."

Her father's eyes twinkled "If you say so."

Bayley put her hands on her hips and glared at her father. "I do expect you to behave."

"I never intended to do anything but that." He gave her a smile that didn't reassure her.

Her father was enjoying this too much. It didn't help her nerves.

At the knock on the door, she hurried to open it. Jenson stood there looking better than a man should. He held a bouquet of daisies in one hand and a bottle of wine in the other. Wearing a knit collared shirt and tan slacks along with brown loafers, he came off as a smart, easy-going man who knew his way around life. All confidence and suaveness. Each time she saw him she waded in deeper and deeper.

He was nothing like she'd originally expected. Even when she'd made fun of him in front of the nurses he'd been good-natured about it. After she'd gotten to know Jenson he'd morphed into someone bigger than life. The man had heart and integrity. There wasn't much he wouldn't do for his patients. He was the polar opposite of a stuck-up rich guy who acted entitled, even though he knew all the women ogled him and were trying to get his attention.

And here she was doing the same thing.

Bayley had to swallow hard to get a word out. Pushing at her hair in a nervous motion, she stepped back with shaking hands. She never let her nerves bother her. Why with this man? "Hey. Come in."

"Hi. Something smells wonderful."

"That's your supper." She pushed her palms down the apron she still wore. Compared to him she must look like a woman who'd crawled out from under a rock.

"Don't you have one of the nurses cooking for you? Or your mother?"

"I haven't had a meal at my parents' in months." He looked directly into her eyes. "And no, I don't have any nurses cooking for me. So I'm really looking forward to this meal."

"I don't know how good it'll be." She closed the door behind him.

"Based on the smells I think it'll be just fine." He looked past her to her father. "Hello, Mr. Dodd. How're you doing this evening? Feeling better after your mishap?"

"I'm fine." Her father touched his forehead briefly. "Bayley removed the stitches yesterday. Just another war wound, I guess."

"It'll probably be to your advantage not to reach for anything above your head. Or at least for Bayley's sake. You really scared her."

"I know. I didn't intend to." Her father hung his head.

In a few words Jenson had managed to do what she couldn't do in a thousand.

Jenson patted her father on the shoulder. "I think that's the way with most people we love. We don't mean to make them worry."

Her father looked at Jenson's hands. "Hey, what do you have there? Did you bring me flowers?"

Jenson smiled at her father. "They can be for you, but actually I brought you the wine."

"I like wine better than flowers. Why don't you give those to Bayley."

"That sounds like a good plan." Jenson offered the daisies to Bayley, who smiled as if he'd given her a new car.

"I love fresh flowers." Bayley took them. An electric

shock went up her arm at his brief touch. "I'll go put them in water. They'll make a nice centerpiece for our meal."

She had to be careful or like everyone else she'd be falling for him. That she didn't need. "While I do that and get dinner on the table you can talk to Dad."

"You don't need help?"

"I can always use that." She returned to the kitchen.

Her father's attention went to the news report on TV.

This was a new concept for her. Other men she had gone out with wouldn't have offered to help or even thought of it. She looked at Jenson. "Have you ever set a table?"

"Not really."

She smirked. "That's what I figured. Someone else did it for you."

"Well, actually, yes."

"Then I'll help you." She went toward a cabinet.

"Just tell me what to do. I'm a quick learner."

She didn't doubt that for a minute. "Here are the place-mats." She opened a drawer and pulled out three green mats. "Place them on the table. Then get the plates that are in this cabinet." She pointed to the one above her head. "The plates go on top of the mats."

"I figured that much." He went about the work with the same efficiency and determination he gave being a doctor.

He came to stand close to her while he reached over her to get the plates. Too close.

Thankfully the heat of the kitchen covered her reaction to his nearness.

"Now what?"

"Fold these napkins in half." She handed him three paper napkins. "The fork goes on top of the napkin to the left side of the plate, knife on the right side with sharp edge facing in. The spoon goes next to it." She turned her back to him while she worked at the stove, pulling the oven open to check on the rolls.

"What's that heavenly smell? Fresh bread?" Jenson leaned over her shoulder.

"It is." He stood too close.

"I may love you forever."

Bayley sucked in a breath and glanced at him.

Jenson looked stricken, as if he'd said something that would cause him to be put to death, and put some distance between them. "I didn't mean—"

"I know what you meant." She looked beyond him. "You did a good job on the table."

Her father clapped. "See? You're never too old to learn something new."

"I guess if being a doctor doesn't work out for me I can work at a restaurant. What else can I help you with?"

Jenson made a quicker recovery than her. "Why don't you get the glasses down and put ice in them? The iced tea is in the refrigerator."

"That I can do without being told how." He started for the cabinet she pointed out.

She said over her shoulder, "That's good to hear."

After she'd filled the containers with food, Jenson set them on the table. She removed the rolls from the oven. Jenson stopped what he was doing and inhaled deeply. "That has to be the most wonderful smell in the world."

She pulled out the rolls.

"Oh, my goodness. Those are homemade." He inhaled deeply.

Glancing over her shoulder, she saw Jenson licking his lips like a hungry wolf.

"I can hardly wait. That's one of my favorites." Jenson stepped closer.

Her cheeks heated and not just from the warmth of the kitchen. "Good to know."

She put the rolls on a platter and put it and bowls of food on the counter. Jenson placed them on the table.

Her father said, "They're a family specialty. Bayley learned to make them when she was just a child. She's perfected them since then."

"Well, I am impressed." Jenson looked at the table. "I had no idea. If I had I might've been over here for dinner a long time ago."

"I think you needed to be invited," Bayley teased as she came around the counter.

Jenson glanced at her. "Some things you don't get unless you give a little push."

She pulled in her bottom lip, giving that thought. "Good to know. I didn't realize you work that way."

"All us Hunts do. You'd be surprised what I'll do when it's for something I want."

"I'll keep that in mind too. All right, I think we're ready here." Bayley took her chair at the end of the table. Her father pulled up to the side next to her. That left Jenson with the one to the other side of her. Over the next thirty minutes they enjoyed a meal together, making small talk about the local news and what was happening around the city.

Bayley had told her dad all about how Jenson had saved Georgie.

"How's Georgie doing?" her father asked.

"Very well. I checked in on him before I left the hospital. He was sitting up in bed and eating when I saw him. Dr. Cowan, the surgeon, is pleased with him."

Her father forked a potato. "Bayley said you were a real hero."

"Dad, I did not." Her voice rose in embarrassment.

Jenson looked at her and grinned. "I don't have a problem with you thinking I'm a hero."

She opened her mouth wide in a fake look of shock. "That figures. Already your ego is being blown out of proportion."

Jenson's eyes turned sad. "A big ego is one thing that has been beat out of me."

Bayley studied him a moment. What had happened to him to make him say something like that? Was he refuring to his ex-wife again? She didn't ask any questions about that statement despite having numerous ones.

She could tell by his tone it was a closed subject.

Jenson looked at her father. "It was more like Bayley was the hero. She's the one who pointed out something was really wrong with Georgie. She's going to be an excellent doctor."

"She should be. She's been taking care of me for long enough."

Jenson looked at Bayley. "Kristy went home today. She'll have a couple more weeks of intravenous antibiotics and home care, but she had a smile on her face when she was discharged."

"She's a good girl who is just scared of everything. After you bought her an ice cream we learned to have some on hand before we went in to do anything major. She took it better knowing she'd be getting ice cream afterwards."

Jenson wiped his mouth. "See, I can be useful."

"I never doubted it."

"Speaking of useful," her father said. "I saw that fancy envelope that came in the mail today."

Bayley's insides clinched. Her dad knew exactly what the letter concerned. It was an invitation to the gala where the recipients of the Wilcott-Ross scholarship would be announced. She narrowed her eyes. "Dad."

He gave her an innocent look.

She glanced at Jenson, whose brows moved closer at his nose. He looked confused by the conversation. Not wanting to appear rude, she felt compelled to explain. "You know exactly what it is, Dad. It's an invitation to the Wilcott-Ross Scholarship Gala."

"Oh, yeah, that's right," her father said in a guiltless fake voice.

Bayley rolled her eyes.

"Are you planning to go?" Jenson asked.

Bayley wasn't. That wasn't her type of event. Anyway, she didn't have anything to wear or extra money to buy something. "I don't know if I'm off work or not."

"Don't you need to be there to find out if you won or not?" Jenson's face turned quizzical, as if he were surprised she didn't plan to attend. "I thought this scholarship was a big deal to you."

She picked up her glass. "It is, but they'll notify me afterwards if I'm not there."

"I think you should go. You at least deserve a nice night out. You should do something for yourself," Jenson said in a firm tone.

"Now, this man is thinking straight." Her father gave her a direct look. "You should be there if they call your name."

Her name better be called. Her future training and her father's well-being depended on her getting the scholarship.

"At least show up to receive something when someone is nice enough to give it to you." Her father continued to apply pressure.

"Dad, I don't know." She looked at her empty plate. "I don't want to do something like that alone."

"I'll go with you," Jenson said.

"No, no, that's not what I meant." She hadn't been hinting for a date. Or had she?

"I know. But I have to be there as well. My family supports the event. It's the one thing I still want to take part in. It's a week from this Saturday at the Governor's Mansion, right? Why don't I pick you up about seven o'clock." Jenson sounded far more excited than she felt.

"Of course you need to go. It's at the Governor's Mansion. How often do you get to go to a party there?" Her father's excitement was audible in each word.

Bayley's heart pounded. How had this happened? But somehow she couldn't bring herself to tell him no. "Okay, I guess."

"I've had patients show more enthusiasm about surgery than you're showing at the idea of spending an evening with me."

She placed her hand on his arm then quickly removed it. "I'm sorry. I'm just out of practice where dating is concerned. If I ever did a good job at it in the first place. I really would like to have a friendly face in the crowd."

Jenson laughed. "I'll take that. It's black tie. I'll have to dust mine off."

She huffed. "I don't own an evening dress to dust off. Maybe I should stay home after all."

"Honey, I have some spare money I've been saving for a graduation present for you. Let me give it to you now.

This is a big deal. You should go and enjoy." Her father's voice held an insistent note.

Bayley started shaking her head before he finished his sentence.

That didn't stop him. "You can get a new dress and also use it for the graduation ceremony. A two for one. How about that?"

That idea did have merit. The bright look of eagerness in her father's eyes told her he really wanted to do this for her. "Okay."

Her father patted the table. "Good."

Bayley sighed. "I don't even know where to start looking."

"I can help with that problem," Jenson stated. "I know just the place. I'll pick you up next Saturday morning at ten and we'll go find you a dress. That'll give you another week to have it altered if you need to."

Bayley shook her head. "I can't ask you to do that."

Jenson said, "You didn't ask me. I volunteered."

"And you want to spend the day shopping for dresses for me?"

Jenson's mouth drew tight for a second in a wince. "Maybe not all day. The store I'm thinking about will have just what you're looking for. It shouldn't take that long."

"I still don't think it's necessary to go to so much trouble for me." Bayley didn't like a fuss over her. She was better in the background.

"I do," both men said at the same time.

She hung her head and shook it. "I'm not gonna win."

Bayley's father smiled. "I believe you are."

Her father must have noticed how uncomfortable she had become with the attention on her because he pushed back from the table a little and put his hands on his stomach. He released a small groan. "I might be full as a tick, but I sure would like to have a piece of that chocolate cake I smelled."

Jenson's head popped up. "Chocolate cake. That happens to be one of my favorites also."

Bayley laughed. "I think everything's your favorite."

"Not everything. I'm not real wild about green beans, but I do like homemade rolls and yours were excellent. And now chocolate cake. Which I have no doubt will be equally excellent." Jenson pushed his chair back as well.

"Especially when it's in my belly." Her father rubbed his middle.

"I couldn't agree with you more, sir." Jenson looked at her. His smile reached his eyes.

Moments later Bayley had slices of cake served on plates and handed out. She watched her father and Jenson all but have a private contest over who could eat theirs the fastest.

She shook her head in disbelief. "You know you guys can slow down. Nobody's gonna take it away from you. In fact, I've got plenty more."

Both gave her sheepish looks and silly grins.

"It's good, honey." Her daddy pushed the plate away.

Jenson nodded. "Really good."

"I'm surprised somebody hasn't snatched you up for your cooking alone." Her father gave her a sly grin.

"That really hasn't been an option." She kept her voice flat. Nor had the right guy come along. Yet.

"It hasn't been," her father said. "Because she won't let anybody in. She's too busy taking care of me and too busy taking care of everybody else. And going to school."

Jenson looked at her as if he were doing a scientific study. "I have noticed that about Bayley."

"Hey, you do know I'm sitting right here, don't you?" She made it sound like she was teasing but she wasn't. Of the guys she might have liked to keep, none had understood her devotion to her father or her desire to become a doctor. She needed a few moments to regroup. The conversation at the table had gotten away from her. "Why don't you two go sit in the living area while I clear up the table and kitchen. I'll fix you some coffee."

"I believe I should help with that as well. It's the least I can do." Jenson dipped his head with an apologetic look. "You'll have to tell me what to do. I don't clean many dishes except for mine and ninety percent of the time I get takeout and throw the leftovers in the trash."

"That doesn't sound healthy," her father said.

"No, it isn't. But when you're single, you're in survival mode, that's just how it is."

Together she and Jenson had the kitchen cleaned and straightened in a few minutes. Finished, they joined her father in the living area. He slept and snored softly.

"I better get him into the bed before he falls out of his chair and I'm back in the emergency room." Bayley started toward her father.

Jenson shifted his weight. "Then I'll get going. Thank you so much for supper. It was really wonderful. I appreciate you inviting me."

"I wanted to say thank you for all you've done." She followed Jenson to the door.

He glanced back at her father. "I'm just glad I could help. Your father is a really good guy. I enjoyed the evening more than you know. Please tell your dad I said bye."

"I'll do that." She opened the door and stepped out on the stoop, leaving the door ajar behind her.

Jenson paused a moment under the dim porch light. "I'd like to kiss you."

Bayley's heart skipped a beat, then kicked into high gear. Her breath caught. She placed her hands on his chest and swallowed hard. "I was hoping you would."

His head came toward hers. Anticipation and excitement swamped her. Too soon, too slow, Jenson's lips found hers. They were warm, firm and full. A hint of chocolate swirled in her nostrils. Jenson pulled her tighter as his lips pressed more intimately against her. Her blood hummed through her veins. Her body heated.

Her fingers traveled along his muscled chest to wrap around his neck. She leaned into him. He released her mouth briefly before rejoining their lips to take the kiss deeper. His tongue requested entrance and she granted it. She sighed. The man could kiss.

"Hey, get a room," a young voice called from the parking lot. A group of male laughs followed.

She and Jenson quickly broke apart, both of them looking in the direction of whoever yelled.

"I better go before I do wanna get a room. Thanks again for dinner. That kiss was the cherry on top of an extra-nice evening." His gaze fixed on hers. "I'll see you soon, Bayley."

Jenson left as if nothing had changed while Bayley was sure the world had stood still while he'd spun her around with his kisses.

The next day Jenson entered a note on the electronic chart on his office computer at the hospital. He clicked Enter and leaned back in his chair, shaking his head. He still had no idea what had gotten into him. The evening he had spent with Bayley and her father had been the most pleasurable one he'd had in a long time. A simple home with wonderful food and pleasant conversation had somehow soothed his soul. The meals at his home while growing up had been formal, tense and demanding. He'd always had everything anyone would want. His parents had been good to him but not necessarily warm. He'd never felt as if he had been understood. Yet with Bayley and her father it had been easy, relaxed.

Then he'd kissed Bayley. After that nothing had been easy or relaxed. Instead, it had been intense, heated and all-consuming. He hadn't planned to kiss her. And certainly not like he had. Why had he? He couldn't figure out what was happening to him. For over a year he'd sworn off women. Nothing serious. One-night stands. He wasn't sure if either of those were Bayley's type of thing He had no interest in getting involved with a woman again. But why couldn't he and Bayley enjoy each other? Remain friends. He would be up front with her. She would understand.

But could he manage that? For someone so sweet and unassuming, Bayley's kisses were fire. When she'd pressed herself against him his body had come alive. He'd had to resist pushing her against the door and having his way with her there on her front stoop. If they hadn't been interrupted…

He hadn't remained celibate after his divorce, but he hadn't been with a woman that often. Maybe that was it. He found Bayley fascinating because he hadn't let himself be around women that much. He shook his head. No, that wasn't it. Bayley was just special.

Pushing his chair back, he stood. He didn't have time

to sit around all day being dreamy-eyed over a woman. He had patients to see. Anyway, Bayley didn't want involvement. She'd even said she didn't have time for it. He didn't want to get in her way. He wanted to help her. Yet he wanted to spend time with her. Show her how to slow down and enjoy life. The gala was a good reason to do that. She had enough hardship in her life. Bayley deserved a nice night out.

With as many hard knocks as life had thrown Bayley, she still managed to have a big heart. She helped out wherever she could and not once had he heard her complain. She deserved wining and dining. By him. At least that was what he told himself.

He looked forward to doing his rounds just to see Bayley, but he pushed down the anticipation. He had other issues to handle before then. He had spoken to the dress store his mother and sister frequented and made an appointment for Bayley. He'd hung up the phone with a satisfied smile. He didn't know why he was making such a big deal of their date, but now that he'd arranged it he would carry through. If he had to go to the gala anyway and Bayley needed to go too they might as well go together. They would enjoy evening then he would back off. He had no desire to hurt her or lead her on, but she had taken so much convincing to agree to go with him that he didn't think she would be interested in a second date anyway.

His phone rang. Expecting it would be a number within the hospital, he was surprised to learn it was his father calling. He and his father hadn't spoken more than a few times since he had left the clinic.

"Dad," Jenson answered.

"Hello, son. Your mother missed you at Sunday lunch."

"I'm sorry about that. I had to work." At least that was an excuse his father could understand.

"Your mother misses seeing you."

"I know." Jenson did feel sorry about that. "I'll come around more often."

"How long are you going to keep this up?" Impatience rang clear in his father's voice.

"I'm not keeping anything up, Dad. I explained I needed to make a change." Why couldn't he be as concerned about Jenson as he was his precious clinic?

"I need you back at the clinic." This came as more of a demand than a request.

The spot between Jenson's shoulders tightened. "Dad, that's not going to happen. I'm happy where I am."

His father softened his voice. "Is there any way to entice you back?"

"None that I can think of." Jenson had no intention of returning to the clinic. It held too many bad memories. More than that he liked working at the hospital. Looked forward to the challenge. To seeing the people he worked with. "But I will see you at the Wilcott-Ross Scholarship Gala."

"You'll be there?" his father asked.

"I'm accompanying a friend. She's a finalist for the scholarship."

His father said nothing for a moment. "Have you taken a personal interest in this girl?"

"Not like you're making it sound. She's a coworker." Jenson's tone sounded more defensive than he'd intended. There were those kisses.

"I can put in a good word if you, say, agreed to come back to the clinic. You know the committee would listen to me."

"No! Absolutely not." Jenson wouldn't agree to that type of sacrifice. No matter how much he admired and wanted to help Bayley.

"If you change your mind—" His father's voice held a thoughtful note, as if he saw more than Jenson wanted him to.

Jenson made a sound of disgust. "I won't."

"The competition is stiff. You know my word could make the difference."

Jenson had no doubt of that. His father made his desires known wherever he went. His word could be the difference between Bayley getting the scholarship or not. Could he give his father what he wanted? How would Bayley feel about him agreeing? Did Jenson want her to have a better chance at the scholarship enough to return to the clinic?

No, he couldn't. "Again. No thanks, Dad."

CHAPTER SIX

BAYLEY'S MOUTH DROPPED open and her eyes widened when Jenson pulled into the parking lot of an exclusive dress shop in the poshest area of Atlanta. "I can't go in here."

"Why not?"

"Because it will be too much. This is the fanciest dress shop in the city. Even I have heard of it."

"Okay. So they sell dresses and you need one." He turned off the engine.

She stared at the building, its pink-and-white-striped awning and windows filled with mannequins dressed in the latest couturier. "I do, but I thought we'd be going to the mall to one of the department stores. Not a place like this."

He looked at her and grinned. "Bayley, are you being a snob again?"

"I am not!"

"Then get out of the car and let's go find you a dress."

Feeling more uncomfortable and out of place than she'd ever been, Bayley entered the store with Jenson right behind her.

A middle-aged woman approached them immediately. "You must by Ms. Dodd. Welcome."

"Uh…hi."

"How may I help you?"

Bayley glanced at Jenson. "I'm looking for a formal dress to wear to a gala."

"Wonderful. I'm sure we have just the thing. Come this way." The woman directed her toward a rack of long beautiful dresses of all shades and colors hanging along an entire wall of the store. "Sir, there's coffee and some donuts in the viewing room around the corner if you would like to wait there."

"I believe I will. Bayley, look at the dress, not the price tag first."

Bayley wrinkled up her nose at him.

"Your father wants you to have what you want." With that, Jenson strolled out of sight.

The woman cleared her throat, bringing Bayley's attention back to her. "Now, do you have any ideas about what you like?"

Over the next thirty minutes Bayley, with the woman's help, pushed dresses around on the racks and pulled others out. With each one Bayley showed some interest in, the woman moved it into a dressing room.

At the end of the row the woman said, "Would you like to try these on now?"

"I guess so." Bayley had dared to look at a number of the price tags. She and her father needed to put their money to better use than buying her a fancy dress. But she had to remind herself that wasn't what he wanted.

With the woman's help she slipped on the first dress. A baby blue one with puffy sleeves. Bayley stood in the small dressing room moving back and forth.

"Come this way. There are more mirrors." The woman led her out to a stage area.

Bayley sucked in a breath. Jenson sat in a cushioned

chair with a coffee cup on a table beside him looking at a magazine. She'd had no intention of modeling for him.

His gaze met hers then skimmed down her body. "That one looks very nice on you."

"Thank you." The words were barely audible. Heat washed through her like Earl Grey after the first frost.

"Now you can see from all sides." The woman encouraged Bayley to look into the mirrors on three sides of her.

The dress looked nice on her. She reached for the price tag. The price she could afford. "I'll take it."

"No, she won't," Jenson said from behind her. "Not until she's tried on all those other ones she picked out."

Bayley looked over her shoulder. "You don't want to hang around here while I do that."

"I don't mind. Especially if the show continues to be this good."

That heat he created went to her cheeks. She glanced away to find the woman had discreetly stepped back to the dressing room area. Her gaze returned to Jenson's.

His look remained level with hers. "Now I'd like to see the next one."

She lifted the hem of the dress. "Since you insist."

"I do."

An hour later Jenson pronounced, "That's the one."

"Really? I've never really worn this color." Bayley turned to see her back in the mirror.

"You look like a lovely yellow rose."

The sunny dress she wore set off her skin color perfectly. Despite the dress being demurer in cut in the front it dipped almost to her waist in the back. A zipper went down the center to the hem of the gown. She shook her head. It hugged her curves too closely. "Don't you think it's a little too…suggestive for an awards ceremony?"

Jenson grinned. "In my opinion the right amount. But you should be comfortable. Confident. If you don't think you can be in this one then don't get it. But I can assure you that you look amazing."

"I've never worn anything so beautiful." She held the skirt, making a small twist one way then the other.

"You should more often. It suits you."

If he liked it on her that much, then she'd get it. Maybe it was time she stepped out of her comfort zone some. "Then I'll get it. Thanks to you I'll be confident about how I'm dressed and not focus so much on my worry over the scholarship."

Jenson wished he could ease Bayley's concerns over the scholarship. He had seen first-hand the help it would be to her and her father. Her angst while buying a dress had more to do with the pressure to win the scholarship and less to do with what the dress looked like.

He could help her; after all, his father had offered. Would it be so wrong for him just to say that Bayley was an exceptional person, deserving of the scholarship? He looked at Bayley again as the saleswoman fussed around the bottom of the dress. Could he return to his father's clinic in order to help her?

Soon they were in the car with Bayley's dress secure on the back seat hanger.

"How about lunch before I take you home?" He didn't want to part with her yet.

"I guess we could do that. But I'd rather stop by the hospital and see Johnny. He wasn't feeling at all well yesterday."

"Why don't we do both? Watching you change dresses made me hungry." In more ways than one.

She gave him a smirk. "Yeah, I'm sure you broke a sweat with all that work you were doing."

He'd broken out in a sweat, but it hadn't been from doing work. She didn't need to know that. "A quick meal and then a visit at the hospital."

Ten minutes later he pulled into an empty parking lot.

"Why're we here?" Bayley looked around.

"For lunch."

"At the food truck?" Her eyes brightened as she unbuckled her seat belt.

"Yep."

"I love food truck food." She opened the door and climbed out.

"I was counting on that." His ex-wife had always turned her nose up at the mention of food truck fare. That was one of many things Jenson liked about Bayley. She wasn't afraid to eat.

He ordered them hot dogs, chips and drinks. They sat at one of the wooden picnic tables facing each other to eat.

"You know, this is fun. I should do it more often." Bayley looked around.

"You should take time to do a lot of things." Jenson took a large bite of his hot dog.

"Yeah. But unlike for you it isn't that easy."

He raised his chin. "Hey, I work for a living too."

"Yes, you do. And hard, I might add. That was unfair for me to say. When I first met you, I thought you would be an entitled, self-absorbed man. I was pleasantly surprised to find out differently."

"Wow. I'm glad I proved you wrong." He paused. "But at one time you might have been right. I'm not sure I was the type of person you would've liked."

"I'm sure you'd have made me come around."

"Thanks for that. I'd like to think so." But would she have really? He wasn't sure he liked who he was back then. "I do know you've helped change my view of life."

"For the better, I hope."

Sweet, kind and considerate Bayley couldn't have done it any other way. "Definitely for the better."

Bayley walked beside Jenson on the way to the nurses' station. She couldn't miss the curious looks of the staff, but she held her head high and didn't flinch. There was nothing wrong with her and Jenson being together. After all, they were there to see one of their patients. At least that was what she told herself.

She knocked on the door to Johnny's room. At the weak "Come in," she pushed open the door. Johnny lay in the bed. The lights were dim and the TV was on but the sound had been turned off. A gloomy heaviness of despondency hung in the air.

Jenson stepped around her. "Johnny, how you doing, bud? I thought I'd find you playing the new-old *Mario Brothers*."

"I don't really feel like playing. I just want to sleep."

Bayley stepped to the bed. "Hey, I don't blame you. It gets tiring to be in the hospital all the time."

"I hate it," the boy all but spat.

"I know you do," Jenson said. "I know you also hate us poking, but I need to examine you. It won't take long. I promise. Bayley, would you help Johnny sit up?"

"Sure." Bayley stepped behind Johnny and slid an arm behind his back. She supported the boy, who was too weak to hold himself up.

Jenson placed the bell of his stethoscope on Johnny's

back and listened. His gaze met hers. Concern filled his beautiful eyes. Johnny was worse than she'd feared. "You can lie back now."

Bayley lowered Johnny with gentleness to the mattress. "You'll get through this. A new heart will come soon."

"I'm okay but I'm worried about my mother."

Bayley tried to put some cheer in her voice but failed. "I'm sure she's more worried about you."

"I don't like for her to worry." The teen settled in the bed.

Jenson continued to check Johnny's heart.

"I think parents just do it anyway. I know I would if I had a kid as great as you." Bayley patted his shoulder.

Her gaze met Jenson's. He had an odd look on his face. As if he wasn't sure what to do next.

Jenson's focus returned to Johnny. "Thanks for letting me check you out. When you feel up to it you let your nurse know and we'll get in a game, okay?"

"Okay," came Johnny's weak reply.

Jenson stepped to the door.

Bayley followed. "Go to sleep, Johnny. I'll see you tomorrow."

In the hall with the door closed between them and Johnny, Jenson said, "He has regressed. I need to check his labs." A minute later at the nurses' station he picked up the electronic pad and typed in his code. Johnny's chart appeared seconds later.

Bayley stood beside him looking at it as Jenson's finger scrolled through the pages of lab work. Her heart sank as her chest tightened. Johnny's lab values were not good.

Jenson shook his head. "He's sicker than he looks. And he looks awful."

She looked down the hall toward Johnny's room. "I didn't want to say it."

"I want to review his last ECHO and EKG." Jenson stepped behind the desk to one of the computer monitors. Seconds later he had the pictures on the screen.

Bayley joined him. A look at the tests confirmed what she'd feared. Johnny had slipped into serious trouble. She took a deep breath and let it go slowly.

"Based on the tests alone he should be moved up on the transplant list." Jenson clicked off the screen.

Bayley blinked to keep the moisture under control. "What if he doesn't get one in time?"

Jenson took her elbow and directed her toward the small conference room down the hall. He pulled Bayley inside.

"Honey." He brought her into his arms. "You're never going to survive being a doctor if you come to tears over every patient."

Bayley wrapped her arms around his waist and hung on. "I know I shouldn't care so much but some patients just get to you. Johnny is just one of those for me."

"He's gotten to me too. I know that tender heart of yours is what will make you a great doctor."

"Thanks." She stepped away from him. "That's if I get that scholarship."

Jenson looked at Bayley's glistening eyes. She had to finish her training. The world deserved the loving, caring and dedicated physician she would be. He would do what he could to help make that happen. Tonight, he'd be speaking to his father about putting a good word in for Bayley.

No matter what it cost Jenson.

* * *

A week later Jenson stood on the doorstep of Bayley's apartment waiting on her to invite him in. Instead, she studied him. A more accurate phrase would be that her gaze traveled over him. He liked it. Her attention remained on him as if she was recording every detail and he was her favorite piece of candy. Yes, he really liked it. Too much.

Bayley looked breathtakingly gorgeous herself. Her wearing the yellow dress still took his breath away. She had pulled her hair back on one side, letting the rest of the waves skim the top her shoulders. His fingers itched to touch the silky strands. The long expanse of neck exposed left him much to admire and desire. Could he get a little taste?

"I like your tie." Bayley's voice sounded breathy, as if she'd been doing physical activity.

The fleeting thought she might sound the same when making love had him pulling at his collar. "Thank you. I thought it added a little splash of color." He fingered his red plaid bow tie.

"I've always thought you got plenty of attention without going to any trouble."

Her teasing tone made his eyes narrow. Did she think he liked the attention? "Thanks. I think."

"You know half the staff at the hospital think you're super handsome."

Jenson leaned closer, his look meeting hers. "I'm only interested in what you think."

She grinned. "Oh, I don't disagree with them."

He smiled. "That's good to hear."

"But there are other things I like more about you." Her gaze remained locked with his.

"That's an interesting statement. Care to elaborate?"

Her eyes twinkled and she shook her head. "I don't think so. I think your ego has been stroked enough for one night already."

There had been a time when he would have said his ego had been stomped out of him leaving nothing but humiliation. But that he could even think back on those days was progress forward. "That dress really suits you. You look lovely."

"Are you using your charm on me, Dr. Hunt?"

Did he want to? Each day it had become more difficult to know. He'd stepped up to help her when he wanted nothing to do with returning to the Hunt Clinic. What did he want? "Is it working?"

"Bayley, don't leave the man standing outside. Invite him in," her father called from behind her.

She startled then stepped back and let Jenson into the apartment.

"You both look very nice." Her father moved his chair until he sat between them. Jenson offered his hand to the older man.

"Thank you, sir, for letting me escort your daughter."

"She's old enough she doesn't need my blessing. But you have it. Y'all enjoy your evening." To Bayley he said, "Ralph's coming over to play cards and will stay until I'm settled in bed, so don't worry about coming home early to see about me, honey. I'll be just fine."

Bayley looked at her father. "Dad, you promise to stay away from the kitchen cabinets?"

Her father raised his hand. "I promise. Now go have a good time. You don't want Jenson to get tired of waiting."

Bayley looked at Jenson.

His gaze met hers. "I don't mind waiting on a good thing."

She kissed her father goodbye.

"I'll have my fingers crossed for you tonight." Her father waved them toward the door. "Go have a wonderful time. Whether you get the scholarship or not we'll make it, Dr. Dodd."

"That's one of many things I love about you, Dad, you're always positive."

Jenson wanted some of that care he saw between father and daughter. What would it be like to have Bayley's concern? If just for a little while. He took her elbow and moved her toward the door.

Sometime tonight they needed to discuss this thing growing between them. He'd not intended to get this involved with Bayley or any other woman for that matter. Yet she pulled at him. Maybe if he just got her out of his system he could move on. Would she settle for that?

And...he needed to talk to her about his agreement with his father. She wouldn't take it well knowing he'd gone behind her back. But would her pride, her father's pride, accept he was just trying to help? Jenson just wanted her to have the scholarship so badly.

With the door closed behind them Jenson led her down the sidewalk to a long, sleek, shiny black car. The chauffeur stood beside it holding the door open.

He grinned when Bayley's mouth opened, then closed, and she stopped to look at him.

"You didn't have to do all of this."

"I know, but I thought it would be fun to be driven tonight. That way I can sit in the back and spend some time with you. Maybe help keep your mind off the scholarship announcements." He took her hand and held it.

Bayley looked around. A few people were out. They

watched them. She chuckled softly. "We look like two roses amongst the thorns in my neighborhood."

"I don't think we stand out that much." He helped her in then climbed in behind her.

"Check out those kids over there." Bayley pointed from behind the tinted glass of the window.

Jenson looked in the direction she'd indicated. Two boys pointed back.

"Okay, maybe we do look out of place." That was just another thing about Bayley that he liked—her sense of humor. Instead of being self-conscious she could enjoy the moment. At least for a moment she didn't look like she wanted to run in the other direction because of frayed nerves.

The driver smoothly drove them through the gates of the Governor's Mansion and up the long drive to the portico to line up behind the other cars unloading. When it was their turn to get out, the driver hurried to open their door. Jenson stepped out, offered Bayley a hand and helped her from the car.

Jenson whispered close to her ear as they entered the house, "Smile. You're much too gorgeous not to. You've got this."

She returned a smile that didn't reach her eyes. "This is such a beautiful place. The light glowing. I feel like I'm in a fairy tale and I'm far too old for one of those."

"You look like a princess, so embrace the moment." Jenson placed her hand on his arm.

A number of people spoke to him as they entered the large room set with tables before a small stage. He placed his hand over hers to reassure her before he introduced her to each of them. Slowly she seemed less prepared to run and her body relaxed.

As they walked away from the third couple, Bayley whispered, "I've never done anything like this before and I don't want to embarrass you."

"Honey, there's no way you can embarrass me. You're the loveliest person here." For months he had slinked around with embarrassment over his stupidity where Darlene and Brett were concerned. Tonight, he had confidence he could handle any remark that came his way as long a Bayley remained at his side.

She made him feel stronger somehow. Her goodness seemed to rub off on everybody, including him. She looked beautiful, timid, yet glorious. In an odd way he wanted to take credit for having brought out those qualities in her, but in reality, they shined through despite him.

"These are just not my type of people." She looked around the room.

"They're not mine either, but we'll make out just fine together."

Bayley stood close, looking at him. "How can you say that?"

His gaze met her darker one. "They're not who I am. I'll tell you what, I'll make a deal with you. As soon as the scholarships are announced you can decide if you want to leave or not."

"Deal." She nodded, looking pleased with his suggestion.

Jenson hoped the evening ended well for her. The strained pull around her lips let him know Bayley's apprehension had grown once more. Her hands trembled slightly whenever the scholarship announcements were mentioned. This night meant so much to her. In turn he found it mattered to him more than it should. Both their lives hung on the name called as winner. He had become too involved with Bayley. After tonight he would back off, he reminded himself. Not let it go any further.

Jenson squeezed her hand. "My mother and father are headed this way. Prepare yourself."

"I hadn't expected to meet them." Panic filled her voice.

"Dad is on the board."

The entire day Bayley hadn't been able to sit still. She'd gone from one worry to another. She didn't want to disappoint Jenson. And she needed that scholarship. She smoothed her hands down the sides of the silky material of her dress.

Despite being pleased with her appearance and not being easily intimidated, the idea of meeting Jenson's parents made her legs shake. She knew and worked with a number of respected and renowned doctors, but Jenson's father's status went beyond the others. But her nervousness tonight didn't stem from the fact that Jenson's father was such a well-respected man in the city, but from the knowledge he was Jenson's parent.

Bayley was no Cinderella. She knew right where her shoes were. Jenson looked like every woman's dream in his black tux with the shiny lapel. And his tie. It just made him more appealing. He had a sense of the dramatic. His hair had been recently trimmed. Clean-shaven and wearing a white shirt she would put him up against any man in the good looks department. He might be handsome but his personality drew her to him. He was an excellent doctor, a man with a big heart and a great sense of humor. She couldn't ask for a more supportive friend.

She didn't know what she had done to gain Jenson's notice. She had to admit his attention built up her ego.

Yet they were so different. From two different worlds. She needed to keep her eyes on the prize: finishing her medical training. There wasn't space in her life for being sidetracked by her fascination with Jenson. She needed to remember he wouldn't always be at her side. A fancy night out wasn't her regular world.

Jenson stiffened beside her. She looked at the older couple coming in their direction. Jenson looked very much like his father. The only difference was the older version was heavier and had a smattering of gray hair. Jenson would age well.

There was no heartwarming, slapping-of-the-back type of greeting between father and son.

"I'm pleased to see you here," his father said in a condescending tone.

"I came to support Bayley." Jenson placed his hand at her waist. "She's a finalist for the scholarship. Bayley, this is my father, Jim Hunt."

"It's nice to meet you, sir. Jenson has been a great addition to Atlanta Children's."

The older man gave her a long look at if he were figuring out a puzzle. "Is that so? We need him back at the clinic where he belongs."

Bayley took a step back, but Jenson held her steady.

Jenson's mother placed her hand on his father's arm. "Jim, let's not do that tonight."

The woman standing next to the older Mr. Hunt was elegantly dressed in a gold gown that worked around her generous curves. Her smile was warm and welcoming. She immediately reached her arms out for a hug from her son, who dwarfed her in height. "Jenson, why don't you come see your mama more?"

This woman Bayley could easily like.

Jenson stepped into his mother's arms. A genuine affection between the two was obvious.

"I'm going to do better. I promise, Mama."

Jenson's mother pulled back and studied her son. "At least you look happy."

Jenson looked at Bayley, bringing her up to stand beside him. "Mom, I'd like for you to meet Bayley Dodd."

His mother's astute eyes swept over Bayley a moment. A smile formed on her lips. "It's a pleasure to meet you."

Bayley smoothed her hands down the material of her dress. "And you too."

"You look lovely, dear." Jenson's mother smiled at Bayley.

A man came to the microphone and asked everyone to find their seats.

"Mom and Dad, we'll see you later. I believe Bayley is supposed to sit at one of the tables up front with the other scholarship finalists."

His mother said, "I had no idea. That's wonderful."

"Honey, I thought I told you that," Jenson's father said, giving Jenson a pointed look. "I expect you to keep your word."

Jenson's skin blanched for a second before the color returned.

Somebody called Senior Dr. Hunt's name and Jenson's parents headed in that direction. What had his comment been about?

"We should find our seats." Jenson took Bayley's hand.

Was something going on she knew nothing about? Whatever it was, it wasn't her business. It didn't involve her.

At their table they introduced themselves to the others seated there. A few people Jenson knew, and one Bayley recognized from the hospital. The conversation became lively around them as their dinner was served. Mostly Bayley just listened.

Bayley didn't taste her food and finally gave up trying. Tonight was it. She needed the scholarship, but she had no doubt others did as well.

Jenson leaned close. "You need to eat something. I can't have you fainting."

"I've never fainted in my life." She sat straighter and picked up a roll. Taking a bite, she tried to settle the army marching through her midsection.

"There's always a first time."

She gave him a weak smile. "I just want this over with. I'm just worried about how it will affect Dad if I don't win. This would really help get him into a place where he could take care of himself. Then give me a chance to save for surgery. Too much of our lives depend on this."

His jaw tightened for a second. "Why don't we just enjoy ourselves tonight and worry about all that tomorrow."

Bayley leaned into him. "Despite how it might appear, I'm glad you came with me."

He chuckled. "I'm glad to know that serious look on your face has nothing to do with me. I'll tell you what, when this is over, I'll take you out for an ice cream."

She smiled. "I'm gonna hold you to that."

Jenson took her hand and squeezed it. "Don't worry about it. It'll be over soon."

"You sound mighty confident as a man who didn't have to worry about putting himself through school."

"That may be so but that doesn't mean I don't understand being nervous, or disappointment. Not that you'll be disappointed." His hurt showed in his eyes.

"I'm sorry. I shouldn't have said that. You've been great. You work hard. I know you're a wonderful doctor because I've seen it. Whatever happens I'm proud to have come with you tonight."

"Thank you. That's the nicest thing someone has said to me in a long time." He brushed his lips against her temple.

Bayley shivered, forgetting all about the scholarship. She looked at him, her lips just an inch from his. Jenson held her complete attention.

"For now, stop worrying over the scholarship. You got it in the bag."

He said that with a confidence Bayley didn't feel.

Jenson couldn't help but feel sorry for Bayley. She was a bundle of nerves. When had receiving something been that important to him? He wanted this for her. If what his father had implied was correct, she would have her wish come true. But she must never know he had been involved.

The chairman of the board stepped behind the podium. "And now for what we're here for…awarding scholarships."

As he announced the winners of the different scholarships Bayley grew more tense. She shifted in her seat, clutched her hands in her lap and then wrapped them in the folds of her dress before twisting the napkin that was still in her lap from dinner.

From the years Jenson had been required to attend the Wilcott-Ross Scholarship Gala, he was aware the largest award would be the last presented. He scooted closer to Bayley, putting his arm along the back of her chair and cupping her shoulder, hoping to ease her anxiety. She gave him a weak smile of thanks.

He wasn't sure if anything he did would help until she knew if she had won or not. He was tempted to offer her the value of the scholarship if just to see her out of pain. Yet she wouldn't accept the money. The strain on Bayley must have rubbed off on him because his stomach had started to roil. She wanted the scholarship badly, and it mattered to him if she received it.

From his father's innuendo it seemed he had put in a good word for her, but that didn't mean it would be successful. If it did work, it would be worth the price to have Bayley happy.

Not soon enough, the chairman cleared his throat. "Now for the Wilcott-Ross scholarship."

Jenson removed his arm from around Bayley and took her hand. It trembled. In a slow movement, he brushed the top of her hand with the pad of his thumb. She held his hand tighter.

"With this scholarship, the recipient may use it as they need," the chairman continued. "Not only for books or tuition, but housing or other needs they might have while finishing up their medical training. There are a number of excellent candidates this year, which is always the case. That makes the decision difficult."

Bayley pulled her hand from his. She clasped both in her lap.

"And this year's recipient of the Wilcott-Ross is…" The chairman paused.

Jenson held his breath. Would his father fail him? Would Bayley's heart be crushed?

"Bayley Dodd."

The room erupted in applause.

Bayley slumped like an unwatered plant against him.

Jenson stood, helping her to her feet. He gave her a hug. "Congratulations. Now you better go up there and get it."

She smiled. Her eyes glistened. "I'll do that."

Jenson returned the smile that covered the sick knot in his stomach. He would have to return to the clinic. But Bayley's joy overrode his sorrow. Maybe he could talk to his father and honor his agreement in another way. More than that, could he keep his part in her winning from her? Jenson would worry about all that later.

With her shoulders held proudly high, Bayley walked to the podium. Jenson's chest couldn't help but swell with pride. He'd done nothing that should have made him feel that way. If anything, he should be experiencing guilt. But the look on Bayley's face made him believe he had done the correct thing.

The chairman handed her the certificate. "Would you like to say a few words?"

Bayley nodded and stepped behind the podium. "I'd like to thank the board and the committee for the honor of receiving this scholarship. I'll work every day to make you proud. Thank you."

The crowd clapped as she made her way back to the table. As she passed people, they spoke to her and patted her on the shoulder in encouragement. She joined him with a bright smile on her face. He brought her in for another hug. Bayley returned it.

Jenson's gaze found hers. "I'm so proud of you."

"I didn't do anything special."

"Just being you is special enough. Apparently, the committee thought so too."

The chairman started to speak again, and they quickly

took their chairs. After a few closing remarks the program was over. Bayley had to join the group of scholarship winners for pictures. Jenson waited for her at the table.

His father's voice came from behind him. "I got her the scholarship so I'll expect you back at the clinic as soon as you can resign. I kept my end of the bargain."

Jenson turned. "Can we meet and talk about it?"

"We can, but I want you back where you belong."

Jenson's heart sunk. What had made him think his father wouldn't hold him to the agreement? Despite his desire not to, he would keep his word. No matter how much he hated the idea. A person's word mattered. Honesty mattered. That was something his ex-wife never understood.

Until then he would enjoy what little time he had with Bayley. Tonight was her night and he would worry about his father and facing all those who had watched his marriage implode tomorrow.

His mother joined them.

"I'm so glad your friend won," his mother gushed. "And she looked just lovely. She seems to be a very special person."

"She is." Jenson didn't know anyone nicer or more deserving of the scholarship.

His mother patted his arm. "I'm glad you found someone special."

"It's not like that. We're just friends. Work colleagues." Or had he started to feel more?

His mother watched him. "Friends don't look at each other like you two do."

Thankfully, his parents were called away once again, which allowed Jenson some breathing room to digest what his mother had said. Did it really look like they were a couple to everyone? He hadn't wanted to become so involved with Bayley. A few weeks ago he would have said the idea of him giving up his new life to return to his old for her sake would have never entered his mind. And look at him now.

Bayley walked toward him with a beaming smile on her face, glowing. She looked so happy. Almost as if the weight of the world had been lifted from her. He wanted to kiss her to feel her delight with her world.

Whatever sacrifice he had to make would be worth it. Bayley could use a break in life and her father needed it. But that's where it stopped. It was time to put some distance between them. Make sure she understood they were to remain friends only.

Her light pulled at him. Made him seek her side. He walked in her direction. Reaching Bayley, he slipped his arm around her waist. "I'm proud of you."

She stepped close. "You ready to go?"

"Only when you are. You deserve to enjoy this moment."

Bayley picked up her purse from her chair. "I'm ready. I just need to step out into the hall to call my father and let him know."

"He'll be anxious to hear. Why don't you do that in the quietness of the car?"

She nodded. "That's a good idea."

Taking her hand, Jenson moved toward the door. There they waited with others for their cars. Soon theirs arrived and they settled inside. Moments later Bayley had her father on the phone. From her tone Jenson could tell how excited her father was for her.

"I just can't believe it, Dad," she kept saying over and

over, then ended the call with "I love you too." Bayley's arms wrapped around one of his as she leaned into him. "I feel like celebrating."

"Practical Bayley Dodd wants to let loose?" He grinned.

"I think she would like that." Her lips curled up.

"It's still early. What would you like to do? Go to a bar? Or we could go to my place. I have a bottle of champagne I've been saving and half a box of ice cream. Interested?"

"That sounds like a pickup line." She leaned her cheek against his upper arm.

He kissed the top of her head. "Maybe so, but I won't make you go if you don't want to."

She studied him for a moment.

Jenson held his breath, fearing she would say no. He would put that distance he promised himself between them tomorrow. Right now, he wanted to experience this happy Bayley. The one who had dropped the weight of the world from her shoulders for a while.

"Yes, I think I'd like that. A quiet celebration between us. And I'd like to see where you live. But I can only stay a little while. I need to get home before my father wakes."

"I'll take you home whenever you're ready to go." He told the limo driver the new address. When they arrived at his apartment complex he told the driver, "I'll see the lady home."

CHAPTER SEVEN

BAYLEY FLEW HIGH in her excitement. Her mind spun with the reality of winning. Or maybe it was the impossible becoming possible. Already the bills she could pay ran through her mind. The apartment she could get for her father. Somehow all her dreams seemed achievable.

The relief in her father's voice was enough reason to celebrate winning the scholarship. It wasn't until hearing it that she realized how much he worried. He carried the burden of not being able to help more. She didn't feel that way despite having most of the financial responsibility while going to school. For the first time in her life, she could think of the future in something more than dollars and cents.

Jenson directed her toward a black door in the large gated complex of two-story apartments.

"I could just squeal."

Jenson looked around. "Go ahead. No one will care."

She'd do it! She swung her arms wide and spun around, letting out a loud happy yell. It was the first time she'd been this carefree since she was a child. Since before her mother left.

Jenson laughed from deep in his belly before he caught her in his arms. The sound of him joining her in her fun had her laughing too. He whirled her around, bringing her feet off the ground. Slowly he brought her to a stop. She leaned against his chest.

Their gazes met, held before his lips found hers in a tender kiss. Too quickly the cool of the evening brushed her mouth. Jenson's warmth had gone.

"I better get you inside before you get cold." His hand lingered at her waist as they continued toward his door.

She liked Jenson touching her. Too much. If she wasn't careful, he could be a distraction on the way to meeting her goals.

Inside he led her down a short hallway to a kitchen/ living combination at the back of the house. The area had only the necessary seating with no extras, not even pictures on the wall. She kicked off her shoes and climbed onto a bar stool where she could watch as Jenson worked in the kitchen. "I still can't believe it."

"I did hear your name called," he teased as he removed his jacket and tie and placed them over the back of another bar stool. He then undid the top two buttons of his shirt.

The man looked good in anything. "Tomorrow I'm going to start hunting for a place for Daddy and me. With the help of the scholarship, I can even pick up one more shift at the clinic. They need me there badly."

"Typical Bayley."

She glared at him "What do you mean by that?"

"Nothing. Just that even in your joy you're thinking about helping others instead of yourself. It's an impressive attribute."

"Shouldn't everyone?"

"Yes, they should. But not everyone does." Did he know many unselfish people?

"I don't think I've ever felt this good in my life." She twisted on the stool.

He popped the cork off the champagne and filled the tall glasses in a practiced matter of someone who had done it often. "I don't know if I think that sounds sad or good."

"Oh, it's definitely good."

He handed her a bubbling glass. "I haven't had champagne but a few times." She took a sip and sighed. Glancing at Jenson, she found him grinning. "Is something wrong?"

"Not at all. I was just enjoying your happiness." He lifted his filled glass in a salute. "To the victor. No one deserves it more than you. It's nice to see you so happy."

They took a sip from their glasses.

"Are you happy?" she asked.

"I'm happier now than I've been in a long, long time." A shadow of sadness flashed across his eyes then was gone. What had he been thinking about? "It makes me happy to see you happy."

"Why were you unhappy?" Despite her struggles and her father's, she'd never thought of herself as being an unhappy person.

"I didn't know I was unhappy during my marriage. It was afterward that I realized it. Now that I'm away from my marriage and the clinic I can see I wasn't as happy as I could have been."

"It's a good thing you made changes. I'm glad you're happy now. I wouldn't like to think you're not."

"You worry about others too much, but it's sweet. Let's go sit in the living room. Get comfortable. I'll bring our ice cream over there." He indicated the sofa and chair arrangement in the middle of a larger living space.

She picked up his glass and carried it with her. "I like a little chocolate sauce on top of my ice cream if you have it."

"Coming right up."

"I love a man who's prepared." Bayley stopped short. She looked back at him. "I didn't mean—"

"I know what you meant."

After setting the flutes on the square wooden coffee table, she sank into the cushions at one end of his buttery leather sofa. It was the nicest piece of furniture she'd ever sat on. She and her father had the same couch they'd had all her life. She ran a hand over the covering. What would it be like to enjoy something like this every day?

Soon Jenson joined her carrying two bowls filled to the top with vanilla ice cream. One covered in chocolate. He handed that one to her. "For the lady."

"Goodness, so much."

"We're celebrating." He sat on the other end of the sofa and looked her up and down.

Bayley's body heated. She liked that look coming from Jenson.

They spent a few minutes enjoying their ice cream and champagne.

"Mmm…" She licked her lips. Placing her spoon in the bowl, she looked at Jenson. He watched her with a particular intensity on his face. "Is something wrong?"

"No, I was just enjoying those sexy sounds you were making."

"Oh." What could she say to that?

When Bayley finished she set her bowl on the table and turned to face Jenson. "That was wonderful. The perfect way to celebrate."

"My thoughts are, if you're going to have ice cream it

might as well be good ice cream. Ice milk and some of that other stuff is a waste of taste buds."

She laughed. "As usual, you're right, Dr. Hunt. Did you always wanna be a doctor?"

"I guess it was more like I never knew you could be anything else. With my family's heritage, being a doctor was expected of me. You know, grandfather, father, son."

"Are your siblings doctors?"

Jenson put the bowl on the table beside hers. "My sister isn't but her husband is. They met when he came to work at the clinic. My brother is a doctor in the Army. When he gets out he will come work for the clinic. My father expects all the males in the family to join his practice."

"You like being a doctor, don't you?" Bayley watched him closely. His eyes brightened.

"I do, very much. I found that regardless of the pressure to become a doctor, it's also the type of work I should be doing. My calling."

"It shows." She tugged at her dress, getting comfortable.

"Would you like more champagne?" Jenson placed his empty glass on the table as well.

She picked up her champagne flute. "No, I still have plenty. Tell me a story about when you were happy." She leaned her head back on the high arm of the sofa.

"We sure are spending a lot of time on happiness tonight."

"That's because I am happy and I want everybody else to be, especially you." She finished her drink.

He smiled. "I'm happy right now being with you."

"Are you dodging the question?"

Jenson sighed. "One summer my family went to this ranch for a week. We didn't know anyone else there. We rode horses, canoed, camped out and ate from a campfire. My father was completely present. He got no calls. We were just there having a good time. I wish there had been more of those times."

She liked seeing the look of pleasure on his face. "That's a nice memory. I've never been away for longer than a few days. A week would be heaven."

"A week on the Riviera for you." He smiled.

"Yes, that would be nice. Very nice. Not likely to happen but really nice." She couldn't stop the dreamy note from entering her voice. She hugged herself. "You know, it really was amazing to hear my name called."

"You are amazing." He tugged her across the sofa until she sat close.

Jenson planned to kiss her. Bayley would let him. She wanted it. Wanted him.

His head bent. His mouth found hers. Heaven.

Bayley curled into him, taking what he would give.

Jenson pulled her into his lap without breaking contact between them. He untangled her dress and adjusted her legs across his. Bayley's arms wrapped around his neck while she pressed into his chest. He took the kiss deeper. His tongue traced the line of her lips, encouraging her to open for him.

Her warm, eager tongue greeted him. His blood ran hot. He hadn't wanted to admit how much he wanted Bayley, but he wanted her badly. After the talk of his past and the reality of returning to the clinic he needed to escape into Bayley to forget. Reality would come soon enough. Facing the matter of what he had done, and the price of having done it, would come later. Right now, his desire for Bayley was all he could handle. One of his hands traveled over her material-covered thigh to her hip to cup her behind.

She shifted toward him. Her fingers threaded through his hair, holding his mouth to hers. Bayley returned his kiss. When he pulled back, she murmured a complaint. Bayley seemed as if she wanted him as much as he needed her.

His mouth traveled over her cheek. She leaned back so he could follow the length of her neck. He nibbled the top of her shoulder.

"You taste so sweet." He kissed the curve of her shoulder. "Much better than ice cream."

Bayley giggled.

The sound, so much like the tinkling of bells, fueled his desire. One of his hands brushed the side of a breast.

"I like that."

He cupped the full orb. Perfect. "What about this?"

"That's nice too." Bayley placed her palms on his cheeks and brought his mouth back to hers. She gifted him with a hungry kiss.

While one of his arms held her secure the other fondled her breast, teasing her nipple. He wanted to touch flesh. Bayley moaned when his fingers left her. His index finger traced the line along one side of her V-shaped neckline to the bottom and just as slowly returned to her shoulder. She shivered.

On his next pass he dipped his finger beneath the edge of the dress at the curve of her breast. Bayley's body tensed. Her breaths came faster. His finger teased her breast. She held her breath, waiting on him to touch her nipple. When he removed his finger, she released the air she had been holding.

His lips left hers to nibble behind her ear. His finger

continued down to the center of the V to return to the spot he'd slipped beneath. This time he went further. Her nipple had hardened, making a peak of the material. He brushed close but didn't touch her ridged tip.

Traveling to her shoulder he pushed at the narrow strap. His lips caressed the skin revealed. He said softly, "I want to see more of you. May I see more of you? Touch you?"

"You'll have to undo my dress." She twisted until her back was to him.

With a hand he was surprised to feel shaking. He hesitated on the zipper.

"As much as I want to do this, I think we should talk first."

She looked at him. "Hey, I'm a big girl. I know the score here."

"Do you?"

"Yeah. I get it. I'm good with it. We have tonight. Neither of us are making any long-term promises. This is for us now. I think that we're adult enough to be friends afterwards. This is a celebration. Sharing some happiness for tonight only."

"If you're sure you want to?" He studied her.

"I can't think of anything I want more."

Slowly he undid her zipper to reveal her tailbone. He ran the back of his hand over the delicate bone before placing small kisses over her back. The hiss of Bayley's breath tightened his already full manhood. He blew over her skin. She shivered. Her reactions fed his need to create more.

With a last brush of her skin, he returned to lowering her zipper as far as her seated position would allow. The skirt flapped open, but the dress remained held in place at the shoulders. "Beautiful."

She squirmed. Her butt brushed against his swollen manhood, sending fire through his already heated body. Bayley flinched when he slipped his hands beneath the material at her waist.

"I'm sorry if my hands are cold." He kissed her shoulder where the dress had once covered it. "I had to touch you. Feel you."

Bayley stilled before he slid his hands up each side of her rib cage. Her breathing came low and shallow as he eased his fingers around just below her breasts. Her hands gripped his thighs. Gradually, inch by inch, his hands moved until they cupped her breasts. With a sigh she leaned back against him, as if offering him the freedom to explore. He accepted the invitation.

He tested the weight of her breasts, enjoying the feel of their fullness in the palms of his hands. His thumbs brushed her already tight nipples. Bayley squirmed. That encouraged him to do it once more. As his thumbs continued to tease, his teeth nipped along the ridge of her shoulder then soothed with kisses over the same spots.

Her hands squeezed his thighs. She whimpered.

His fingers left her breasts to go to her shoulders. "This dress, as pretty as it is, needs to go."

Bayley made an unintelligible noise.

He pushed the straps down. Bayley removed her arms from the dress, letting it fall to her waist. She leaned her head back against his shoulder. Jenson didn't wait to take her breasts in his hands again. Looking over her shoulder, he enjoyed the sight of his large hands holding her full creamy breasts.

"So beautiful." He lifted them and lowered them. "Truly lovely."

Bayley twisted in his arms, coming to lie against his chest, her body between his legs. "I want to see and touch you."

"Maybe we can take this to a more comfortable place." His gaze met hers.

"I'll agree to that." He helped her to her feet.

She held her dress over her incredible breasts with one hand while he took the other. He led her up the stairs to the large bedroom above. To his delight she didn't hesitate at the door. He shouldn't have been surprised. When Bayley made up her mind she stuck with her decision. She had decided she would be with him tonight. He was honored.

Jenson brought her into his bedroom and up to his bed. Clicking the bedside light on, he turned to her. She watched him while holding her dress secure. The need to taste those luscious breasts grew. He gathered her into his arms and kissed her as he tugged the dress from her hands. Her fingers gripped his shirt as the dress puddled on the floor.

His hands found her waist then followed her curves. Her satin-smooth skin rippled beneath his fingertips as he moved to explore her back. He shifted so he could see her. She was full curves with only a small slip of pink for underwear. "So beautiful."

Lifting one of her breasts, he took the nipple into his mouth. Heaven. He sucked. Bayley moaned. Quivered from head to toe. Her fingers bit into the top of his shoulders. His tongue twirled around her nipple. Her hands cupped his head. She was so responsive. He wanted to see what other parts of her would react to his touch. There was such passion in her.

Her fingers worked the buttons of his shirt undone. While his lips skimmed the top of her shoulders, she pushed his shirt wide and placed kisses over his pectoral muscles. His skin quaked wherever she touched. What Bayley could do to him with a simple touch humbled him.

She stepped back, pushing his shirt off. While he worked to release his cuff links, she continued to kiss him, going down as far as his belly button before he took her by the arms and brought her to standing. "That's far enough."

"Making you uncomfortable, Doc?" She looked at him with her eyes twinkling.

"No. I just want this to last a long time and if you keep that up I'll be done before we even get started."

"You that easy?" She dipped in again as if she planned to kiss his chest.

"Only where you are concerned." He continued to fuss with his cuffs. To his shock he realized that was true.

"Let me do that for you." She took his hand and turned the wrist up. With swift, sure movements she removed the link. She carefully placed it on the table. "Let's see the other one." He offered his other hand. She followed the same procedure.

Jenson shrugged out of the shirt not caring if it fell to the floor.

"Let me help you with this." Bayley's fingers moved to the zipper of his slacks.

Her hands brushed his straining manhood causing his ache to climb to painful. The back of her hand rubbed him as it lowered the zipper. On purpose or not, he wasn't sure.

"There. All done," she said with satisfaction.

"Hardly." His voice had gone rough and needy even to his own ears.

"Hard, I would agree with."

"Are you teasing me?" He shucked his pants, stepping out of them.

Watching him she said, "Maybe a little. I like those tight boxers. They show your assets well." She rolled her lips in as if resisting a need to lick them.

Mercy, the woman would kill him, and she wasn't even touching him.

"Come here, Bayley," he growled.

She took a large step forward.

Jenson brought her against him. His lips found hers as his hands cupped her butt, lifting her and pressing her against him. Her hands went around his neck as his manhood snuggled between her legs.

Bayley wrapped her legs around his waist. Stepping backward until his legs hit the bed, he sat. Her heated center ran the length of his straining manhood. She lifted and did it again.

"Bayley." His voice was harsh.

She giggled. "Like that, do you?"

He loved it. "Two can play this game." He held her steady as his mouth found a nipple and pulled. She flexed against him. He continued to tease that breast and moved to the other. Her movements had become an endurance test.

He widened his legs, which made hers open. With a finger he followed the line of her panties to her sweet, warm, wet center. His finger slid beneath. He captured her gaze. Watched it turn dreamy with desire. Holding it, he slipped his finger into her core.

Bayley's eyes widened. Her lips parted. He pulled away. She whimpered. He entered her again. This time he received a sigh of pleasure.

"Like that, do you?" he mimicked her with a smile.

She nodded.

"Maybe you'd like some more?"

"Uh-huh" was but a whisper on her lips. She lifted her hips.

"I wouldn't want to disappoint." His finger pushed inside her.

Soon she rode his finger with a pace that matched his movements. Bayley's hands clutched his shoulders. Her eyes closed, head falling back as her body tensed. She squirmed, went rigid before moaning her release.

Jenson had never seen anything more amazing and liberated than Bayley at that moment.

CHAPTER EIGHT

BAYLEY HAD NEVER experienced anything like that before. She wasn't completely lacking in experience, but Jenson had sent her over the moon and hadn't even entered her. The man had talents. She slowly returned to earth and the bedroom.

Jenson rolled her over and upward across the bed. His skin was tight across his cheeks, his jaw set. He stood and reached for her underwear, stripping them down her legs before dropping them to the floor. He removed his boxers before pulling out the drawer of the bedside table and reaching in for a square package. "I need to know you really want this."

Should she really do this? If this went any further would she be able to just see him as a friend? But they had trust and honesty between them. They had agreed. Their friendship and respect for each other was strong enough to risk crossing the line.

She looked into his eyes. He desired her. She might die if she didn't have him. Bayley opened her arms in welcome. "I'm saying yes. I understand what's between us."

Tearing the package open, he covered himself. His lips found hers as he adjusted his hips between her legs. He raised up on his hands. Looked at her. His manhood nudged her center. "I want you so badly."

"I'm here." She flexed slightly, encouraging him.

With a forward motion of his hips Jenson filled her. With a sigh of delight, she felt him throughout her body.

Jenson rocked back and forth, creating a heat in her that ignited into a flame, then a roaring fire. Her hands traveled over his chest to embrace his neck. She flexed toward him. He pushed into her. The fire blazed. Then ran wild. As he pumped, she clawed for release. Bayley squeezed her eyes closed. She wanted this desperately. Finally she touched it, found it, and broke apart like embers into the night. She soared beyond.

Slowly, gently she returned to reality. Jenson was there. Jenson. The man who made her feel as she never had before. Her mouth found his. She rewarded him with a wet, passionate kiss as he pumped into her and groaned his release. He came down on her, but his weight was reassuring.

Before he became heavy, he rolled to his side. With his breathing still labored, he brushed the back of his hand over her stomach. "Bayley, you have hidden talents."

She smiled. "I'm glad you think so."

"I do, indeed."

He shifted onto his side facing her. "You deserve something special for your efforts."

"And what would that be?"

A wicked grin formed on his lips. "Another bowl of ice cream?"

Bayley giggled. Jenson had a way of bringing those out in her. Before meeting him, her life had been so serious all the time. He'd taught her that she could work hard and still find fun in it.

Jenson wrapped his long arm around her waist and pulled her close. She snuggled into his warm, hard body.

Moments like these were what she wanted out of life. Now and forever.

He reached over them and pulled at the coverlet until it covered them. For once someone was caring for her. "It was nice to meet your parents tonight, and a bit scary."

"I can't imagine you scared of anything or anybody," Jenson murmured.

"I'm afraid of many things."

"Such as?"

Of not having more moments like this. That I could be falling in love with you. "I was afraid of not being able to care of my father. Or not finishing my training. Or not paying the bills. But thanks to the scholarship that has been lifted off my shoulders."

Jenson's body tensed then he kissed her shoulder. "I'm glad."

Had she said something wrong?

Moments later he softly snored.

Jenson woke to a warm body curled against him. Bayley. What was he doing? He'd stepped over the line big-time. He looked at Bayley. Her hair covered her face while her arm lay across his chest. His first thought was to wake her with a kiss but that would lead to other things. It would be harder to leave her.

He couldn't, wouldn't offer her forever. That was a fantasy. He had learned that lesson well. They had agreed this would be simple and easy. No expectations. Everything he felt about Bayley screamed forever, but he knew well that didn't exist. And then there was his secret. They had talked of trust and honesty but he hadn't managed to achieve either. If she ever found out what he'd done their friendship might be gone as well.

A brush of something against his skin drew his attention. Bayley stirred. Her lips made butterfly kisses on his chest. She brought back memories of the night before, the pleasure, the heat and desire like he'd ever experienced. He would never forget it.

His manhood grew with just the thoughts of their time together. He had to put a stop to the want boiling in him or he'd never be able to leave Bayley alone. It would already be hard enough to resist her.

"We need to get you home if you want to be there before your father wakes." He found the idea sweet she didn't want to make it obvious she had spent time in his bed. She was a grown woman who wanted to honor her father. He wished he and his father had the same type of respectful relationship.

Everything about Bayley revolved around kindness. If she ever appeared angry, she had never shown it to him. Regardless of the situation she remained more concerned about others than herself. Except where her mother had been concerned.

Her mother leaving had made her become a people pleaser. That way she wouldn't get left behind again. She feared hurting anybody's feelings. She worried she'd caused her mother to leave, even though he believed Bayley consciously knew better. Bayley was a strong person to live through something like that. What amazed him the most was she didn't act bitter about her situation. She proudly made the most of what life gave her.

How would she react when she learned he was leaving? And what if she found out why? He feared it would be the end of her good humor.

"Bayley." He shook her gently.

"Uh…?"

"We fell asleep. I need to get you home."

"I like it here." She snuggled in closer.

He liked her there too. Too much. That was the problem.

"What time is it?" she muttered.

"It's four thirty in the morning."

Bayley sprang to a sitting position, her beautiful bare breasts bouncing. "I've got to go."

He couldn't help himself. He ran a finger down the top of one breast to the nipple. He watched as it stood to attention. "Yes, you do. I hate it too."

"You better stop that, or I might not get out of here."

Why did that idea not send a bolt of fear through him?

She hustled off the bed in all her naked glory. He took the moment to appreciate it and bemoan its loss.

"I've got to go. I can get a taxi. You didn't get much sleep."

There was that kindness again. "Neither did you. You won't be getting a taxi. Just give me a minute." By the time he found his jeans she had already pulled on her dress.

"Will you help me zip this up?"

He stepped behind her. Disappointed at covering all that lovely skin, he pulled the zipper into place. The temptation to kiss her back was almost overpowering. He wouldn't do it; that would be a step in the wrong direction.

She turned her head back and forth, as if she were looking for something.

"Your shoes are in the living room." She looked in his direction then came to an abrupt stop.

"What's wrong?"

Bayley continued to stare. "You are the most handsome man I have ever seen."

She stood in front of him, placing her small sure hands on his chest, coming only as high as his shoulders. Going up on her toes, she gave him a sweet kiss. "Thank you for last night. It was wonderful. You were wonderful. I'll always remember it."

His hands of their own accord went to her waist and brought her against him. He kissed her with all the passion he'd felt the night before. Bayley had a way of getting to him. All thoughts of his commitment to put distance between them had gone out the window the moment she touched him. At least temporarily. He'd gather his defenses after he took her home.

When he would've taken her back to bed, she stepped away. "I've gotta go." She headed out the door.

Disappointed, he picked a T-shirt off a chair and pulled it on before slipping on a pair of loafers.

He found her in the living room with shoes on and purse in hand. "Let's get you home."

A few minutes later they were in his car, headed into the dark, trafficless streets.

He pulled into a parking spot and then moved to open the door. She put a hand on his forearm. "Don't get out. I'll be fine. Thank you for being there for me at the gala. And the extra celebration afterward." Her face softened. "It was very special."

Jenson controlled the wince threating to form. "Bayley, I..." He couldn't tell her now. It could wait until tomorrow. He wouldn't ruin the sweetness of what they'd shared for her. Hell, for him. Not yet.

She brushed his arm. "You're a good man and an amazing person."

"I could say the same about you. But you're certainly all woman."

Bayley chuckled. "Hey, I'm off Friday and I think you are too. Why don't you come over for dinner and we'll have a celebration with Dad?"

"I don't know. I have to be gone for a couple of days this week for a seminar. If the plane is late coming back, then I wouldn't be able to make it. I don't want you to be waiting on me."

Her look dropped to her lap. "Okay, maybe we can do it later."

His chest tightened. Jenson reached for her hand, held it. "I'll let you know how things are going. How does that sound?"

She brightened. "That'll work." She gave him a quick kiss on the lips before she opened the door.

He watched her hurry up the walk with a sadness of loss. It was for the best.

Bayley stopped before she went inside and looked back, giving a little wave. Once she was safely inside, he drove away with a heavy heart.

Bayley hadn't heard from Jenson in two days. Granted they had agreed to a one-night stand, no strings attached or expectations afterward, but he'd never been this distant. They'd been on different shifts before but somehow seen each other coming or going from the hospital. Even in the last few weeks when she'd worked at the clinic he'd turned up. Despite knowing he would be out of town, not hearing from him for two days disturbed her. She sensed something had shifted when he had dropped her off early that morning after their night together. One she'd relived a hundred times in her dreams. She was in love, had no doubt about it whatsoever.

Even having never experienced it before she recognized the pure bliss of love. The knowing she'd found her soul mate. The person she belonged to and with. She wanted to shout to the world that Jenson belonged to her. Sadly, apparently Jenson didn't feel the same.

She'd have to accept the feeling was one-sided. What she couldn't accept was him not holding to his promise they would maintain their friendship. If he did still want her as a friend, then why hadn't she heard from him? The least Jenson could do was text, even if he was out of town. Was Jenson trying to put some distance between them? Why would he? She had put no demands on him.

Never before had she been muddled or distracted at work. Her mind had always been clear where medicine was concerned. The last few days she'd had difficulty concentrating. Just what she had feared had happened. Getting involved with Jenson took her off her goal path. When she should be thinking about her and her father's future, finishing her training and going into practice, Jenson scrambled her thoughts, made it hard for her to think Even her excitement over the scholarship had been dampened by Jenson's lack of attention. This had to stop.

She picked up a tech pad to review Johnny's chart. The teen's health had quickly become critical. Was Jenson calling in to check on him?

By the middle of the week she still hadn't heard from Jenson. If he wanted nothing to do with her then she wanted nothing more to do with him.

She continued to lie to herself. Until a text came through. Her heart jumped.

Sorry I haven't texted sooner. Been busy. See you soon.

That wasn't the most warm and fuzzy text she had ever received, but it was better than nothing. She couldn't help but be excited.

Her fingers quickly typed.

I understand. I look forward to seeing you too.

The next two days were long and slow. She anticipated Jenson's coming home on Friday, that he would call or just show up at her door to see how she was doing. Yet her phone remained silent. The night passed without his appearance. Sadness shadowed her the entire weekend, the only bright spot being she and her father going house-hunting. They found a nice small home that would be perfect. All that had to be done was signing papers and moving.

By Monday she advanced into anger. She believed Jenson was better than this. Friends didn't treat each other this way. It was time to accept he didn't even want that now. Still, she wouldn't let this dark cloud continue to shroud her. The time would come when he'd have to face her. Account for his inactions.

"Hi, Bayley, I heard congratulations are in order. You got that scholarship," one of the floor nurses said from where she sat behind the desk.

Bayley looked away from the pad. She smiled for the first time in days. "I sure did."

Another nurse wearing a grin walked up beside Bayley. "I also heard you won the jackpot for the night."

Bayley tilted her head. "How's that?"

"Dr. Hunt went with you."

"Yes, he did." They'd had a beautiful night together. Then nothing.

The nurse beside her narrowed her eyes then asked, with disbelief circling her words, "You didn't have a good time?"

"Oh, yeah. I did. I had a great time." Flashes of Jenson standing at her door looking dashing in his tux, with his arm around her shoulder as he supported her before the scholarship was announced, and later in his bed all ran through her mind. Yes, she'd had a good time. The best of times. Until…

"I bet you did," the nurse behind the desk said. "You were there with the most eligible bachelor in town. Who knew the dark horse would come from behind and win the race."

Bayley looked up. "What're you talking about?"

"You were the last one we expected him to latch on to. He seemed so disinterested when he arrived."

This conversation had turned catty. "We're just friends. He had to go, and I needed to be there."

"Yeah, yeah, that's what they all say," the first nurse said.

Two more nurses joined them. They all laughed.

Apparently, she and Jenson had made the hospital rumor mill, or at least the one for the floor. Little did they know she hadn't heard from him in days. Some friendship.

A telemetry staff member interrupted them. "The patient in 334… Heart rate is down to twenty-six beats per minute."

The group sobered.

Bayley dropped the tech pad on the desk. That was

Georgie's room. He was back for a heart catheterization. She called over her shoulder as she ran down the hall in the direction of the patient's room.

"Page the cardio person on call," one of the nurses shouted.

Steps behind her were two of the code team. They had practiced for emergencies like this one. They all knew their responsibilities and positions around the bed.

Bayley shoved open the door. Georgie lay in the bed. He appeared asleep. She knew better. He was in distress. Bayley headed straight for the bed. The monitors leading to his chest rang and lights flashed.

She whipped her stethoscope off from around her neck and placed the bell on the boy's chest, hoping she had learned enough to be able to help him. Other staff joined her, but her concentration remained on listening to his heartbeats. They were still too far apart.

" He needs epinephrine."

"Bayley's right."

She knew that voice. Jenson's. She didn't have time to deal with those emotions. She'd already wasted too much of her time on him.

The syringe of epinephrine was placed in her hand. Bayley looked at the amount and called the number out. The nurse with the code card confirmed the figure. Bayley emptied the liquid into the already placed IV. Another nurse placed the bag over his mouth and nose then managed the oxygen bulb with gentle squeezes. Other hands started doing compressions on the boy's chest.

Jenson's hands entered her view holding electric paddles.

"Clear." His voice commanded everyone's attention.

Bayley stepped back making sure she didn't touch the

patient. She glanced around to make sure the others had moved as well. "Clear."

Jenson placed the paddles on Georgie's chest. He jumped from the electric shook.

Bayley watched the monitor.

Come on...beep. Show me a heartbeat. The words went in a circle around in her mind as a lifesaving mantra.

Nothing.

"Clear," Jenson called.

He placed the paddles again.

Bayley held her breath, repeated the mantra and watched the monitor.

Beep. Beep. Beep, beep, beep. The monitor voiced the heartbeats.

"We got it."

His gaze met hers for the first time in days.

"We need to stabilize Georgie. Pull a full blood panel. Order an X-Ray, EKG and ECHO stat. Then let's get him to CICU. Call Dr. Sewell. Have her meet us there. He's going to need a pacemaker ASAP."

The respiratory therapist squeezing the oxygen bag resumed his work.

Seconds later Georgie left the room with Jenson beside him.

So, Jenson had returned to town. And not contacted her. If only he'd shown her the same consideration and care he'd given Georgie.

Jenson looked up from where he sat behind his office desk at the hospital. Not because of a sound he'd heard, but from the sense someone was at the door. He faltered when he saw Bayley. She didn't appear happy. Not that he'd believed she would. The look in her eyes wasn't one of jubilation over a success like when their gazes had met over Georgie. Instead, it held sadness. An emotion he'd put there.

The lack of brightness in her eyes and the tight line of her mouth suggested this wasn't going to be a conversation he would enjoy. In fact, he was sure of it. He'd been running from her for over a week. That disgusted him. That was becoming a habit. Their meeting now might be one of the worst of his life. And he'd had a number of bad face-offs. He could only blame himself.

"I've been asked to check whether your report on the code is finished."

The tone of her voice cut like a rusty scalpel. His chest tightened. He deserved that and more.

Her warmth and smile were missing. At least for him, Bayley's light had gone out. He'd seen it when she had been determined to save Georgie. But it was gone now.

"I'll take care of it. Bayley—"

"Then I'll let you get back to work." She left without a backward glance.

What a tangled mess he'd created for himself. Once again, his personal life had become knotted in his professional world. Couldn't he ever learn? Why couldn't he have left things at friendship with Bayley? Kept her at arm's length like he'd promised himself he would.

Instead, he'd become involved in the scholarship process. That meant keeping secrets from Bayley. He'd become everything he detested. Dishonest and untrustworthy. Even when it was for a good reason.

Yet his body wanted her. Begged for her. Craved her. But going there again would only make matters worse.

"I thought better of you."

His head jerked up. Bayley had come back. Apparently to tell him off.

"You don't think I understood I was a one-night stand."

Jenson's jaw ticked. She didn't give him time to say anything before she continued.

"We talked about it. Agreed. Friends don't treat friends like you did. I'm a big girl. I can take it. My mother left me, so I have a lot of experience with rejection, so one more wouldn't hurt. I'll get over it and move on. But I gave you more credit than I should have. You seemed to be a nice guy. That's what disappoints me the most. I believed we were adult enough to remain friends. Sadly, I guess we're not."

That was a punch to his chest. Hadn't he done to Bayley the same as Brett had done to him? What kind of person did that make him?

"You could have had the guts to have at least faced me and said how you feel."

He winced. Bayley wasn't holding back. She came at him full-on.

"I know the score. I'm an adult. I make my own choices. I can live with them. You didn't have to wait until there was a crisis with a patient to actually show up in my life again."

He stood. "Bayley—"

She waved a hand. "I shouldn't have come back. It's on me that I expected more. I'm sorry to have bothered you."

Jenson stared at the empty doorway. When she didn't return he hurried around the desk, out the door and down the hall. He reached Bayley just seconds before she went through the exit leading to the main hall. He grabbed her elbow.

She looked around, surprise covering her face along with moisture floating in her eyes.

Bayley crying almost dropped him to his knees.

The last week had been a living hell. He'd lost count of the number of times he'd wanted to pick up the phone to call Bayley. But he hadn't. Wouldn't let himself. Yet now...

"We should talk. About us."

Bayley's eyes widen into an incredulous glare. "Us?"

"Yeah, about us."

She tugged her arm from his hold, her stance determined.

Jenson lowered his hand. "Please, come back to my office. We don't need to do this in the hall."

Time ticked by long enough he wasn't sure she would agree.

"Okay. I guess you deserve a chance to explain yourself."

Relief washed the fear away. At least she was being reasonable. He waited on her to start down the hall, then followed her. With them both inside his too small office he closed the door. The last thing he wanted or needed was a public show of his personal life. He'd had enough of that with Darlene. He wouldn't let that happen here.

Bayley stood her ground. He stepped beside the desk, putting space between them, but remained standing as well.

He watched her trying to gather her thoughts. Saying the wrong thing here would do him no good. "We need to work this out."

"There is no *we*. There was a one-night stand between two consenting adults."

Jenson had the good grace to wince. The woman had a way of cutting to the point of the matter.

"Come on, Bayley, let me at least try to explain. I never intended to hurt you."

"Hurt's what I felt Wednesday, Thursday and Friday. I became numb over the weekend. Today it eased into anger."

This time his face contorted as if she had slapped him. Despite his best intentions he'd hurt her anyway. "I want us to be friends."

"Friends discuss things with their friends."

"That's what I'm trying to do." He gripped the edge of the desk.

She glared at him.

"I should've called. I realize that."

She stuck her neck forward. "Then why didn't you?"

What had happened to the sweet, big-hearted Bayley? This one he didn't recognize but he liked her equally well. Both Bayleys had backbone.

"Well?"

"Because I didn't want to hurt you." It sounded weak even to him.

"Well, you missed the boat with that."

She'd made that perfectly clear. Jenson's fingers tightened on the desk to keep from reaching for her.

"How could you treat me that way? It made me feel cheap and used."

He stepped toward her, then stopped. "That wasn't my intent."

"Then what was it?" Bayley glared.

"I know you. You'll want a marriage and a family once you finish medical school I can't give you that. That dream for me is gone. My ex blew it out of the water."

"I don't remember asking for any promises. I agreed to an arrangement and intended to honor it. I didn't ask for you to give me more. But you haven't talked to me. At the very least we should have enough trust between us to say what we're thinking."

"I didn't mean to hurt you." There should be trust, but how would she feel when she found out he'd been keeping a secret from her? That fact ate at him. He'd been holier-than-thou about Darlene and Brett and look what he was doing to Bayley. He was no better than his ex-wife and former best friend. Jenson sighed. "I just don't trust like I used to."

"Then I feel sorry for you. You need time to work on that, so I'll give you room to do so. I'll stay out of your way. Starting now." Bayley left before he could say another word.

Why did he feel as if he'd just let something vital to his life slip through his fingers? At least he would be leaving the hospital soon and not have to face Bayley every day.

CHAPTER NINE

"WHEN'S THAT SMILE going to return?" Bayley's father asked a couple of days later. "It would be nice to see it again. When are you and Jenson going to come to your senses?"

Her father sat in the middle of the living room with boxes Bayley had packed stacked against the wall. Since finding the new house she had been in frenzied mode. Bayley placed the last item from the cabinet into the packing box. It had been a whirlwind experience of winning the scholarship, finding a place for them to live, scheduling appointments with her advisor around work and now the actual move.

At the hospital she and Jenson maintained a working relationship of professionalism around the staff and patients. Whenever they were alone, which wasn't often and even then only briefly, the sexual tension sizzled between them. Just the smallest of accidental touches was enough to cause her heart to flutter. With each meeting the pressure built from the time before. Her need grew more intense with the not having and the wanting. "How do you know my mood has anything to do with Jenson?"

"Honey, your father isn't blind or dumb. I know something happened between you and Jenson."

"We're just friends. Busy people. We came to an understanding about our free time."

"An understanding? Is that what they're calling it these days?"

She wrapped another glass and placed it in the box. "I don't know what others call it but that's what we've agreed on. Friendship."

"Am I to get grandchildren someday out of this agreement?"

Bayley shook her head, her heart heavy. She didn't want to think about that. "No, Dad. He had an awful breakup with his ex-wife. He's not interested in returning to that type of situation."

"Situation? As in marriage?"

"Yes, Dad, I don't know if he'll ever marry again. If he does it won't be to me." Bayley gave him a short summary of Jenson's past with his ex-wife and his best friend.

"It's understandable he's a little skittish. How do you feel about this understanding?"

She looked at her father. "I love him, Dad. But he doesn't feel the same about me. I have to respect that. We're work colleagues. That's all."

"I suspected how you felt. I'm not fooled. You're more than work colleagues."

Her father had always been able to read the full picture. What surprised her was that he'd taken this long to question her about them. "I don't know what to do about it but move on and pretend it doesn't matter."

Her father pursed his lips, nodded in a thoughtful manner as if organizing words of major importance. "Come, sit down, Bayley."

"I don't have time today. I've got packing to do before I go to work." She continued to pull dishes out of the cabinet.

"You've got time. Sit." Since her father rarely spoke to her that way, she did as he said.

"It's time that we talk about your mom."

This Bayley hadn't expected. Her father rarely spoke of her mother.

"I suspect from what you said that Jenson is much like your old man in some ways. He's lost his sense of trust. Worse, he's putting his ex-wife's failings on other women. Including you. You don't know this, but your mother could never be satisfied. Nothing was ever really good enough for her."

Bayley started to rise. "I don't wanna talk about her. Mine and Jenson's relationship has nothing to do with her."

Her father waved her down. "You might find there's more in common than you think. We should've had this conversation a long time ago. It might've helped you with Jenson. It certainly would've made you less focused on everything else you were doing and let you learn to live."

Her father paused. "Your mother chased after me. She dated a lot of men. I think she settled on me because she thought I was her best way out of a bad situation. Back then I had the potential to earn a good living. Yet nothing was ever good enough for her. She'd go on a shopping spree and then hide things from me. When that didn't give her enough excitement, she started running around on me. There were telltale signs here and there, and then you came along. I wanted you and not part-time, so I convinced her to stay with me. After you were born, she really felt stuck. Then there was the accident. She said she couldn't stay. Taking care of a child and a man in a wheelchair was too much for her emotionally. There was no way she could stay and survive. I knew it. She knew it."

Bayley sank into the chair.

"Some people are just selfish. That's their makeup. No matter how much they might care for someone else, they care for themselves more. Your mom was one of those people. It sounds like Jenson's ex-wife is one of those people too.

"The problem is they leave devastation in their wake. Those left behind have to pick up the pieces of that loved one's needs and inadequacies. I know you certainly had to do that."

"Dad, I have no complaints."

"Yes, but I do."

He took her hand.

"Because of your mama's leaving, you've had to help take care of me. You have a big heart to care for others, but you don't take care of yourself enough. What I want you to understand is some people are weak. We can't let them define our lives. We have to live and be happy despite them. Jenson has taken a hard hit. It's difficult for him to trust again. To believe that somebody can want him, to stand by him. That's where Jenson is. I believe he'll come around. You're just the person to heal his heart."

"And how do you know that?"

"Because I know you and he won't be able to resist your heart."

She straightened. "He says he doesn't want another relationship."

"You stand your ground." Her father made a firm nod.

"You do it at work, at the clinic, and you do it with him. He'll come around."

She put her arms around her father's neck and hugged him. "I love you, Dad. And I sure hope you're right."

He patted her arm. "Trust me on this. It'll become clear to him how he feels about you when you and he least expect it."

Jenson went in search of Bayley. He asked at the nurses' station if they had seen her. One of the staff said Bayley was working in one of the consultation rooms doing some charting. He headed that way. After six in the evening, they both should have been at home but instead they were still at the hospital. He'd stayed at the hospital late so he'd be busy. If he was then he wouldn't have time to think about Bayley. Facing his apartment where they had been together made it difficult to go home. His life had become a mess again.

He knocked on the consultation room door. At a soft "Come in," he opened the door.

The shock and panic on Bayley's face when she saw him was like having an incision without anesthetic. They had been so close and were now so distant. It was all his fault.

"They have a heart for Johnny. Would you like to tell him?"

Bayley's face lit up. A broad smile formed on her lips. She jumped up and threw her arms around his neck.

He brought her against him, holding her tight. It had been too long. She fit so right.

Too soon she pushed away from him. She tugged at her scrub shirt, adjusting it. "You bet I would."

Jenson had to hurry to keep up with Bayley as she all

but ran down the hall toward Johnny's room. She stayed three steps ahead of him along the tile floor in her eagerness to get there. She had become emotionally invested in Johnny's case. Not a particularly healthy spot for a medical professional to be in but certainly a human one. It was just one more thing to admire about Bayley.

She stopped at the door. "You are sure you want me to do this?"

Jenson nodded. "I'm sure. I think he'll like it coming from you."

Bayley straightened her shoulders. She drew in a deep breath and slowly released it.

He studied her a moment. "Are you going to be able to do this?"

"Sure I am. I just don't want to appear too excited. I know how many things can go wrong."

"Good idea. Take your time." Jenson kept his smile to himself.

A few seconds later she said, "Okay, I'm ready." She knocked on the door.

Jenson followed her into the room. Johnny lay in his bed with a body that looked like a longtime prisoner of war's, too gaunt and with haunted eyes. The teen needed a new heart. Another day might have been too late. Johnny's parents sat in chairs in the corner.

Bayley stepped to the end of the bed. She looked directly at Johnny, almost humming with excitement. He felt it. Did the others? Or was he so in tune with Bayley that he was the only one who did?

"Johnny, do you think you're up to getting a new heart tonight?"

The boy's eyes widened. He looked at his parents, who had jumped up from the chairs.

"There's a heart?"

"Yes."

Jenson stepped forward. "There is, but I have to caution you that a lot of things have to fall into place just right."

Johnny's mother and father came to the bedside. His mother said, "Thank goodness."

Bayley took Johnny's mother's hand. "You do know this is going to be a long, drawn-out process, don't you?"

"Yeah, I have listened and read and talked to people. We're ready for this. Johnny is ready for this."

Jenson spoke up. "He'll feel a lot better when he's got a new heart, but it's not a complete fix. It's changing one set of problems for another. He'll have a long road ahead."

"We understand," Johnny's mother said. "We appreciate both of you being here. It's nice to have someone you know around."

"They'll be coming in soon to start the long process of getting you ready. I'll be around for a while if you have any questions." Jenson extended his hand to Johnny. "Congratulations, man."

Johnny shook his hand.

"I'll be checking in with you. It'll take all night so settle in." Bayley smiled.

She followed Jenson out of the room. "Thanks for letting me do that. It's nice to give good news for a change. We spend our time giving bad news too often."

"I'm glad you were still here so you could."

"Would you have called to tell me?" She watched him closely.

"I would have."

That put a smile on Bayley's face. "That's good to

know. I better go help with the orders. See that things get done correctly."

"I'll be around if needed."

"Thanks again, Jenson."

He looked at her a moment longer then started down the hall. They had been so close once and now they were little more than polite strangers.

Three hours later Jenson walked down a floor to where the surgery waiting room was located. Johnny's mother sat with some others inside the glass-enclosed room. He passed Johnny's father pacing the hall and nodded. He wasn't surprised to see Bayley sitting in a chair beside the mom.

"What're they telling you?" Jenson asked.

"There's a delay getting the heart here. There was a paperwork issue, and they're getting that straightened out. Also, one of the other organ teams is running late." Bayley offered him a resigned look.

"How's Johnny holding up?"

"He is stable. Sleeping," his mother said. "The nurse said we'll just be in a holding pattern for most of the night until they get everything in order. Oh, and Johnny said before he went into surgery that he wanted a new game so he could play Dr. Hunt."

Jenson grinned. "I look forward to the game." He looked at Bayley and nodded his head toward the door. She followed him out. When they were out of hearing range from the others, he said, "It's going to be a while before anything happens. I think you should go home and come back."

"I'm good. I'll sleep in one of the doctors' overnight rooms." Bayley turned back to the waiting room.

"Don't you need a few hours' sound sleep before you're supposed to be at the Intercity Clinic tomorrow?"

She looked at him for a long time. "Yeah. I guess I do."

"You won't get that in the doctor's sleeping room. I'll tell you what. I live closer than you do. Why don't you use my spare bedroom. We'll have the surgery call when the heart is on the way. We should be here before it arrives."

Jenson watched the indecision in her eyes.

"No pressure." He held up his hands.

"Okay. You do live closer. I have been here since six this morning. I'm tired. Plus I want to be close when they call about Johnny."

As they walked to Jenson's car Bayley said, "Heart transplants never seem to happen at a convenient time. In the middle of the day would be nice."

"They're pretty notorious for being done at late hours." Minutes later they were in his car leaving the parking lot. "Will your father be worried about you not coming home?"

"I've already called Dad and told him I wouldn't be home tonight. I had already planned to stay."

"How's he doing?" Jenson missed seeing the older man who had started to feel like a friend.

"He's doing fine. The new house may be farther from the hospital, but it is worth it for my father. He has all the adjustable conveniences he needs to make his life easier. I hope next year he can have that surgery."

"I'm glad to hear it about the house." The price he would be paying was worth it just to hear Bayley say her father was safe. Jenson drove into his garage and turned off the car.

Bayley yawned.

"Come on, let's get you inside." In his kitchen he asked,

"Are you hungry? I haven't eaten. I've got enough ham and cheese for a grilled sandwich. Want one?"

"That would be nice. I haven't eaten since breakfast. Let me help."

"Okay. How about fixing us some iced tea. I'll get the sandwiches done."

She fixed the drinks and set them at the bar. Taking a seat, she watched Jenson finish up a sandwich. He put it on a plate and pushed it toward her.

"Don't wait on me. Eat it while it's hot."

She did as he said. "Do you think they're going to get the heart here in time?"

Jenson looked over his shoulder at her. "I do."

"He's so sick I'm worried he might get a heart and still not recover."

"Johnny is sick but he's young. He has people who love him. He has those things going for him." Jenson slipped his sandwich onto a plate and came around the bar to sit beside her.

"I know I shouldn't get so involved but it's hard for me not to."

"He's one of those kids that get to you." Jenson took a bite of his sandwich. Bayley hadn't eaten but half of hers. "You need to eat. We could be called at any time."

"The waiting is awful. I know it's far worse for his parents. I just haven't had to do it like this. Have it matter so much."

Jenson stood. "Let's go sit on something more comfortable than these bar stools to talk. I think you need to."

To his surprise Bayley didn't argue. That was a sign she was really upset, tired or both.

She settled into the corner of the sofa. He took the cushioned chair beside her not wanting to have her feel pressured by him. He wanted that friendship they'd once had back. It was nice to have her in his home. To talk to her. To reassure her.

"Johnny's bloodwork numbers are so bad. He's so weak."

"I've seen worse do just fine." And he had.

"I've studied this stuff, but the reality is the variables are so different with each patient." She wrapped her arms around her waist.

"That's true but Dr. Swartz is a great surgeon. He knows what he's doing." Bayley's sad eyes made his chest tighten.

"I know I'm being silly. What kind of doctor am I going to make if I fall apart over difficult patients?" She wiped the back of her hand against her cheek.

Jenson moved beside her, taking her in his arms. "Honey, you're going to be a fine doctor. A better one for your tender heart."

She wrapped her hands around his waist and buried her face in his shoulder.

He held her tight. His hands traveled up and down in a gentle motion over her back. He'd missed this. Holding Bayley. Feeling her heat. Being alive.

The touch of her lips against his neck sent a shot of sexual desire though him. Jenson took her mouth. Her chest met his. Bayley turned, putting a leg over his lap to sit facing him, placing her knees on either side of his hips. She pressed her center against his buldging length. Jenson groaned. His blood ran hot. While his lips stayed fixed to hers, he ran his hand under her shirt and found skin. Smooth, warm, and oh-so-touchable skin. All that had been his once and could be again.

Bayley's hands went to his shoulders.

He broke the kiss. "If we don't stop now, we might not be able to. I think you're emotional right now and I don't want you to regret anything that happens between us. I should show you your bedroom."

"I'd rather stay with you. I need to be held."

He wouldn't have her accusing him of misunderstanding what she wanted. Jenson's heart thumped against his chest wall. "I don't think I'm capable of just holding you. You're going to have to say it, Bayley."

She looked into his eyes. "I want you."

His mouth found hers. His hands moved to her waistband, released the button and opened the zipper. Bayley went up on her knees, letting him push her pants and underwear down. She stood and pushed her clothing off then climbed on his lap again. His fingers skimmed her center. Wet, ready for him.

She lowered to his lap once more, pushing back to sit on his knees. Her small, capable hands worked at releasing him. He lifted his hips to give her room to push his pants as far away as possible.

Too soon and not soon enough her hand circled his throbbing manhood. Jenson sucked in a gulp of air, easing the pain in his failing lungs as she pumped him. He made quick work of removing her shirt and the front hook of her bra. Pushing it away, his mouth found the sweet, tender offerings just at the right level.

His tongue flicked against her ready hard nipple before his mouth surrounded it. No woman had ever been more responsive to him than Bayley. As he continued to taste, her grip on him tightened.

His index finger found her center and pushed into her heat. So ready. "Say it again, Bayley."

"I want you," she whispered in a low sexy voice against his jaw before kissing it. "Now."

Jenson raised her with his hand under her arms. He bit out, "Find my wallet."

Bayley found it after an agonizing length of time and handed it to him. He pulled out a packet. Bayley took it from him with a lift of her mouth. "I'll do it."

The sweet pain of her manipulations only heightened his anticipation. Sweat dampened his brow before she finished.

Her gaze rose to his, held. She lowered, twisted, filling herself with him. A dreamy look entered her eyes. The sadness of earlier had disappeared.

His heart shook. No one had ever looked at him as she did.

Bayley lifted and settled on him again. He flexed to meet her movements. Her fingers bit into his shoulders, his into her waist. Her delicious breasts bounced with her pleasure. Their raptures erupted at the same time, sending them spiraling off.

She collapsed against him, her head coming to rest on his shoulder as she took large drafts of air. He wrapped his arms around her. Held her tight.

How could he ever let her go? She would leave him when she learned of the secret he kept. Would he be able to pick up the pieces this time? No, not after Bayley. He must find a way to make her understand. But now wasn't the time. She needed rest. "Honey, it's time for bed. We both need to get some sleep." When Bayley didn't move, he kissed her ear. "Sweetheart, you're going to have to get off me."

"Can't. Sleep right here."

He chuckled. "Let me help roll you to the side."

"Ugh..."

Jenson gently moved her to the sofa beside him. He pulled his pants up. He steadied Bayley on her feet. He led her up the stairs to his bedroom. "Definitely sleep."

Bayley looked around as if in a daze. He liked the idea he had that type of effect on her. She murmured, "I don't have anything to wear to bed."

"I'm good with you in nothing." He walked to his chest of drawers, pulled out a drawer and removed a worn-out T-shirt. "Here. You're welcome to wear this if it'll make you more comfortable."

Bayley took the shirt.

He stood in the middle of the room. "You can have the bathroom first. We're both tired. I'm just glad you're here. Now go do what you need to in the bathroom so we can get some sleep."

By the time Jenson had taken his turn in the bath, Bayley lay in his bed with the covers pulled up. She looked so right there. He turned off the lights, then slid under the covers. He circled her waist with his arms and pulled her soft body against the wall of his chest. Jenson's chin rested on top of her head. She snuggled against him, igniting that want once more, but he resisted the desire.

It was still dark when Jenson woke to the warmth of Bayley cuddled against him. Could there be a better way of waking? He couldn't think of one.

They had stepped over the line again. But really that would happen over and over again between them. They would never be just friends. He'd fallen in love with her. Soul-stealing, canyon-deep, till-death-do-us-part love. He'd been fooling himself.

He'd tried for weeks to resist her, to not let her invade his world, but that hadn't worked. Maybe embracing her and her special essence was what he should be doing. He could be hurt if he did. But what if he always felt this way and she never really belonged to him? Wouldn't it be worth the risk to find out how good life could be?

He rose from the bed slowly not to disturb Bayley. In the kitchen he called and checked on Johnny. He returned to bed.

Bayley asked in a sleepy, sexy voice, "What time is it?"

"Midnight."

She moved. "I've got to check on Johnny."

He slid in beside her taking her in his arms. "I just did. No news yet. He's still waiting. Sleeping."

The tension in her body eased and she relaxed. Bayley showed that type of caring to everyone. What would life be like living under that shelter of care and concern? To have a refuge to run to when life knocked him down. She obviously felt something for him. Last night the look in her eyes as she'd filled herself with him had told him that. Yet she hadn't come out and said the words.

Could he handle hearing them? Could he take the chance on returning them?

Bayley's first thought was always for others. She had nothing compared to him monetarily but everything emotionally. The shelter of Bayley's love was there and open for him to step under. All she wanted was her love returned.

She cared enough to make a relationship personal. To help others, touch them, to make them feel important. She made him want to be a better person, share the same values.

Bayley had pushed at the doors of his heart and broken the lock. She had made him examine his feelings to recognize he couldn't stay walled off from others, especially not from her.

Yet the truth of the scholarship stood between them. What about him leaving? She would ask questions. Demand answers. How was he going to handle that? He couldn't lie to her. He had to come clean, but if he did, he felt confident it would explode in his face. That would only put him back in the misery he'd lived in the last few weeks. He had to talk to her.

The time he had spent with Bayley was the difference been daylight and darkness. He didn't want to return to the person he'd been before. Bayley needed to hear from him that he was resigning, about his agreement with his father, before she got word some other way. "Bayley, we need to talk."

Her phone rang. She scrambled for where it lay on the nightstand. "Yes, this is Bayley." She listened a moment. "Thanks for letting me know. That was Johnny's mother. The heart is finally on the way." Bayley pushed the covers back. "I have to go."

Before Bayley could get out of the car in the hospital parking lot, Jenson stopped her with a hand on her arm. "I owe you something?"

"What's that?"

"This." He pulled her to him and kissed her. It was as if he were trying to pour all he felt into the one action. "A thank-you for last night."

Bayley smiled. "I owe you one as well." She gave him a sweet kiss on the cheek. "I can't trust myself to do more because it would be indecent in the hospital parking lot."

"Maybe you could show me later," Jenson climbed out of the car and took her hand as they hurried into the hospital.

She liked the security of having her hand in his. Something had happened between them last night. A barrier in Jenson had come down. It was as if he had let her in. All the way in. She would talk about it with him later when they had time.

Bayley turned to him when they were inside the hospital. "I'm going to sit with Johnny's parents for a while."

"I'll go with you."

"Really?"

"Yes, really. I've become fond of the boy as well."

They entered the waiting room.

Bayley asked Johnny's mother, "How's it going?"

"Somebody from surgery came to tell us they are opening Johnny's chest and that he's doing well. That the new heart looks good and it's on its way."

"Dr. Hunt and I are going to sit with you awhile if you don't mind," Bayley said.

"No, I'll be glad to have you." Johnny's mother looked grateful and worn out.

"Can we get you anything before we do?" Bayley looked at the group of family and friends around them.

"No. We're fine. Just ready for this to be over," Johnny's mother said.

Bayley took an empty seat across the room and Jenson sat beside her.

Jenson leaned over to whisper, "This is worse than anything I've done. This waiting."

"Yeah, it makes you hope you never have to do it with your own child."

She glanced at Jenson. He would make a wonderful father. If only he believed it.

"Do you think we could go to the OR and check in on how things are going?" Bayley whispered.

"I don't see why not." He stood.

Bayley said to Johnny's mother, "We'll return in a little bit. We're going to see if we can get a report."

He and Bayley walked in silence down the hall and through the OR department doors. "I'm Dr. Hunt and this is Nurse Dodd. We wanted to know if we could get a report on the boy having the transplant?"

The person behind the desk picked up the phone. "Let me call back and check." Moments later she hung it up. "He's stable. The heart should be here any minute."

Just then the door swung open and two people, one carrying a small cooler, entered. They continued down the hall to the OR.

"Will you let them know in the OR we'll let the family know the heart is here?" Jenson touched Bayley's arm.

The clerk nodded. They left and started back to the waiting room.

Bayley eagerly told the parents Johnny's heart had arrived. "Someone should be out soon to let you know that Johnny has a new heart."

The mother took Bayley's hand. "That's wonderful news. Thank you for being so kind to us."

Bayley smiled. "I'm glad I could be here."

Jenson nudged her elbow, and they went out the door again. "Let's go get a cup of coffee."

Bayley hadn't realized it was getting so close to morning. She'd been wrapped up in Jenson and then Johnny's heart arriving. Each of Jenson's actions showed he cared but he never said how he felt out loud. How long could she continue before she'd have to tell him she couldn't see him any longer in order to save her heart? She didn't even want to think about how painful it would be to lose him.

"Let's go down to the cafeteria." Jenson's phone buzzed. He pulled it out of his pocket and looked at the text. "I'm needed upstairs. Someone said they had seen me in the hospital, so they paged me. I'll be back as soon as I'm done."

"You're a good guy. Most doctors would be angry to be paged on their day off."

"You would never be. You care so much." He touched the tip of his fingers to hers. "I'll see you in a little while."

Bayley didn't know what to say. It touched her Jenson thought so highly of her. "I'll get a cup of tea and return to the waiting room." She watched him walk away.

Two and a half hours later Jenson returned to the waiting room. Bayley's heart quickened at the sight of him.

He took a seat beside her. "How's Johnny doing?"

"The new heart started beating on its own. They're closing his chest now," Bayley said with a smile.

CHAPTER TEN

JENSON'S HEART TIPPED OVER. Bayley's happiness filled him. She had a becoming tint of pink in her cheeks. All the more becoming because the sight of him had put it there. She looked at him as if he had hung the moon.

He sank into the chair beside her. He still carried secrets and had things he needed to tell her. Things that he had thought at the time wouldn't matter, but now they did. He had broken their trust. It ate at him not being honest with Bayley. He had to come clean. He would tell her what he had done the first chance he got and beg for her forgiveness.

Jenson's attention remained on Bayley. He would miss her when he left the hospital. He'd already put in his resignation. The department head hadn't been happy to receive his letter, complaining that the hospital needed him. Jenson had apologized for his short stay but explained that there wasn't anything he could do about it.

Being a man of his word, Jenson had no choice but to honor his agreement with his father. Bayley had gotten the scholarship. She and her father were at least set financially until she finished her training. Jenson would leave knowing she would be secure. Somehow, he would see that her father had the operation for his back soon

If the situation were different, Jenson would be staying at the hospital. He had never felt more like he belonged.

Bayley leaned close. "How are things upstairs?"

"Stable for now."

"Good to hear."

An hour later Bayley told Johnny's family goodbye since he was on his way to CICU and he was doing well. Bayley and Jenson headed out of the hospital. She was due at the clinic in less than an hour.

They were walking down the hall toward the parking lot door when one of the other cardiologists approached them.

"Hey, Jenson. I'm sorry to hear that you're leaving us. You've been a nice addition while you've been here."

Bayley stopped dead still in the hallway.

Jenson glanced at her, his jaw tight.

The other man continued as if he didn't see the strain on either of their faces. "When is your last day?"

"Friday." The word sounded forced from Jenson.

Bayley made the sound of a hurt mouse. Her blood ran cold. How could he have not told her?

Jenson looked at her. She glared at him in disbelief. Acid filled her throat. Only with a great effort did she manage not to turn and run for the nearest restroom. Jenson leaving! Why?

Bayley moved past the two men. She needed a moment alone. Why would Jenson do it? He'd said he planned never to return to his family clinic. His words had been firm, determined, as if that would be the last place he'd work. So why?

Was he leaving because of her? Had he decided he couldn't work with her like he had his former best friend?

Had she driven him away from somewhere he said he was happy? She just couldn't understand. Jenson must be leaving for an extraordinary reason.

She only made it as far as the next hallway before Jenson caught up with her. "Bayley, wait."

"For what?"

"I want to explain." His frustration rang clear in his voice.

"That you're leaving and didn't bother to tell me?" She started walking again.

"It's not like you think."

Bayley stopped in the middle of the hall with her hands on her hips, glaring at him. "Then tell me what I should think."

Jenson placed a hand on his chest and rubbed. He looked around. "Let's go somewhere private so we can talk."

"What's wrong with right here? Everyone but me seems to know you're leaving. Why didn't you tell me? I thought we were friends."

"Bayley, keep your voice down. I don't want everyone to know my business."

She huffed. "Including me."

Jenson looked around. Taking her elbow, he led her into the open door of a storage room. He closed the door.

She rounded on him. "I have to go. I'm due at the clinic. You don't owe me any explanation."

Jenson hissed, "I do. I told you I wanted to talk to you."

"You've been with me for the last almost twenty-four hours and you couldn't work in the three words I am leaving in that amount of time."

His shoulders sank. "Come on. Be reasonable. When was I supposed to have this conversation? When you weren't talking to me? Or while you were upset over Johnny? Oh, I know, while we were making love. Or maybe in front of Johnny's family. Please be fair and listen to me."

She glared at him. Maybe he had a point. The time hadn't been right. Her mouth tightened. "Okay, tell me what's going on. Why I'm the last person to know you're returning to Hunt Clinic when you said you'd never do that. Explain to me why you've been lying to me."

Jenson blew out a breath. "I should have told you sooner. But it's not what you think."

She narrowed her eyes. "And just what should I think?"

"Look, my father offered me an opportunity that I couldn't refuse. It was too important for me not to return."

"And that would be…?" Bayley took a step toward him.

"He promised me that I could run the clinic as I wished. Most of all, fund a lab at the Intercity Clinic."

"But will you be happy there?" She didn't miss the skin across Jenson's cheeks tightening. Her question had hit a sore spot. "I will say this. I do hate the thought of you being unhappy. I know how you felt about going back to work at the Hunt Clinic."

"I'll survive. The benefits outweigh the negatives." The sadness of that statement showed in his eyes.

"I still had to learn about it by accident in the hallway. Where's all that honesty you say is so important to you?"

Jenson winced.

At least she'd pricked him. "I don't understand why you didn't say something sooner."

"At first it didn't matter because we weren't in a re-lationship. In fact, I thought you might be glad to see me leave. Then I wanted to pick the right time. It didn't come soon enough."

"And you thought keeping that information to yourself would make it better? What was the game plan? For you to just not show up one day and for me to figure it out?" Bayley all but spat the words.

"No, and just because I'm leaving the hospital doesn't mean we can't still be friends. We just won't be working together."

"Jenson, who do you think you're kidding? We are not friends," she spat. "We haven't been for weeks. We've been lovers. And if we had been real friends, you wouldn't have kept something this big from me. Friends don't keep secrets from friends. I expect to be able to trust the people I have real relationships with. Everything about ours has been shallow. I want more out of my friendships. I'm done playing bedroom games. It's been nice knowing you. I hope you enjoy your new job."

She opened the door and didn't look back.

Jenson's chest hurt as his heart cracked down the middle. This was true heartbreak. He'd lost all he'd ever really wanted when Bayley walked out the door. What had his life become? Not even when he'd found Darlene and Brett together had he felt such pain. Did Brett love Darlene as he did Bayley? If he did, Jenson could better understand some of what he had done.

The humiliation at the time was what had hurt the most. Jenson recognized that now. He understood love and the pain of losing it. He should have told Bayley he loved her. But she had been so angry—would she have believed him or thrown it back in his face? How could he ever get her to believe anything he said?

The only thing he could do now was take heart in the fact that Bayley could finish her training and her father's future would be secure. He would find a way to get her father the surgery he needed. Now that he had lost Bayley, she'd never need to know if he was involved.

His last days were spent primarily in the hospital clinic. That limited any contact with Bayley. He was mostly glad because he figured she would be relieved to have it that way. He wrapped up visits with patients and introduced them to new caregivers. Since he was leaving, he left all admissions to other doctors. Johnny was the only patient he made a point to see. First in CICU and then by the end of the week on the floor.

Johnny was doing well enough that they played a short game together. They were at the end of it when there was a knock on the door. It was pushed open and in walked Bayley.

She jerked to a stop when their looks met. "Uh, I didn't know you were in here."

He was sure she hadn't, or she never would have entered.

"I'll let you two finish your game and come back."

Just like that, Bayley was gone.

He would have been hurt but he already ached so deeply and profoundly that he couldn't feel further injury. Or at least that's what he would have believed until this moment. To have Bayley turning from him scalded him. He'd hoped with some time she would relent enough to accept his apology.

Over the weekend he'd spent hours gaming. By Sunday evening he was more depressed than he ever had been. He'd been so happy spending time with Bayley. Just having ice cream with her had been exciting. Now nothing seemed worth doing.

Monday morning and the return to Hunt Clinic came

too soon. He returned to his old office with all the usual people still on staff. They were nice enough, said all the correct things, but this wasn't home any longer. The differences between here and the hospital were everywhere. Even the patients didn't seem the same. Somehow, they were less receptive to his suggestions about care.

Tuesday evening, he sat behind his desk finishing up for the day when Brett loomed in his doorway. Jenson hadn't seen him since his return because he now worked on a different hall of the clinic. No doubt Jenson's father had seen to that. That was a point in his father's favor.

"Hello. Welcome back."

Jenson could be civil now where he couldn't have been before. "Hey, Brett. Come in. It's nice to see you."

To Jenson's surprise he meant it. With the loss of Bayley he'd somehow adjusted his view of his past. In order to really move forward he needed to come to terms with what happened between him and Brett and Darlene. This was as good a time as any.

"Why don't you close the door."

Brett's brows rose with a look of concern, but he did as asked.

"Have a seat." Jenson leaned back in his chair and indicated the one in front of the desk for Brett.

His old friend eased into the chair with an unsure look on his face.

"Don't look so defensive. I'm not planning to beat you up or yell at you."

Brett relaxed some. "It wouldn't be because I don't deserve it."

"On that we can agree."

Brett flinched.

"Since I've returned, I know we must figure out a way to work together."

"It would be for the best. Before you say more, I'd like to say I've never had a chance to tell you how sorry I am about going behind your back. I'll never forgive myself for not being man enough to face you."

"It would have been nice. Did you love her or were you trying to hurt me?"

"You don't know?"

"Know what?" What had he missed?

"Darlene and I married six months ago. We are expecting a child in a few months."

Why didn't it hurt that Brett had everything he'd wanted with Darlene? Because she wasn't his soul mate. Bayley was. He wanted that with her.

"In answer to your question, yes, Darlene and I love each other. We didn't mean to hurt you. We didn't plan it and tried to stay away from each other. The day you found us was the first time we had been together. I'm so sorry we did that to you."

"Sounds like you needed to get that out."

"I did. I have carried the weight of what I did to you too long. I want to ask for your forgiveness but will understand if you can't give it."

"If you would've asked a few months ago I don't think I could have, but now I understand better. I'd have liked you to have been honest with me about your feelings but I kind of get why you couldn't be. That is all in the past. I don't see us being best friends again, but I do think we can work under the same roof and be civil."

Brett studied him a moment. "You have changed. For the better is my guess. You seem more settled. As if you know what you want."

Jenson did know what he wanted. But Bayley didn't want him. "I know what true happiness is. And isn't."

"I'm sorry for my part in any unhappiness. That was never what I wanted."

"I'll tell you this, you did me a favor. If it hadn't been for you and Darlene, I might never have found what I truly wanted and needed in life." Now he just had to figure out how to get it back.

Brett had just left when Jenson's father entered without knocking. One more thing Jenson hated about working at the clinic. His father treated him as if he weren't an adult who needed space.

"How can I help you?" Jenson asked. "I'm just on my way out."

"Did I just see Brett leave?"

"You did." Jenson cared nothing about sharing that conversation with his father. The man hadn't cared when Jenson's world had been destroyed, so why should he care now? Unless it involved his precious clinic.

"And?" His father glared down at him.

"And what?"

"What did he have to say?" Demand filled his words.

"That was between us." Jenson wouldn't share with him.

"Okay," his father said, terse. "How did your week go?"

"Fine."

His father huffed. "That's all you can say."

Jenson straightened his desk. "Yes."

"I wish you'd act more enthusiastic about being back." His father paced the room.

"I wish I could be more enthusiastic about it."

"It's just the first week. It'll get better." His father left with a disgusted look on his face.

Jenson doubted that.

Bayley had thought about what Jenson had said and become angrier with each passing day. How dare Jenson's father manipulate him into returning to the clinic when she knew Jenson hated it there? His father deserved to know what a great doctor Jenson was and how valued he was at the hospital. And how happy he had been working there.

As she stalked toward the door of the Hunt Clinic, she let her full indignation boil to almost overflowing. She gripped her purse. It was up to her to see that Jenson's father knew what he had done. At the reception desk, she announced, "Bayley Dodd to see Dr. James Hunt."

The woman made the call. With a surprised look on her face, she said, "You may go back."

Bayley walked with quick, sure steps as she followed the directions the woman had given her. Was Jenson's office nearby? What would he say if he saw her here? She hadn't thought that through in all her righteous anger.

She found the office she was looking for and rapped on the door. At the sound of "Come in," she entered.

Jenson's father stood as she approached his desk. "Ms. Dodd, this is an unexpected pleasure."

Dr. Hunt's syrupy welcome did nothing to calm Bayley's ire. "Dr. Hunt, thank you for seeing me."

His eyes narrowed. "What can I do for you?"

She clasped her hands in front of her holding her purse tight. "I wanted to let you know that I think it's wrong what you did to get Jenson to leave the hospital. He was happy there. The children need good, caring doctors like him."

Jenson's father sank into his chair. "And exactly what did I do?"

She forced herself not to move on the plush carpet, wanting to place her hands on the desk and glare down at the self-assured older man. She settled for waving a hand around. "You manipulated him with money for a lab and the chance to run the great Hunt Clinic."

"And you don't think he wants to do that?"

Her voice rose. "I know he doesn't want to work here. He does want the lab but not with strings attached."

"You know this how?"

"He told me so. No parent should do what you have done to Jenson."

Dr. Hunt leaned forward so that the desk chair dropped with a click. "Now, wait just a minute, young lady. I don't invite people into my office to lambaste me."

She raised her nose. "'Bayley Dodd,' not 'young lady.'"

"Sit down, Bayley. I think you're working under erroneous information."

"I'll stand." She didn't move a step.

"As you wish." Dr. Hunt leaned back in his large brown desk chair again and crossed his arms. "For your information my son made a deal with me to see that you won the Wilcott-Ross scholarship. He asked me to put in a good word to the committee. If I did, he would return to the clinic."

The wind died in her sails. That's what Dr. Hunt had been referring to the night of the gala. She sank to the chair beside her. "He did that?"

"He did. I expected him to keep his word and he has."

Bayley felt lower than a worm. And she'd accused Jenson of being dishonest. Which he had been but to help her. Now she understood why he'd not told her he was leaving. Or why he hadn't wanted to tell her why. Instead, he'd given her half-truths. "I'll repay the money. I don't want the scholarship."

Dr. Hunt looked shocked. "You want to give the money back?"

"I do and I will. I won't accept it under those circumstances. I wanted to win through merit and I would never let Jenson make such a sacrifice for me. Why would he give up his happiness for the rest of his life to help me?"

Guilt washed over Jenson's father's face. "His happiness?"

"Sure. He was happy at the hospital. He didn't tell you that?"

"I never asked him." He paused. "Or gave him a chance to say so. I think I have done my son and you a big disservice. The committee had already picked you by the time I said something about you being a good candidate."

Bayley shot out of her chair. Her heart raced. "You tricked your own son?"

Dr. Hunt hung his head. "I did."

"Why would you do that?" Disbelief circled her words. She understood none of Dr. Hunt's actions.

He looked at her. "Because I wanted him back at the clinic where he belongs. This building has his name on it."

"And you would trick him to make that happen?" She shook her head, sadness filling her. She couldn't imagine her father ever doing something like that to her. "A name and money aren't everything. You can't throw it around and manipulate people's lives with it. But you've done that to Jenson and me. I have pride too. I won't be manipulated for money. I won't be bought by the likes of the Hunt family. I'll be returning the scholarship."

"It must be nice to stand on that mountain of pride. Not accepting help."

"How dare you? You've had everything you've ever wanted in life except, apparently, a relationship with your son. You dare question how I feel about taking a hand-out?"

"You're taking this the wrong way. I was trying to help Jenson and make him see he should be working here. I didn't go against any rules. Jenson never asked me for anything before. Our relationship has never been easy. He's always had a mind of his own. But maybe I went too far this time."

"Maybe?"

Dr. Hunt's lips thinned. "Okay. I misstepped. Badly."

"Have you thought about talking to Jenson? And really listening to what he has to say about how he feels and what he wants? You might be surprised by what you find out." Dr. Hunt didn't respond. "Thanks for your time and the enlightenment. I need to have a talk with your son as well." She turned toward the door.

Dr. Hunt hurried around the desk with a pleading hand out. "Please don't be angry with Jenson. He knows nothing about me tricking him. He asked something from me to help you. Based on what you've told me, he must really care for you to make such a sacrifice. I know of no one else who would have done the same. I have to admire Jenson for that. I think you should as well."

"I'll think about it," Bayley said before walking out the door.

Bayley was more perplexed than she had been before

she entered Dr. Hunt's office. Jenson had done all of that for her. Weeks ago. Why?

For weeks Jenson hadn't been honest with her. Had kept a huge secret that'd affected both their lives. Even if she forgave him, could she trust him not to keep secrets in the future—or with her heart?

CHAPTER ELEVEN

BAYLEY STOOD IN front of Jenson's condo door the next afternoon. She had needed time to absorb what his father had told her before she faced Jenson. And face him she would. If not today, then sometime. Some of what Jenson's father had told her she still found hard to believe.

What kind of father tricked his son to get his way? She shook her head.

Jenson had sacrificed his entire life to help her. Why would he do such a thing?

Then not telling her about what he'd done... It all swirled in her head.

She looked at the grain of the door trying to gather her thoughts. And her emotions.

Bayley had only seen him once briefly since Johnny had gotten his new heart. She missed Jenson with every fiber of her being. Despite all that had happened between them, she still loved him. Would always. That made what she knew now even more difficult to accept.

Over the last twenty-four hours she'd rehearsed what she planned to say over and over yet hadn't settled on a speech that covered everything she felt. She was torn between indignation, shock and being immeasurably grateful.

To make matters worse she wasn't sure what her reception would be when she saw Jenson. The last time they had seen each other she'd said some strong words. He'd have the right to slam the door in her face. But she had to try to see him. At the very least she owed him an apology along with a dressing-down. To add to her stress her heart just wanted to see him.

Bayley raised her hand and rang the doorbell. It was time to stop stalling. She waited, shifting her weight from one leg to another. Still the door didn't open. She rang it once more. Nothing. He must not be home. She'd made it halfway down the walk before the door opened.

"Bayley?"

Her stomach tightened. She returned to him. Jenson looked nothing like the man who was normally immaculate in his grooming. His hair stood on end in a number of places. He hadn't shaved and had a day's worth of a dark shadow along his jaw. Dressed in an old T-shirt and jeans that had seen better days and with bare feet, he looked completely different from the man she had expected to see. Still good looking and sexy, but also disturbing. Had he been as miserable as she had?

Yet it was good to see him. Her heart skipped a beat. "Hi, Jenson."

He just looked at her.

"May I come in? I'd like to talk to you."

He watched her as he stepped back and opened the door wider.

Bayley's hands shook. She hadn't been sure of her reception and now Jenson's actions made her more nervous. She continued to the living area then turned to face him.

Jenson came to stand in the space between the kitchen and living room. His face remained immobile but his gaze focused on her.

Before she'd entered his home her confidence had been a sword of righteousness and now it slipped to the floor with a clunk. "I, ugh…came to tell you that I spoke to your father yesterday."

Jenson's brows rose.

"He told me what you did. You shouldn't have."

He took a step toward her then stopped. "You deserve that scholarship. You need the money. What about your father?" Jenson shoved a hand through his hair, adding to the unkempt look.

"You shouldn't have interfered. Your father shouldn't have either."

Jenson stepped closer, a pleading look on his face. "I know. But in my defense, I was thinking of you. Your father. You needed it."

"You shouldn't have hidden what you did from me."

"I knew you would never take the scholarship if I told you."

"I thought we had trust and honesty between us. At least I did on my side."

"I knew I'd made a mistake, but I was worried that if I told you, I would lose you. I've missed you." He said the last words softly.

The warm resonance of his voice rippled through her body. Pulled at her. "Jenson."

"What?"

"Why did you do it?"

Jenson swallowed. He'd done so much he regretted. He couldn't believe Bayley was here. For the first time in days the ache in his chest had eased. Just seeing her had been a balm to his damaged heart. He didn't care if she was angry with him; she was here and that was all that mattered.

"What?"

She stepped closer for the first time since she'd arrived. "Make that deal with your father. Agree to return to the clinic. Sacrifice your life for mine. What made me more important than you?"

"You needed the help."

She nodded. "That's true, but what was the real reason?"

He didn't say anything. What was she getting at?

"Why would you agree to do something that would make your life miserable?"

"I don't know."

She made a step closer. "I believe you do."

He could reach out and touch her.

"Why? Tell me why, Jenson. Why?"

"Because I love you," burst from him. The words were out before he realized he had said them. A smile he'd not seen in too long formed on Bayley's lips. But he had no doubt in his mind or his heart that they were true. Loving someone meant putting their needs over your own even if you didn't know why at the time.

"Now, that wasn't so hard to say."

He returned her smile.

"I love you too."

He reached for her and brought her against him. It felt right to have Bayley in his arms again. This time he would do whatever it took to keep her in his life. His lips found hers. Her arms went around his neck as she returned his kiss.

Sometime later they lay in bed. Their lovemaking

had been passionate and poignant at the same time. He'd found contentment.

Bayley's fingers traveled over the skin of his chest up to touch his face. "I like this rough-looking Jenson. Just a little edgy."

"Edgy, huh?" He hugged her close. "What I like is knowing that the woman I love stood up to my father. I wish I had been there to see it. Few have ever gotten away with it. You must have been amazing in your fury."

She hung her head. "I might have come on a little strong."

"I'm even more flattered by the fact you stood up for me than you appreciating my looks." He'd never had someone stand up for him like Bayley had. And even after he'd deceived her.

Her gaze met his. "Hey, that's what people do when they love someone."

"Bayley."

"Mmm…" She used the tip of her finger to draw circles on his chest.

"You need to keep the scholarship. You won it fair and square."

She opened her mouth.

"Hear me out. I want to start a scholarship for doctors who will work at the Intercity Clinic. If you give yours back, I'll want to help you and your father. So use the scholarship. It's yours anyway."

"You sound like your father. A little bit of trickery there."

"What do you mean?" Jenson sat straighter.

"He told me that he tricked you into returning to the clinic. That he went to put in a good word like you asked but the committee had already decided on me. He didn't do anything."

"Why, that—"

Bayley placed her palm on his chest, keeping him in place. "Jenson, he's your father. He loves you. He just wanted you to work beside him. What he did was wrong, and I think he realizes that now. Talk to him. I really do think he wants you to be happy."

He moved her so she lay across his chest. "You are truly an amazing woman. You not only defend me but my father."

"But I will always be in your corner no matter what."

"That's good to hear. You'll keep the scholarship then?" He looked into her eyes.

"I'll keep the scholarship. But there is one more thing."

Jenson groaned. "What have I done now?"

"Don't ever lie to me or keep a secret from me ever again."

"You have my word." He raised a hand.

"I'm going to hold you to that." Her tone implied she would do just that.

"I'm going to have to come up with a graduation present for you."

She shook her head. "You don't have to do that."

"I was thinking about maybe taking you to the Riviera for a week. But if you don't want to go…"

She sat up so she was looking down at him. "I would love that. But it would be too much."

His hand caressed her hip, his fingertips teasing toward her center. "Not if it makes you happy."

"It would." She kissed his chest and studied him a moment. "Are you happy?"

"Yeah. I'm happy. Anytime I have you in my arms I'm happy."

She smiled. "I'm glad. I thought you a very unhappy man when I first met you. A handsome but unhappy one."

"Was I really that bad?"

She shook her head. "Not bad, just sad."

"Well, I'm not sad now. In fact, I've never been happier. With you is where I belong—forever."

EPILOGUE

BAYLEY LAY IN the hospital bed watching Jenson hold their baby girl. The rapture on his face filled her heart with joy. Louisa already had her father wrapped around her finger.

"Russ, come see your baby sister," Jenson said to their three-year-old son, who had found the controls of the adjustable bed.

Russ looked at the buttons with regret and went to his father. The youngest male in her life was a copy of the older one. Bayley smiled. The day would come when she would have to use a stick to keep the girls away from Russ.

Women still looked at Jenson when he passed but Bayley took comfort in knowing he was hers. Not once had she caught him acting interested in another woman. Jenson took their wedding vows to heart. Nor had they kept anything from each other. Honesty and truth were the cornerstones of their relationship.

A knock on the door ended her musing. Her father and Jenson's parents entered. Jenson's mother made a direct line to Jenson and Louisa. Bayley didn't mind. Her mother-in-law couldn't be a lovelier person. Many of the attributes she loved most about Jenson he'd received from his mother. She'd become the mother Bayley never had.

Jenson and his father's relationship had improved over the years with the help of Russ, who formed a bridge between them. After Russ was born Jenson better understood his father's need to honor the Hunt name and its heritage. Father and son, along with grandson now, met for breakfast once a month. Russ had just gotten old enough to join them. Still, Bayley hoped for Jenson's father to better understand her husband. She watched the three Hunt males who favored each other so closely admiring Louisa. Yes, they were making progress.

Her father shuffled to the edge of the bed and took her hand. "Louisa is so beautiful. She reminds me of the day you were born."

"Stop, Dad. You're going to make me cry."

"Nothing wrong with a few tears on a day like today." He moved over to join the group surrounding her husband.

Jenson had insisted on paying for back surgery for her father. It had worked. Her father could walk for short distances and best of all function well enough to live on his own. He liked the fact he could give Bayley and her family space.

Half an hour later the group bustled out of the room, Jenson's mother with Russ's hand in hers. Russ would be staying with his grandparents until she, Jenson and Louisa got home.

Bayley fed Louisa and handed her to Jenson to place in the bassinet. He treated his daughter like a piece of fine china. Jenson worked with children every day but having his own to care for took his abilities to a new level.

With Louisa settled he pulled a chair up close to the bed. He kissed Bayley with a sincerity and depth of feeling that took her breath. "Thank you."

She studied him. "For what?"

"For making my life more than I ever dreamed it could be. For loving me. For giving me two beautiful children. For being you. I love you so much."

"You're welcome." She smiled. "You put fun in my life. We added some more today. I love you too."

* * * * *

COMING SOON!

We really hope you enjoyed reading this boo
If you're looking for more romance
be sure to head to the shops when
new books are available on

Thursday 18th
January

To see which titles are coming soon, please visit
millsandboon.co.uk/nextmonth

MILLS & BOON

Introducing our newest series, Afterglow.

From showing up to glowing up, Afterglow characters are on the path to leading their best lives and finding romance along the way – with a dash of sizzling spice!

Follow characters from all walks of life as they chase their dreams and find that true love is only the beginning...

Stories published every month. Launching January 2024

millsandboon.co.uk

MILLS & BOON®

Coming next month

ER DOC'S LAS VEGAS REUNION
Denise N. Wheatley

'Do you have a minute?' Brandi asked. 'I'd like for you to meet someone.'

As the men walked toward them, Eva's entire body went numb.

'Nooo,' she whispered. 'It can't be…'

'I'm sorry?' Brandi asked her.

'That's—that's Dr *who*?'

'Dr Malone. Dr Clark Malone to be exact. He's one of our emergency room physicians, so you two will be working very closely together.'

Eva's knees gave way. She leaned against the wall, her racing heart palpitating inside her throat as she struggled to grasp Brandi's words.

Clark Malone…

He and Eva shared a tumultuous past that she'd buried deep in the corners of her mind. Up until now. Because as he approached, a whirlwind of memories came racing to the forefront, the first being that he was no longer a handsome yet wiry young medical student. Clark had matured into a full blown, broad shouldered, extremely fine-looking man.

They'd met during their first year of medical school. Despite the undeniable chemistry between them, Eva and Clark had formed a tight platonic bond. Together they'd helped one another adjust to a new city, an extremely challenging course load and a rigorous schedule. While free time was sparse, they'd sneak off on occasion to Cedar Rapids, Iowa's Black Sheep Social Club for live jazz music, or Pub 217 for veggie black bean burgers. The friendship they'd built was solid, inimitable even. But all that had changed one night during their third year.

Losing Clark as a friend had hurt her deeply. But Eva's aspirations had taken precedence over her emotions – she'd worked too hard to risk getting distracted. But she'd thought about him many times over the years—particularly that one steamy night they'd shared. While it had been amazing, Eva couldn't help but regret how it led to the demise of their friendship. She'd contemplated contacting Clark on numerous occasions but had always talked herself out of it. After the emotional rollercoaster ride they'd endured, she didn't think he would want to hear from her. Since he'd never reached out to her either, Eva had figured he'd moved on and decided to do the same.

Now here he was, standing before her at Fremont General Hospital of all places.

What were the odds?

Continue reading
ER DOC'S LAS VEGAS REUNION
Denise N. Wheatley

Available next month
millsandboon.co.uk

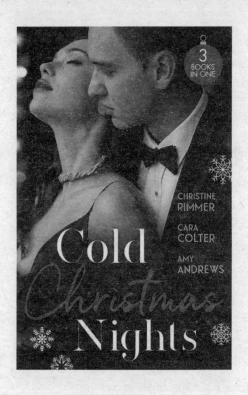

LET'S TALK

Romance

For exclusive extracts, competitions
and special offers, find us online:

- **f** MillsandBoon
- **X** @MillsandBoon
- **⊙** @MillsandBoonUK
- **♪** @MillsandBoonUK

Get in touch on 01413 063 232

MILLS & BOON

THE HEART OF ROMANCE

A ROMANCE FOR EVERY READER

MODERN

Prepare to be swept off your feet by sophisticated, sexy, seductive heroes, in some of the world's most glamorous romantic locations, where power and passion collide.

HISTORICAL

Escape with historical heroes from time gone by. Whether passion is for wicked Regency Rakes, muscled Vikings or Highlanders, awaken the romance of the past.

MEDICAL

Set your pulse racing with dedicated, delectable doctors, high-pressure world of medicine, where emotions run high, passion, comfort and love are the best medicine.

True Love

Celebrate true love with tender stories of heartfelt romance, from the rush of falling in love to the joy a new baby can, and a focus on the emotional heart of a relationship.

Desire

Indulge in secrets and scandal, intense drama and sizzling action with heroes who have it all: wealth, status, good looks... everything but the right woman.

HEROES

The excitement of a gripping thriller, with intense romance at its heart. Resourceful, true-to-life women and strong, fearless men face danger and desire - a killer combination!

To see which titles are coming soon, please visit

millsandboon.co.uk/nextmonth